Witness Protection 8
Midnight Requisition

Holly Copella

ISBN:
ISBN-13: 978-1-947694-18-7

To all my wonderful, imaginary friends ~
Sorry for the hell I've put you through.
Please forgive me when I do it again!

Love,
Holly Copella

ACKNOWLEDGMENTS

Copella Books: First Paperback Edition 2019
Cover Artist: Daniela Owergoor
Dani-owergoor.deviantart.com
Model by Grafvision
Model: Attila Hajnal
Stock Photography by NeoStock www.neo-stock.com
Printed by KDP, an Amazon.com Company

PUBLISHER'S NOTE

Chapter 1

Operation Midnight Requisition.   Twenty-three years ago. The boating marina, located a few miles north of Boston, was becoming busy with activity as the sun warmed the morning air.   The docks contained dozens of slips, although half the vessels were already out on the water heading to sea.   It was late morning, and there were more than two dozen vehicles already parked within the lot.   Just about all the fishermen were out in their boats getting a jump on the early morning catch.   A few whale watchers and tourists arrived early, but the majority of tourists wouldn't show up until that afternoon.   A man in his late twenties to early thirties, Zack, approached a white delivery van within the marina parking lot.   Despite the number of vehicles in the lot, the parking area was void of life.

Zack Kinsley was shorter than average but had a surprisingly athletic build, which would almost certainly go unnoticed beneath his khakis and a casual button shirt.   His brown hair was kept short and neat, although moderately spiky on top, lending a look that was somewhere between intimidating and cuddly.   Zack casually looked around before tapping on the side door of the van.   Without waiting for a response, he climbed into the back of the van.   The van's interior had bench seating on one side and a row of back facing seats in the front allowing space in the middle. There was a console alongside the left wall. It contained monitoring equipment that resembled something the FBI might use during surveillance.

There were three men already in the back of the van. Two of the men seemed to be hanging out with little purpose while one man fiddled with the electronic equipment. Zack collapsed onto the bench seat along the right side wall and eyed his three teammates, Ross, Abbott, and his commanding officer, Jackson. Jackson Remus was an impressive man befitting the title, Navy SEAL Lieutenant Commander. The man in his early thirties was tall, moderately muscular, and more than intimidating in appearance. His clean shaved, bald head added to his commanding presence. Ross Madrid, who was about the same age as Jackson, was a handsome man with a full head of prematurely graying hair. As were most Navy SEALs, he was in amazing physical shape with enough muscle mass behind him to put much younger men to shame.

The last man was possibly no older than twenty or twenty-one and had only been part of the Navy SEAL team, Whiskey Tango Foxtrot, for a little over a year. Abbott Renshaw was a tall, somewhat attractive, well-built man. Although not muscle-bound, he had enough muscle mass to be imposing. He kept his light brown hair buzzed close to his head, giving him the stereotypical military appearance. Zack was obviously distressed about his assignment, which was unusual for the hardened Navy SEAL. He never allowed life-and-death situations to influence his emotions before, but this time was different. His life and his entire world was about to come to an end. It was possible he was having second thoughts on his decision.

As the three men discussed the sequence of events, Zack didn't even seem to be paying attention. Jackson finally stopped talking while staring at his best friend and teammate.

"You okay, Zack?" Jackson asked.

Zack shifted his attention to Jackson and mechanically nodded. "Of course."

"We can still call it off," Jackson insisted while seemingly reading Zack's emotions. "We can move to our backup plan. Our version of witness protection isn't so bad."

"No," Zack retorted and sat up straight. "No one else should have to pay for my sins. A life of looking over one's shoulder isn't much of a life." He tensed and held his breath. "Not in this case."

"We all have targets painted on our backs, Zack. You know that," Ross informed him. "That doesn't mean we have to give up living."

"Yes, we all have targets on our backs," Zack agreed then raised his brows. "Mine is just a bit bigger and a lot bolder. I was wrong to think I had a life outside of the military. I was wrong to think I could have a family."

"I have a family," Jackson insisted.

"Entire countries want me dead," Zack remarked. "It's not the same."

Abbott suddenly touched his ear transmitter and looked at the guys. "Our man in the field has eyes on her," Abbott announced. "She's leaving the restaurant."

"Man?" Zack scoffed at the comment. "That kid, Gil, is barely old enough to shave." He eyed Jackson with some irritation. "Where did you find that one? Navy daycare?"

"He's one hell of a pilot," Jackson remarked.

"He crashed a Sea Hawk," Zack reminded him.

"It was already going down," Jackson countered while waving him off. "Besides, he managed to set her down, saving every man on board."

"So he can crash with finesse," Zack launched back. "I can do that."

"Give the kid a break," Ross scoffed.

"You don't like anyone, Zack," Abbott muttered.

"No one asked for your opinion, Abbott," Zack responded while glaring at his teammate.

Abbott was about to comment when he touched his ear transmitter. "She's heading back to her apartment."

"Her apartment?" Zack asked with surprise. "She was supposed to be going to her parents' house."

"Maybe she forgot something," Abbott insisted then looked at his watch. "Our window is about to open."

All eyes were on Zack. He frowned and nodded. "Let's do this."

Zack sprang up from his seat and approached the side door. He hesitated, drew a deep breath, and looked back at the three men.

"See you on the other side," Zack announced.

"Avoid the bright light," Jackson teased.

Zack managed a tiny smile, opened the side door, and jumped out of the van.

§

A compact car pulled into the parking garage and found the first available spot closest to the elevators. A black sedan pulled into the lot a moment or two after and parked in one of the spaces just out of view of the car he'd been tailing. The man behind the wheel of the black sedan put the car into park and silently watched the woman's car. Gil Rafferty looked to be just a kid. He was a tall, slender eighteen-year-old boy with short dark hair. Despite his youthful appearance, Gil was far more advanced than most men his age. He had graduated high school when he was just fifteen and spent two years in an accelerated college program before enlisting in the Navy at seventeen. Although the Air Force had wanted the aspiring young recruit, Gil wanted to follow in the footsteps of his father and become a Navy SEAL.

A young, attractive woman got out of the car and headed for the elevators. Maggie Wayland was a short, petite woman in her mid-twenties. She was a natural beauty with clear blue eyes, and her long, dark hair hastily pulled up into a messy ponytail. Gil sat within his car and silently watched the attractive woman, possibly admiring her beauty, before finally touching his ear transmitter.

"She's entering the building through the parking garage entrance," Gil announced.

"Keep eyes on her car," Abbott responded through his transmitter. "Make sure she doesn't leave."

"And if she does?" Gil asked.

"Stop her," Abbott replied with some annoyance.

"Roger that." Gil frowned and avoided broadcasting his concerns. "Yeah, sure," he muttered aloud to himself. "I'll just tackle Zack's girlfriend to the pavement. That'll go over real well." He shook his head. "That crazy bastard is going to kill me no matter what I do."

Gil appeared bored while watching the elevators in the event that the woman returned. She was supposed to be traveling back home to visit her parents in Maine, but it was possible she'd forgotten something for her trip. Gil's boredom didn't last long. When the elevator doors opened less than twenty minutes later, Maggie bolted from the elevator and made a frantic dash for her car. Something had the woman upset. Gil cursed under his breath and took only a moment to debate what to do. At the pace she was moving, he'd never be able to cut her off before she reached her car.

As her car backed out of the parking space, Gil shifted his vehicle into reverse and backed out at the same time. He didn't stop and instead gunned it, ramming the front of her car with the back of his. Gil threw his car into park, leaped from the driver's seat, and hurried to the driver's side of the young woman's car. Maggie was halfway out of her car when she saw Gil approaching.

"I'm so sorry," Gil announced while instantly and convincingly transforming into a helpless teenage boy. "Are you all right?"

She stared at him a moment with surprise then slowly nodded. Gil immediately looked at the wrecked back end of his car and ran his fingers through his dark hair.

"My father's going to kill me," he cried out then looked back at her. "I am so sorry. I've never been in an accident before. Are we supposed to call the police? Exchange insurance cards?"

Maggie stared at him and seemed unable to respond. She shook her head. "I don't have time for this," she announced and ran for her car door. "I have to go. Tell your father you backed into a garbage container."

She jumped into her car, threw it in reverse, and then drove around him. Gil watched her speed away through the parking garage and stared with disbelief. He touched his ear transmitter.

"Abbott, we have a problem," Gil announced while hurrying for the driver's side of his car. He jumped behind the wheel. "I'm positive Zack's girl is heading for the marina. With the way she's driving, she'll be there in ten minutes."

"Copy that, Gil," Abbott responded. "Return to base."

Gil hesitated and seemed to consider questioning the order. He held his breath and thought better of it. "Roger," he replied. "Returning to base."

§

Zack sat on the bow deck of his boat, the *Dame Margaret*, where she was docked in the marina. He leaned on the lower railing while his legs dangled over the edge of the vessel. He stared into the ocean and seemed twice as far as he stared. Zack allowed his head to rest against the middle rail a moment before he finally glanced at his watch. It was show time. He pulled himself up from the ship's deck and headed for the gangway onto the dock. Abbott was seen just up ahead close to a few prime witnesses. Zack avoided looking at Abbott and even pretended he didn't see his teammate approach him. After making sure they had enough witnesses who were just close enough to see what was happening but not interact, Abbott lunged for Zack and nearly took him to the ground. Zack retaliated with a few fast punches of his own, which were meant for Abbott to block easily.

Abbott went for the hidden gun down the back of his pants. Zack kicked him in the chest, knocking him back several steps then took off for a less populated area along the path not far from the cliff. Abbott grabbed his discarded gun and ran after Zack. Several fishermen stopped to watch the excitement. Zack ran up the path leading to the cliffs. He was almost to the woods, running past several whale watchers standing on the cliffs with their binoculars. A gunshot rang out, and Zack fell to the ground. He rolled twice before springing back up to his feet. Zack clutched his bleeding leg and attempted to limp for the woods. He finally stopped and gasped for breath, no longer able to run. Zack then turned to face the man pursuing him. Abbott raised the gun.

"No," Maggie was heard screaming.

Zack stood before the cliff and stared at Maggie with surprise as his expression shattered. Three gunshots rang out, startling Zack almost as much as they startled his girlfriend. Maggie watched in horror as the bullets struck Zack in the chest and blood exploded outward. Zack felt the intense pain in his chest, but it had nothing to do with the bullets striking his bulletproof vest beneath. He fell backward over the cliff as the onlookers watched.

"Zack!" Maggie screamed and ran for the cliff.

Jackson, who had been standing near the cliff pretending to be a whale watcher, caught her and stopped her from running too close to the edge. He sneered and shot a glare at Abbott, who took off and disappeared into the woods before some brave onlooker would attempt to intervene. Maggie struggled to reach the cliff while sobbing as Jackson held her back.

"No," she wailed and attempted to pull free from the strong man's hold but ended up sinking to the ground.

Jackson assisted her to the ground and attempted to comfort her while cradling her in his arms as she sobbed.

"He's gone," Jackson announced softly into her ear as he held her head to his chest, comforting her like an old friend while blinking away his own tears. "I'm sorry."

§

Zack trudged through the surf onto shore not far from the cliff while shedding his jacket. Abbott, who had shot him a few minutes earlier, walked across the beach toward him. Zack saw him and immediately sneered as he approached the surf.

"We have to hurry," Abbott announced while pausing before Zack on the beach. "If anyone sees you, this entire operation will have been for nothing."

Zack looked up, met his gaze, and suddenly punched Abbott in the mouth, stunning him. Abbott held his mouth and stared at Zack with surprise. Zack tore off the special vest he wore containing bullet holes with fake blood and tossed it onto the beach. He straightened then pointed a warning finger at the stunned man, who gingerly rubbed his bleeding mouth.

"She wasn't supposed to be there, Abbott," Zack cried out in anger. "She wasn't supposed to see that. I didn't want her to see me die!"

Abbott wiped the blood from his mouth and glared back at Zack. "It wasn't my fault. It was planned perfectly," he announced. "That new guy, Gil, was supposed to make sure she didn't leave her apartment."

"And I told you not to use the new guy on this mission. He has the attention span of a puppy," Zack snarled as his anger increased. "He's a pilot for Christ's sake." His hostility continued to rise. "The plan was perfect. Your execution was sloppy."

Abbott shook his head defensively and with some anger. "We did everything according to the book. Either way, the mission was a success. You're officially dead, and your girlfriend is free from your past," Abbott informed him although harboring some resentment from the accusation. "Jackson should be on his way to the marina where Ross is waiting for us. We should go before someone comes this way and sees us here."

Zack pulled his pants leg up and removed the wrap containing the fake blood from his perceived leg wound. "That's the last time I count on you, Abbott," he growled. "You never should have taken the shot with her there. I won't forgive you for that." He snatched the special vest and walked along the beach with both wraps containing fake blood.

"I'll add it to the list, Zack," Abbott muttered then followed him.

Chapter 2

Present day. Thursday, July 10th. Early morning. Vernon Heights, Virginia. The split-level home was nestled in a quiet development with other charming homes in what would be considered an upper-middle-class neighborhood. Despite the rumor that the owner had moved to Colorado, the yard surrounding the house was well manicured. The home appeared to be in excellent condition, and it was obvious someone had been tending to the lawn and garden on the owner's behalf. There was a lot of mystery surrounding the old Remus homestead. Despite that the owner no longer resided within the house, there was an endless parade of overnight guests invading the home. That most of the visitors were men had raised a few eyebrows in the small development.

It was after three in the morning, and streetlights dimly lit the quiet neighborhood. Most of the homes were dark as expected for a weekday night. Jackson Remus' old house seemed to be the only one with any sign of life. The faint appearance of lights inside indicated someone was up and possibly watching television. The homey living room was dimly lit by the glow of the television with the volume barely audible. An attractive young woman in her mid-twenties sat on the floor with her back resting against the sofa. Jackie Falcone, the late Lt. Commander Jackson Remus' daughter, wore an old, black tank top and sleep shorts, revealing her athletic build and ample cleavage. Her long, dark hair hung down, appearing wild and untamed as if she had slept on it. Given the hour, that was probably the case. She sat on the floor alongside Zack and listened to the story.

Despite all the stories he'd told her regarding his past, he had never mentioned Midnight Requisition. Zack seemed to be off in his own world as he stared at the television, although it was evident he wasn't actually watching it. That he hadn't said a word since he finished the story was somewhat unnerving to Jackie and forced her to shift uncomfortably.

"I'm so sorry, Zack. I didn't know what you'd done to protect Maggie," Jackie almost whispered, hoping to bring him back to reality. "That must have been the hardest thing you've ever had to do."

"If you love something, set it free," he announced in possibly the softest voice she'd ever heard from the rarely emotional man. He finally looked at her through the dim glow of the television. "None of it mattered. She died anyway. My past caught up with me, and she died because of it. Maybe if I'd stayed; maybe I could have done something to prevent it." He hesitated while holding his breath, then stared into her eyes. "Maybe I never should have been in her life to begin with. I'm like cancer, Jackie. I infect others."

Jackie shifted uncomfortably and returned the stare. "No, Zack," she announced in a firm tone. "We're not going there again. I can take care of myself. I've been living with the demons of my own father's past. I can handle yours too. I'm safer with you in my life than without you."

"I wish I believed that," Zack whispered and seemed to drift out.

Jackie tensed and eyed him. "I didn't realize there was bad blood between you and Abbott." She shuttered slightly and rubbed her chilled arms as the pain and trauma from a not so distant past again invaded her memory. "I trusted that man. Loved him the way I loved the rest of the team," Jackie remarked. Her eyes then narrowed as she fought her anger and betrayal of the day she'd lost her father. "I was a different person just a few years ago. I'd have handled that whole situation a lot differently." She shuttered slightly and glanced at

Zack now feeling a little lost herself. "I often wonder if me of today could have saved my father."

§

Around four years earlier. Jackie stood alongside her father, Jackson, at the private airfield as Abbott, who was nearly two decades older, checked over the vintage plane. Despite only being in his early forties, Abbott had rapidly aged since Jackie knew him as a child. He was still in excellent physical shape and had most of his hair, but he seemed tired and anxious. Abbott eyed Jackie's father and appeared humored.

"Old Marge, huh?" Abbott teased. "Nothing newer? A sexier model, perhaps?"

"Not for your first time out," Jackson replied with a cheap grin on his face.

Although Jackie's father had ten years on Abbott, her father had aged more gracefully than his former teammate. Jackson took care of himself both mentally and physically, although Jackie may have been part of the driving force behind his youthful appearance.

"You never did like to share your toys," Abbott remarked then indicated the plane. "Well, what are we waiting for?"

Jackie looked at her father and smiled innocently. "So is it okay?"

Her father groaned then looked back at Abbott. "Do you mind if Jackie rides along?"

"Mind? Of course, I don't mind," Abbott replied. "The more witnesses to my act of valor, the better."

"I call point," Jackie cried out with delight.

Jackson rolled his eyes then looked at Abbott. "It's okay," he announced with defeat. "I'll ride in the back."

Abbott's expression dropped slightly, although he attempted to cover with a tiny smile. "Maybe I should ride in the back," he remarked, seeming a little tense. "You know, in case you need to assist Jackie."

Her father snorted a laugh. "Don't be ridiculous," Jackson replied. "Jackie's been piloting small planes since she was in diapers. Soon she'll be moving on to commercial airliners. She's more than capable of getting us out to the old airfield. Once there, we'll get you in the pilot's seat and give you a crash course in flying."

Jackie rolled her eyes. "Oh, Dad, those puns are getting old fast."

Abbott didn't appear convinced but nodded his acceptance. Only a few minutes later, they were airborne. Jackie enjoyed flying the older plane. She was loud, and she was cranky. All three wore pilot aviation headsets in order to communicate with one another above the roar of the engine. Abbott sat rigid in the co-pilot's seat, obviously nervous about his young pilot. Jackie knew it wasn't that he was sexist. The men from her father's SEAL team had accepted her as one of the boys a long time ago. She was sure he was just uncertain about her flying abilities. Little did he realize she was a better pilot than her father. They were only halfway to the deserted airfield when Abbott fidgeted and seemed oddly uncomfortable.

"You know," Abbott finally spoke after near silence the entire flight, "it's nothing personal."

Jackie glanced at him with surprise to his remark. She didn't understand what he'd meant until she saw the gun in his hand held close to his chest. It was aimed at her. She met his gaze and stared with alarm.

"Abbott--?"

Her father was alerted to the conversation, noting the look on Jackie's face. He attempted to lean forward to check out the situation. Abbott aimed the gun at him. The look on his face conveyed he was serious.

"Just sit back and relax, Commander," Abbott growled.

Jackson tensed and slowly sat back without taking his eyes off the man holding the gun.

"What's going on?" Jackson demanded.

"Just a little change of plans," Abbott informed him. "We're not going to the abandoned airfield."

"Where are we going?" her father asked, seeming unusually calm.

Jackie already knew something bad was about to go down, and it wasn't going to end well for any of them.

"I need an exit," Abbott informed him. "I need to leave the country before certain people catch up to me, and you're going to help me."

"What people?" Jackson demanded.

"Just people," Abbott replied. "That's all you need to know. Just do as I say, and you'll both live to fly another day." He handed Jackie a paper. "Here are the coordinates."

She glanced at the paper, stared a moment with surprise, and then handed the paper to her father behind them. Jackson looked at the coordinates then back at Abbott.

"This won't take you out of the country," her father announced boldly. "This will take us to Washington, D.C."

Abbott stared at him with a look of surprise. "Wow, you decoded that pretty fast."

"Yes, that's why I'm a lieutenant commander," he snarled while keeping his eyes on Abbott. "We're not flying you to Washington for some suicide mission."

"What makes you think it's a suicide mission?"

"I know my men, Abbott," Jackson replied firmly. "I know you had a difficult time with PTS. We can get you help, but I can't do that with you pointing a gun at me and certainly not at my daughter."

"I'm going to do a lot more than point this gun, Commander," Abbott announced in an icy tone. "You're going to fly to those coordinates or one of you is going to eat a bullet."

There was an awkward silence. Jackie watched the tense scene from the corner of her eye in silence. Abbott aimed the gun at Jackie, keeping it close to his chest so Jackson couldn't disarm him before he would squeeze the trigger.

"What's it going to be, Commander?" Abbott demanded.

Jackson finally looked at Jackie. His look wasn't that of defeat but that of the Navy SEAL she rarely saw.

"Jackie, take him to Washington," her father announced firmly. "Take Old Marge down to conserve fuel, if we intend to make it there. You'll want to bring her around in a buzz saw."

Jackie held her breath, kept her eyes locked on the countryside before her, and fiddled with a few switches.

"Yes, Commander," she replied faintly and accepted her new orders.

Jackie inhaled deeply and flipped another switch. The propeller suddenly slowed, and the engine shut down. Abbott looked around with surprise then to Jackie. She sharply turned the control wheel to the right, sending the plane spiraling. Abbott cried out with surprise and attempted to hold on despite his shoulder harness. He aimed the gun at Jackie and squeezed the trigger. Jackie held her breath and kept the plane steady in a spiral. Her father leaped for Abbott from the rear and attempted to take the gun from him. The gun fired, and a bullet struck the control panel. The panel smoldered. The gun fired again as the men struggled for control over the gun in the spinning plane. Jackie kept the plane spiraling until the weapon flew from Abbott's hand. She corrected the spin and immediately restarted the engine. The engine sputtered as lights flashed and alarms sounded. She fought to level the plane before the engine seized altogether. Old Marge was tough, but she'd given it her all and had nothing left. Her father released his safety harness, lunged forward, and punched Abbott in the face several times.

Abbott only got in one shot, being restricted by his safety harness, but it was enough to send her father into the backseat. Abbott immediately dived on Jackie, attempting to force her to crash the plane. She managed to punch him away from her, his seatbelt restraining him from getting any leverage on her. She saw the lake up ahead and feared crashing into it. Abbott released his safety harness and attempted to jump on her. Jackie sent the plane to the right, tossing him against the door. As he tried to recover, she partially turned in her seat and kicked him in the chest, throwing him backward and against the door. The door gave, and Abbott plummeted from the plane. Jackie struggled to regain control of the now rolling plane. Her father weakly climbed into the co-pilot's seat, strapped himself in, and engaged the controls on his side to assist her. They leveled the plane as the engine continued to sputter. Jackie looked at her father fighting the controls alongside her. She saw the large amount of blood on his abdomen. He'd been shot!

"Keep her steady," he shouted as they fought the controls and the failing engine. "We'll need to find a clearing and glide her in for a landing!"

"You've been shot," Jackie cried out in panic.

"I've been shot before," he launched back at her. "Land the plane!"

Jackie continued to fight the controls as the engine suddenly seized. There was an eerie silence. She saw a clearing just beyond some trees. They were going down, and that's where she was going to land.

"Up ahead," she yelled to her father.

As she fought to keep the plane in the air long enough to reach the clearing, she looked over at her father. He was slumped in the seat with the harness holding him upright. Jackie stared at her father with horror then looked back out the windshield. She needed to clear the trees. The plane struck the tops of the trees and teetered wildly. Jackie fought the controls, but she was coming in too hot. The plane hit the clearing with incredible force, tearing the wheels off the bottom. Jackie was thrown violently within her seat. She felt several contact points of pain as the sound of tearing metal echoed loudly throughout the cockpit. Jumbled images turned to darkness.

§

Jackie felt a tremendous stinging sensation throughout her entire body. She wanted to open her eyes, but she couldn't seem to wake. Something warm and sticky ran past her eyelid. She soon tasted a horrible, familiar liquid. It was blood! She desperately tried to open her eyes. The light hurt at first. She didn't know where she was, but something was wrong. Jackie slowly lifted her head. It pounded in response. Blood ran freely from a gash on her scalp and streaked down her face. She was in the wreckage of Old Marge. At first, she didn't know what had happened or how she even got there. She remembered the dreadful alarm sounding and several lights on the control panel flashing but very little after that. All she knew for certain was she crashed Old Marge. Jackie looked at the co-pilot's seat. Her father was reclined back in the seat with blood streaking the side of his face. For a moment, she could only stare at him. He wasn't breathing! She removed her harness and slid closer to him.

"Dad," she gasped and touched his face.

His skin was already excessively cool to the touch. He'd been dead too long for any hopes of bringing him back. As reality set in, she found herself staring at the blood saturating his abdomen. There was so much blood! His hands were covered in dried blood as well as the controls before him. He'd attempted to help her land the plane as she went down. Once again, he'd completed his mission, but it was his last. He died a hero, as he always wanted to die. He died *her* hero.

Chapter 3

Present day. Jackie shifted uncomfortably on the floor before the sofa, sniffed, and wiped the tears from her eyes even though Zack couldn't see them in the dim lighting within the living room. With a trembling hand, she snatched his glass of whiskey from the nearby coffee table and finished the rest of the contents while Zack watched her. Although most people wouldn't be able to tell, Zack was drunk. He held his liquor well and functioned almost normally except he tended to talk a little more. Jackie suddenly felt like getting drunk herself, but she had to resist the temptation for Zack's sake.

"With everything I've been through, that is one of the memories that haunts me most," she whispered as she set the empty glass down. Jackie cast a glance at Zack with tears in her eyes. "There was only one other moment that was equally horrifying."

Zack stared back at her as if feeling her pain. He placed his hand on her shoulder, gave it a gentle squeeze, and managed a tiny smile

"My perfect ending. I would have gone out in a triumphant blaze of glory," he announced then frowned. "And you wonder why I loathe *that* woman."

Jackie groaned and rubbed her tired, tear-filled eyes. "Don't drag Mac into this again," she announced then cast a look at him. "If you insist on bringing her up, I'm going to demand an explanation. You're almost drunk enough that I could probably get it out of you."

Zack removed a carefully hidden, full bottle of whiskey from beneath the coffee table and refilled his glass. Jackie held her breath when she saw the bottle. She thought she'd successfully ended his drinking binge when she found the empty bottle on the coffee table.

"Relax," he announced as he recapped the bottle and set it alongside him furthest away from her so she couldn't confiscate it. "I don't have the energy to discuss Mac."

Jackie watched as Zack took a healthy swallow of whiskey from the glass.

"I'd rather not discuss Abbott either," she insisted and was unsuccessful at hiding her sneer. "I know I'd certainly feel better if they'd found his body." She shuttered slightly. "Part of me always feared he'd show up again one day." Her look turned to anger and hatred. "Maybe I'd welcome it. Killing him slowly with as much pain as humanly possible would be excellent therapy."

Zack snorted into his glass as he took another swallow of whiskey. "Now you sound like your father," he teased then set the glass on the coffee table before him. Zack placed his hand on her hand and squeezed it affectionately.

Jackie glanced at Zack as he stared into her eyes with a somewhat creepy grin.

"You don't ever have to worry about Abbott," he announced. "That honor was all mine."

She stared at him with a strange look and wondered what he meant.

§

Over four years ago. The cemetery was peaceful in the early morning hours. The sun had barely risen, and the grass was still wet with morning dew. The elaborate marble headstone of Lieutenant Commander Jackson Remus and his wife, Beverly Remus, sat stately on the immaculate cemetery grounds. Several flower arrangements remained from the burial just two days earlier, giving the grave a bright, cheerful look. A shadow was cast over the headstone. Zack stood proudly before the grave wearing his best suit and perfectly shined shoes. He had a solemn look on his face and kept his hands clasped firmly in front of him.

"I'm sorry I didn't make the funeral, Commander," Zack said gently. "I know you understand, considering the trouble you and the guys went through so I could go dark." He inhaled a deep, shaken breath. "My premeditated death aside, I did have other business that required my immediate attention. I know you'd understand how important this particular mission was." He offered a tiny, devious smile. "And, maybe one day, we'll swap war stories again, if they'll let me in wherever it is you've gone." His look again turned solemn. Zack saluted the headstone and fought the tears in his eyes. He laid something at the base of the headstone and straightened. "*Now* you may rest in peace, my friend."

Zack turned and walked away. At the base of the headstone lay a severed finger wearing a decorative Purple Heart ring.

§

Present day. Back in Jackie's living room in Vernon Heights, Zack affectionately held Jackie's hand in his as she stared at the grin on his face. She was slightly chilled at what he'd finally admitted after all this time. There was a certain amount of satisfaction she'd felt as well as a hint of uneasiness. Perhaps it had more to do with Zack's darker side. She knew it existed, but she rarely saw it. Jackie placed her free hand on top of the hand that held hers and stared into his mostly drunken eyes.

"You know how much you mean to me, Zack," she whispered while caressing his hand on hers. "I love all the guys, but you and I have something special. An unbreakable bond." She turned on her hip to face him without releasing his hand. "I'd kill for you, and I'd die for you."

He snorted a laugh. "I used those words when I proposed to Maggie," Zack teased.

Jackie raised her brows demandingly, immediately silencing him. "If you plan on making that trip to hell," she informed him while staring into his eyes with a strange seriousness, "I intend to follow you."

His expression dropped.

"We're a team," she insisted without taking her eyes off his. "Where you go; I go."

Zack stared into her eyes and couldn't look away. "I almost believe you," he whispered.

Jackie nodded without flinching. "Good," she replied then removed her hand from his and held it out. "Then give me the gun."

There was a long silence as Zack stared at Jackie. He drew a sharp breath, picked up the gun from the floor alongside him, and handed it to her. Jackie skillfully ejected the magazine and the bullet already in the chamber. She set the gun aside and removed the bullets from the magazine one at a time into his glass of whiskey. Zack groaned and gently rubbed his burning eyes.

"I'm tired," he muttered in a drunken tone then placed his head on her shoulder.

Jackie set the empty magazine aside and gently stroked his head on her shoulder. "Let's get you to bed."

Chapter 4

Thursday, July 10th. Late evening. Colorado Springs, Colorado. It was already late evening when the attractive, twenty-two-year-old woman entered the luxury hotel suite. Scorpio Wayland was moderately petite, barely making five foot four, but she was excessively toned, indicating the young woman was athletic. Her long, dark hair was slightly mussed from the long road trip from the ranch that she and her friends had called home the last few weeks. Scorpio looked around the suite with an approving grin. It was possibly one of the nicest hotel rooms she'd ever seen. Considering she traveled extensively with her wealthy grandparents, that said a lot. Scorpio's boyfriend, Rayner Roderick, entered behind her with their overnight bags and marveled at the room as well.

Although undeniably handsome, Rayner, who in his early thirties, had a nerdish genius sort of look about him. His light brown hair was cut short, and his face was clean-shaven to the point of meticulous. Despite appearing exhausted, he seemed enthusiastic with the luxury accommodations.

"Nice," he announced and nodded his approval.

The suite had a massive, king-sized bed, fireplace, large screen television, and a fully stocked bar. French doors led to the terrace that overlooked the city lights. Scorpio glanced back at Rayner.

"It was nice of Sig to put us up in this classy hotel for the night," Scorpio announced. "After what he paid us for the assignment at his ranch, it wasn't necessary."

Rayner approached the bathroom, poked his head inside, and then looked back at her while grinning. "Luxury garden tub for two," he announced with enthusiasm. "I'm thinking champagne and a bubble bath."

Scorpio nodded her approval then glanced at her watch. "If you want champagne, you'd better hurry before the hotel's gift shop closes."

Rayner kissed her quickly but warmly on the lips and flashed a smile. "I'll be back in twenty minutes," he announced then hurried for the door and nearly collided with Scorpio's twin brother, Kane, who was entering the suite.

Kane, who was traveling under an assumed last name of Templeton, was a handsome young man in his own rights with an almost steampunk sort of appeal. His brown hair was kept short although moderately spiky on top, and his neatly trimmed beard looked more like a five o'clock shadow. His piercing blue eyes attracted plenty of female attention dating back from when he was just a boy. Kane was slightly shorter than average, being a tick over five foot eight. Although he wasn't built very muscular, he was excessively toned, which was difficult to notice beyond his moderately worn clothes keeping in theme with his whole steampunk look.

Rayner glared at Scorpio's brother. "You have twenty minutes then she's mine the rest of the night."

Kane watched Rayner hurry from the room. He raised his brows then closed the door and turned to face Scorpio. "He's a brassy nerd, I'll give him that much."

Scorpio watched her brother flop on the excessively large, king-sized bed and make himself comfortable. She raised her brows with some annoyance.

"Off."

Kane frowned and sat up on the bed. There was a knock on Scorpio's bedroom door.

"Come in," Kane cheerfully announced from where he remained comfortably seated on the bed and received a loathing sneer from his sister.

The remaining two men from their team, Maverick and Stone, entered the room leaving the door open behind them. Both men were in their mid to late twenties. Ben Stone was about six foot four and built sturdy if not slightly muscular. He was a clean-cut, moderately attractive African-American man with his black hair kept short. Stone could fit in just about anywhere. He looked just as good in jeans as he did an expensive suit. Blake Maverick was devilishly handsome with flowing dark brown hair kept in a short, businessman cut. Although not as tall as his friend, he had a solid, athletic build. Unlike Stone, Maverick looked more like a hitman for the mob and didn't blend nearly as well.

"We're grabbing a bite to eat in the restaurant downstairs before it closes," Stone announced and pointed to the suite door. "Mac's already downstairs getting us a table. You guys coming?"

"Rayner and I are ordering room service," Scorpio informed them with a sly smile.

Stone chuckled while grinning. "I sort of thought that," he teased.

"Did you book a flight for tomorrow?" Maverick asked with interest.

"Not yet," she replied then eyed Kane, who fiddled with his cell phone. "Will that be four or six for that flight to Maine?"

Kane drew a deep breath, reluctantly sighed, and waved her off. "Yeah, I'll come back home," he replied then eyed her sharply while pointing a warning finger at her. "But I'm not promising I'll stay."

"What about Mac?" Scorpio asked.

Maverick cast a look at Kane while pretending to be disinterested.

"She'll probably come along," Kane replied then grinned playfully. "My little badger can't live without me."

"That's one hell of an ego you've got on you," Stone remarked.

Maverick hid his sly grin at the news that Mac would be traveling back to Maine with them. Stone saw his friend's look and rolled his eyes.

"Either way, we both need a vacation from this last job," Kane announced then pressed a button on his cell phone to check his voicemail.

"Why do you call her that?" Maverick asked.

"Call her what?"

"Your little badger," Maverick remarked and appeared curious.

Kane shrugged. "She's cute and cuddly, but she'll rip your throat out when provoked," he remarked then grinned. "Respect the badger." Kane listened to his cell phone and shook his head. "Ten voicemails while we were at the ranch without cell phone service." He listened to the first voicemail and frowned. "Telemarketer." He hit a button then listened to the next message. "Telemarketer." Kane hit another button and again listened. He suddenly became interested in the voicemail.

Maverick and Stone were about to leave when Kane's look caught their attention. Stone hesitated, shut the door, and leaned against it. Kane's expression nearly dropped. He pressed a button on the phone and stared at Scorpio with an indescribable look.

"A man who used to work for Sal Romano called two days ago," Kane informed his sister with a look that concerned her. "He wants to meet to discuss our father."

Scorpio tensed and held her breath. She then shook her head with disapproval. "Let it go, Kane," she insisted. "Nothing good is going to come from looking for him. There's no telling what he's mixed up in."

"I can't, Scorp," Kane announced while staring into her eyes. "I have to settle something with him. I need to bury his memory even if it means burying him."

"I don't like this," she insisted.

"Maybe we should stay another day or two," Stone suggested while straightening. "Provide backup."

Scorpio didn't look away from her brother, who maintained his stare at her.

"Don't you want to know?" Kane asked in a docile tone. "Aren't you the least bit interested?"

"No," she replied firmly then drew a deep breath and held it a moment. "But I'm not going to let you meet this guy alone either. We can stay a few more days. Maine isn't going anywhere."

"Actually," Kane announced. "He wants us to meet him in Virginia tomorrow evening."

Scorpio's expression suddenly dropped. "Oh," she groaned and vigorously shook her head. "I have a bad feeling about this."

"Virginia?" Maverick asked while studying them. "Isn't that where your father was originally from?"

Kane nodded then pleaded with his sister. "This is it, Scorp," he announced. "This is the one."

"Which one?" she demanded. "The one that gets you killed?"

"I'm doing this with or without you," he insisted.

"What about Mac?" Scorpio asked.

Kane immediately shook his head. "No, she can't know," he announced. "I think she knows more about our father than she's willing to tell me. She worked for Sal Romano. I want to trust her, but I can't risk her warning him. This is too important."

"She doesn't even know Zack Kinsley is our father," Scorpio insisted. "What would she possibly be warning him about?"

"Mac stays out of this," Kane announced with noted annoyance. "She can go to Maine with you, and I'll catch up with you after I've met this guy in Virginia."

Stone and Maverick immediately tensed and shot looks at Scorpio.

"Don't do it," Stone announced boldly. "You can't let him meet this guy by himself. We've been down this road before. I'll go with him. He can't go alone."

Scorpio drew a deep breath and stared at her brother. "You're not meeting this guy without a plan," she insisted then groaned. "Discuss the details of this meeting with Rayner. He can check things out. We'll decide how to approach it from there."

Kane managed a smile and hugged his sister. She groaned and reluctantly returned the embrace.

"You're the best, Scorp," he announced then pulled away but remained cheerful.

"What about Mac?" Maverick again asked and shifted uncomfortably. He appeared disappointed. "Are we really keeping this from her?"

"Not a word to Mac," Kane replied with a firm insistence while locking eyes with Maverick. "She's to stay far away from this one. I'll find something for her to do here in Colorado Springs for the next few days. Perhaps have her spy on some poor, unsuspecting person. I'll book her a flight to Maine for later next week."

Chapter 5

It was a few minutes before ten o'clock that night, and the luxury hotel's restaurant was getting ready to close. Sections of the elegant restaurant were already shut down, leaving only the small portion lit near the register. The restaurant contained many romantic booths and smaller, romantic tables as well as larger tables for groups and families of four or more. A large bar lined the back wall not far from the kitchen, and a wall of windows allowed a generous nighttime view of the city outside. The sole waitress on duty was wiping down the counter while the busboy cleaned the tables. A cleaning lady vacuumed the carpet in the vestibule as well as the hotel hallway beyond the restaurant.

Only one table remained occupied. Kane, Stone, Maverick, and one woman, Macbeth sat at the table and finished their nightcaps. Mac was an attractive, dark-haired woman in her mid-thirties. She wore her long hair pulled back in a neat ponytail and usually had a stray lock falling across her face. Her athletic build suggested she worked out extensively. Although she could pass for a sophisticated woman, the truth was less flattering. Kane wearily leaned back in his chair, glanced at his watch, and sighed.

"Looks like we closed this place," he announced then stretched while attempting to stay awake. "I'm still living on ranch time. I'm beat."

"So what's on the agenda for tomorrow?" Mac asked almost eagerly. "Are we heading to Maine or what?"

Maverick was the only one who flinched at the question. Mac didn't react, but she noticed the way he tensed.

Kane glanced at Mac and offered a charming smile. "No agenda tomorrow," he replied cheerfully. "You've earned the day off."

Mac stared at him a moment before her eyes narrowed suspiciously. "What's the catch?"

He chuckled at her suspicious nature and slipped her a folded piece of paper. Mac opened the paper, read the name and address, and then eyed Kane.

"I need you to do a quick weekend follow-up on our previous stalker case," Kane informed her. "Our client is heading out to the clubs with some friends on Saturday night, and I need you to make sure Romeo doesn't find his way to the same club."

"Why me?" Mac asked.

"You look better in a dress," Kane teased.

"I thought you didn't like the way I handled the situation the first time around," Mac insisted and appeared curious. "Why the change of heart?"

"It's easy money, and I'm not expecting the guy to show up," Kane replied while grinning as he leaned back in his chair. "It'll also be beneficial if you and I don't show up together at my grandma's house. She'll think we're a couple, and it'll be a whole thing."

Mac hesitated while staring at Kane. "Would you prefer I didn't go to Maine?" she asked as if reading between the lines. "If you don't want me there, just--"

"Don't be ridiculous," Kane announced without letting her finish the question. "Of course, I want you to meet my family and friends. In fact; I intend to spread rumors around about us." He straightened proudly and grinned with an abundance of charm. "You're my little badger. If anything, you're going to be embarrassed by me."

Mac managed a tiny laugh. "Point taken," she replied and placed the paper in her pocket.

"I'll email you the boarding pass in the morning," Kane informed her. "You're booked on a flight to Maine early Monday morning."

"If the job is supposed to be Saturday night, why not Sunday?" Mac asked.

Kane stared at her as if she were talking nonsense. "Do you have any idea how much plane tickets cost for a Sunday departure?" He rolled his eyes. "It's insanity."

"God, you're so cheap," Mac scoffed.

"It's been a long day," Maverick announced and was about ready to leap from his seat. "We're keeping these poor people from going home."

All four stood and approached the checkout counter. Stone, Maverick, and Mac kept distance between them and the register. Kane eyed the three, frowned, and shook his head.

"By all means," Kane announced dramatically. "Let me pay. I insist." He shook his head while approaching the cashier and handed her the bill and his credit card.

Once they paid for their meal, they left the restaurant and headed across the hotel's massive lobby in order to reach the bank of elevators. The lobby was abandoned much like the restaurant. Its plush leather furniture was freshly cleaned, and the tacky, red and gold carpets recently vacuumed. A weary desk clerk manned the large front desk, although there would be little activity throughout the night. All four approached the elevators and waited for one of the four elevators to return to the lobby. Kane glanced at his three teammates and shifted uncomfortably.

"Okay, rather than play musical sleeping bags later tonight, let's address the sleeping arrangements now," Kane finally announced with a sigh. "Would anyone like to switch rooms? Speak now."

Kane and Stone cast looks at Maverick and Mac. Both appeared slightly embarrassed and avoided looking at each other. The elevator dinged and broke the silence.

"And not share a room with you?" Mac teased with Kane then laughed. "I'll stay with Maverick." She then cast a look at Stone. "Good luck with that one." Mac indicated Kane. "He talks in his sleep almost as much as he does when he's awake."

Mac entered the elevator without further explanation. Maverick and Mac's recent, long lasting, one-night-stand was a poorly kept secret. Maverick smiled proudly, grinned at his friends, and then hurried into the elevator after Mac.

Chapter 6

Friday, July 11th. Morning. Maverick's luxury hotel suite had two queen-sized beds, a fireplace, large screen television, and a fully stocked bar. French doors led to the terrace that overlooked the city just before sunrise. Maverick slept peacefully beneath the expensive sheets pulled up to his waist, allowing a generous view of his toned, bare chest and broad shoulders. He woke when the sheets moved. Mac pounced on top of him, straddling his hips while on all fours hovering over him. He met her gaze as she smiled deviously.

"What time is your flight?" she asked as she made herself comfortable on top of him, pressing her naked body against his.

Maverick immediately grinned and firmly caressed her bare buttocks beneath the sheet. "Not until early afternoon," he replied. "Why? Did you feel like waking the neighbors this morning?"

"You read my mind," she teased and kissed him quickly on the lips.

He held her against him and kissed her passionately with added aggression. Maverick assertively flipped Mac onto her back and took the more dominant position. He warmly kissed her neck and worked his way lower as his hand firmly traveled her body. Mac smiled contentedly while rubbing her body against his. Her eyes opened briefly, and she watched as his lips brutally assaulted her shoulder. She caressed his back while playing with his hair and sighed her pleasure. Maverick suddenly stopped kissing her, lifted his head, and met her gaze.

"Did you just sigh?" he asked with some surprise.

She stared back at him and managed to hide her smile. "I'm pretty sure I groaned," she replied.

Maverick grinned and laughed. "No, you sighed," he announced proudly. "You're even smiling."

She gave him a playful shove. "Don't read too much into it," Mac insisted and attempted to hide her smile. "You're not half bad in bed."

"What every man wants to hear," he remarked while chuckling. His look then turned playful. "You're going to miss me, aren't you?"

Mac rolled her eyes but didn't respond.

Maverick laughed at her eye roll. "Admit it." His hand traveled her body beneath the sheets.

She suddenly cried out then laughed and stopped his hand. "I can't believe you found my one ticklish spot," she launched. "Stop it."

"You're going to be without me for three days," he announced while grinning. "Admit you're going to miss me or I'll tickle you straight to hell."

Mac laughed then looked at him, caressed his chest, and again sighed.

"You did it again," he proclaimed. "You sighed."

She managed a playful frown, groaned, and slipped her arms around his neck. "I have to admit," she began then hesitated while staring into his eyes. "I sort of enjoy sex on demand."

"Who doesn't?" Maverick remarked while giving her a strange look.

"It's just, well, it's been a long time since I've had that," she admitted. "It's nice being able to roll over on top of someone." Mac grinned and patted Maverick's chest. "Especially someone who's always, well, ready to go."

Maverick laughed at the comment. "Is that a polite way of saying 'horny as hell'?"

"Like the "Energizer Bunny"," she replied.

"I don't know what that is," Maverick remarked in all seriousness while grinning.

Mac's expression dropped, and she groaned. "God, you're too young for me."

"Not for what you want me for," he teased then resumed kissing her neck.

"True," she replied and clung to him.

§

Maverick held Mac in his arms while both panted heavily after their aggressive lovemaking. He affectionately kissed the top of her head as she rested against his chest. His cell phone dinged, indicating he had a text message. On the second ding, Maverick groaned.

"I'm starting to hate Kane," Maverick informed her. "He's so needy with all the texting."

Mac gave him a bewildered look. "When did he have time to text you?" she asked. "Our cell phones didn't work on the ranch, and we just got in last night."

"When you were in the shower last night," Maverick announced. "He sent me twenty texts reminding me about the flight, what time we needed to leave for the airport, and his last but not least--" Maverick rolled into Mac and snatched his cell phone from the nightstand. He quickly scrolled through his text messages then showed her the one from last night. "Tuck Mac in and give her a kiss goodnight from me."

Mac stared at the text and raised her brows. "He's seriously disturbed."

"No, the guy needs to get laid," Maverick informed her.

The phone dinged again while in his hand. Maverick groaned and reluctantly checked the last three text messages Kane had sent already that morning. He snorted a laugh at the last one.

"What?" Mac asked and attempted to see the message.

"He said he booked the hotel room here for you through Monday," Maverick informed her then flashed the message for her to see. "I guess he feels bad for making you work the weekend."

"Pretty impressive for the cheap bastard," Mac remarked and laughed.

Maverick cast a look at her while holding her against him in one arm and the phone in his free hand. "Why doesn't he just text you directly?"

"Because my phone is turned off," she informed him while grinning. "He drove me crazy the first day he had my number. I like my mornings quiet." Mac indicated the phone. "Send him a text back for me."

Maverick groaned, handed her his phone, and got out of bed. "I may be your sex slave, but I'm not your messenger boy," he announced. "If you want to banter with your boss, keep me out of it."

Mac grinned deviously and typed a response to Kane on Maverick's cell phone. Maverick took a moment to stretch his naked body in the sunlight flooding through the partially open curtain. Mac darted a look at his naked body from the corner of her eye and hid her approving smile. She aimed the phone at him and hit a button. Maverick lowered his arms and gave her a surprised look.

"Did you just take a picture of me?" he demanded.

Mac grinned and laughed. "It's okay," she replied. "It's on your phone. I promise not to send it to mine."

He attempted to take the phone from her, but she rolled onto her side and kept it from him. He waved her off and didn't seem too concerned.

"Go ahead," he announced. "Send it to yourself. You're going to need it for the next three days." Maverick headed to the bathroom and paused in the doorway to look back at her. "Shower for two is now available."

She didn't bother looking at him and continued typing on the phone. "Start without me," Mac announced. "I want to have a little fun with Kane first."

Maverick groaned and frowned his displeasure. "Please don't send him any dirty messages while pretending they're from me," he announced. "I hate when he gives me those funny looks."

Mac grinned and snickered. "Why send dirty messages?" she teased. "Sending him a dick pic has far more entertainment value."

"Don't you dare," Maverick growled.

Mac laughed and cast a quick look at him. "Relax," she teased. "I wouldn't do that."

Maverick rolled his eyes and entered the bathroom while muttering something under his breath that she easily ignored. Mac hit send then sat up in bed while holding the sheet to her naked body. She stared at the messages left by Kane that morning. Her brows knitted as she read the last message from Kane regarding the expensive hotel.

"Why's that cheap bastard suddenly being so generous?" Mac muttered then scrolled back several text messages on Maverick's phone. Something then caught her attention. "Vernon Heights?" She sank into thought. "Where have I heard that town before?"

She pulled up the internet and typed Vernon Heights into a search. It immediately came up from a previous search Maverick had done just last night. Mac's brows knitted.

"Vernon Heights, Virginia?" she whispered with confusion. Her eyes suddenly widened in near horror as realization hit her. "Vernon Heights!"

Mac frantically searched Maverick's phone and brought up his GPS app. She opened it and saw the last thing entered was directions from a motel in Vernon Heights to an airplane boneyard. Mac stared at the destination with her mouth hanging open and a frozen look of horror on her face.

"No," she gasped and pressed a button with a trembling finger.

She stared at an image of the all too familiar airplane boneyard. Unfortunately, Mac had been there once before. She'd been there with Zack! Mac sat on the bed clutching the sheets to her now chilled, trembling body while staring at the cell phone in her hand.

"They're going to Virginia," she gasped softly and repeatedly ran her fingers through her hair while just about pulling it out by the roots. "They're going to Virginia, and they don't want me anywhere near it."

Mac reached across the bed, snatched her own cell phone from the nightstand, and pressed a button. She placed the two phones back to back while watching her phone pair with Maverick's cell phone. Once the pairing was complete, she

37

scrolled through Maverick's text messages and found the one indicating their flight time. She set his phone on the bed and frantically worked on her phone. She checked the flight information at the Colorado Springs Airport. There weren't any flights leaving for Maine at that time, but there was one leaving for Virginia. Mac cursed under her breath.

"It's getting lonely in here," Maverick called to her from the shower.

"Coming," Mac replied as she frantically worked on her phone.

Mac found another message from Kane giving an address, date, and time. It was today's date! The address was the boneyard, which meant they were going to the boneyard to meet someone tonight! Mac checked additional flights to Virginia, found an earlier one, and booked it. When the payment information came up, Mac typed in a sequence of numbers she had memorized. It asked for the name on the credit card, she swiftly typed Kane Templeton. Payment was accepted. Mac dropped both phones onto the bed and held her head a moment. She cursed softly then looked at the open bathroom door and listened to the running shower.

"Damn it," she muttered then collected herself.

Once she calmed her nerves, she got out of bed and headed into the bathroom.

Chapter 7

Late afternoon. The abandoned airfield in Virginia was home to a large aircraft boneyard. Considered an eyesore, the boneyard was located in a secluded area of mostly junk land far from anywhere. Barely considered an airfield and its seclusion made it the perfect rendezvous for illicit activity. Mac had parked her rental car in a secluded area of woods two miles from the boneyard where it wouldn't be spotted. She needed to arrive early enough to make it to the abandoned airfield before anyone from her team or the party they were meeting was to show. Mac found a secluded spot hidden in a tree line more than two hundred yards from the massive junkyard of planes. She spent nearly thirty minutes scoping out the boneyard through a pair of binoculars.

There weren't any signs of life that she could see. In the amount of time she took to stakeout the area, someone would have revealed him or herself in that time. Just to be safe, she kept low in the tall grass to remain hidden from sight. The few snakes she encountered weren't poisonous and therefore didn't bother her. She made it to the edge of the boneyard with nearly two hours to spare before her team would show up. Mac was careful to keep out of sight as she passed the old, abandoned planes. One caught her attention. The four-passenger prop plane had the name Old Marge elegantly painted on the side. The wheels and one wing had been torn off possibly when it crashed. The underbelly was severely scraped, and burn marks were visible beyond the seams of the engine compartment.

Mac could make out an old bloodstain resembling a handprint on the windshield on the passenger side of the craft. The open doorway, missing its door, was level with the ground. The sight of the plane sent a chill down her spine. She'd spent enough time with the team and heard enough stories to know Jackie's father died in the plane before Jackie crash-landed it. The longer Mac stared at the aircraft, the more obvious it became. If her team was meeting someone in the boneyard to discuss Zack, it would be poetic to meet around or in Old Marge. Mac looked around and found the perfect hiding spot just beneath the old, wrecked plane. The opening beneath the tail end of the plane was just big enough for her to stretch out and take a little nap while she waited. She removed her jacket, bunched it up on the ground, and used it as a pillow.

§

Mac woke where she had fallen asleep beneath the belly of the wrecked plane. She wasn't sure what woke her. Mac silently rolled onto her belly in the cramped space. The sun had already set, and the boneyard was rapidly becoming dark. She could see someone approaching the plane. Mac repositioned herself for a better look at the man. It was dark enough that she wouldn't be noticed beneath the plane. As the approaching man came into view, horror swept over Mac. She stared at the familiar man in complete disbelief. It was Bogart, Jackie's brother and newest member of Whiskey Tango Foxtrot. Bogart was a tall, well-built man in his late twenties. The charming country boy was 'hunky actor' handsome with flowing golden-brown hair.

What was Bogart doing at the boneyard? Her team was meeting Bogart? It didn't make any sense. She watched him get closer to the plane then heard him enter the wreckage. She could hear his movements within the old plane. The metallic thumping was loud and the entire hull vibrated. After several minutes of movement, the plane was finally silent. Bogart was meeting her team. Now it was just a waiting game. An hour later, it was mostly dark except for some moonlight, which was only light enough to make out the old, wrecked planes. Mac remained silent where she lay on her belly beneath the tail section of Old Marge.

From her hidden position, she could see Maverick approach the old, wrecked plane. In the dark, no one would spot her now. Maverick studied the plane a moment and squinted at the windshield through the moonlight. He grimaced at the sight of the faint, bloody handprint then cautiously entered the dark plane with his baton flashlight brightening the way. Mac remained silent beneath the tail section and attempted to listen for any sounds. Having flown on a commercial airliner, she was unable to bring any weapons with her to this unauthorized rendezvous. Even if she had, whom would she defend?

The moment Maverick stepped into the plane wreckage, a large light blinded him and prevented him from seeing the man he was supposed to meet.

"You realize we could have met at some nice, cozy coffee shop," Maverick announced while shielding his eyes from the blinding light. "I'm not a fan of all this cloak and dagger business."

"You want Zack Kinsley or not?" Bogart's voice snarled from the darkness beyond the light.

From Mac's position beneath the plane, she could clearly hear the conversation within the wreckage through several rusted areas.

"Yeah, I want Zack Kinsley," Maverick replied while keeping his hand to his eyes. "Where do I find him?"

"Not so fast, pretty boy," Bogart remarked. "I'd like to know why you want him. You have some sort of grudge against him?"

"Me?" Maverick shook his head and appeared almost disinterested. "Never met the guy. My boss is really interested in meeting him though."

"Who's your boss?"

"Midnight Requisition," Maverick replied.

There was a brief moment of silence.

Bogart suddenly chuckled. "What sort of stupid ass name is that?"

"You ask too many questions," Maverick replied without appearing fazed. He cocked his head slightly while squinting at the light. "Where will I find him?"

"I'll arrange a little introduction," Bogart announced. "I know exactly how to lure him out of his comfort zone and into whatever kill box you want."

Just beneath the plane, Mac listened in horror to Bogart's words. She mouthed the word 'kill box' then concentrated on listening to the rest of their conversation.

"I never mentioned killing him," Maverick remarked without flinching.

Bogart chuckled within the darkness in an almost sinister manner. "Yeah, but they all want to--" There was a pause. "Eventually."

"How do you intend to lure him onto our playfield?" Maverick asked.

"Now who's asking too many questions?" Bogart teased with a sinister chuckle. "I intend to lure him to you with the siren's call."

"Siren's call?"

"Yes," Bogart continued. "See, I know his weakness. Every man's weakness, I suppose. Women. In his case, one woman. A *special* woman."

Mac considered the words 'special woman'. There was only one special woman in Zack's life. Jackie. Mac was chilled by the words.

"You won't hurt this woman," Maverick demanded. "There won't be any innocent blood spilled. No *collateral* damage."

"No, I won't hurt her," Bogart continued. "But he'll show up if he thinks he's there to rescue her. He always does. She's his Achilles heel."

A booted foot appeared from the darkness and slid an envelope across the plane floor to Maverick.

"There's the time and place," Bogart announced. "Don't be late. You'll only get one chance at him. If he suspects a setup, you'll never get another shot." There was a brief pause. "And he'll probably kill you."

Maverick picked up the envelope, placed it in his inner jacket pocket, and again shielded his eyes from the bright light. "Why are you handing him over? What's he done to you to warrant such betrayal?"

"Zack Kinsley is a plague upon this earth and needs to be taken out," Bogart announced with a vengeful hiss in his tone. "He's poisoned the mind of someone I love deeply and turned her against me." The light went out, and the plane was once again dark. "He claims he loves her, but I know he's not capable of loving anyone or anything. He'll eventually take her from me, and she'll wither and die like everything else he's ever touched."

"Hmm, yeah," Maverick announced and fidgeted. "That's not at all dark and sinister." He gave a half-hearted salute. "Thanks for the rendezvous."

Maverick turned and left the plane. Mac watched Maverick head across the boneyard and for the main entrance. She could hear faint movement within the wrecked plane as well as the distinct sound of a cell phone. She then heard Bogart's voice, and his words chilled her.

"One down; one to go," Bogart replied into the phone with little emotion. "Operation 'Witness Protection: Midnight Requisition' is a go."

Mac quietly slid out from beneath the plane on the opposite side from the doorway. Since it was dark, she wouldn't be noticed leaving the boneyard the way she came. Bogart would undoubtedly head out the way he came, which was the direction of the main road. Mac hurried across the dimly lit boneyard while keeping within the shadows of the wrecked planes. She finally made it to the field surrounding the junkyard. She surveyed the area in all directions before being reassured no one was around to see her. Mac hurried back through the field while keeping low and finally reached the darkened woods. Once within the woods, she used her small flashlight to find her way back to her hidden car.

Mac approached her car, scanned the area surrounding it, and then cautiously checked the back seat. As she reached for the door handle, she felt the warmth of someone's breath against the back of her neck. Mac spun around, prepared to strike, when she was suddenly thrown against the car door with tremendous force.

Chapter 8

Saturday, July 12th. Evening. An hour from Vernon Heights. Jackie drove her father's ten-year-old black Mustang along the winding back road. Her father had bought the car brand new and rarely drove it, since he wasn't home much while overseas, leaving the car in near mint condition. Although Othello had delivered the car to her in Colorado, she had it shipped back to her father's home in Virginia, where it spent most of its time in the garage. Jackie couldn't deny she had been in her own world most of the journey, but her travel companion wasn't exactly talkative either. Jackie glanced at her half-brother, Bogart, who sat silently in the passenger seat while off in his own thoughts. When they finally reached the large cemetery, Bogart snapped out of his daze.

"You weren't kidding about the drive," Bogart announced and shifted with some stiffness. "Why did he want to be buried this far out?"

"My mother loved this area when she was a little girl," Jackie informed him as they drove through the vast cemetery. "She grew up in a farmhouse not far from here."

"There doesn't seem to be anything around," Bogart countered.

"The cemetery bought up most of the land on this side of town," Jackie informed him. "If you continue on the old road through the woods, you'll find the original cemetery from the seventeen and eighteen hundreds. My great grandfather's farmland ended just on the other side of the old cemetery. It was in the family for generations." Jackie sank into a different world and smiled as she reminisced. "I was able to see what was left of the house before it was torn down."

"I wish we could have grown up together," Bogart remarked then seemed to drift back out again. "I'd give anything to have all those memories and stories to tell."

She glanced at Bogart and appeared almost humored. "Are you kidding?" Jackie asked. "You tell tons of great stories."

"Some are even real," Bogart remarked.

Jackie eyed him with a strange look. He flashed a humored smile. She was no longer sure if he was telling the truth or joking around at that point. Jackie parked the black sports car along one of the many paved branch-off roads in the main cemetery. Both got out of the car and walked past dozens of headstones. The sun was getting low, and it would be dark in less than an hour. Jackie paused before one of the headstones, flashed a smile, and gave a slight nod. Bogart looked at the black marble headstone and let a tiny laugh escape his throat. It was Zack's headstone.

"I think I was twenty when we laid Zack to rest that time," Jackie informed Bogart.

"Jesus," Bogart scoffed and eyed Jackie. "How many times did you plant the guy?"

"I'm only aware of three headstones, but I think he's been dead more than that," Jackie replied and again indicated the plot. "I distinctly remember burying a big toe. Had a tiny casket and everything."

"You buried Zack's big toe?" Bogart just about demanded.

"No, we buried *a* big toe," she replied then grimaced. "Turns out it wasn't actually his. Surprisingly, he has all his."

Bogart stared at her in disbelief. "Then whose big toe was it?"

"I don't know," she replied then shook her head, "and I'm certainly not asking."

They continued onward until they reached her father's headstone just a few plots away. Jackie indicated the fancy headstone.

"There's the commander," Jackie informed him. "That's our father's grave."

Bogart stood solemnly over the grave and stared at the headstone with the names Jackson and Beverly Remus etched onto it.

"I wish I had the opportunity to know him," Bogart announced just barely above a whisper. He then cast a look at Jackie. "Do you think he would have accepted me? Or would he have been disappointed?"

Jackie offered a warm smile and affectionately touched her brother's arm. "He would have accepted you with open arms," she announced. "And he'd be proud of the way you look after his little girl."

Bogart seemed unusually tense. Jackie cast a look at him and noticed his slightly odd behavior.

"Is everything okay?" she finally asked.

Bogart shifted, seemed unable to make eye contact with her, and managed a tiny nod. "Yeah, it's just been a rough couple of weeks, that's all."

"Tell me about it," Jackie remarked then sighed with defeat. "Holden wanted to whisk me away on some romantic, tropical vacation. I'm almost grateful for all his added paperwork from our last fiasco. At least I don't have to feel quite so bad about all this extra time I'm spending with Zack's issues."

Jackie then heard a strange sound in the near distance coming from the area beyond the woods. She stared at the rarely traveled dirt road leading to the old cemetery.

"That can't be good," Jackie muttered then shook her head. "We should probably check it out."

Bogart and Jackie walked along the paved roadway within the newer cemetery before heading along the dirt road through the woods. Bogart's tension seemed to increase.

"I know it's a sore subject," Bogart announced, "but I'd like to discuss Zack with you."

Jackie groaned with mounting irritation. "We're not doing this again, Bogart," she insisted. "There's nothing to discuss. My relationship with Zack is complicated. I can't explain it to you. I barely understand it myself."

"I just think--"

She turned to face Bogart with a threatening look. "No," she announced firmly. "Discussion over."

Jackie walked on the dirt road ahead of Bogart. He stared after her while frowning then nervously scratched the days' worth of stubble on his face. He cursed softly under his breath then followed her in less of a hurry.

§

Night. The small motel on the outskirts of Vernon Heights had seen better days, but the town was small and lodging within a fifty-mile radius was difficult to come by. The motel consisted of twenty, no-frills rooms. The ten, standard rooms faced the parking lot and what constituted a main road while the other ten were considered premium rooms, which basically meant they faced the small swimming pool. The bland looking motel was clean, as was the pool, although the landscaping lacked curb appeal.

Within the first room facing the in ground pool, Maverick paced the small area before the double beds. Kane and Rayner sat on the edge of one of the two double beds and studied the aerial view of the old cemetery almost an hour away from Vernon Heights. The two men were discussing their hastily thrown together plan while Scorpio leaned in the connecting doorway to the adjoining room and watched her brother and boyfriend conspiring. Scorpio wasn't thrilled about the situation she'd mistakenly allowed herself to be thrown within, but she was here now and needed to see it through for her brother's sake. Stone sat casually reclined on the second bed and watched Maverick pace.

"Will you stop pacing," Stone finally erupted while losing patience with his friend. "You're exhausting me."

"I can't help it," Maverick announced unable to settle down. "I don't like this. I don't like any of it." He nervously ran his hand along the back of his neck. "We never should have excluded Mac."

Kane looked up at Maverick and showed little emotion. "You know why we couldn't bring her along," he announced.

"As much as I love her, she's hiding something about her relationship with our father. If she would warn him, we may never get another opportunity to find him again."

"I told you what our contact said," Maverick remarked. "He doesn't have a high opinion of your father. If he's a ruthless killer, Mac could be the only one standing between us and certain death."

"He's not going to kill us," Kane insisted although his actual motive seemed less clear with each passing moment. "We're just going to have a little talk with him, that's all."

"Our contact didn't make it sound like he's someone you have 'little talks' with," Maverick informed him.

"Relax, Maverick," Kane announced in a firm and confident tone. "There are four of us and one of him."

"Five of us," Rayner muttered without looking up from his laptop then shook his head. "It's like I'm not even here."

"Sorry, Rayner," Kane replied. "No disrespect."

"None taken," Rayner scoffed under his breath.

"It's very simple," Kane continued. "I'll meet him alone. The rest of you will just take a lookout position and watch my back."

"And what about this woman?" Rayner finally asked and looked up. "Who is she? What did our mysterious man mean by he'll show up if he thinks she's in trouble? We have no idea who your contact is and what he's capable of doing. What if he's abducted this woman? What then?"

Kane glared at Rayner alongside him. "Whose side are you on?"

"The side that doesn't get an innocent woman killed," Rayner insisted with some irritation. "If this mysterious man kidnaps or inadvertently kills this woman, we're all accessories after the fact."

Kane groaned and held his head a moment. He finally looked up and straightened. "You know what?" he announced. "This is between my father and me. The rest of you shouldn't get involved. I'll go alone."

"That's not happening," Scorpio muttered and folded her arms across her chest.

"Then we need to go over the plan again," Kane announced with a deep sigh then indicated the overhead view of the cemetery on Rayner's laptop. "We'll arrive an hour early, stakeout the area, and position the rest of you in a few strategic spots."

"Are we expecting trouble?" Stone finally asked and raised a curious brow. "You realize, apart from Scorpio, we don't have any weapons."

"Good," Scorpio launched with some hostility and straightened. "We're not pulling weapons on a man who's quite possibly a trained assassin. That's not going to end well for any of us." Scorpio fidgeted then groaned and raked her fingers through her hair. "We've discussed it before. This is a non-confrontational meeting. *If* he shows up, you tell him who you are and why you wanted to meet him. He tells you he wants nothing to do with you or me, and we all head back to Maine where I'm never leaving my hotel on the bluff ever again."

"I second that," Rayner muttered.

"That's the plan, Scorp," Kane insisted while glancing back at his sister. "I'm just being cautious, that's all."

"What time do we leave?" Maverick asked and finally stopped pacing.

Kane looked at his watch.

"Three in the morning," Rayner replied without looking away from his laptop.

Kane eyed Rayner. "I was thinking more like four o'clock."

"It takes an hour to get there," Rayner informed him. "You wanted to be there an hour prior to his arrival. I think you have to take into account the possibility of him showing up early. We're supposed to be there at five in the morning, so we need to get there by four."

"Okay then," Kane agreed with a sigh. "We leave at three in the morning. We should try to get a couple of hours of sleep before heading out."

Maverick removed his cell phone and flashed it. "I'm going to call Mac and check on her," he announced. "See how it's going in Colorado Springs."

Maverick just about bolted out the hotel room door. Rayner cast a look at Scorpio. She caught his look then turned and headed into the connecting room. Rayner shut his laptop, sprang from the bed, and hurried after her. Kane saw the way Rayner darted after Scorpio.

"We're sharing a room," Kane called after them in a threatening tone. "Don't even think about doing anything--"

The connecting room door shut and locked behind Rayner. Kane groaned and shook his head.

Stone cast a stern look at Kane from his bed. "Don't even think about getting into bed with me," he announced. "Maverick and I sprang for our own room so we'd each have our own bed."

"Fine," Kane scoffed and grabbed the extra pillow from the first bed. "I'll sleep in the rental car."

Chapter 9

Sunday, July 13th. It was an hour before sunrise. Scorpio, Kane, and the rest of the team appeared on the old roadway before the cemetery that was more than two hundred years old. Moonlight dimly lit the area, making it possible to see enough without the use of flashlights. They had hidden their rental car just before the woods beyond the main cemetery so it wouldn't be spotted. Kane fiddled with his watch and appeared slightly apprehensive now that they were actually there. He gathered his courage and looked at the others.

"Everyone take your lookout position," Kane instructed. "We have an hour before he's supposed to show up. Scorpio and I are going to have a look around."

Maverick, Stone, and Rayner remained close to the woods and went their separate ways to find their lookout positions. Kane and Scorpio walked along the worn path in the eerie cemetery.

"This is not creepy at all," Kane muttered.

The old cemetery, which was enclosed by woodland on all sides, was larger than it had appeared on the online aerial view. Most of the worn and chipped headstones were from the seventeen and eighteen hundreds. There was an old, family crypt toward the far end. Scorpio carried the two swords wrapped in a blanket in her arms rather than in the dual holster on her back. She didn't want to give the impression that they were armed, especially since she was the only one carrying a weapon. They could see the partially crumbling family crypt just ahead of them causing Scorpio to shiver at the sight. As they got closer, Kane suddenly stopped his sister and stared at the tomb.

"Oh, hell--"

Scorpio squinted at the distant crypt. A woman dressed in black pants and a black leather jacket lay on the ground. It was possible she was only unconscious, but Scorpio feared she was dead. Rayner's chilling words at the motel came back to haunt her. If their mysterious contact had killed someone, they would be accessories after the fact.

Kane held his hand up to Scorpio. "Stay here," he instructed. "Keep watch. I'll check on her."

"This is bad," Scorpio whispered while looking around then focused on the motionless woman. "He wasn't supposed to hurt anyone. What if she's dead?"

"Just--wait here," Kane announced while attempting to sound calm, but he wasn't fooling her.

Kane hurried toward the crypt. As he got closer, Kane slowed and looked around. It was possible that the man who did this was still around. When Kane didn't see anyone, he approached the motionless woman on the ground just before the tomb. Kane kneeled before the woman and gently rolled her over to reveal Jackie. He stared in horror at the woman he'd recognized as their pilot a few weeks ago during their trip to the ranch in Colorado.

"Oh, no," Kane gasped as he tried to make sense of what he was witnessing then nervously looked around the cemetery for signs of whoever did this.

Scorpio nervously waited several yards away from the crypt and scanned the area around her with concern. Although she didn't see anything, she could hear her friends moving around within the nearby woods. Despite what they were witnessing, they had to remain hidden or risk compromising everything. Scorpio strained to listen for anything unusual, but the sound of crickets chirping was almost deafening. She prided herself on her exceptional hearing, but she was hearing too much and couldn't pinpoint any one sound. Scorpio looked back at the crypt, met Kane's somewhat frightened look, and silently questioned the woman's condition. Kane remained tense while placing his fingers to Jackie's neck and felt a pulse. He breathed a sigh of relief that she was alive and gently tapped her face to rouse her.

"Hey, wake up," he announced just loud enough for her to hear.

Kane looked back across the cemetery and no longer saw his sister. Scorpio was gone! Kane quickly straightened and scanned the dark headstones for signs of his sister. The headstones cast hundreds of shadows, any one of which could contain Scorpio. Kane was about to call out for her when he felt a slight gust of wind and suddenly tensed. He spun around and stared at Zack standing only two feet from him. Kane's expression suddenly dropped at the familiar yet older man. It was like seeing a ghost. Time stood still in what seemed like an eternity, although it was actually no more than a split second. Raw emotion and rage suddenly exploded within Kane.

"You ruined my life!" Kane cried out.

"Take a number," Zack scoffed while showing little reaction.

Kane allowed his emotions to take control in a hate-filled attack on the man before him. Kane threw several fast punches and kicks that Zack easily seemed to block with his own defensive moves. Although it seemed as if Kane was putting up a good fight, the reality was less flattering. Zack was toying with him like a cat with a mouse. Kane's anger continued to rise with each failed attempt to take down his father, and his frustration was starting to show as he attempted several fancy kicks in desperation.

"What have you done with my sister?" Kane yelled then continued with his assault on his father.

Zack easily blocked the next punch and the kick that instantly followed without reacting to Kane's emotional outburst. "Never met her," Zack replied without care. "But if she crossed me, I assume she's dead."

Zack's words were all it took to send Kane over the edge. Kane spun into two fast kicks, one forward and one backward, and nailed Zack in the chest with both. Zack stumbled back a step and was briefly surprised at the young man's ability to strike him. Kane went after Zack with more aggression and was able to connect with a few more hits, but he was successfully wearing himself down while Zack seemed to exert minimal effort.

§

Scorpio was face down on the ground behind one of the headstones and struggled beneath the large man who had managed to sneak up on her. She discovered too late that the man had been hiding in the shadows of one of the nearby headstones. If it hadn't been for all the damned crickets chirping, she was certain she would have heard him. His massive body was just about crushing her while his hand covered her mouth to keep her from screaming for help. His hand smelled strongly of tuna, onions, and gun oil.

"You're a feisty little thing," the man announced close to her ear, which didn't calm the situation or her struggling. "What are you trying to prove? I weigh twice as much as you. Quit struggling, or you're going to hurt yourself."

The man pinning her to the ground was Kirk Mandel. Kirk was a large, muscle-bound man who stood an imposing six-foot-four. He had broad shoulders, a large chest, and biceps the size of tree trunks that were barely hidden beneath his tight, black shirt. His buzz cut and thick facial stubble made him look moderately intimidating although undeniably handsome.

Kirk remained almost casual about keeping Scorpio pinned to the ground with his entire body covering hers. "I get it; I'm intimidating, but I don't intend to hurt you," he continued with the one-sided conversation. "If you'd just relax and calm down, you won't hurt yourself."

Scorpio's pointless struggling had just about exhausted her, and it was obvious the large man had height and weight over her. She decided he was right. Scorpio allowed her body to relax, which also relaxed the man on top of her.

"Now that's more like it," Kirk continued. "No one needs to get hurt--"

Scorpio suddenly threw her head back and struck him in the mouth with her head. There was no denying it hurt her almost as much as it did him, but he was stunned just enough to allow for a counterattack. Kirk clutched his mouth in response and groaned, quite possibly more surprised than injured. With her now freed arm, she rammed her elbow backward and into his side. Due to her position and lack of momentum, she wasn't able to hit him with nearly as much force. She immediately followed through by kicking him on the side of his knee with her freed leg. It was the advantage of being shorter against a taller man. Kirk cried out from the fast assault giving Scorpio just enough time to toss him off her and roll out from under him.

She made it to her knees before Kirk attempted to pounce upon her. As he lunged for her from his knees, she flipped back and kicked him on the side of the face with her booted foot. Kirk flew backward from the hard hit giving Scorpio a chance to spring to her feet.

Chapter 10

Kane continued his attack on Zack, getting a few shots past his father's defensive maneuvers, although they seemed to produce little to no injury. Zack continued to toy with him and seemed to mock his rage. When Kane attempted a low blow for Zack's groin, Zack stopped playing and switched from defense mode to attack mode. Kane suddenly found himself attempting to block kicks and punches coming at him with frightening fury. Kane took a punch to the ribs, one to the abdomen, and a knee to his side. He managed to block the next two punches that turned out to be a distraction for the kick to the chest that followed. Kane was thrown backward against an old headstone, which crumbled when he struck it. Kane scrambled to his feet, at which point Zack could have easily delivered another shot or two permanently ending the fight, but for some reason, he gave the young man time to catch his balance.

Once Kane was on his feet, Zack flipped through the air, caught Kane around the neck, and threw him to the ground with him. It was usually Zack's signature move to use enough force to break his opponent's neck or follow through with a neck break, but Zack seemed to hold back possibly due to the fact that the man hadn't been armed and wasn't nearly as much of a threat as anticipated. The landing was rough enough on Kane. While still on the ground with Kane, Zack followed through with a heel to Kane's chest, which successfully knocked the air out of him. Zack used his booted foot to roll the gasping man off the leg that had been pinned beneath him. Zack then sprang to his feet and stood over the writhing young man. Kane clutched his chest while attempting to catch his breath both from exhaustion and from the painful shot to his sternum.

"Now that we have the pleasantries out of the way--" Zack began.

Zack was about to proceed with his interrogation of the young man when a black, booted foot struck him in the chest. Zack stumbled back a step from the hard hit and looked up at his new adversary in time to see the blade of a samurai sword coming at him. Zack threw himself to the ground as the sword clashed with the two-foot, retractable steel baton. Scorpio coiled her sword back with some surprise and stared down her opponent. Jackie now stood before Scorpio with her wuss sticks grasped firmly in each hand and a cold, emotionless expression on her face. Despite Scorpio's surprise of the con job, she twirled both samurai swords and aggressively attacked Jackie. Unlike Kane's initial attack, Scorpio was playing for keeps, and she intended to draw first blood.

Jackie blocked each of Scorpio's aggressive blows with her steel batons. Zack had already backed away from the fight in progress, allowing them room to maneuver. Kane managed to roll onto his stomach but couldn't catch his breath enough to make it to his hands and knees. He watched his sister wildly attack the woman who was supposed to be unconscious. Despite that Jackie held her own against the dual swords with her wuss sticks, the playing field seemed a little unbalanced. Jackie blocked Scorpio's next two strikes then kicked her in the abdomen, temporarily stunning her. Jackie then kicked her left arm, jolting the sword free.

As the sword flew up in the air, Jackie threw herself into a roll across the ground, tossing aside her batons, and caught the samurai sword on its way down. Jackie sprang back to her feet and spun around with the sword now clutched in an attack stance. Although mildly surprised at the loss of one of her swords, Scorpio didn't let it throw her off her game. She intended to take this woman down. Scorpio resumed her aggressive assault on Jackie, clashing swords with her.

Kane panted as he managed to pull himself up to his hands and knees and watched in horror as Scorpio and Jackie clashed swords with fury. Scorpio's fast strikes were blocked by the woman who had tricked him into thinking she was the victim in all of this. At the rate Jackie was deflecting Scorpio's blows; it was no longer certain Scorpio was the better fighter. Kane attempted to move to his feet but lacked the strength to help his sister. Zack placed his booted foot to Kane's side and pushed him back to the ground. Kane attempted to catch his breath while looking toward the woods.

"Intercept!" Kane shouted out after finally catching his breath.

The entire cemetery was suddenly flooded with light from several spotlights and possibly a few vehicles. Kane's body twitched as he looked around at the ambush that had already unfolded. Bogart and three men with assault rifles pushed Stone, Maverick, and Rayner into the old cemetery. All three of Kane's teammates were bound with zip ties and had duct tape covering their mouths to keep them from shouting any warnings. The expression drained from Kane's face at what he was witnessing. He'd been played, and he never saw it coming. The four men forced his friends onto their knees while keeping their weapons aimed close to the bound men's heads.

A struggle could be seen within the woods as Mac was finally forced into the cemetery. Despite that her hands were bound behind her back and her mouth was covered with duct tape, she resisted, putting up one hell of a fight. She glared back at the man behind her. The man, Monroe, attempted to move her, although he lacked enthusiasm for what he had to do. Monroe Dallas was a tall, lanky man in his mid-thirties with more of an athletic than muscular build. His light brown hair was neatly trimmed, and his face mostly clean-shaven. Once Monroe forced her into the cemetery clearing, Mac spun into an almost perfect roundhouse kick despite her bound hands. She came close to hitting Monroe, but when he moved, she ended up falling to the ground.

Mac managed to pull herself to her knees with the rest of the team and soon saw what was happening within the cemetery. A large, silver sable German shepherd dog approached Mac and sat proudly alongside where she kneeled. The dog, Darth, turned his head now on level with her face and licked her nose. Mac groaned and glared at the dog, who now happily panted and watched the action in the cemetery.

§

Although aware of the spotlights suddenly brightening the cemetery grounds, Scorpio was focused on her adversary. She didn't even notice what was happening with the rest of her team. She couldn't afford to lose concentration for a second. Scorpio clashed swords with Jackie and attempted a snap kick. The woman she fought was good; a little too good. Jackie blocked Scorpio's kick and responded with her own kick, striking Scorpio in the abdomen. Jackie's sword immediately followed and nearly sliced the young woman. Scorpio managed to block the sword strike and instantly realized she wasn't nearly as fast as the woman she faced. When Jackie came to the same conclusion, she added a few more kicks into their sword fight and threw Scorpio off her game each time she made contact with her foot.

Scorpio's aggressive strikes turned into defensive blocks as her confidence rapidly diminished. Jackie was coming at her too strong, and Scorpio was running out of options and strength. Scorpio had one last trick up her sleeve. She forced Jackie to block a strike from her sword and then attempted to kick Jackie's legs out from under her. Jackie seemed to anticipate the move and avoided Scorpio's leg while spinning into her own roundhouse kick. She caught Scorpio in the chest and sent her backward. Scorpio tripped over a headstone and crashed to the ground. Jackie knocked the sword from Scorpio's hand with her booted foot then flipped the sword in her hands and prepared to plunge the tip downward into Scorpio's throat. Kane realized the woman was about to end his sister's life and panicked.

"Scorpio!" Kane cried out in horror.

Zack's body suddenly tensed as if a thousand thoughts exploded in his mind. He saw Jackie about to plunge the sword into the young woman's neck and, for the first time, fear filled him.

"Jackie, no!" Zack shouted.

Jackie plunged the sword downward to several horrified screams. Scorpio remained motionless while holding her breath. She cast a look at the samurai sword embedded in the ground alongside her face. Jackie glared down at Scorpio and took a step back. Kane held his head a moment from where he remained on his knees with Zack standing over him. Kane released the breath he'd been holding and now trembled. Scorpio quickly sat up and scrambled backward and away from Jackie, who pulled the sword from the ground. Scorpio then felt the stinging on the side of her face. She gently touched her cheek and felt the freely bleeding scratch where the blade grazed her. It was a frightening reminder of just how close she came to being impaled through the face with her own sword.

Zack gave Kane's shoulder a slight push with his knee as if secretly signaling for him to get up. Kane sprang to his feet and ran for Scorpio. He dove to her side and pulled her into his arms. Scorpio clung to Kane and felt her body trembling along with his.

Chapter 11

The team forced their bound prisoners deeper into the cemetery to join Kane and Scorpio, who remained huddled on the ground clinging to each other. The men removed the duct tape from their prisoner's mouths now that it wasn't necessary to keep them from shouting a warning. Scorpio and Kane looked at their bound friends and finally realized what sort of trouble they'd gotten themselves into. Among the men holding the team captive was Ross Madrid. Ross, who was now in his early fifties, was completely gray and had a refined, distinguished appeal about him. Ross slung his assault rifle over his shoulder and eyed Zack, who stared at the young man and woman huddled together.

"What's going on, Zack?" Ross asked with a curious look. "Holden is standing by. Should we call him in?"

Zack didn't acknowledge Ross, which was surprising. Without a word, he approached Scorpio and Kane. Kane saw him approach and shielded Scorpio in his arms, keeping her from looking at Zack. Scorpio could feel her brother's fear. It was something she rarely felt from her brother. Kane nervously looked up from his defeated position and met Zack's cold gaze. Zack crouched before them with a look that successfully intimidated Kane. He'd been defeated and now cowered before his father.

"Kane Templeton?"

Kane nodded but was unable to speak. Zack's focus shifted to Scorpio. Kane tightened his arms around her in an attempt to protect her from the frightening man.

"You," Zack gruffly announced to her. "Your name is Scorpio?"

Kane refused to release his sister and kept her face pressed tightly against his chest.

Zack loudly snapped his fingers near her. The sound was intense and frightening, causing her to twitch in her brother's arms.

"Look at me," Zack ordered.

Scorpio had to struggle to free herself from Kane's overly protective grip. She drew a deep breath, buried her fear deep inside, and proudly raised her head while meeting her father's gaze. No matter how frightened she was at that moment, she wasn't going to show that fear in front of this man. As she met his gaze for the first time, Scorpio almost couldn't believe he was actually real. All the times her brother insisted their father was alive; she never actually believed it was true. It was almost as if she were staring at the Loch Ness Monster, although twice as frightening. As Zack stared into her eyes, his expression suddenly shattered.

"Maggie," he gasped then sprang to his feet and took two, quick steps away from Scorpio. "Who are you?"

Scorpio saw the look in Zack's eyes and felt his panic. "Scorpio *Margaret* Wayland," she boldly announced as some of her confidence returned. She could almost see him putting the pieces together. "This is my twin brother, Kane *Zachariah* Wayland."

Ross twitched at the name, Margaret Wayland, and looked at his teammate, Gil, standing alongside him. Gil, who was now in his late thirties or possibly early forties, had aged over the last twenty-three years, and his dark hair was now peppered with gray. Gil had also been involved in Midnight Requisition, and he knew the name well. Both men seemed almost as stunned as Zack. Mac shifted looks from Zack to Kane and Scorpio, uncertain what was happening. She'd been left out of the loop and had no idea why Kane was looking for Zack. Jackie leaped to Zack's side, took his hand, and placed her free hand on his shoulder.

"*That* Maggie?" she whispered close to his ear.

Zack couldn't take his eyes off Scorpio and Kane as he nodded in response to Jackie's question. He then backed up a few more steps and pulled away from her. Without a word, Zack turned and walked away. Jackie cursed under her breath then hurried after him. Ross shook his head and indicated the others.

"Cut them loose," Ross ordered.

Gil and Bogart cut Stone and Maverick free. The last member of Whiskey Tango Foxtrot, Beck, cut the zip ties binding Rayner. Beck Larue was a ruggedly handsome man in his mid-thirties. He stood over six feet tall and maintained an impressive athletic build. Once Rayner was free, he sprang to his feet, ran to Scorpio's side, and fell to his knees alongside her. She threw her arms around his neck and clung to him. Monroe cut the zip ties binding Mac's wrists behind her back. Mac gingerly rubbed her wrists and met Monroe's sympathetic gaze.

"I'm sorry about the rough treatment, Mac," Monroe gently announced. "We just felt--"

Mac punched Monroe in the crotch. He gasped while clutching himself as he doubled over. Maverick was about to approach Mac when he witnessed her reaction to Monroe's apology. Maverick immediately backed away. Mac hurried toward Kane, where he remained on his knees alongside Scorpio and Rayner. He appeared to be in his own world. Mac fell to her knees alongside Kane and stared at his profile.

"I'm so sorry, Kane," Mac whispered and placed her hand on his shoulder. "I didn't know--"

Kane cast a glare at Mac, which immediately silenced her. He sprang to his feet and walked away. Mac remained on her knees and allowed her gaze to fall to the ground before her. Hot breath blew into Mac's face. She lifted her eyes. Darth stared at her then licked her face before spinning around and running back to join Gil. The guys slung their assault rifles over their shoulders and collected the rest of their equipment. They had been excessively prepared for the ambush, and it showed.

64

Maverick approached Ross, who stood with Bogart while discussing their bugout.

"Are you the man in charge?" Maverick asked while maintaining a non-threatening demeanor.

Ross eyed Maverick. "Yeah, I'm the man in charge," he replied with little emotion.

"This has all been a big misunderstanding," Maverick informed him. He offered his most charming smile and extended his hand. "I'm Maverick."

"Yes," Ross replied and ignored his extended hand. "Blake Maverick, Petty Officer 3rd class. You'd spent four years in the Navy with your friend, Petty Officer Ben Stone."

Maverick stared at Ross with some surprise then collected himself. "You guys are thorough."

"You have to be in our line of work," Ross replied.

"What line of work is that?"

Ross stared at Maverick with limited patience. "You're free to go," he announced. "Isn't that enough?"

"I know Mac meant well," Maverick insisted. "You have to understand; she wasn't in the loop. If she had been, all of this could have been avoided."

"Sticking up for Mac, huh?" Ross remarked and tilted his head. A strange grin crossed his face. "Despite what you may think, Mac doesn't work for us, but I'm guessing she works for you."

"If Mac didn't give you inside information on us, how did you get the information?"

Ross chuckled and shook his head. "You're going to need a lot more experience if you're going to make it in our world," he announced. "Your boss, Kane, was shopping around his business, Midnight Requisition, while tracking down Zack. Every person he spoke with reported back to us. Little by little, we learned all we needed to know regarding your team, its players, and Mac's involvement." He then hesitated and considered his comment. "I suppose if we had heard the name Wayland, we might have put the pieces together a little better, but your boss was careful to leave his sister out of it while using the assumed name Templeton."

"You were tracking us in Colorado, weren't you?" Maverick asked.

"You willingly gave up a lot of information to some fed friends of ours when you stopped that kidnapping attempt near that ranch," Ross informed him.

"Now that whole situation makes a little more sense," Maverick remarked as if reflecting back.

"Everything else fell into place from there," Ross informed him. "If Mac hadn't stopped to help my wife when she was injured, we probably never would have placed her with your group. Naturally, my wife confided in me, although I won't deny that I'm grateful to Mac for her assistance that day." Ross drew a deep breath while staring at Maverick. "Let this be a warning to you and your friends. Forget the name Zack Kinsley. *Our* attention is the least of your worries. Zack has more than enough enemies who would have no issues torturing or even eliminating you and your team to get their hands on him."

Maverick seemed surprised by Ross's words and stared at him in disbelief. Without further comment, Ross walked away from Maverick, looked at his team, and circled his finger in the air.

"Move out!"

Maverick watched as the men from Whiskey Tango Foxtrot vanished into the woods, leaving as quickly as they had appeared. Rayner collected Scorpio's discarded samurai swords and extended them to her as she stood. She eyed the swords and without a word, Scorpio turned and walked away. Rayner returned the swords to their sheaths and hurried after Scorpio, who joined Kane. Rayner followed the brother and sister duo as they walked in silent shame back down the old roadway to the newer cemetery beyond the woods. Maverick and Stone filed in behind them.

Mac remained on her knees in the same spot still staring at the ground in front of her. Despite that her team was walking away, she didn't bother getting up. It was entirely possible she was no longer welcome and another family would once again abandon her. A few drops of rain started to fall. Within a few minutes, the rain became steady and almost instantly soaked her. Even then, Mac didn't move. A hand was extended before her face. Mac tensed and looked up. Maverick stared down at her and raised his brows in question while offering a tiny, sympathetic smile. Mac reluctantly placed her hand in his and allowed him to help her to her feet.

Maverick placed his arm around her shoulder, pulled her against his side, and held her as they walked along the old roadway through the cemetery. She found herself clinging to him as if her life depended upon it. It appeared as if she still had one friend left.

§

The team returned to the Remus' homestead in Vernon Heights a little before seven o'clock in the morning. Since Jackie and Holden moved to Colorado, the team's former commander's home had turned into a layover for the guys and others in their military family. The guys were exhausted after their early morning activities and made themselves at home in the spare bedrooms. The four-bedroom home allowed for enough beds for the entire team. Zack typically took the sofa in the living room since he was the shortest of the guys and was less likely to share a bed with any of his teammates. He didn't mind buddying-up with Jackie, but Jackie's husband, Holden, was along for the ride and would almost certainly mind. Zack already spent half his time at their home in Colorado Springs. Sharing their bed was out of the question. Zack never understood the problem.

Gil would fly Beck, Ross, and Holden back to Colorado around one o'clock that afternoon, which would give the guys plenty of time to get a decent amount of sleep, even though they could sleep on the more than six-hour flight. Gil was the only one who actually needed to stay awake for the trip since he was the pilot. Zack, Kirk, and Bogart opted to stay in Virginia for a few days and fly back with Jackie in her helicopter, which was a much longer flight back home with more frequent stops. Monroe made plans with Gil to later return for some fun in the sun to his home off the coast of Florida.

Jackie entered her father's master bedroom while casting her leather bomber jacket onto the nearby chair. She flopped across the bed with exhaustion as her husband, Holden, entered the room and closed the door behind him. Holden hesitated then turned the lock on the door. Jackie's federal agent husband was a ruggedly handsome man in his mid-thirties with neatly trimmed, nearly black hair and the darkest brown eyes. He wasn't built excessively muscular, but he had broad shoulders and a toned chest. Holden approached the bed and removed Jackie's 'kicking-ass' boots for her then sat on the bed and eyed her.

"Are you okay?" Holden asked while studying her where she remained sprawled across the bed without moving.

"A little exhausted," she replied as her arm draped over her eyes.

"And--?" Holden asked while raising clever brows.

Jackie groaned, allowed her arm to fall from her face, and sat up on the bed. "You should have been there, Holden," she announced and shook her head as she pulled the hair tie from her hair. She flicked the hair tie across the room and frowned. "Zack's kids." Jackie leaned forward and held her head. "I can't believe I was that close to slicing up his daughter." She turned her head and met her husband's gaze. "I'm feeling a lot of things right now. Guilt, anger, fear."

"Fear?"

"She tried to kill Zack," Jackie informed him. "She attacked me with not one but two samurai swords. I could have killed her. She's lucky I didn't shoot her first and ask questions later."

"Why didn't you shoot her?" Holden asked with a curious tilt of his head.

Jackie held her breath and stared at him. "Because I looked at her, and I saw me," she admitted. "God. They were barely over the legal drinking age!"

"Yeah, I met the boy at Ross's training facility," Holden replied. "Not a single red flag went up."

"Tell me about it," Jackie groaned as she vigorously ran her fingers through her hair. "He was freaking out when he found me playing victim. He didn't strike me as the violent criminal type. When he went after Zack, it was raw emotion. He wasn't angry. He was hurting. And his sister--? She went berserk when she thought Zack was going to kill her brother. I think that's why I couldn't do it." She held her breath. "The moment I heard her brother scream her name, Scorpio, I knew something wasn't right."

"Why's that?" Holden prompted.

"Because Zack said if he ever had a kid, he wanted to name him Scorpio after a botched mission that killed an entire team of good men," Jackie replied. "The second I heard that name, it was like an alarm went off in my head. I knew I couldn't kill that girl."

Holden placed his arm around Jackie's shoulder and pulled him against her. She rested her head on his shoulder and fought her emotions. Holden placed his cheek on the top of her head and nuzzled her.

"It's over now," Holden gently replied. "You made the right call. No one was hurt."

"Everyone was hurt," Jackie whispered while nuzzling Holden's shoulder. "My heart broke."

Holden kissed the top of Jackie's head as he held her.

Chapter 12

Twenty-two years ago. It was a sunny, warm afternoon in the on-base housing community. A beautiful, three-year-old girl with big brown eyes and long dark hair sat on the front lawn of the little house and played with her toy Sea Hawk helicopter. Little Jackie made puttering sounds as she spun the movable rotor and moved the twelve-inch toy through the air. She sprang to her feet while sputtering loudly and teetering the toy helicopter.

"Abort, abort," she cried out as she veered the toy down toward the grass. "Take the stick!" At the last minute, Jackie lifted the toy helicopter upward. "Mission accomplished! Alpha Mike Foxtrot!"

She spun around with the toy helicopter while skillfully 'flying' it and bumped into someone. Jackie jumped back with surprise, stared at the sandstorm camouflage pants and boots, and looked up at the man standing over her. Jackie's eyes lit up.

"Zack!"

Jackie leaped into Zack's open arms. He picked her up off the ground. She threw her arms around his neck and happily hugged him. Zack laughed and held her in his arms, squeezing her until she screamed. He pulled back far enough to look into her big, brown eyes.

"Where's the commander?" he asked.

Jackie seized the opportunity to play with Zack's dog tags. "Daddy's doing that thing with the grill," little Jackie informed him.

"Burning dinner?" Zack asked with a teasing smile.

Jackie grinned in response. "Yeah, that."

Zack laughed, set Jackie down, and crouched before her. His look was serious as he stared into her eyes. "Have you been practicing what I taught you?"

She eagerly nodded.

"Show me," Zack announced.

Jackie leaped into a defensive karate stance, cried out loudly, and snap kicked Zack's open hands. He laughed then shook his hand.

"That was good," he announced then picked up the toy helicopter. "I need emergency extraction to the backyard. Can we get this bird airborne?"

Jackie nodded, spun the rotor, and made the puttering sound. Zack sprang to his feet then ran after her and her toy helicopter around the house and into the back yard. Jackie hovered her helicopter near the grill where her father flipped the hamburgers while talking with Ross.

"Deploy, deploy," Jackie cried out while hovering near her father.

"Dust off and wait for my signal," Zack informed her.

She saluted him. Zack returned the salute then tussled her hair. Jackie flew her toy helicopter across the yard to her father's youngest teammate, Gil, who sat by himself at the picnic table. Jackie landed the toy helicopter on the table near Gil, flopped on the wooden bench alongside him, and gave him an inquisitive yet serious look.

"Do you fly Daddy's Sea Hawk?" Jackie asked.

Gil eyed the little girl, smiled, and laughed at the question. "Yes, I fly your daddy's Sea Hawk."

Raised voices were heard near the gas grill. Gil glanced across the patio. Zack and Abbott were arguing again. This time, Zack looked ready to strike. Jackson said something, and Zack headed into the house. Abbott seemed to get a few more words in before Ross directed him to the beer keg chilling on ice. Jackie didn't even seem to notice the commotion.

"Daddy's going to teach me to fly Old Marge," Jackie informed Gil.

Gil's attention shifted back to the little girl, and his smile returned. "That's quite the honor," he announced. "He won't even let me fly her."

Jackie appeared puzzled. "Why not?"

Gil waved her off. "He said I'm not old enough."

"How old do you need to be?" she questioned with childlike confusion.

"He said something about when I'm old enough to shave," Gil teased. "And maybe another derogatory remark."

"What's derogatory?"

"A fancy term for the way men talk to one another when there aren't ladies present," Gil replied while smirking.

"Oh," she announced while nodding with understanding. "You mean poker."

Gil laughed and played with the toy helicopter. "Close enough."

"Zack cheats at 'Go Fish'," she announced.

"Yeah?" Gil remarked with a curious look. "He cheats at poker too."

"I drew a picture of Old Marge," Jackie announced while beaming with delight. "Want to see it?"

"I'd love to," Gil replied.

"Be right back," she announced then ran to the house.

Gil watched the little girl excitedly enter the house and had to smile at her innocence. He then examined the Sea Hawk toy replica and opened the side door. A small action figure fell out. Gil picked up the Army action figure with an automatic rifle super-glued to its hand. Gil shook his head.

"No one's messing with that girl," he muttered.

Gil again looked across the patio to the grill where his commander and Ross were having a serious conversation. Gil attempted to mind his own business until he heard the words 'midnight requisition'. He fiddled with the toy helicopter and secretly listened to the conversation.

"You're making a mistake, Jackson," Ross insisted. "Let it go. Zack made that decision. Going behind his back is a bad call."

"I'm aware that he made the call," Jackson remarked defensively, "but he didn't want it to go down that way. We botched that mission, and it's up to us to make things right."

Ross shook his head. "That concussion of yours is affecting your mind," he announced. "You aren't even cleared to drive. There's no way you're flying to Boston."

"She's not in Boston," Jackson replied. "She moved back home with her parents in Maine. I did some digging."

"Hmm, even further away," Ross remarked. "How do you intend to get there?"

Jackson shrugged. "I'll have the kid fly me there," he replied.

"Yeah, sure," Ross announced then shrugged. "Why not? Zack already hates him for screwing up at his girlfriend's apartment building. May as well put him at the top of Zack's hit list."

"It'll all work out," Jackson insisted. "In the end, Zack will be happy about it."

§

The following afternoon. The rental car pulled up to the large home in the small coastal town in Maine. Gil sat behind the wheel of the rental car and eyed Jackson, who stared at the mansion-like home with some apprehension.

"Is this the right place?" Gil asked snapping Jackson out of his thoughts.

Jackson nodded and still seemed reluctant to get out of the car. Gil studied his commander who was dressed civilian business for his secret meeting. He carried a briefcase, which was even more puzzling.

"Did you want me to go along?" Gil then asked.

"No," Jackson replied while remaining distant. "I need to do this alone."

"If you don't mind my asking--?" Gil began then hesitated. "I overheard you and Ross talking."

Jackson shot a glare at Gil. "You just forget what you heard," he snapped with irritation then seemed to tense. "Zack can't know we were here."

"Why are we here?" Gil then asked.

"To right a wrong," Jackson replied then indicated the large house. "That young lady has a right to know the truth. She should be the one to make the decision. She can live on the base under military protection. If Zack wants out, we can put him into our own witness protection. Point is; they should be together if they want to be."

"Didn't Zack already make that decision?" Gil prompted. "After all, didn't he do what he did to protect her?"

"There's something you haven't learned yet, Gil," Jackson announced. "Zack did what he did because he knew he couldn't protect her, but Zack forgot something important. He's not in this alone. *We* look out for one another. He never had to do it alone." Jackson drew a deep breath. "I'll speak to her in private. She can then decide what she wants to do. If the answer is no, Zack doesn't need to know I was ever here." His look turned demanding. "Agreed?"

Gil tensed then nodded. "Yes, sir."

Chapter 13

Present day. It was almost eleven o'clock in the morning. Ross, Gil, Holden, and Beck would be leaving for the private airport around noon in order for Gil to fly them back to Colorado Springs. Beck and Holden could be heard moving around within their respective rooms, possibly planning on taking showers before leaving. Gil and Ross were already up and in the kitchen with a freshly brewed pot of coffee on the main counter. Both men sat at the kitchen table with their mugs of coffee and seemed uncomfortable.

"Maybe we should tell Zack," Gil remarked to Ross while staring at his coffee mug.

"What purpose would that serve?" Ross just about demanded.

Gil looked up at Ross and appeared surprised by the question. "Doesn't he have a right to know what Jackson did that day?"

"It doesn't matter what Jackson did," Ross insisted. "It doesn't change the outcome, and it's not going to make Zack feel any better."

"Maybe not," Gil insisted, "but we've been keeping it from him all these years. It just seems as if he should know."

"What are you girls gossiping about?" Jackie asked from the kitchen doorway.

Both men straightened with surprise to Jackie's sudden and quiet appearance. Ross put on a false smile and appeared unusually cheerful. Gil just frowned and refused to look at her.

"Good morning, Jackie," Ross announced. "How did you sleep?"

Jackie raised a skeptical brow at Ross then crossed the kitchen to the coffeepot. "Cut the crap, Ross," she announced with some irritation. It had been a rough night. "I heard the two of you plotting." She poured herself a cup of coffee then turned at the counter, leaned against it, and eyed both. "What should Zack know?"

Gil cast a look at Ross across the table and raised his brows in silent comment.

"Some things are better left unspoken," Ross informed her. "You know that."

Jackie eyed Ross then turned toward the counter, removed another coffee mug from the cupboard, and poured a second cup of coffee. Ross eyed the novelty mug that was the shape of a hand grenade. He suddenly frowned but didn't bother looking at the doorway behind him.

"Good morning, Zack," Ross announced with less enthusiasm.

Zack crossed the kitchen and accepted the grenade-shaped coffee mug. He leaned against the counter alongside Jackie, sipped his coffee, and eyed the two men at the table.

"Tell me about these unspoken things," Zack calmly announced.

Ross leaned back in his chair and sighed. "When we returned home from one of our missions less than a year after Midnight Requisition, Jackson got it in his head to right the wrong of that botched affair," Ross announced.

Zack appeared curious and tilted his head, although he didn't offer any comment.

Ross met Zack's gaze and tensed slightly. "He went to see Maggie at her parent's house in Maine."

Zack's expression dropped then turned slightly angry. "Why?" he just about demanded.

Gil turned in his seat and met Zack's hostile gaze. "He told her you were alive," he confessed.

Zack's expression was frozen and hard to read.

"Jackson offered to take her to you. He set up a date and time for her to meet him," Gil continued then held his breath. "She was supposed to meet him the day she died."

The room became tense as all three awaited the explosion that was bound to follow. Zack placed his mug on the counter and left the kitchen for the patio without a word. Jackie released the breath she'd been holding then shook her head.

"This is going to require a lot of damage control," she muttered then set her mug down and headed out of the kitchen after Zack.

Ross and Gil exchanged uncomfortable looks then frowned in response.

§

It was around six o'clock in the evening Colorado time. Gil's newly purchased plane landed at the Colorado Springs Airport at the private terminal away from the busy commercial area. The Pilatus PC-12 was a luxury, eight-passenger plus two crew, single-engine turboprop plane. It had a wingspan of fifty-three feet and a body length of forty-seven feet. Once the plane stopped, the door opened downward revealing the built-in steps. Ross, Beck, and Holden walked down the steps to the tarmac. Gil and Darth were only a minute or two behind them. The rest of the team remained in Virginia at their former commander's house in Vernon Heights.

Gil would be returning to Virginia in the morning after he picked up one of their dearest friends, Sal Romano. They would then meet up with Monroe, Gil's on-again-off-again ex-wife, and another friend, Othello. The group would then fly to a small island off the coast of Florida and spend a week or so at Monroe's beach house. The men were nearly exhausted as they headed across the tarmac toward the parked cars.

"It's been a long couple of days," Holden announced to the men as he glanced at their weary faces. "Are you sure you wouldn't prefer staying at my place before making that long trek back to the lodge?"

"Thanks," Ross announced, "but we have wives waiting for us. They've been sorely neglected recently."

"And the lodge won't repair itself," Beck added then cast a disapproving glare at Gil.

Gil snorted a laugh then grinned. "I'm not going to apologize," he announced boldly. "Monroe offered Ellie and me a week at his beach house. Ellie actually said yes. That's where my priorities lie."

"Not much of a romantic week at the beach," Beck teased while casting a devious glare at his friend. "Othello, Sal, and Monroe are tagging along."

"Ellie will be there," Gil again insisted. "That's the important part."

"Don't listen to them," Holden announced and waved off Ross and Beck. "You and Ellie have a good time. Sal will keep Othello and Monroe busy."

"Possibly even get them arrested," Beck muttered.

Holden ignored Beck's comment and eyed Gil. "Did you need a lift to Sal's place?"

"I was hoping you'd ask," Gil teased while grinning.

Gil, Darth, and Holden parted company from Beck and Ross.

"See you next week," Beck called after them.

"Or the following week," Gil teased back without turning to look at them.

They approached Holden's official, black SUV. Gil opened the back door for Darth, who eagerly jumped inside. Gil then hopped into the passenger side and immediately sank in the seat, shutting his eyes. Holden started the vehicle and drove away from the airport.

"So Zack has kids," Holden announced and shook his head.

Gil didn't bother opening his eyes. "Yeah, that should mess him up for a while." He then opened one eye and glanced at Holden. "It's nice that you're so understanding about Zack's PTSD. Obviously, you have no reason to feel threatened by Jackie's relationship with Zack, but you have to be a saint to put up with him around so much."

"I don't necessarily get their relationship," Holden announced while watching the road, "but he's saved her ass enough times that I can't really question it." He sank into thought a moment and again shook his head. "Zack has kids. I just can't fathom it."

"If those are the only two, I'd be surprised," Gil remarked while resting his head back against the seat with his eyes closed. "I love the guy, but Zack's a mutt in heat."

"I know that," Holden responded. "It's just, well; it's hard to imagine him in a serious relationship." He then eyed Gil, who almost appeared asleep. "Were you with the team back then? Did you meet this woman that meant so much to him?"

"Meet? No," Gil replied without opening his eyes. A sly smirk crossed his face. "I did stalk her once. Insanely beautiful. She'd have to be to have two good-looking kids like that. They didn't get their looks from him, that's for sure. And his daughter certainly has his attitude."

"Never met her," Holden responded. "I hope I never do. A female version of Zack sounds frightening."

Gil snorted a laugh. "Funny you say that, considering you married one."

Holden glared at Gil and didn't share his amusement.

Chapter 14

Sal Romano's Colorado Springs country mansion was nestled on a large parcel of land beyond tall, stone walls. The professionally landscaped estate didn't have a hedge out of place. Weeping willow trees and faux split rail fencing lined the long driveway. The driveway split off to circle a large fountain outside the front door while the remaining driveway branched off to the kitchen, staff wing, and eventually to the massive, detached, eight-car garage. A man in his mid-forties sat in his study and stared at his computer monitor. The wealthy homeowner was Salvatore Romano. Sal was a robust man with a round cherub face and a youthful appearance. Even when dressed casual, he still had impressive taste in clothing. Although nothing was ever proven regarding his past dealings, Sal remained everyone's favorite mob boss.

Sal stared at the computer screen and seemed to be lost in his own world. Every few seconds, he'd stretch his shoulder and gingerly touch his healing injury. The gunshot wound to his shoulder was almost a week old, but it was still as sore as the day he'd received it. There was a light tapping on his open study door. Sal looked up and caught the disapproving look from his devoted housekeeper, Rosa. Rosa was a plump, older woman in her mid to late fifties with short hair she regularly dyed black. The older woman shook her head in what could be perceived as motherly disapproval.

"I told you to see the doctor about that shoulder," she scolded him.

Sal maintained his sense of humor with the smothering woman. "I already saw a doctor," he informed her.

"And did he tell you to rest your arm and not work so much?" she demanded.

"No," Sal casually replied while grinning. "He told me to stop getting shot."

The older woman rolled her eyes and shook her head. "You're going to be the death of me," Rosa announced.

"Why are you still here?" Sal teasingly demanded. "You're supposed to be heading to your sisters while I'm away for the week."

"I was waiting for your friend to arrive," she insisted. "I thought you boys might be hungry."

Sal stood, rounded his desk, and approached the woman. He lovingly guided her from the office. "If we get hungry we'll order a pizza," he replied.

"Pizza," she lashed out while gesturing with her hands and shook her head. "You need to start eating healthy. I've left some healthy snacks in the refrigerator for you."

"Yes, I'll get right on those," Sal teased, mocking the woman. "What's the point of my taking a vacation if you won't take advantage of the time off?"

"Knowing you, you'll probably get yourself shot full of holes again," she scolded as he guided her down the broad hallway toward the kitchen.

"Unlikely," Sal replied cheerfully. "I'm spending a relaxing week at my friend's beach house with some of the boys."

"I've met 'some of the boys'," Rosa announced boldly. "You should probably see about getting some new friends. Maybe some new lady friends instead. They'd be less hazardous to your health."

Sal chuckled and patted her on the shoulder as he guided her into the kitchen. "I've been shot by women too. Believe me; they're far worse. They rarely miss," he teased. "Go. Grab your bags, and have a relaxing week away from me. You need it."

The gate buzzer sounded from the kitchen monitor, alerting them to visitors. Sal indicated the monitor and the black car at the front gate.

"There's my friend now," Sal announced and pressed a button to open the gate. "I'll leave the gate open for you and the pizza delivery guy."

The older woman attempted to hide her smile then shook her head. "I'll see you in a week."

"Drive carefully," Sal announced cheerfully.

"I'm not the one always getting shot," she retorted then grabbed her purse and headed out the side door for her car.

Once Rosa was out the door, Sal turned on the small light above the sink and opened the cupboard door. Where the bag of chips should have been, there was a note that read, "Eat healthy!" Sal groaned, shut the cupboard door, and opened the back closet door. He removed a grocery bag filled with chips and pretzels. He opened each bag and emptied them into decorative baskets then removed two bottles of beer from the refrigerator. It was a little too obvious that Sal was dying to have a guy's night. Sal could hear Rosa's car leaving and the car from the gate pulling up. When he heard the car shut off, Sal hesitated. Had Holden planned on staying for a while as well? Sal hurried to the refrigerator and removed a third bottle of beer just in case. As if timed perfectly, there was a knock on the door.

"It's open," Sal called out while twisting the cap off the first bottle of beer.

When Sal turned toward the kitchen door, his expression dropped at the familiar yet uninvited guest and his two hired henchmen.

"Giovanni," Sal just about gasped as he stared at his old friend with surprise. "What brings you here?"

Giovanni was a handsome, moderately athletic built man in his late forties with dark hair and a classic Italian look about him. Although he was somewhat imposing standing a little over six foot tall, his reputation as a powerful mob boss was his most intimidating feature. His accompanying muscle consisted of two men who were both around six foot four and looked like professional wrestlers. Between their large, muscular chests and arms, the additional girth of their hidden shoulder holsters almost kept their arms from touching their sides. Neither man looked particularly friendly.

Although Sal didn't seem intimidated by the much-feared man, he didn't make any sudden moves either. It wasn't often someone as notorious as Giovanni showed up in person and unannounced at anyone's home. As of late, Giovanni rarely left his personal island, which was a long way from Colorado Springs. His unexpected visit was somewhat concerning. Giovanni suddenly laughed and smiled while holding out his open arms to Sal. Sal laughed in response and gave his old friend a manly hug. Giovanni pulled back, grinned, and lightly slapped Sal's face.

"You've trimmed down since our last meeting," Giovanni announced and eyed Sal's frame. He appeared disappointed and shook his head. "That surly housekeeper of yours not feeding you enough?"

Sal frowned and waved him off. "She has me on a diet," he announced. "I'm reduced to sneaking snacks in the house after she's gone to bed."

Giovanni laughed and indicated the kitchen table. "Let's sit a moment," he announced. "We need to catch up."

Sal nodded and handed his old friend one of the bottles of beer then took a seat at the table.

Giovanni accepted the bottle, eyed it, and shot a look at Sal. "What's this? Lite beer?" He shook his head and sat at the table across from Sal. "At this rate, you may as well marry the old girl." He suddenly hesitated and cast a quick look around. "She's not hanging around, is she?"

"No, she was leaving for her sister's house when you pulled in," Sal replied.

Giovanni sighed with relief then took a swig from the bottle. "She knows my house manager, Gretchen," he announced. "If they get to talking, I'll be drinking lite beer too."

Sal grinned in response. "We've come a long way, huh?" he teased.

"Having grown kids will do that," Giovanni replied then sighed deeply and eyed Sal. "You know how it is."

"I can't complain about my daughter," Sal announced. "Since she's been with Beck, our relationship is pretty solid."

Giovanni stared at the bottle of beer in his hand and appeared distant. Sal noted his look.

"Something troubling you?" Sal asked. "You traveled a long way for an unannounced visit."

The intimidating man shifted uncomfortably in his chair then met Sal's gaze. "It's my son, Marco," he replied. "After his wedding day massacre, he became understandably angry. I figured he'd eventually get it out of his system. You know, meet a nice girl and all." Giovanni shook his head and looked back at his bottle of beer. "He refuses to move on. He's dwelling on that day. The more he dwells; the angrier he becomes." Giovanni frowned and met Sal's gaze. "He blames everyone for his shattered life. He blames me, you, and your friends."

Sal stared at Giovanni and revealed his concern. "My daughter?"

Giovanni nodded. "It's as if he's completely forgotten what his lying fiancé did to him," he announced. "He's placing blame on everyone but the ones who deserve it."

"What are you saying?"

"I'm saying my son is out of control," Giovanni informed Sal while staring at him in all seriousness. "I came out here to warn you so that you could warn your friends. He's my son, and I love him, but I think he's been monitoring my business. That's why I came out here unannounced. I couldn't risk him finding out."

"You think he's monitoring your calls?" Sal asked with surprise.

"Someone is," Giovanni replied. "Normally, I'd seek out the rat and destroy him, but I'm afraid the rat this time is my own son. I can't harm my boy. Honestly, with the way he's been acting, I could be the one in danger."

"What do you intend to do?" Sal asked.

"Currently, I'm avoiding him," Giovanni replied. "He left a few days ago, and I'm making an effort to keep him off my island until he cools down. I have a few men keeping tabs on him, but I don't even know who I can trust in my own ranks anymore." Giovanni held his breath and seemed distressed. "Just keep an eye out for Marco. Even if he has lost his mind, your daughter should be safe. I don't even know the location of your friends. Just look out for yourself. If you happen to see my son, avoid him."

"Thanks for the warning, old friend," Sal announced.

The outer kitchen door opened without warning to reveal Gil, Holden, and Darth. Both enforcers simultaneously reached inside their jackets for their semiautomatics hidden in their shoulder holsters. Darth suddenly stopped and snarled viciously at the two men while Gil and Holden reached for their weapons at the same time.

"No," Sal cried out and sprang up from his chair while waving his hands then turned oddly calm. "We're all friends." He motioned gently with his hands to keep anyone from making any sudden movements. "Everyone just relax."

Gil and Holden released the handles of their hidden weapons while Giovanni's men did the same. Once everyone relaxed, Darth stopped growling. Giovanni stood and grinned when he saw Gil. He took a step toward him with his hand extended. Darth closely watched the man moving toward Gil. Although his eyes remained focused on the questionable man, he didn't growl.

"I remember you," Giovanni announced cheerfully. "You're one of Sal's *special* friends."

As Gil and Giovanni shook hands, Holden's expression immediately dropped, having recognized the man.

"Uh, I don't think I should be here," Holden announced while tensing.

"Relax, Holden," Sal assured him. "Giovanni is an old friend just visiting while he's in town."

Giovanni grinned and extended his hand to Holden as he took a step closer. "You're a nervous one," the mob boss teased.

Holden uncertainly accepted Giovanni's hand and shook it while keeping his eyes on the man.

"This is Jackie's husband, Holden," Sal informed his friend. "The fed."

Giovanni looked Holden in the eyes then grinned and laughed. "That explains a lot," he teased and laughed some more before releasing Holden's hand. "Your wife is lovely." Giovanni then shrugged. "Maybe a little crazy but lovely. You're a lucky man."

"I was just about to order some pizza," Sal announced cheerfully while clapping his hands together. "Will you be joining us, Holden?"

"I'm not sure I should," Holden replied while remaining tense. "The Bureau may consider that a conflict of interest."

"What conflict?" Giovanni teased and laughed. "Sal's an old friend. We were just catching up on old times." His smile cheapened. "Not hiding a body or anything."

Holden raked his fingers through his hair and shifted uncomfortably. "I really need to go," he announced. "It was nice meeting you." He then pointed at Sal. "I'll talk to you later."

All five, as well as Darth, watched Holden leave the kitchen in a hurry. Once he was gone, Sal and Giovanni exchanged curious looks then laughed.

"He's a great guy," Sal informed his friend.

"A little nervous though," Giovanni teased while maintaining his humored grin.

"He used to be that way around me too," Sal announced with a laugh.

Chapter 15

It was a little after nine o'clock that night in the quiet neighborhood within Vernon Heights. Nearly all the homes had lights on indicating their occupants were still up despite being a weekday night. Neighborhood kids were riding their bikes back home before getting the dreaded call from their mothers. Since it was summer, most of the children played until dark, pushing their curfew to the limit. Jackie's childhood home seemed quiet despite just about every light being on, but it was actually quite noisy inside. Kirk, Bogart, and Monroe shouted at the television while watching the ending of a baseball game. Bogart and Monroe were fans of the local team while Kirk was a fan of the rival team.

Jackie stood before the kitchen counter while making two mugs of tea. It was obvious she wasn't going to be missed by any of the men in the living room. She took both mugs and headed onto the back porch. She didn't bother turning on the patio light since there was still enough light to see the large yard. Jackie saw Zack's chair was vacant, although she wasn't too surprised, then scanned the rest of the yard. When she didn't see him, she approached the edge of the patio beneath the covered porch, paused, and extended the first mug of tea up to the porch roof. She only waited a moment before the mug was removed from her hand. She held up the second mug, which was also taken. Jackie jumped onto the half wall and easily climbed onto the porch roof where Zack sat holding both mugs while patiently waiting for her. Jackie sat alongside Zack and accepted her tea mug.

"Are you okay?" she asked in a soft, sympathetic tone while studying her friend.

"I'm fine," he responded without looking at her then sipped his tea. "Why wouldn't I be?"

"Offhand; I can think of two reasons," Jackie replied as she cast a look at his profile.

She didn't know why he always insisted on lying to her about his emotions when she easily saw through him.

"I haven't even given it a second thought," Zack remarked without care.

"Bullshit," Jackie scoffed, no longer wanting to play that game. She then relaxed and joined him at staring across the neighborhood.

Zack groaned and shook his head. "I want to believe it's a con," he remarked. "Somehow, someone from my past is using these two kids to flush me out." Zack held his breath. "I just can't get past the girl. She looks so much like Maggie. For a moment, I thought I was seeing a ghost."

"You know, if you want to talk to them--"

"No," Zack launched and shifted uncomfortably. "They hate me, and by all rights, they should. It's my fault Maggie died. I exposed her to my past, and my past came back and took her away. I never should have gotten involved the way I did." He then hesitated. "Maybe I never should have left. I don't know." He then glanced at her.

Jackie gently touched Zack's lower arm. "You did everything in your power to keep your past from going after her," she insisted. "You threw yourself off a cliff, for heaven's sake."

"Abbott should have aborted," Zack snarled. "Gil told him she left the apartment. When he saw her there, he should have scrubbed the mission." He hesitated and drew a deep breath. "I don't blame your father for going back and telling her I was still alive. He wanted to right a wrong. Unfortunately, it makes me feel even worse. Before she died, she knew I was alive. I can't imagine what she had to be thinking." He shook his head. "I killed her long before she died in that car wreck."

Zack then eyed Jackie alongside him. "What sort of man does something like that?" He sank into his own thoughts then groaned. "She was pregnant, and I never even knew it."

"I doubt she even knew yet," Jackie reassured him. "You couldn't have possibly known."

"She named my daughter Scorpio," Zack gasped and fought his tears.

Jackie placed her arm around Zack's head and pulled it to her shoulder.

"Twins," he whispered while resting his head against her. "Maggie gave me twins, and neither of us got to see them grow up."

"You need to make peace with this, Zack," Jackie informed him as a million different scenarios raced through her mind. "You should talk to them."

"They hate me," he replied softly. "I hate me. Why shouldn't they?"

"I'm not saying you need to be their father or make them like you," Jackie announced while patting his head on her shoulder. "I'm just asking you to talk to them. They went out of their way to find you. I'm sure they have something to say too."

"They wanted to kill me," he remarked. "You were there. Wasn't it obvious? The sword was a giveaway."

"There were some raw emotions," she responded back. "That doesn't mean they don't have something they want to say to you. If they want to scream and yell, tell you they hate you, it's unimportant. None of you are going to heal until the three of you get it out in the open."

"I can't do it," Zack replied timidly. "Being confronted with what I did to their mother is the only thing I can't do." He nuzzled her shoulder. "I've hit bottom, Jackie. I just can't do this anymore."

"You're not a quitter, Zack," Jackie insisted while staring at him. "You don't give up on anything. If you want, I'll talk to them."

"No, I don't want that either," he replied softly.

"Othello and Ellie are arriving early tomorrow morning. They're supposed to meet Gil and Sal at the airport by eleven o'clock," Jackie reminded him. "You and I can drive them to the airport. We'll take the helicopter to one of your little secret hideaways so you can work this out."

He straightened and gave her a surprised look. "You actually trust me to be alone in one of my hideaways with a cache of weapons?"

"No, I don't," Jackie replied while glaring at him then released the breath she'd been holding. "I'm going to stay with you. You just need a few days to clear your mind, that's all." She studied him a moment then quoted the Navy SEAL motto. "*The only easy day was yesterday.*"

Zack cast a look at her and offered a tiny smile. "Yes, Commander."

Jackie smiled smugly and sipped her tea. He may have meant it as an insult, but Jackie was damned proud of that particular insult.

§

Evening. It was after ten o'clock that night, and the Vernon Heights motel was mostly quiet. Sunday was a big checkout day, so there were few guests remaining that night. Mac sat on one of the lounge chairs at the poolside while clutching her knees to her chest as she stared at the clear water glowing from the underwater lights. Maverick sat on one of the nearby lounge chairs and watched her in silence. Stone walked across the patio and approached them with a defeated look. Mac didn't bother looking at him. Maverick looked up and appeared hopeful.

Stone frowned and shook his head. "Rayner said Scorpio still doesn't want to talk to anyone," he announced. "And Kane isn't even answering his door."

"He won't even text me back," Maverick remarked. "We haven't heard from either of them since we got back from the cemetery this morning."

Stone sat on the lounge chair with Maverick, hunched over, and clasped his hands between his knees. "Can't say I blame either," he remarked with little emotion. "Kane got his ass kicked by a man twice his age, and Scorpio was nearly piked by a she-ninja."

"Let's face it," Maverick muttered and rubbed the back of his neck. "We had our collective asses handed to us today. We weren't ready for what came at us. Damned lucky they didn't want us dead."

"It's all my fault," Mac finally muttered without looking at either.

"A little maybe," Stone replied.

Maverick smacked Stone on the arm with added vigor and gestured angrily with his hand.

"What?" Stone demanded while glaring at Maverick. "I didn't say it was *all* her fault. Kane acts like he and Mac are so tight. If he had been truthful with her in the first place, we might have avoided all this drama." He gingerly rubbed his shoulder. "And bruises."

"Kane has every right to hate me," Mac informed them then held her breath. "You all do. If I had come clean about my entire history with Whiskey Tango Foxtrot, we could have avoided all of this." She shook her head. "I tried to warn Kane. I knew Zack would tear him apart if provoked. You can't serve two masters. I knew better, but I played the odds anyway."

"Why didn't you say something?" Maverick asked while studying her profile.

Mac groaned and finally stretched out on the lounge chair. She now stared at the stars in the clear sky. "My relationship with them is a complicated one," she informed him. "Like trying to win the attention of an abusive mother. Any attention is better than none."

Maverick looked at his watch, sighed, and stood. He extended his hand to Mac. She eyed his hand before meeting his gaze and showed little reaction.

"Come on," he announced in a sympathetic tone. "It's late, and you need some sleep. I'll buy one round from the minibar before bed."

"Why are you being so nice to me?" Mac asked and refused to move. "Why aren't you mad?"

"I am mad," Maverick informed her with little emotion. "I'm mad at myself for listening to Kane. I'm mad that I caved and excluded you on his insistence. I'm mad that we all got our egos and bodies bruised this morning." He drew a deep breath. "We could both use a hot shower, a strong drink, and a lot of sleep to forget this day."

Mac didn't take her eyes off his. She exhaled, accepted his hand, and allowed him to pull her to her feet. Stone eyed them as they crossed the patio.

"So where does that leave me tonight?" Stone called after them.

Maverick glanced back at his friend. "You'll probably want to get a room for the night," he announced and guided Mac back to his room.

Stone groaned and shook his head. "I had a bad day too," he muttered to himself. "Anyone care about my bad day?" He shook his head as he walked toward the motel lobby. "I need some new friends."

§

Kane sat on the bed in his room with his back against the headboard, his knees up to his chest, and his head in his hands. He subconsciously raked his fingers through his thick, dark hair while staring at the duvet. His knuckles were scraped and covered in dried blood that he still hadn't washed off. Kane allowed his head to fall back against the headboard revealing the large bruise on his cheek from where his father hit him in the face.

§

Scorpio lay on her bed, curled on her side while clinging to the extra pillow. Despite her blank expression, she was reliving the entire scene at the old cemetery one blow at a time. Rayner sat on the bed and stared at her back facing him. He left the television on so it would keep the room dimly lit and offer some white noise to soothe his traumatized girlfriend. Rayner leaned over Scorpio and gently brushed the hair from her face revealing the scratch on her left cheek where Jackie nearly impaled her with her own sword.

"Can I get you anything?" Rayner asked while gently stroking her hair.

He was unable to take his eyes off the small scratch on her cheek. It obviously disturbed him that he nearly witnessed her death. One split second and a skilled woman's amazing self-control were all that stood between Scorpio and death. He wasn't surprised when she didn't answer him. She hadn't said much since they left the cemetery that morning.

"What happened?" she finally whispered without moving or looking at him.

"We followed Kane," Rayner replied with some disgust.

Scorpio tensed from his words then rolled onto her back and looked at him by the glow of the television. "If you're trying to make me feel better, you're doing a lousy job."

"No, I'm not trying to make you feel better," Rayner informed her. "Kane poked the bear. He flushed out a man who didn't want to be found, and it nearly got both of you killed." He hesitated and reconsidered the comment. "Possibly all of us, if it had been their intention."

Scorpio pulled herself up into a sitting position and leaned against the headboard next to Rayner. "What was he thinking?" she gasped softly with limited understanding.

"I suspect he wasn't," Rayner replied. "Kane was looking for redemption from the man he felt abandoned him, his sister, and his mother."

"That wasn't Kane," Scorpio informed him and again relived the scene in the cemetery. "I don't know who that was." She held her breath. "Maybe it was that part of me he carries buried deep inside him. That same monster I've been trying to keep locked away."

"I'll admit; his actions shocked me," Rayner remarked and shook his head while seemingly reliving that morning as well. "I thought your brother was reserved and level-headed. I guess everyone has their breaking point."

Scorpio drew a deep breath and stared into Rayner's eyes. She knew what needed to be done, and it was time she said it.

"It's time we went home," Scorpio announced. "We're on the first flight out of here."

"I'm certainly not going to argue with you," Rayner remarked then held his breath as he studied her expression. "What about Kane?"

"He's going to listen to reason this time," she insisted.

"And if he doesn't?"

"Then we're going to tie him up, rent a van, and drive all the way back to Maine," Scorpio informed him.

Rayner raised his brow with some surprise by the comment. "Sounds like a plan."

Scorpio moved into Rayner's arms and clung insecurely to him. He pulled her against him and warmly kissed the top of her head.

Chapter 16

Monday, July 14th.   One o'clock in the morning. Scorpio twitched in her sleep, jolting Rayner who had been asleep while holding her against him from behind. He had just barely woke when Scorpio sharply cried out and just about flew up in bed. Rayner jumped away from her with surprise and looked around a moment with disorientation while holding his chest. Scorpio gasped several times before allowing her head to fall into her hands then sobbed softly. Rayner immediately pulled Scorpio into his arms and held her against him.

"It's okay," he gently reassured her while caressing her hair. "It was just a bad dream."

Scorpio finally got a hold of her emotions, wiped her tears, and pulled away from Rayner. She met his gaze through the dimly lit room. "I dreamt he killed Kane," she whispered while insecurely rubbing her chilled arms. "I screamed for him to stop, and then he came after me."

"It was just a dream," Rayner reassured her. "Despite what happened yesterday, your father isn't coming after you or Kane."

She lifted her head and eyed Rayner with a serious look. "It wasn't him," Scorpio replied while trembling. "It was my grandfather."

Rayner was slightly surprised by the response then resumed comforting her. "He's never going to hurt you again," he gently replied. "He can't. He's dead."

"I know," she whispered while running her trembling fingers through her hair. "I hate sleeping. Nothing but nightmares and bad memories just waiting for me to close my eyes."

Rayner affectionately brushed the stray tear from her cheek. Scorpio met Rayner's gaze and couldn't get over how sweet he was despite everything she'd put him through since the day they'd met. She threw the covers off and got out of bed.

"I, uh, need to check on Kane," she informed him. "I need to make sure he's okay."

"The connecting door is locked," Rayner reminded her as she approached the door dividing the two rooms.

They heard the deadbolt on the other side of the connecting door unlock. Scorpio looked back at Rayner, who seemed surprised that Kane had heard their conversation from the next room.

"No point in you losing sleep," she informed him. She needed to spare him some of her drama. He needed his sleep too. "I'll be back."

Scorpio opened the connecting door and entered Kane's motel room. Kane was already back on his bed sitting against the headboard and staring at the blank television screen. Scorpio closed the door behind her and joined Kane on the bed. He didn't bother looking at her and offered no emotion.

"Thanks for unlocking the door," she announced timidly.

"I had to pee anyway," he replied then cast a docile look at her. "Are you okay?"

"Just needed a break from all the rainbows and unicorns," she replied as she rested her head against the headboard and stared at the blank television screen with him.

"Well, you came to the right place," he muttered. Kane drew a deep breath and finally looked at his sister. "I'm sorry, Scorp. I'm sorry I ever started this quest, and I'm sorry for dragging you into it." He tossed his head back against the headboard with a loud clunk. "I nearly got you killed. I don't know that I can forgive myself for that."

Scorpio clung to Kane's arm and rested her head on his shoulder. "You met our father, and you got your answer," she gently replied. "It's time to go back home."

Kane was silent a moment then seemed to relive the trauma. "Their level of organization was beyond comprehension," he remarked while shaking his head. "We were like puppies taking on a wild pack of wolves." He groaned and remained lost in yesterday's beating. "Did you see their weapons?"

"I can't say I noticed," Scorpio replied and subconsciously shivered. "I was too busy fighting that psycho ninja woman trying to take my head off."

"Our pilot," Kane moaned and again shook his head. "Our damned helicopter pilot in Colorado. The moment I saw her, I knew we'd been played. They were onto us before we even knew they were there. I feel so stupid." Kane then hesitated. "And small. We never stood a chance against them. They were two steps ahead of us from the beginning. While I was asking questions about our father, they were organizing and moving into position." He finally looked at her, held his breath, and gently touched the scratch on her cheek. "I am so sorry, Scorp."

Scorpio placed her arms around his neck and hugged him without comment. Kane pulled her against him and held her in his arms.

§

It was just about five o'clock in the morning. Mac lay naked in Maverick's arms while he slept bundled beneath the sheets on the double bed. She stared at the ceiling for the longest time then glanced at the bedside clock. She slipped out from his arms while attempting not to disturb him. Mac found her discarded clothes on the floor and quietly dressed. When she looked back at the bed, Maverick's eyes were open, and he watched her.

"Where are you going so early?" he asked.

"I can't sleep," she informed him. "The diner up the road should be opening soon. I'm going to walk up there."

"Want me to come along?"

"No, there's no point in both of us losing sleep," she insisted.

Maverick nuzzled the pillow and had a difficult time staying awake. "We're probably leaving today," he informed her. "Don't be gone long."

"I won't," she replied then kissed him quickly on the lips. "Get some sleep."

She didn't have to tell him twice. Maverick closed his eyes and was out almost instantly. Mac approached the motel room door, unbolted it, and then glanced back at the sleeping man. When she was certain he was asleep, she picked up her duffel bag by the door and slipped out of the room.

§

The private airfield on the outskirts of Vernon Heights seemed busy for almost seven in the morning. Being it was Monday, a lot of businessmen were seeking private flights to undisclosed locations for meetings. Mac entered the small terminal building and approached the tired man at the main desk. The older man gave her a quick once-over, appeared puzzled, and then seemed to recognize her.

"You're Izzy's friend, aren't you?" he asked.

"Yeah, I'm Izzy's friend," she replied then managed a tiny smile. "Is Izzy around?"

"You just missed him," the man announced then looked at his watch. "He wasn't going far. He should be back in two hours. Did you want to wait for him?"

"I've got nothing but time," Mac replied with a sigh. "Is the coffee still free?"

"Yeah, but it tastes like shit," the man informed her. "I'd know. I'm the one who made it."

Mac snorted a laugh. "I'll be in the break room making a fresh pot of coffee."

"Be my guest," the man replied and seemed to appreciate the idea.

§

Almost two hours passed. It was a little before nine o'clock in the morning. Mac sat on the worn sofa in the private airport lounge and flipped through an outdated aviator magazine. She was bored and tired from lack of sleep. The sound of a dog's pattering feet on the tile floor caught her attention. Mac lowered her magazine and saw Darth standing directly in front of her just about on eye level where she sat.

"Darth?" she asked with some surprise.

Darth woofed, wagged his tail, and panted happily before licking her chin. Mac laughed and scratched Darth behind the ear.

"Hey, boy, what are you--?" Mac's expression dropped. "Oh."

Chapter 17

Gil refueled his plane a little after nine o'clock that morning while Sal paced with his cell phone to his ear. Despite the number of planes on the tarmac, there didn't seem to be any signs of life at the private airfield, although there was some laughter coming from one of the hangars. Many pilots knew one another and often hung out when they were running ahead of schedule or waiting on passengers. Sal finally disconnected the call and eyed Gil, who seemed to stare off into the sky. When Sal approached him, Gil popped out of his thoughts and gave him a curious look.

"What did they say about us being early?" Gil asked with a teasing smile.

"I hadn't tried calling them," Sal replied then indicated his cell phone. "I was trying to get a hold of Pinto on the satellite phone at the lodge."

"I'm sure no one answered," Gil informed him with a humored laugh. "Too early for Beck and Pinto on a Monday morning."

"It's seven o'clock in Colorado," Sal countered.

Gil eyed him and appeared humored. "Not everyone is up with the sun, Sal," he announced. "When we're not working, we like to sleep in."

"Seven o'clock is sleeping in," Sal countered.

"Are you sure you didn't serve with the commander?" Gil teased.

Sal chuckled then glanced at his watch. "What time are they meeting us here?"

"Eleven," Gil replied. "We're early. Make yourself comfortable."

Sal groaned and shook his head. "Vacations are too stressful for me," he remarked. "I'm going to get some coffee. See you in there."

§

Sal entered the airport lounge, which was void of life except for the German shepherd dog sitting by the water cooler as if waiting for someone to get him a drink.

"Have the place to ourselves, huh?" Sal teased to the dog. "I didn't want to make small talk with pompous, rich guys anyway."

Darth woofed in response. The lounge door shut behind Sal. Sal immediately spun around in response. He was rather quick with his reflexes as a man accustomed to surprise attacks would be. Mac leaned against the closed door with her arms folded across her chest and a sneer on her face.

"Not exactly the bastard I was expecting to run into here," Mac snarled.

Sal relaxed and frowned when he saw his former employee. "Good morning to you too," he remarked with little emotion. "To what do I owe the honor?"

"I get why you don't trust me," Mac announced in a calm tone. "I even understand why you stood firm with the team and blacklisted me from ever working for you again." She allowed her arms to fall to her sides while glaring at him as her eyes narrowed. "But rolling me over to get to my friends? That I can't forgive."

Sal frowned and nodded. "Your new *friends* were displaying stalker level, mercenary behavior," he informed her. "Naturally, I was going to alert the team to everything I knew." His brows rose sharply. "I'm sorry you had to go down with

101

your new friends, but you didn't exactly stop them from poking around in the team's affairs. You had to know the hammer was coming down."

"Yeah, I knew," she scoffed defensively. "That's why I flew all the way the hell out here. I wanted to stop a massacre. When you learned I was involved with them, did it ever occur to you to come to me first? Is our relationship so fractured that you can't even extend me that common courtesy?"

"I picked a side, Mac," Sal casually remarked. "Zack doesn't trust you. Considering you attempted to steal millions from me, I'd say he's more trustworthy."

Mac shook her head while frowning. "I saved your ass on Giovanni's island," she reminded him then sneered. "I doubt I'll make that mistake twice."

She turned and left the lounge while nearly plowing down the man from the front desk. The man watched her leave with some surprise. Sal frowned and looked at Darth, who looked back at him while tilting his head.

"It's complicated," Sal told the dog.

§

A few minutes later, Sal carried two cups of coffee onto Gil's private plane, where they could wait in comfort for their travel companions. Gil's private plane wasn't top of the line luxurious, but it was plush and comfortable. It was certainly nicer than the small, airport lounge. Sal joined Gil in the fuselage, handed him the extra cup of coffee, and sat on one of the plush chairs across from the pilot. Gil sipped the coffee and seemed pleasantly surprised.

"Better than usual," Gil remarked.

"I suspect someone *else* made it," Sal reported then frowned. "I ran into Mac in the lounge."

"Mac?" he gasped with surprise then appeared curious. "What's she doing here?"

"I suspect she's fleeing the scene of the crime," Sal replied then shook his head in disappointment. "I wanted to give her the benefit of the doubt, but the last few weeks haven't helped her case any."

"I disagree," Gil announced surprising Sal.

"Oh?"

"They're good people," Gil informed him. "She didn't sell us out to a bunch of mercenaries. She just found someplace where she fit in."

"Do you honestly believe she was acting in anyone's best interest but her own?"

"Absolutely," Gil replied without hesitation. "Lee confessed to Ross that Mac was the one who patched her up after she'd been shot. She also asked Lee if she thought we needed her help when those mercenaries came after us. That's not someone protecting their own hide. That's someone desperately seeking approval. Unfortunately, until Zack loses his hostility toward her, there's no place for her with us."

"Did he ever say what happened between them?" Sal finally asked.

"No, not even to Jackie," Gil remarked then held his breath. "It had to be pretty bad. Zack was willing to forgive and forget with Katya, and she threatened to castrate him *and* kill Jackie."

"What could Mac possibly have done to piss him off to that degree?"

Gil shrugged. "He's not talking, and no one is asking," he replied.

Darth suddenly perked up and ran down the steps and off the plane.

Sal watched the dog then looked back at Gil. "What's with him?"

"One of the guys has a wealthy widowed woman that he carts around," Gil remarked and waved off the dog's piqued curiosity. "She owns this cute miniature collie. Darth has the hots for that collie." He shook his head. "She's going to be pissed when she sees those puppies."

"Careful, she may sue you and Darth for puppy support," Sal teased.

"I should stop him from roaming," Gil confessed then grinned. "But you only live once, right?"

Sal laughed then sank into thought and seemed less jovial. He sighed deeply. "At least someone's having a good time," he finally admitted.

Just outside the plane, Darth rounded the steps and sniffed around the plane's wheels. He followed his nose a few feet as if tracking something of importance then stopped and snarled at the partially open storage compartment near the tail section. The compartment opened partway. Darth snarled and lunged for the opening. The compartment door was vigorously pulled down and struck him on the head. Darth barely yelped before hitting the tarmac.

§

Sal and Gil sat in the comfortable chairs within the fuselage and laughed like old friends over some of their adventures. It was only nine-thirty. They still had another hour and a half until Monroe arrived with Othello and Ellie. Neither man seemed to mind the wait.

"Othello said he's bringing his drone along to check out the 'scenery'," Sal teased while grinning. "Since the beaches are mostly private, he said he'll teach me how to fly the drone. You know, where I won't accidentally kill anyone with it."

"Ellie and I are going to take Zack's old yacht out for a day cruise," Gil announced while drifting off into his own romantic fantasy.

"Zack has a yacht?" Sal asked with surprise.

"Yeah, he left it docked at the island marina after it sustained some damage from the hurricane," Gil replied. "Monroe lived on it for a while when his house was being rebuilt, uh, the first time."

Gil looked toward the steps then eyed his watch. "I should probably see what trouble Darth is getting into," he remarked then shook his head. "He's starting to beg for food from strangers. Holden's been spoiling him again."

"I'll check on him," Sal announced and sprang up from his seat. He instantly regretted the action and rubbed his sore shoulder. "I must be getting old. I don't remember gunshot wounds being this painful before."

"It's been too long since you've been shot," Gil teased then grinned. "It always hurts."

Sal laughed then headed for the nearby steps and disappeared from the plane. Gil finished his cup of coffee then heard Sal on the steps. He looked up as Sal returned to the fuselage with a strange look on his face and his hands held up in front of him. Gil reached for the gun in his shoulder holster before he even saw the man holding the gun to Sal's head from behind.

"Do it, and your friend dies," the man announced.

Sal was forced into one of the nearby seats while the man kept the gun to his head. A second man hurried onto the plane, approached Gil, and removed the semiautomatic from his shoulder holster. He tucked Gil's gun down the back of his pants then removed a pair of zip ties and indicated for Gil to turn around. Gil frowned and did as instructed in fear Sal would be killed. The man secured the zip ties to Gil's wrists behind his back then shoved him into the plush seat. His partner then approached Sal with a second set of zip ties. The man with the gun motioned for Sal to turn around. Sal frowned and did as he was instructed, allowing the man to restrain his wrists behind his back as well. He cringed with some discomfort in his already injured shoulder. Once the zip ties were secure, Sal was pushed into one of the vacant seats. The first man replaced his weapon to his hidden shoulder holster then nodded his partner to the cockpit.

"Let's get this thing airborne," he announced.

The second man hurried up the aisle toward Gil and the cockpit while the first man turned toward the steps. A black, booted foot struck the man in the face, throwing him backward and almost into Sal. Mac leaped into the plane as the man recovered and punched him in the face. The second man stopped on his way to the cockpit and reached for the gun he'd removed from Gil. Gil kicked the man in the knee, dropping him to the aisle. He then jumped from his seat and kicked him in the groin for good measure. As the first man recovered from the hard, fast punch, Mac kicked him in the face. He was thrown backward against the plane's interior and collapsed into the empty seat next to Sal. Sal stared at Mac with some surprise then grinned and laughed. Mac sneered back at him. Sal's expression suddenly dropped.

"Behind you," he cried out.

Mac spun into a roundhouse kick and struck a third man coming up the steps. He was thrown down the steps but managed to catch his balance before hitting the bottom. As he leaped back up the steps, Mac attempted to snap kick him in the face, but limited space and his position on the steps allowed him to avoid her flying foot. He tackled her into the unconscious man in the seat next to Sal. Mac immediately punched the man in the face to get him off her. Her position beneath him gave her little leverage and lessened the harshness of her punch. The man was minimally fazed and punched her back. She took the hit to her cheek. Despite the hard hit, Mac managed to kick him off her. As he caught his balance, Mac sprang to her feet. The man pulled a switchblade knife from his pocket. Mac only took a second to plan her course of attack.

As the man slashed the knife for her, she avoided the blade and immediately blocked his arm. She went for a low kick while keeping his hand with the knife at bay. The first man recovered and blocked her kick. Sal head-butted the man in the chair next to him. Sal and the man in the chair both suffered from the connection, but it got him out of Mac's way. Mac went for a second kick while keeping the knife away from her. Due to the tight quarters, the man was able to block her kick. She released her hold on his wrist and threw a left-handed punch. The man plunged the switchblade into her shoulder just before she punched him under the chin. The man was thrown off balance as Mac stumbled backward while clutching her bleeding shoulder. As the man lunged for Mac, Sal attempted to kick his legs out from beneath him.

The man avoided Sal's legs, punched Sal in the face with his left fist, and then continued on his mission to take down Mac. Despite the blood seeping between her fingers, Mac straightened and snap kicked the approaching man. She kicked the knife from his hand but had a difficult time maintaining her balance in the tight quarters and from the injury. The man punched her in the face, sending her to the floor. Once she was down, he punched her in the head. She no longer moved. Despite his hands tied behind his back, Gil was just about on top of the man standing over Mac. The man alongside Sal pulled his gun while springing to his feet and aimed it at Gil's face, stopping him in his tracks.

"Don't," the man snarled in anger.

Chapter 18

The black sports car raced into the private airport parking lot, drove up to one of the hangars, and spun into a circle as it came to a squealing halt in what had to be a precision parking job. Zack sat behind the wheel and laughed in his throat while another man, Othello, sat in the passenger seat and hooted excitedly. Othello was a heavyset man in his late twenties to early thirties with wild, curly dark hair. At first glance, the man wearing a superhero novelty t-shirt didn't look like someone to be taken seriously, but Othello was anything but an ordinary computer geek. He was possibly one keystroke away from being a criminal mastermind.

"That was freakin' awesome," Othello cried out.

Zack glanced at Othello while grinning. "I'm a great driver, right?"

"You totally missed that rabbit in the road," Othello responded and laughed. "I loved the part where we were airborne for a second."

"I don't understand why no one ever lets me drive," Zack countered.

Othello and Zack turned their heads and looked into the back seat. Jackie sat between Monroe and Gil's on-again-off-again ex-wife, Ellie. Ellie Rafferty was an auburn-haired beauty in her mid to late thirties. Ellie and Monroe clung to the seat and the side of the car while panting heavily from the experience while Jackie just about clung to Monroe. She was frozen in fear as her life seemingly flashed before her eyes. Othello and Zack exchanged looks.

"Are they okay?" Othello asked.

"Just being a bunch of drama queens," Zack announced and waved Othello off. "They're fine."

"Can I get out now?" Ellie gasped while staring straight ahead and seemed unable to blink.

Othello and Zack got out of the car and pushed their seats forward to release the hostages from the back seat. Monroe and Ellie jumped out of the car. Jackie slid over from the middle seat, climbed out on Zack's side, and met his gaze. Despite that he grinned like a schoolboy, Jackie's look was scathing.

"You're never driving again," she scoffed.

Zack allowed the driver's seat to fall back into place. "Drama queen," he muttered.

Once they recovered from their death ride, Monroe and Ellie looked around the tarmac for Gil's plane, but neither saw it.

"I guess we're early," Ellie reported then glanced at her watch.

It was a quarter until eleven, and they agreed to meet at the private field around eleven o'clock.

"Maybe they had a weather delay in Colorado," Jackie remarked as she also glanced at her watch. "Gil's never late if he can help it."

"I guess we should leave the bags in the trunk until they arrive," Monroe announced then eyed Jackie. "If you and Zack want to get going, you can leave the trunk unlocked. There's no reason for you to hang around."

"We're not on any sort of schedule," Jackie replied. "Just a little nature retreat. We'll wait with you. If they're going to be more than an hour late, I can always take you to Monroe's beach house. That way, they can make up time by heading straight there. I'll try to contact them in the air from my helicopter and check on their ETA."

"I'll stow our bags in the helicopter," Zack announced and popped the car's trunk. He grinned at Jackie as he removed both their duffel bags from the trunk containing Ellie, Monroe, and Othello's bags as well. "Maybe you'll let me fly the helicopter part of the way."

Jackie cast a glare at Zack. "You know my rules about you flying."

Zack frowned and playfully pouted. "Only over your dead body, when hell freezes over, or if there's a zombie apocalypse." He then grinned. "Whichever comes first."

"You'd totally rock a zombie apocalypse," Othello announced from a few feet away.

Jackie rolled her eyes. She couldn't handle another one of Othello's zombie apocalypse 'what-ifs'.

§

A little while later, Jackie and Zack entered the airport lounge where Monroe, Ellie, and Othello impatiently waited. It was a quarter after eleven o'clock, and Gil was late. The three eagerly eyed Jackie for some word on Gil's arrival. Jackie wished she had better news or even any news.

"What time will they be here?" Ellie asked while tossing her magazine aside.

Jackie frowned and shook her head. "I couldn't get ahold of them on the radio," she replied. "Gil only maintains radio silence in an emergency."

"What does that mean?" Ellie asked as her concern increased.

"Since we're not on a mission, there shouldn't be an emergency. I'm guessing he's just not in the plane for some reason," Jackie responded although she wasn't convinced there wasn't some diabolical reason for it.

"Where else would he be?" Monroe asked and now shared Ellie's concern.

"I didn't see any bad weather between here and Colorado," Jackie informed them. "So he shouldn't have been diverted to a different airport due to weather." She gave the others a curious look. "He didn't leave a voicemail with any of you?"

"I didn't get any messages," Ellie replied.

"Sal didn't call me either," Othello added.

Jackie frowned and sank into thought. She couldn't come up with a rational explanation for Gil's lack of communication that didn't involve foul play. Monroe seemed equally tense, as he must have come to the same conclusion. Something happened to them.

"It hasn't been that long," Othello chimed in. "I'm sure there's no reason to worry." He then raised his brows as if not convinced. "Right?"

"If he were delayed due to issues with the plane, he'd call from wherever he landed," Jackie remarked. "If he's in the air, he'd have his radio on."

"What are the chances there's an issue with his radio?" Othello asked.

Jackie considered the possibility.

"Minimal," Zack announced, coming out and saying what the others were thinking. "He knows he's expected. It's not like Gil not to check in." He then eyed Ellie. "Especially with Ellie waiting. He wouldn't do that."

Ellie tensed and appeared ready to panic. "You think something happened?"

Jackie held her breath and looked from Monroe to Zack. She didn't want to say what she was thinking. Monroe sprang to his feet and eyed the others.

"We'll give him another half an hour before we assume something has happened," Monroe announced. "I'm sure there's some logical explanation."

"The voice of reason has spoken," Zack informed them. "That being said; as the ambassador of paranoia, I intend to patrol the perimeter and do a little recon." He then nudged Jackie. "You have friends at the airfield in Colorado Springs. See what you can dig up on Gil's plane." He then shot a look at Othello. "See what you can extract from the desk jockey's computer on all inbound and outbound flights at this airfield this morning." Zack then pointed at Ellie. "You call Jackie's house. See if Kirk or Bogart heard anything." Zack then turned to Monroe. "You call the lodge and see if they've heard anything. If not; call Holden."

Zack turned and left the lounge. Jackie and Monroe exchanged baffled looks.

"What just happened?" Monroe asked. "Zack's never given orders before. He barely follows them."

"I couldn't tell you," Jackie replied while shaking her head then removed her cell phone. "But I'm not about to make him ask twice."

§

Othello stood before the reservation desk and watched as the attendant poked at the computer keyboard with one finger while attempting to pull up some information on Gil's plane. Othello leaned on the desk and stared in a nearly catatonic state before vigorously scratching his brow. The attendant stopped and looked at the screen. He then made a face.

"No, that's not what I wanted," the man announced. "Let me try that other screen. I still haven't gotten the hang of this new system."

Othello bolted upright, hustled his large frame behind the desk, and edged the man aside.

"Let me give it a try," Othello announced.

"It's a complex system--"

Othello rapidly struck keys. Despite his thick fingers, his keystrokes were precise and fluid. The attendant stared at the screen in disbelief while watching screens pop up and then disappear.

"You're good with computers, huh?" the man asked.

"I dabble," Othello replied without taking his eyes from the screen.

He finally stopped typing and read the screen before him. "Arrived at nine?" Othello announced with some surprise then appeared concerned. "Departed at nine-forty-five?" Othello looked at the attendant. "How is that possible?"

"I'm guessing he just refueled," the attendant replied. "That doesn't take long." The man then considered the comment and snapped his fingers. "You know, I think I remember seeing your friend's travel companion. Balding guy in his forties. He left the building with that dog I see around here a lot."

"Yeah, that's the other guy," Othello responded with some hope. "Do you remember seeing them takeoff?"

"A lot of planes took off around ten," he replied. "The pilots were playing cards in one of the hangars while waiting for their VIP passengers to arrive."

"This is important," Othello announced while staring at the man standing alongside him. "Did anything unusual happen while my friends were here? A fight? Anything at all suspicious?"

"No, not that I saw," the man replied then shrugged. "Well, apart from Izzy's friend ripping the bald guy a new one."

"Izzy's friend?" Othello asked while cocking his head with concern. "Who's Izzy's friend?"

"Attractive woman," the man replied then grinned. "Nice body."

"You don't know her name?"

The man shook his head.

"What were they arguing about?" Othello pressed.

"He said he didn't trust her," the man reported then gave it some thought. "Something about her stealing money and picking a side."

"You said she tore into him," Othello prompted. "What did she say?"

"Something about saving his ass on some island and not doing it again," the man remarked then raised his brows. "She was really heated. Nearly knocked me over storming from the lounge."

"Saving his ass on an island?" Othello asked and appeared bewildered. A strange realization swept over him. "What did the dog do during this argument?"

"The dog?"

"Yeah, the dog," Othello practically cried out. "You said the bald man was with the dog. How did the dog react to this woman?"

"I don't recall the dog's reaction at all," the man replied. "Why?"

"Son-of-a-bitch," Othello muttered under his breath and shook his head. "If Darth didn't defend Sal, it means he *knew* and *liked* the woman." Othello slammed his palms on the desk. "I need to find the guys."

Chapter 19

Zack left the empty hangar where the pilots had earlier collected. The few planes remaining on the tarmac were grounded for the morning. He walked past the remaining planes while carefully scanning them and the tarmac for any signs of his teammate or indications that he'd been at the airport that morning. Zack paused by one of the planes and studied a damp mark on the front wheel and the tarmac beneath it. Zack crouched beneath the front of the plane, dabbed his finger in the damp spot, and smelled his fingertip.

"Someone's been marking their territory," Zack announced then looked around as he wiped his finger on the tarmac. He straightened and rounded the plane.

Zack continued across the tarmac and paused when he saw a trail of dark spots. At first, it appeared as if something had leaked. Perhaps something dripping from a passing plane. Zack crouched before the first dried droplet and scratched his finger across it. He stared at the red stain on his finger then immediately straightened and followed the line of droplets with his eyes. He again looked at his finger and wiped the blood onto his pants. As gross as it seemed, having a sample for potential DNA didn't hurt, and Zack was no stranger to wearing the blood of others on his clothes. He followed the droplets nearly twenty yards before they suddenly stopped. He looked around a moment.

Jackie approached Zack and was unable to hide her concern. "I spoke with some friends who frequent the airport in Colorado Springs," she announced. "One of them said Gil and Sal took off early this morning. They should have arrived here around nine o'clock our time."

"That's concerning," Zack replied then nodded to the trail of blood droplets. "Taking into account the dryness of that blood, someone was injured at least an hour ago. At the rate of bleed, I'm guessing it was a decent wound."

Jackie studied the trail of blood droplets, and her expression dropped. "Gil or Sal?"

"A male dog marked that plane over there," Zack informed her. "I'm guessing sometime in the last couple of hours. We need to hear what the others have learned."

§

Jackie and Zack entered the small terminal building and saw Othello standing in front of the desk with his laptop open and the terminal's computer screen turned toward him. He alternated typing into his computer and onto the terminal computer. The attendant didn't even attempt to stop Othello, who had essentially taken over the airport's computer system. Monroe paced the small lobby with his cell phone to his ear then disconnected the call when he saw Zack and Jackie. He hurried to join them.

"They were here. Terminal flight logs have them landing at nine and taking off forty-five minutes later," Monroe announced with a look of dread on his face. "The attendant said a woman fitting Mac's description was in the lounge arguing with Sal." He shook his head. "I've been trying Mac's cell phone, but she's not answering."

Ellie hurried across the lobby from the lounge and approached them with her cell phone in her hand. "No one has seen or heard from them.   Kirk and Bogart are on their way here."

"It's possible we have a situation," Zack informed them.   "I found a trail of blood on the tarmac covering twenty yards. I'm assuming someone was injured in one plane and ended up in a second plane."

"Gil," Ellie gasped as panic swept through her.

"How badly--?" Monroe asked then stopped himself and fidgeted while shifting a concerned look at Ellie.

Zack didn't answer the question but raised his brows in silent response so as not to upset Ellie.   Monroe cursed under his breath.

"Did you get in touch with Holden?" Jackie asked while attempting to mask her concern for Ellie's sake.

"He's running Gil's plane tail registration number through the FBI computer," Monroe replied.   "Hopefully, he'll be able to discover if and where it landed."

Zack glanced at Othello at the terminal desk.   "Anything, Othello?"

"Sal has GPS on his cell phone," Othello informed them without looking up from his laptop as he continued to type. "It's not responding with his location."

"What if his phone is turned off?" Ellie asked.   "You'll never be able to track him."

"It doesn't work that way," Othello replied.   "The only way it won't respond is if the phone is destroyed or they're out of range."   Othello glanced back at Ellie.   "I think they're still in the air."

"So that currently puts them a little over an hour away by plane," Monroe announced then looked at Jackie for her input on the situation.

"I can get a map from the helicopter and give a projected area, but I have no idea which way they went," Jackie informed him.

"Already working on it," Othello informed them.   "As soon as Sal's cell phone comes back online, it'll show up on my map."

"So we just sit here and wait?" Ellie demanded while nervously wringing her fingers together.   "Isn't there something else we can do?"

Monroe tensed then eyed the others. "There's one phone call we haven't made yet," he announced then grimaced. "But it's going to make everyone extremely uncomfortable."

"I don't care who's uncomfortable," Ellie cried out. "Whoever it is; call them."

Monroe, Zack, and Jackie exchanged looks and seemed to simultaneously tense.

Othello eyed all three. "Who do you need to call?"

There was a tense moment as they stared at one another. Zack drew a deep breath and raked his fingers through his hair. He released his breath and looked back at Monroe.

"Make the call."

Monroe removed his cell phone and pulled up his call list. He hesitated before pressing 'call' beneath the name 'Midnight Requisition'.

§

Mac lay unconscious in the cramped cargo hold of a small, private plane. The otherwise dark compartment was lit by a glow stick near the exterior door, which was clearly stained with bloody handprints, indicating she had attempted to escape through the door. The sound of the engine was nearly deafening as the area around Mac vibrated. Her bloodied shirt had been removed and was bunched on the floor not far from her, leaving her in her lacy, black bra. The stab wound on her blood covered shoulder was black and singed. A cigarette lighter remained in her outstretched hand. The smoky compartment smelled of singed flesh.

A dog whimpered softly but was barely audible above the loud hum of the craft's engine. Darth licked Mac's face repeatedly. When that didn't work, he clawed at her chest. His toenails caught the cleavage of her bra several times and jolted her body. Mac groaned as her head turned slightly. Darth woofed and again whimpered as he resumed licking her face. Mac again groaned and opened her eyes. She immediately cried out in agony while placing her hand to her shoulder, which hurt even worse. She pulled her hand away from the cauterized wound then looked around the cramped cargo hold.

Darth let out an excited woof that echoed through the cargo hold. Mac attempted to sit up, but she was weak from loss of blood and in a tremendous amount of pain. Darth placed his head under her arm. She clung to his collar and allowed him to pull her up into a sitting position, which was all the room she had before her head touched the top of the compartment. Mac endured the pain in her shoulder, panted several times, and then weakly patted the dog.

"Good boy," she whispered.

She looked around the compartment and the few bags she had rummaged through to find the lighter. Mac found a man's button shirt among the pile of clothes she'd torn from the bags. Her blood seemed to be everywhere within the compartment. Mac gingerly slipped her injured arm into the shirt followed by her good arm then buttoned the three middle buttons. She was exhausted after the small task. She then patted one of the duffel bags that was open but hadn't been routed through.

"Darth," she announced and thumped the bag. "Search." Mac hesitated then spoke in German. "Suche."

Darth sniffed the bag then tore items from it with his paws and teeth. Mac remained reclined against the suitcase behind her back and watched the useless items being thrown across her feet. She shut her eyes a moment to rest. Darth whimpered and licked her face. Mac gasped and woke. Something rattled from nearby. She reached into the shadows of the compartment and felt something metal, which was possibly a toolbox. She attempted to pull it toward her but couldn't even grip the edge. She thumped the small toolbox.

"Darth," she announced while thumping the metal box.

Darth trotted across the scattered clothing, jumped over her extended legs, and sniffed the metal box. She again thumped the box.

"Darth, bring it," Mac announced. "Bring es." She felt herself fading back out.

Darth barked as everything went dark. Mac opened her eyes as the dog licked her face while whimpering. The sound of the engine now sounded different, and the vibration decreased. Mac's ears were popping, indicating they were descending.

Panic filled Mac. She was in no condition to fight whoever opened the compartment, which meant she needed to escape before they came for her. It was a calculated risk. Mac looked alongside her and saw the metal toolbox. Darth had managed to pull it closer to her. Mac opened the case and found a large, flat-head screwdriver and a hammer. With all her strength, she scooted herself closer to the compartment door and rested her shoulder against the area alongside the door.

With her bad arm, she held the screwdriver against the seam by the latch and used the hammer in her good hand to pound on the end of the screwdriver. Each strike jolted through her body, causing agonizing pain in her injured shoulder. Darth tilted his head and watched her. He then woofed and scratched at the door as if attempting to help her. Mac managed a weak, humored smile.

"That's a good boy," she whispered.

§

Mac opened her eyes as Darth pressed his nose against her chin to wake her. He whined softly. She looked around and felt the plane rolling along the tarmac. They had landed and nearly stopped. Mac picked up the hammer that had fallen from her hand and moved just enough that she fell to the floor on her back. She scooted closer to the door on her backside until her booted feet were against the lightly clanging cargo door and her knees were halfway bent. She coiled her legs close to her chest, drew several deep breaths, and then kicked the door with both feet. It jolted but didn't open. Darth barked with encouragement, or so it seemed. Mac took another deep breath, pulled her knees up to her chest, and again kicked the door.

The door flew open, flooding the compartment with light that nearly blinded her. Mac cried out while sitting up with the hammer raised in her good hand, prepared to strike first. An older man jumped away from the compartment when he saw the deranged woman covered in blood, holding the hammer in the air. Mac stared at the older man while Darth barked at him, although he lacked viciousness. Mac attempted to focus on the man and realized he wasn't one of the men who attacked her. She groaned, dropped the hammer, and collapsed onto her back. Darth barked at her and attempted to nudge her awake with his cold nose.

§

Mac couldn't move her body, and it felt as if she were tied down. Her body was jolted, causing immense pain in her shoulder. It then felt as if someone punched her in the chest. She heard Darth growl low and long.

"We can't take the dog with us," a man announced.

"Yeah, well, you tell him that," another man responded.

Mac opened her eyes and saw Darth lying on the ambulance stretcher half on her and half to the side. He rested his head on her chest while staring into her eyes and whimpered softly.

"Good boy," Mac whispered and patted his back paw near her hand.

The EMTs loaded Mac and the dog on top of her into the back of the ambulance.

Chapter 20

The rental car pulled into the private airport's parking lot a little after eleven-thirty and parked next to the black sports car. Kane got out of the driver's seat, removed his sunglasses, and stared at the black Mustang. He raised his brows while admiring the car.

"Wow," he announced and nodded his approval.

Stone got out of the front passenger seat while Maverick, Scorpio, and Rayner got out of the back. Scorpio tensed and glanced across the tarmac at the distant, familiar helicopter. For the first time, fear and panic swept over her. She looked back at her brother.

"Are we sure we want to do this?" she timidly asked and rubbed her chilled arms.

"They're positive Mac was here this morning," Maverick announced without hesitation. "Two of their friends are missing, and they found blood on the tarmac. Someone's been seriously injured. It could be Mac."

Kane met Scorpio's gaze. "Maverick's right," he announced then held his breath. "If something's happened to Mac, I'm responsible. It's my fault she came to Virginia. We should have been in Maine."

"Yesterday was brutal," Scorpio delicately reminded him. "Do we really want to face them?" She then hesitated and choked on the next part. "Do we really want to face *him?*"

"Yes, Scorpio," Kane announced without missing a beat. "This is all on me. I fucked up everything from the moment I left Maine in the first place. I need to take responsibility and make it right. I'm not going home until I find Mac."

"I'll live with the humility if it helps find Mac too," Maverick announced. "I'm just as responsible for pushing her over the edge."

Rayner placed his hand on Scorpio's shoulder and gave it a gentle nudge. "No one's forcing you to face them," he informed her. "If you want to leave, we can leave."

She eyed Rayner and felt her entire body stiffen. "What do you think we should do?" Scorpio asked while putting on a brave front.

"I'm not making that decision for you," Rayner insisted. "I'm comfortable with whatever you decide."

Scorpio drew a deep breath and wiped a stray tear from the corner of her eye. "Those people scare me to death," she announced timidly then eyed her friends. "I don't remember ever being this scared of anything before."

Stone approached Scorpio and Kane and shifted looks at each of them. "You know what's scary?" he announced in a bold tone. "The two of you. Professional hitmen were sent to put you down, yet you both walked away. You tracked down and found a man you thought was dead. You don't quit, and you don't walk away from danger."

"That's different," Scorpio informed him while frowning. "We had help with all those things. We didn't do them by ourselves."

"And you won't do this by yourselves either," Stone insisted while holding his head up proudly. "You have us to back you up." He took a moment to reflect then nodded. "Yeah, we got our asses handed to us yesterday, but we're still here. We're still together. That makes *us* the scary ones."

"Make your point a little faster," Maverick announced then nodded across the parking lot. "More of their scary people are arriving now."

They looked across the parking lot and saw Bogart and Kirk get out of a car. Stone cast a look at Kirk's large frame and shook his head.

"Son of Mary, that man is big," Stone muttered then cast looks at Scorpio and Kane. "Lacking confidence? Fake it. It's all in how you're perceived. Inside. Now."

Scorpio drew a deep breath then nodded and headed for the small terminal building. The other four followed her wanting to avoid the two approaching men. Kane and Scorpio entered the building and stopped a few feet inside the door. Rayner, Maverick, and Stone stopped just behind them. Monroe, Zack, and Jackie stopped what they were doing a moment and stared at the five. Jackie turned to face Zack, placed her hand on his shoulder, and spoke softly to him. Zack focused on their private conversation then nodded. He removed her car keys from his pocket and headed for the door. Zack didn't even look at the five as he left the building. Monroe cast a look at Jackie, who remained across the room and made no effort to move. He groaned then approached Scorpio and Kane.

"Let's just agree to put the unpleasantness of yesterday behind us and attempt to figure out what happened to our friends," Monroe announced.

"We haven't heard from Mac, and she's not answering her phone," Kane informed Monroe.

"She's not returning my phone calls either," Monroe replied. "Though, under the circumstances, I'm not really surprised."

"She'd return mine," Kane announced with confidence. "I groveled for her forgiveness. Trust me; she'd be all over that message just to rub it in."

Monroe snorted a laugh and smirked. "Yeah, no kidding." He then pointed at Othello, who stood before the counter with his laptop. "That's Othello. He has GPS access to one of our friend's phones. He's not registering anything yet."

Rayner glanced at the large man standing before the desk then tapped Scorpio on the shoulder. "I'm going to brainstorm with Othello."

Scorpio nodded and watched Rayner head toward the desk. Kirk and Bogart entered the building, eyed the four, and then continued past without a word, making a beeline for Jackie.

"What are they doing here?" Bogart asked Jackie while indicating the four across the lobby.

Jackie scooted them further away from the four, so they could talk privately. Scorpio tensed at what she witnessed and insecurely clutched the back of Kane's jacket while attempting to maintain her air of confidence.

"Does anyone know what Mac was doing here in the first place?" Maverick asked Monroe. "She took her bag and snuck out of the hotel early this morning."

"The attendant said she was waiting for a pilot named Izzy," Monroe replied. "He said she was here at seven this morning then had an altercation with our friend around nine. A little before ten, our friend's plane left, and none of them had been heard from or seen since."

"Does this place have a lounge?" Kane asked.

Monroe nodded and pointed toward the back. "First door on the right."

Kane removed his cell phone and headed for the lounge. Scorpio hurried after him wondering what her brother was up to. Monroe appeared curious and followed them to the lounge. Kane looked around the lounge and pressed a button on his cell phone. They heard a faint ringing sound. All three looked around. Scorpio pointed to a set of lockers. They followed the ringing to one of the lockers containing a lock. Kane groaned and removed his lock pick kit from his jacket pocket. While he fumbled with his tools, Monroe approached a nearby toolbox. Kane moved closer to the lock but was edged out of the way. Monroe held a large bolt cutter in his hand and easily cut the lock off the locker. Monroe casually cast the heavy bolt cutters onto the nearby toolbox with a loud clatter.

"If you're going to break into something," Monroe announced, "do it right."

Kane eyed Monroe with some surprise then turned back to the locker and opened the door. He removed Mac's duffel bag from the locker, dropped it to the floor, and routed through it. He removed her cell phone and her identification, including her passport. He then looked up at his sister and Monroe and flashed the passport.

"I don't think she left willingly," Kane informed them.

"Someone hid her bag in that locker," Scorpio remarked and eyed her brother.

Kane replaced the items, closed Mac's duffel bag, and straightened while facing Monroe. "These friends of yours," he announced while regaining some of his confidence. "Did they have a grudge against Mac? Is it possible they'd hurt her? Do we know what the altercation was about?"

"They didn't hurt her," Monroe assured him with some hostility. "The man she was arguing with was her former employer. She saved his life. He didn't have a grudge against her, but she did have one against him."

"Her employer?" Kane suddenly asked and appeared curious. "Sal Romano?"

"Yeah, Sal Romano."

"You are aware that he's a mob boss, right?" Kane just about gasped. "You don't think he's capable of hurting her, do you?"

"Sal's reputation has never been proven," Monroe informed him. "Even if he were a mob boss, he'd never hurt her. He has a soft spot for her."

"Then why were they arguing?" Kane demanded.

Monroe groaned and raked his fingers through his hair. "Mac's been after Sal to hire her back, but he won't because of whatever happened between her and Zack."

Kane was silent a moment and didn't ask the question he obviously wanted to ask. "Yeah, she mentioned that," Kane easily lied.

Monroe suddenly appeared interested. "She told you what happened between them?" he asked with surprise.

"Of course she did," Kane replied and seemed almost casual about his lie. "She may have lied about not knowing where to find Zack, but she did admit she knew him."

Technically, the statement was true.

"Zack hasn't been nearly as forthcoming about their last interaction," Monroe remarked.

"Mac and I have a special bond," Kane admitted while attempting to gauge Monroe. "Naturally, she'd tell me about her sexual relationship with Zack."

It was a wild guess on Kane's behalf, and Scorpio had to keep from shooting a look at her brother. It was difficult pretending the comment didn't surprise her. There was no way Scorpio believed Mac would have slept with Zack.

Monroe gave Kane a strange look. "Everyone knows about that," he scoffed.

Kane's expression suddenly dropped. "She slept with him," he cried out in near horror.

Monroe was stunned by the outburst. "You said you knew."

"I was playing you," Kane cried out and remained horrified. "She never said anything about having sex with him!"

Monroe's expression suddenly dropped as he stared at Kane. "Oh, God," he gasped. "Don't tell me you've slept with her too."

"What do you mean by 'too'?" Kane cried out while staring at Monroe. "Did you sleep with Mac?"

Monroe stared at Kane and was suddenly at a loss for words, which just about confirmed the question. Scorpio groaned and placed her hand over her face while shaking her head.

"I think we've gotten way off topic here," Monroe announced while hiding his embarrassment.

"Oh, my God, you did," Kane gasped with horror.

Monroe threw his arms in the air and avoided looking at Kane. "This topic is closed for discussion," he launched then shot a look at Kane. "Zack can't know you and he slept with the same woman, especially Mac."

"I *didn't* sleep with Mac," Kane boldly announced. "We don't have *that* kind of relationship."

"But you just said--" Monroe became frustrated. "If she's not your girlfriend, why are you so upset?"

"Because she slept with my father," Kane launched. "Seriously. Ewe!"

Monroe stared at Kane as his mouth fell open. "Did you just say 'ewe'?"

Chapter 21

Othello hustled behind the counter to the front desk printer. He snatched the paper as it finished printing and slammed it on the desk. Jackie hurried to the desk and looked where he pointed.

"I've got the location of the plane that took off just before Gil's plane," Othello declared excitedly. "It just touched down at Blue Grass Airport in Lexington, Kentucky."

Monroe turned toward the attendant, who appeared unwilling to engage the gathering of people now taking over the small terminal.

"Are you sure the plane we're tracking was alongside our friend's plane on the tarmac?" Monroe asked.

"Yeah, I'm sure," the man replied. "They were the last two planes to leave. The two just out front."

Jackie and her team exchanged looks. She was already calculating the time it would take to fly to Kentucky. It wasn't going to be a short trip, and they had already wasted enough time.

"What's our ETA?" Monroe asked.

"It'll take about two and a half to three hours by helicopter to Lexington," Jackie informed him.

"No chance for a rental plane?" Zack asked her as he approached.

"No," she replied as she glanced at Zack. "It's Monday. This place is a ghost town."

"We'd better move out then," Monroe announced.

"I'll prep the helicopter. Meet me on the tarmac in fifteen minutes," she informed him then ran from the terminal.

Kane hesitated only a moment then ran after Jackie. Bogart saw the young man take off after Jackie. He sneered, cocked his head, and then hurried after them.

Zack tossed Othello the keys to Jackie's sports car. "Take Ellie back to Jackie's house," he announced. "Keep us posted from there. When you get tracking on Sal's phone, let us know."

"Yeah, sure," Othello replied with some uncertainty.

§

Kane followed Jackie to her helicopter where it sat on its landing pad. Jackie's Bell helicopter was a commercial, fourteen-passenger aircraft with a spacious cabin, sliding side doors, and adjustable seating. She'd bought the helicopter new after scoring a huge payday from their last assignment, Alpha Dogs. The helicopter was her baby. Jackie knew Kane was following her, but she didn't bother looking back at him.

"Stop following me," Jackie snarled with some irritation while she removed the straps tying down the rotors.

"If Mac's in trouble, I want to help," Kane informed her and continued to follow her despite her harsh tone.

She spun and nearly collided with the handsome man. He jumped away from her, clearly unfazed by her annoyance with him.

"Good for you," Jackie scoffed.

"I want to come along," he insisted.

"You're asking the wrong person," she replied and opened the pilot's door and nearly hit him with it. "I'm not in charge."

"I beg to differ," Kane announced.

Jackie ignored the comment, sprang sideways on the pilot's seat, and fiddled with several switches.

"If not you, who's in charge?" he then demanded. "Whom do I ask?"

"I suggest asking your father," she remarked and almost cursed herself for how snarky she sounded.

Kane stared at her and seemed slightly stunned by the comment. "Ouch, that hurt." Kane placed a hand on the doorframe and the door while partially hovering over Jackie as her legs remained outside the craft. She continued with her prep and ignored him. "Yesterday was intense. I get it. I'm very disappointed in myself, and I'm sorry for the way I behaved."

Jackie didn't acknowledge him and pretended to ignore him even though she shared some of his guilt.

"I realize you and Zack have some sort of unshakable bond, and I can see how you'd take my attacking him a little personally," Kane continued then drew a deep breath despite that Jackie didn't acknowledge him. "You'd throw your life down for his as I'm sure he'd do for you." He hesitated. "Well, that's how I feel about Mac."

Jackie stopped working and stared at the helicopter controls a moment. She drew a deep breath and then cast a look at Kane. Despite what happened yesterday, she saw nothing but sincerity in his blue eyes. Jackie groaned and rolled her eyes.

"You'll want to wear your seatbelt," Jackie informed him. "Zack's been known to throw people out of moving helicopters."

Kane released a breath and smiled gratefully and with relief. "Thank you," he announced and straightened. "You won't regret this."

She frowned and waved him off. "I regret it already," Jackie scoffed. "Get whoever's going together and meet me out front in five."

Kane offered a relieved smile then hurried away from the helicopter. Bogart shot a look at Kane as he passed then joined Jackie by the helicopter.

"What did the kid want?" Bogart demanded.

Jackie eyed her brother with little emotion. "What do you think he wanted?"

Bogart groaned and shook his head. "You're not seriously considering taking them with us, are you?"

Jackie ignored the question and continued with her helicopter prep.

"Damn it, Jackie," Bogart scoffed and pointed back at the terminal building. "You're going to create more tension than we already have. Zack is a powder keg. If he explodes, even you aren't safe from the blast."

She flipped several switches, and the engine started. Jackie cast a look at Bogart. "You may want to get inside," she announced. "It's about to get breezy."

Bogart frowned then cursed under his breath as he jumped into the back of the helicopter. The rotors picked up speed, and the craft lifted off the tarmac. Bogart sat in the back with the door open as they flew only a few feet above the tarmac for the nearby terminal building.

§

Once the helicopter shut down outside the terminal building, Bogart jumped from the back and hurried inside. Jackie leaped from the pilot's seat and entered the back section. She folded down the middle row containing four seats to make room for eight rather than twelve. As she turned toward the open side door, Zack jumped into the back, crowding her personal space, and stared her down.

"What the hell do you think you're doing?" he demanded with a look that was more than disapproving.

"I'm collapsing the middle row," she casually informed him. "It's going to be a long flight, and we'll need the leg room."

"That's not what I meant, and you know it," Zack snarled and just about pinned her by the last, back-facing seat.

Jackie wasn't easily intimidated by Zack, but he'd been under a lot of stress the last few days. She couldn't deny his closeness coupled with hostility set her on edge. Jackie knew she wasn't helping decrease his stress any by letting Kane come along. After she'd made her decision, she fully anticipated Zack taking his frustration out on her. She actually preferred he took it out on her than option number two. Taking it out on Scorpio and Kane. Zack didn't give her an inch of space as his eyes pierced through hers. She pressed her back against the closed side door and braced her palm against his chest to keep him from crowding her further.

"They aren't coming along," Zack informed her in a low, chilling tone while putting pressure against her hand on his chest.

She stared back into his eyes while refusing to be intimidated by him. "It's not your call," Jackie responded in the same low tone.

"They're bringing nothing to this party," he snarled back without giving her an inch. "They're unnecessary and unwanted collateral damage. No unauthorized civilians allowed on potentially dangerous assignments, and I don't want them tagging along." Zack's look was commanding. "You're supposed to be on my side."

Jackie removed her hand from Zack's chest that had unsuccessfully held him back and gently touched his face. "I am on your side," she announced while searching his eyes. "I nearly impaled your daughter through the face with a samurai sword. I'm wrestling with my own demons here. Just this once, I need you to consider *my* emotional state."

Zack held his breath a moment then groaned with defeat while pulling her into his arms. He held her against him. "I'm sorry," he whispered close to her ear. "I don't mean to keep dragging you down with me."

Jackie clung to him and sighed softly. "You aren't dragging me down, and I'm not complaining," she announced gently. "Just give me this one."

He nodded while pulling his head away from her shoulder. "You've got it," Zack replied then met her gaze without releasing her. "I can't be confined back here with them for over two hours."

"You're honorary co-pilot," she replied.

Zack managed a smile, kissed her quickly on the lips while releasing her, and then slipped into the front. He sank into the co-pilot's seat just as Monroe opened the co-pilot side door. Zack glared at Monroe without emotion.

"Too late," Zack casually announced. "I already called shotgun."

Jackie approached the open side door and was about to jump out when she saw Kane standing just outside with his hand up to assist her. Jackie took a moment to eye him. He was a little too charming for his own good. Normally, she wouldn't accept a chivalric gesture by someone outside of the team, but she felt compelled to accept. Jackie grasped his hand as she would one of her teammates, locking thumbs, and jumped from the back. Her unfeminine approach seemed to set Kane back, as he was expecting something more delicate.

"I'm confused here," Kirk scoffed loud enough to catch everyone's attention. "What are *they* doing here?"

Stone flashed a charming smile meant to mock Kirk. "We're here for comic relief," he boldly announced then leaped into the back of the helicopter past the large man.

Kirk cast a disapproving glare at Jackie and Monroe. "Who authorized this?"

"I did," Jackie announced while glaring at Kirk. "My helicopter; my rules. Get your ass in there. We're burning daylight."

Kirk took a step toward Jackie, towered over her, and stared her down with an intimidating look. "I'm telling Ross," he huffed then climbed into the back of the helicopter.

Jackie hid her smile then twirled her finger, signaling for everyone to climb aboard. Kane, Scorpio, and Rayner were in a tight huddle while seemingly holding things up as they spoke among themselves.

"Guys," Jackie announced gruffly to the three. "Ass in seat or we're leaving without you."

Kane frowned while turning toward Jackie and nervously raked his fingers through his hair. "My sister got sick on our last helicopter flight to the ranch. She's sort of freaking out about it."

"It's a long flight," Jackie informed him. "Her anxiety is only going to make her motion sickness worse."

Jackie turned and headed for the pilot's seat. Kane groaned and looked back at Scorpio, who was already holding her stomach.

"She's going to leave without us," Kane insisted while indicating the open back door. "We need to go now."

"Just go without us," Rayner informed him.

Kane frowned then looked back at the helicopter. Jackie was now standing in front of him and nearly startled him. She met his gaze, raised her brows, and held up a syringe.

"Her choice," Jackie announced.

"What is it?"

"A mild injectable sedation," she replied. "It's too late for her to take OTC airsick pills."

Kane drew a deep breath then looked back at Scorpio. "Your choice, Scorp," he announced.

Scorpio held her breath a moment while staring at the syringe. She groaned then removed her jacket and rolled up her short sleeve. Jackie approached her, pulled the cap off with her teeth, and met Scorpio's gaze.

"A little pinch on three," Jackie announced with the cap between her teeth. "One, two--"

Jackie jabbed the needle into Scorpio's upper arm. She yelped with surprise. Jackie removed the syringe cap from her mouth and smiled mockingly.

"Three," she teased.

Scorpio rubbed her arm and then slipped back into her jacket. Her eyes rolled back, and she started to sink to the tarmac. Rayner caught her.

"I may have exaggerated the 'mild' part," Jackie remarked while capping the syringe. She nodded to the helicopter. "Get her strapped in."

Scorpio's eyes opened, and she started laughing. "Wow, I'm all tingly."

"Oh, boy," Rayner groaned.

Kane helped Rayner escort his sister to the back of the helicopter. Stone grabbed her hands from inside while both men gave her a boost from outside. She stumbled across the back of the craft while laughing the entire way. Maverick caught her around the waist from behind as she just about fell on top of Bogart. She braced her fall with her hands on Bogart's thighs, surprising him. Maverick pulled her away from Bogart and into the vacant, front facing seat alongside him. Rayner was already in the back and attempted to secure her with the harness. Scorpio laughed while placing her hand on Bogart's leg.

"I'm sorry," she giggled and patted his thigh. "I didn't mean to grope you. Purely by accident."

Jackie stood outside the open side door with a broad grin on her face. She laughed and shut the side door before hopping into the pilot's seat. Zack stared into the back of the helicopter and watched as Rayner and Kane strapped the giggling young woman into her seat. Bogart released his harness and jumped into the vacant, back facing seat alongside Kirk. His motive was unclear. Kane and Rayner took the now vacant seats on either side of the giggling woman. Zack turned his head and glared at Jackie as she strapped herself in. She met his gaze and grinned.

"This trip won't be so bad," Jackie teased. "We have inflight entertainment."

Chapter 22

Gil woke to warm, bright sunlight shining on his face. He slowly opened his eyes to see tattered sheer curtains covering the large windows not far from his bed. Judging by the amount of sunlight flooding the room, it had to be close to noon. He blinked several times in an attempt to wake himself, seeming somewhat groggy. He struggled to move his arms and found some resistance. Gil made a second attempt to free himself then looked down. Although he was still dressed in his street clothes from that morning, nylon wrist and ankle restraints bound him to what appeared to be an old hospital bed. He thrashed a moment in an effort to free himself, but it was no use, the binds weren't letting loose.

He attempted to compose himself and scanned the unfamiliar room. There were six, old-fashioned hospital beds within the deteriorating institution room. The plaster was chipped and crumbling in several areas, particularly near the top of the tall ceiling. Tattered partition curtains were just about falling down separating his bed from the one next to his although he could make out others in the room occupying the beds. There weren't any dressers, but there were rolling carts containing instruments and supplies not far from the bed.

Gil again looked at the window while struggling against his bindings. Behind the tattered curtains, steel bars could be seen covering the windows. Wherever he was, it was evident no one was meant to leave. Gil finally glanced at the man in the bed across the room from him and saw Sal staring at the ceiling. His friend appeared unharmed, although his lack of movement was concerning.

"Sal?" Gil called out and attempted to get his attention.

Sal seemed unresponsive at first despite his open eyes. He blinked, indicating he was alive, and then peered through his small, round glasses at Gil in the bed across from him.

"Hey, Gil," Sal announced in an oddly calm tone.

"What's going on?" Gil demanded without sharing Sal's calm demeanor. "Where are we?"

Sal looked back at the ceiling with little emotion. "Well, it would appear we're strapped to beds inside some old, abandoned mental institution."

Gil stared at Sal tied to the bed past the foot end of his own bed. "You're rather calm about our situation," he huffed at his friend.

Sal continued to stare at the ceiling. "Actually, I'm terrified beyond comprehension," he announced while barely blinking. "I have a tiny phobia regarding mental institutions. My grandfather was clinically insane, and my father forced me to visit him once a month." He seemed to slip into a past time. "There was an unkempt woman roaming the hallways clinging to her headless baby doll. She'd talk to herself and periodically scream for no reason."

"Okay, Sal," Gil announced while fidgeting. "Find your happy place." He then looked around. "I'll work on getting us out of here."

"I was here an hour before they brought you in," the man in the bed alongside Gil's responded.

Gil glanced at the partially pulled, deteriorating partition curtain. He could only see the man's booted feet.

"Who brought us in?" Gil asked the stranger.

"Two psychopaths dressed like doctors," the man replied. "Both were wearing surgical caps and masks. They were dressed in scrub uniforms."

"So you don't know who they were?" Gil again asked.

"No, I never saw their faces," he replied. "I'm John, by the way."

"If you say 'Doe', I'm finding a way out of this bed and punching you," Gil informed the man.

The man chuckled in a mildly jovial manner. "No, but I have gone by John Smith on numerous occasions," he boasted.

"Do you know how you got here?" Gil pressed. "Why someone brought you here?"

"I just assumed my past caught up with me," John informed him.

"I was sort of thinking the same thing myself," Gil muttered then eyed the man's boots. They were definitely military style, although not necessarily military issued. "Are you a merc?"

"Yeah," John replied. "You?"

"To save time, I'll go with yes," Gil remarked, although that wasn't entirely true.

Mercenaries typically did unethical work for the highest bidder. Whiskey Tango Foxtrot maintained some sort of ethics and didn't consider themselves above the law, although they worked within the gray area most of the time.

"So there's nothing you can tell me about our situation?" Gil pressed the man whose face he couldn't see.

"I know about as much as you," John replied. "The man in the bed diagonally across from you said I was unconscious when they brought me in."

Gil strained to see the man in the bed diagonally across from him. He could just about see the man's chin. He, too, was strapped to the bed and still wearing his street clothes.

"He's Barton," John announced then hesitated. "Barton! Yo, Barton!"

"What do you want?" the man grumbled.

"Just making sure you were still alive over there," John teased.

"Still alive; still tied," Barton replied under his breath. "Still pissed off."

"He's not the talkative type," John informed Gil. "The bed alongside him and the one across the room from that bed are both occupied, but we haven't heard anything from either of them the entire time we've been here."

"They're either heavily sedated or dead," Barton muttered.

Gil reached for his thigh pocket while squirming around on the bed.

"Gil is it?" John questioned then seemed sedate. "Fighting those restraints doesn't work. They're designed to restrain crazy people."

"I may be able to reach my pocket," Gil informed his neighbor.

"I'm sure they emptied your pockets," John announced with little enthusiasm. "I had all sorts of fun tricks in my pockets, but they took them all."

"I have a special hidden pocket," Gil remarked while struggling to pull open the seam of his pants. The Velcro on the seam was unforgiving and difficult to pull apart with his index and middle finger.

They heard footfalls in the outside corridor.

"Tell me it's something useful and sharp," John announced with concern in his tone. "Because I hear someone in the corridor."

"Working on it," Gil moaned while struggling with the Velcro.

Gil finally slipped his fingers inside the small opening and removed a thin switchblade knife from the pocket. He was able to flick it open with the press of a button. John must have heard the sound. Sal was now alert to the person outside the room and the sound of the switchblade.

"Easy, Gil," John announced softly. "Company is right outside the door."

Gil managed to turn the blade around and easily cut through the heavy material binding his wrist to the bed. Despite that the sharp blade easily cut through it, the thick material was two inches wide and required some skill to use the switchblade on the backward angle. Someone entered the room. The man's footfalls were louder now. Sal tugged against his restraints while attempting to watch Gil across from him. As the footfalls passed through the room, Gil hid the switchblade under his thigh. A man decked out in a surgeon's scrub suit, hat, mask, and bloodstained apron appeared in the aisle. He didn't even bother looking at Gil, although Sal and Gil watched the creepy man.

The fake surgeon paused before the cart near the back wall and slipped into a pair of latex gloves. Gil watched as the man approached a rolling table containing rusted, bloodstained tools. He removed a bloodstained scalpel and eyed it almost as if fascinated. Since he wore the mask over his face, it was difficult to read his facial expression. Gil and Sal stared at the man with concern and possible fear. The surgeon then replaced the scalpel and pushed the rolling cart containing the assorted surgical tools along the aisle and past John's bed. The moment he was out of sight, Gil removed the switchblade and resumed cutting through the wrist binding.

The curtain between Sal and Barton was suddenly pulled further closed, although it remained partially open at the foot end, allowing John a peek at what was happening.

"What the hell--?" Barton cried out in something resembling a mixture of anger and fear.

Barton suddenly cried out in agony. His continuous screaming was enough to cause Sal and John to bounce within their beds, as they seemed to imagine what was happening to the fourth man. Gil kept his head while cutting through the last of the binding, sprang up in bed, and easily sliced through the strap binding his left arm. Barton's agonizing screams echoed throughout the room. Gil slashed the ankle restraints as the sound of the scalpel hitting the metal tray was heard. A loud crunching sound sent chills through the remaining three men. Barton's cries suddenly subsided. As Gil sprang from his bed, they heard a second crunching sound that was almost certainly the sound of Barton's chest being spread apart.

Gil ran for the mostly closed fourth curtain and ripped it open. The demented, blood-soaked surgeon spun to face Gil while still holding the jagged chest spreader in his hands. He immediately swung the chest spreader at Gil's face. Gil ducked the rusted, bloodied blade then lunged forward with his switchblade knife and stabbed the man in the neck. The man cried out in anguish while clutching his profusely bleeding neck. Gil pulled the blade free. As the surgeon collapsed to his knees, Gil saw Barton strapped to the bed with his chest spread open as blood saturated his open shirt and the sheets beneath him. Gil leaped back with horror and placed the back of his hand to his mouth as if about to vomit. He took only a moment before slipping into Sal's area and sliced through his wrist restraints rather than wasting time untying them.

Sal popped up in bed with a pale expression on his face while Gil easily cut through his ankle restraints.

"Is he--?" Sal asked while still looking rather pale from what he'd heard.

"For his sake, I hope so," Gil just about gasped.

Once Sal was free, Gil ran to John's bed. He barely took a moment to eye the man strapped to the bed before cutting him free. John was a tall, athletically built man in his mid to late thirties. He had short, light brown hair and a few days' worth of stubble on his otherwise clean-shaven face. John was classically handsome with a definite military appeal.

"Grab whatever you can find for weapons," Gil instructed both men. "We need to move."

Sal pulled back the curtain between him and Barton and nearly gagged when he saw the man with his chest spread open. He controlled his gag reflexes and removed the rusted, blood-soaked scalpel from the tray. John avoided looking at Barton and snatched the discarded chest spreader from the floor. All three hurried across the room and paused only a moment to eye the men in the first two beds. The first man was sliced open from sternum to groin. His insides were hollowed out, and his internal organs appeared to be missing. The blood was mostly dried, and maggots covered the wound, indicating he'd been dead quite some time. The second man was missing the top of his skull as well as his brain. Most of his blood was dried, although there was some still wet enough to indicate he hadn't been dead longer than twenty-four hours.

"What the hell is this place?" John demanded while nearly gagging at the sight of both dead men.

"I don't know, but we're going out there blind," Gil informed him. "We move fast and quiet."

Sal and John nodded.

Chapter 23

Gil, Sal, and John hurried along the creepy corridor while keeping watch in every direction surrounding them. They didn't hear any movement. The corridor resembled an atrium lined with tall, floor-to-ceiling windows all covered in bars. Surprisingly, most of the windows were intact. Only a few were cracked or broken. Since they didn't hear or see anyone, Gil paused by one of the windows to look around outside. His expression dropped. Sal and John paused alongside him and looked out as well. There was a large, overgrown field with a tall, chain link fence just before the woods. Despite the age of the fence, it was lined with newer barbed wire across the top. The barbed wire made the mental hospital seem more like a prison, and maybe it was.

"Well," Sal announced with a sigh as he stared off. "That's not good."

"No, it's not," Gil agreed then looked along the creepy, paint chipped corridor before them. "Let's see where this leads. There's no telling how many men are waiting to take us out so stay frosty."

Both men followed Gil along the corridor until they reached a set of double doors. The doors contained windows, so they could peer into the next area without opening the door first. When nothing moved, Gil pushed open one of the doors and entered a large, common room, which was possibly the patient's lounge. There was a large nurse's station containing a solid half wall and then glass the rest of the way up to the ceiling. The old nurse's station seemed to have chairs, equipment, and other nursing supplies that had been left behind. The lounge itself was extraordinarily creepy. In addition to the plaster crumbling and peeling, there were chilling frosted glass windows containing bloodied handprints, old rotting furniture, and dried bloodstains on the floors and walls.

What stood out most within the room was a large chunk of floor that had collapsed, leaving a ten-foot-by-ten-foot hole in the floor. Sal nervously took a step closer to the opening and peered down to the floor below. He could see the crumbled floor debris covering what was once the kitchen. Sal took a step away from the pit and looked around.

"This place is rotting from the inside out," Sal announced with concern. "It's possible any of the floors could give away at any time."

John looked up then indicated the ceiling. "There's your source," he remarked.

Gil and Sal looked up and saw the large hole in the ceiling, which revealed exposed beams and broken water pipes. A large portion of the ceiling contained water stains as well. Water dripped from the broken pipe suggesting the water to that area had been shut off, but the facility must still have running water. John indicated the door across the room then led the way. He passed through the second set of doors with Gil and Sal only a few steps behind him. The patient's bedroom wing was a broad hallway with wooden doors containing small glass windows at eye level. The long hallway must have contained twenty doors on each side. The arched ceiling was frayed and peeling, leaving plenty of debris on the floor. Despite being a throwback from the sixties, the patient's wing had a medieval sort of feel. They passed a random stretcher and wheelchair, which both contained leather straps to tether the patient to the device.

"This place is cheerful," Sal muttered then subconsciously shivered.

"Looks like a tomb," John remarked while making a disgusted face.

As they continued down the broad corridor, they heard a faint, metallic banging sound. Gil nodded toward the end of the hallway while gripping his switchblade. John was content to lead the way, which Sal and Gil didn't seem to mind. John paused before a door on the right with frosted glass windows. A sign on the door read 'morgue'. All three exchanged concerned looks. The banging sound was louder. It was definitely coming from the morgue.

"I don't like this," Sal muttered while nervously flexing his hand around his bloodstained scalpel.

When John entered the morgue, Gil felt compelled to follow him. Sal groaned and reluctantly trailed behind. The morgue contained a concrete floor with a metal table that almost looked like a surgical table. It was possibly an autopsy table, which seemed odd for a mental institution. The slightly rusted table contained large amounts of old bloodstains. There were bloodstains surrounding the drain on the floor directly beneath the table as well. Chipped tile lined the walls surrounding the six freezer doors. The sound had almost certainly come from one of the freezer doors, but it was quiet now. John approached the first door, gripped his chest spreader in one hand, and held the door handle in the other. He eyed Gil and Sal as if silently signaling them.

Both men raised their weapons. John pulled open the door. It made a chilling sound, but there wasn't the telltale sign of frozen air, indicating the freezers hadn't worked in some time. All three were greeted by the foul odor of rotting flesh. A man's badly decomposed body was awkwardly positioned on the tray. Since the freezers hadn't been turned on, it was entirely possible the man died a slow, agonizing death from dehydration. All three men gagged on the foul smell. John slammed the door shut. The door alongside it suddenly vibrated. All three men turned toward the next freezer door.

Gil was closer than John was. He held his breath then pulled open the door. The drawer flew out by a man pushing on it from inside. The man, Wyatt, immediately sat up while gasping then looked at the three men staring at him. Wyatt wasn't as tall as John was, but he had more muscle mass behind him, indicating he worked out extensively. Wyatt kept his dark hair in a neat, military buzz cut. His outward appearance gave off a definite military vibe, which seemed to be the theme for all those they'd run into so far. Wyatt was defensive at first, raising his fists, then seemed to relax when he realized they were there to help him.

"Thank God," Wyatt gasped. "I thought you were more of *them* for a minute."

"Them?" Sal asked. "Them who?"

"The crazies," Wyatt remarked with hostility in his voice as he jumped off the metal tray. "Those bastards locked me in there and left me to rot."

Wyatt swayed slightly and had to grab onto the metal tray to catch his balance. It was uncertain how long he'd been stuck inside the morgue freezer.

"We ran into one of them," Gil remarked. "Killed a man in the infirmary."

"Yeah, there's a good dozen or more of those nut bags running around here," Wyatt informed them while looking around. "We need to get out of here before we're next."

"We were looking for the way out when we heard you knocking," John remarked while eyeing the man suspiciously. "Do you know the way out?"

"The main entrance is through the lounge and to the doors on the right. If you were in the infirmary, you had to have come that way," Wyatt replied. "That'll take us to the lobby and the front doors. I made it that far. Problem is; we need a set of keys if we want to unlock the door."

"Where are the keys?" Sal asked.

"Back in the nurse's station," Wyatt replied. "The sealed office in the lounge with glass surrounding it. I saw it right before those bastards jumped my friend and me. I'm not sure what happened to him. I think he got away."

"We need to get that key," John insisted.

"We can send help back later to find your friend," Gil informed the man.

There was a round of introductions before they headed into the broad corridor, and they soon learned Wyatt was also former military. The coincidences were a little concerning, which suggested it might have been Gil who had been the intended target and not Sal. As the four headed back down the corridor toward the lounge, they heard a faint sound coming from one of the patient's rooms. If it hadn't been for Wyatt's pounding from the morgue, they might have heard it on their way through. Wyatt stopped them before one of the rooms. He peered inside but didn't act as if he'd seen anything. They heard the sound again, which definitely came from the same room. Rather than just take a quick peek, Wyatt and Gil stepped into the room and looked toward the back corner, which couldn't be seen from the doorway.

Four filthy looking men and one woman all in tattered clothes were crouching in the back corner with their backs to the men. Wyatt tapped Gil and motioned him from the room, obviously not wanting to gain attention from the small gathering. Gil strained to see what the men and woman had been doing in the corner. Their actions were puzzling. Just then, one of the men turned his head and looked back. Gil could see the fresh blood down the man's chin and covering the front of his bloodstained shirt. Gil then saw the chunk of flesh the man held in his blood-covered hand. The woman alongside him, who was also covered in blood, turned as well and straightened, allowing both men a view of the dead heap of flesh that was once a man now piled in the corner.

"Christ," Wyatt gasped. "They ate him!"

The others were now alerted to their presence, and all five stared at them while chewing on chunks of flesh. Gil subtly motioned Wyatt from the room. Both men backed toward the open door. Gil shut the door behind them then motioned for the others to hurry. They ran along the broad corridor toward the lounge.

§

Gil, Sal, John, and Wyatt hurried into the lounge and ran for the nurse's station. Wyatt pointed at the reinforced glass door on the side of the office.

"The keys are in there," Wyatt informed them. "We need to find a way to pick the lock--"

Gil picked up the pace, passed Wyatt, and roughly kicked the door near the handle without missing a beat. The door was thrown open with enough force that it struck the inside wall and cracked the shatterproof glass. Gil entered the nurse's station with Sal only two steps behind him.

Sal snatched the ring of keys from the peg on the wall and jingled them. "Got them," he announced.

Gil removed a large, baton-style flashlight from the nurse's station desk.

"That won't work," Wyatt informed him. "This place has been shut down for close to twenty years. The batteries are long dead."

Gil casually flipped the flashlight in his hand and raised a clever brow. "I didn't plan on using it to see better," he replied.

"I like the way you think," John announced while grinning deviously.

Wyatt darted out of the nurse's station and motioned for the others to follow. "Come on," he called out excitedly. "This way!"

The three men hurried after Wyatt. Once they passed through the second set of doors, they entered what used to be an elegant lobby. The institute would want the patients' families to see a nice, clean facility. The lobby had a beautifully patterned, tile floor now cluttered with debris from another hole in the cathedral ceiling revealing the sky and the outside world. The area above the lobby was only one-story, unlike what they saw in the lounge. Dead, dried leaves were spread out across the once elegant floor. A beautiful, dual staircase extended to the second floor from both sides of the lobby, which meant there were other floors in the area beyond the lobby. The wood and marble banister on the staircase was beautifully detailed, as were the wooden steps.

Windows extending from the floor to the ceiling lined the front of the one-story lobby allowing natural light to flood into the once grand room. Although there were bars on the windows, they were less noticeable and more intergraded. Bars weren't family friendly. The expensive furniture sporadically placed around the room was now tattered and torn with stains resembling blood, although it was possible the stains were just mud from whatever debris that had fallen through the hole in the ceiling. A massive, walk-in stone fireplace was the showpiece of the once ritzy lobby. All four men hurried for the large, heavy front doors. Wyatt stepped out of the way and allowed Sal to unlock them with the keys on the large ring. It took Sal a couple of tries to find the right key. The large doors unlocked. Wyatt shoved the doors open and charged onto the covered, front porch.

Wyatt and John led the charge down the overgrown driveway for the distant metal gate. Certainly one of Sal's keys opened the front gate lock as well. Sal kept pace with Gil, who seemed to slow while looking around the distant woods and the nearby trees. Something about the area before the gates troubled him. Tree branches were heard creaking loudly as they got closer to the front gate. Wyatt and John either didn't notice or didn't care. Gil slowed even more and looked at the trees as they neared the massive gate. A man's bare feet could be seen dangling from within the trees and nearly stopped Gil in his tracks. More tree branches creaked and groaned from excessive weight on them. Gil then saw a light glimmering off something in the woods, alarming him.

"Everyone down!" Gil cried out while tackling Sal to the overgrown driveway.

John threw himself to the ground upon command. Too many years in the military taught soldiers to react to certain words or risk losing their lives. Wyatt ignored Gil's fearful command and continued for the gate. Two nearly silent shots struck Wyatt. One hit him in the chest and the second struck him in the head, exploding the back of his skull. He dropped to the ground. John rolled back to his feet and retreated to the institution while collecting Gil and Sal along the way. The ground exploded near their heels, motivating them to pick up the pace. They ran back onto the safety of the porch and hid behind the large columns. All three stared at the distant gate and the dead man not far from it.

"What did you see?" Sal asked while attempting to catch his breath from their short sprint.

Gil nodded toward the trees. "Dead men hanging," he announced. "There must be a dozen of them hanging by their necks from the trees near the gate."

"Why?" John suddenly cried out where he remained hidden behind his own pillar. "Why would someone do something like that?"

"As a warning," Gil informed him. "Someone or several someones are out there waiting to pick us off if we try to leave."

"Who the hell did we piss off?" John demanded in a cross between anger and panic.

"Good question," Gil muttered then nodded for the open, front door. "We need to get back inside. At the moment, we're safer inside than we are out here."

Chapter 24

During the first hour of the flight, Scorpio hung on Rayner's shoulder and gleefully sang old road trip songs in her euphoric state. Kane was amused by the less serious sister he hadn't seen in years. Thankfully, everyone had their own headsets, so her singing went unheard by those on a different frequency. Jackie glanced at Zack, who seemed to be off in his own world.

"Hey, you okay?" Jackie asked.

Zack didn't respond. She reached across the seat and nudged him. Zack changed his headset frequency and repositioned his microphone.

"What were you saying?" Zack asked.

Jackie stared at him a moment with a strange look then glanced into the back at the happily singing woman reliving a moment from her childhood. Jackie looked back at Zack and raised her brows.

"Were you listening to her singing?" she asked with some surprise.

"I don't know what you're talking about," Zack scoffed and focused on the scenery before them.

"You know," Jackie began while casting looks at him. "No one's saying you have to stand up and be a father to them, but that doesn't mean you can't get to know them a little." She studied his profile and raised her brows despite that he seemed to ignore her. "After all; they *are* Maggie's children. That should be reason enough to make an effort."

Zack frowned and refused to look at her. "I love you, Jackie," he announced with a sigh. "Don't make me shoot you."

After the first hour in the air, Scorpio fell asleep snuggled against Kane despite the harness holding her back. Kane had his cheek resting on top of Scorpio's head and drifted in and out of sleep as well. Jackie glanced into the back, saw the brother and sister duo, and admired their unbreakable bond. She cast a look at Zack and made a mushy face.

"Oh, they're so adorable," Jackie announced. "Like a kitten and puppy snuggling together."

Zack turned his head and glared at Jackie. In the back, Kirk slept with his head against the window, which was the only reason he ever wanted a window seat. He usually fell asleep on flights over an hour even back in the day. Monroe, who sat on the other side of Rayner, played a game of computerized chess on his laptop with him. They talked and laughed while enjoying their game to pass the time. Stone and Bogart spent the second hour talking overtop of Maverick. Maverick finally removed his harness and forced Stone to take the seat next to Bogart. Maverick was preoccupied and stared out the window rather than get involved in any conversations.

§

It was around two-thirty that afternoon when Jackie's helicopter landed at Blue Grass Airport in Lexington, Kentucky. Many of the private planes were either grounded or still away on business travel for their clients, leaving the private portion of the airport almost as quiet as the one they'd left in Virginia. Scorpio was the last to leave the helicopter and required the assistance of Stone, Rayner, and Kane.

"Are you okay?" Rayner asked with concern to her slight unsteadiness.

"Yeah," she replied while having a difficult time keeping her eyes open. "That was probably the best sleep I've had in years."

Monroe nudged Jackie and nodded across the tarmac toward one of the smaller hangars. An older man was seen scrubbing the rear compartment of his private plane. There was a clear plastic bag filled with bloodstained clothing. Jackie and Monroe approached the busily working man while Kirk and Zack held the others back just far enough so they wouldn't make the man nervous.

"What happened?" Jackie asked the man while eyeing the bag of bloodied clothing.

Monroe glanced at the compartment door that was also stained with blood. The older man looked at Jackie and Monroe and shook his head.

"Damnedest thing I've ever seen," the man informed them then indicated his plane. "I heard this clunking coming from the back compartment the moment I hit the tarmac. I went to open the door, and the door was kicked open by some woman trapped inside." He shook his head. "I have no idea who she was, but she'd been pretty badly mangled. The paramedics said she'd been stabbed, but I caught a glimpse of her shoulder when they exposed the wound. Looked and smelled like burnt flesh."

"Early thirties, dark hair?" Jackie asked.

The man nodded. "Yeah, attractive woman," he replied. "Don't know who'd do that to her and then stuff her in my storage."

"How long ago?" Jackie asked.

"About three hours ago," he replied. "Took the police that long to investigate my plane. The way they questioned me, you'd think they suspected I abducted the woman."

"The paramedics took her to the nearest hospital?" Monroe eagerly asked.

"Yeah, her and the dog."

"Dog?" Jackie asked with surprise.

He nodded. "Yeah, she was trapped in the compartment with this German shepherd dog," the man announced then shook his head. "That dog wasn't leaving her side. Rode on the stretcher with her."

Jackie and Monroe exchanged concerned looks. "Darth," Jackie gasped and shook her head. "Gil and Sal are in trouble, Monroe."

Monroe motioned Jackie back to the others and offered a sympathetic smile to the older man. "Sorry about the mess."

He shrugged. "I'm sure she didn't mean to bleed all over my things," the man replied. "If she's a friend of yours, I hope she's okay."

"You didn't see anyone else messing around with your plane in Virginia?" Monroe asked.

"No, I didn't see anyone," he replied. "There was only the one plane not far from mine, but I didn't see anyone there either."

"Thanks," Monroe replied then hurried after Jackie.

"They took Mac to the nearby hospital," Jackie informed the others.

Maverick and Kane tensed at the information.

"Is she okay?" Kane asked.

"She'd been stabbed," Monroe offered. "Sounds like she cauterized the wound. Our friend's dog was trapped with her in the cargo compartment of the man's plane. Darth probably tried to help her and our friends."

"We need to get to that hospital," Maverick insisted, revealing his concern.

Monroe turned to Kirk. "See about renting a van," he announced. "We'll need a few things from our bags." As Kirk headed for the smaller, private terminal, Monroe looked at the others. "Do you need anything from your bag?"

"No, we're good," Kane replied. "Rayner has his laptop with him."

"We should call the hospital and check on Mac," Maverick announced and removed his cell phone.

"Don't do that," Zack informed him.

Maverick looked at him with some surprise. "Why not?"

"We don't know what she's told the police and if anyone else is looking for her," Zack replied.

"He's right," Monroe announced. "The police are probably keeping an eye on her. We'll need to proceed carefully. We'll send only one or two people in to check on her."

Jackie eyed Kane and Scorpio and considered their options. "They should go in," she announced. "Mac's concerned brother and sister."

"Good plan," Monroe replied. "She'd probably be happier to see them than us anyway." He cast several looks at Scorpio and Kane as they headed toward the terminal. "Get as much information as you can about what happened at the airport in Virginia. We still need to find our friends, and the situation is probably not good."

Chapter 25

The black rental van pulled up to the curb outside the main entrance to the hospital just a little before three o'clock that afternoon. The side door opened. Kane and Scorpio climbed out and were joined by Monroe.

"Play dumb," Monroe instructed them. "You're looking for your sister; you heard she may have been brought here. Give her name. If they don't have her registered, she may not have given her name. Ask if there were any Jane Does."

Kane nodded, grabbed Scorpio's arm, and hurried her for the hospital entrance.

"This isn't happening," Scorpio announced to Kane while running her fingers through her slightly mussed hair. Her mind was reeling about what must have happened to their friend. "What are they into that got Mac attacked?"

"I don't know, but keep up the anxiety for the receptionist," he announced. "This isn't the situation to play it calm."

Scorpio and Kane approached the front desk and remained tense.

"We're looking for our sister," Kane announced with a sense of urgency to the receptionist. "We heard she may have been brought here."

"What's her name?" the woman politely asked.

"Macbeth Lamar," Kane replied.

The receptionist checked the computer then shook her head and looked back at Kane. "I'm sorry," she replied. "There's no one here by that name."

"She wasn't carrying her purse," Kane informed the receptionist. "We're not sure how badly she was hurt. Were there any Jane Does brought in between eleven this morning and one o'clock?"

The receptionist consulted the computer, found what she was looking for, and then nodded. "Yes, there was," she announced then looked at them. "She's on the fourth floor. The room number isn't given, although I'm not sure why. Ask the nurse's station for her room number."

"Thank you," Kane announced then hurried Scorpio for the nearest elevator.

The elevator was filled on their ride up to the fourth floor, which left Kane and Scorpio silent on their journey. Scorpio could feel her brother's anxiety regarding Mac's condition. She knew there wasn't any romantic involvement between them, but Kane took to Mac for some reason. If anything happened to his newly found friend, he wasn't going to handle it well. They hurried out of the elevator on their chosen floor and approached the nurse's station. Two police officers were talking to one of the nurses and an orderly. Kane caught Scorpio's arm and slowed her while watching the heated exchange.

"Hold up," he announced cautiously.

Kane approached one of the visitors standing nearby who seemed to be watching the commotion. "Hey, what happened? Some sort of emergency?"

"One of their patients made the great escape about half an hour ago," the man reported and shook his head.

"Did you see what happened?" Kane asked.

"No," he replied. "A dog was brought in with one of the patients. Shortly after one of the nurses took the dog outside to do his business, they discovered the patient was gone."

"And that requires the police?" Scorpio asked while attempting to assess the situation in the corridor.

"No, they were keeping an eye on the woman," the man announced. "Not sure what happened to her, but the police were standing guard outside her door."

"And they didn't see her walk out of the room?" Kane asked with surprise.

"I guess she slipped out when the dog was causing the commotion," the man replied.

Kane thanked the man and hurried Scorpio back to the elevator. "How much do you want to bet the nurse that took the dog outside was actually Mac?"

"How did she get a nurse's uniform?" Scorpio asked.

"I'm guessing we should ask the dog," Kane muttered and hurried her into the nearest elevator.

§

Scorpio, Kane, Stone, and Maverick sat in the back of the van and watched while Rayner used the hospital's Wi-Fi to pull up a map of the surrounding area.

"I can hack into all the local cab company's call centers," Rayner informed them. "I can then cross-reference them and see if any of the cabs picked up a fare within a block or two from the hospital."

Monroe, Kirk, Bogart, and Jackie stood just outside the van's open side door and watched Rayner work his computer magic.

"He's like a mini Othello," Monroe teased then looked around and appeared curious. "Where's Zack?"

Jackie didn't bother looking at Monroe. "Why do you even ask?"

"Got it," Rayner excitedly announced. "In the last hour, there were five cabs in the area. One was called to the area, and two others were a little too early to have been Mac. That means two cabs picked up random fares in this area around the time she left."

"Can you find out where they dropped off?" Maverick eagerly asked.

"Checking now."

"We should probably split up and check both destinations," Monroe announced.

Jackie glanced across the sidewalk toward the hospital's valet. Zack talked with one of the men at the podium. Jackie didn't bother interrupting the men while they were brainstorming over the taxi theory, but she already knew what was coming next. Zack approached the van and paused alongside Jackie.

"Mac left in a powder blue, Hyundai Elantra," Zack informed them.

All eyes were suddenly on Zack with a shared look of bewilderment.

"She stole a car?" Monroe asked with surprise.

"Of course she stole a car," Zack replied while eyeing him with disbelief then shook his head. "Am I the only one here who actually knows this woman? The valet is missing a car, and we're missing a mentally unstable woman with sticky fingers. The valet podium isn't heavily guarded. A two-year-old could walk off with a set of car keys."

"What made you check with the valet?" Stone asked with some surprise.

"Mac had no identification, no money, and no cell phone," Zack informed Stone. "If I needed an exit and had nothing on me, that's what I'd do."

"Now we just need to figure out where she went," Kane remarked.

"My guess would be back to the airport," Jackie informed them and received several looks. She shrugged. "She'd want to get back to Virginia. She'll find a phone somewhere along the way and eventually call someone."

Monroe's cell phone rang. There was an eerie moment of silence.

He removed his cell phone and looked at the caller ID. "It's Othello," Monroe announced then answered the call. "Hey, Othello. What do you have?"

"You didn't call me back," Othello announced from the other end. "Don't you check your messages?"

"We were in the air most of the time," Monroe insisted. "We tracked Mac to the local hospital. She'd been attacked and tossed into the cargo hold of some guy's plane."

"Yeah, I'm guessing you didn't run into her at the hospital either," Othello remarked.

"How did you know?" Monroe asked his friend with some surprise.

"Because I got a phone call from Beck," Othello informed him. "Apparently, Mac called Sal's housekeeper and instructed her to call one of the guys. Her only contact was Pinto, so she called the satellite phone at the lodge."

"What did she tell Sal's housekeeper?" Monroe eagerly asked alerting the others to the conversation.

"It's not so much what Mac told the housekeeper as what the housekeeper told Mac," Othello responded. "It would seem Sal's housekeeper also has GPS tracking for Sal's phone. I guess he gave it to her in the event of an emergency. Mac got her to give up the information. It's the same information I had called you about shortly after you were in the air. Sal's phone must have come back online while we were heading back to Jackie's house."

"Where's Sal?"

"Bridgewater Corners, Vermont," Othello replied from his end.

"Where the hell is Bridgewater Corners, Vermont?" Monroe demanded.

Jackie turned to Rayner and immediately indicated his laptop. Rayner typed in Bridgewater Corners, Vermont to find it on the map for her.

"I don't know, but he's there," Othello insisted from the other end. "Apparently, Mac is heading there too." There was a pause. "I have his last known coordinates, but you should know that I lost the signal."

"What does that mean?" Monroe asked.

"That means his phone has been rendered useless," Othello informed him from the other end.

"Useless?"

"Probably smashed," Othello replied from Monroe's phone. "The coordinates will take you to the last known location of his cell phone."

"Thanks, Othello. We'll catch up with Mac at the airport," Monroe announced then disconnected the call. He drew a deep breath and eyed the others. "Mac was in touch with Sal's housekeeper and had her call Beck at the lodge. She's probably at the airport by now looking for passage to Vermont. I'm sure we'll be able to catch her there. Without any money or identification, she's not getting very far."

"We need to go," Kane announced without hesitation as his concern grew.

"Vermont? That's about nine hundred miles from here," Jackie remarked and eyed the guys. "It'll take too long by helicopter. Gil and Sal need us now. We're going to need to rent a plane. We're looking at a good three and a half hours just by plane."

"Then you'd better start making some phone calls on the way to the airport," Monroe informed her.

§

It was nearly four o'clock by the time the two teams reached Blue Grass Airport. While Kirk returned the rental van, Jackie was on her way to meet a man about a plane. Bogart and Stone found the powder blue car Mac had 'borrowed' from the hospital. Kane and Maverick led the investigation into locating Mac within the small, private terminal, but she wasn't anywhere to be found. Stone found the rest of their team and hurried for them while shaking his head regarding his find.

"She actually found someone to fly her to Vermont," Stone informed them. "Apparently, she knows a lot of Izzys. She left in a plane half an hour ago."

"She's crafty," Kane remarked then held his breath while looking at the others as Scorpio and Rayner joined them. He then nervously rubbed the back of his neck and frowned. "There's no reason to involve the rest of you in this. Maybe you guys should catch a flight to Maine. When I find Mac, we'll join you there."

"And leave you?" Stone asked with surprise.

"I don't know what's going to happen," Kane informed them. "She's attempting to locate two guys that are in enough trouble that she was stabbed. It could be dangerous, and I can't ask you to traipse across the country because of something that's at least partially my fault."

"If Mac is in trouble, I'm going," Maverick informed him without hesitation.

"We're not leaving you," Scorpio insisted. "We'll stick together and find Mac."

Kane glanced at Stone and Rayner.

"I've made my position clear," Rayner remarked. "I go where Scorpio goes."

"I'm not leaving without Mac either," Stone insisted. "We're in this together."

Kane drew a deep breath then tensed, revealing his concerns. "Then we need to find those guys before they attempt to leave without us."

"You don't think they'd do that, do you?" Stone asked with some surprise and immediately received glares and raised eyebrows from the other four. "You're right. We should find them before they take off without us."

Chapter 26

It was four o'clock that afternoon. Sal, Gil, and John had camped out in the game room where they locked and barricaded the door from the inside for added security. They chose the game room due to its close proximity to the lobby, and their eventual extraction point. The game room wasn't the sort of game room one found in a posh hotel or even a one-roach motel. It was the sort of game room found in a mental hospital. It contained a ping-pong table, a foosball table, and assorted games meant to entertain underdeveloped minds. Most of the activities were designed for smaller children, which included coloring books, blackboards, and drawing tables. For a bunch of former military types, it was quite demeaning to their character. The men needed a chance to collect their thoughts and formulate a plan. Sal sat on the floor against the wall and glanced at his watch. He groaned at the hour and rubbed his abdomen.

"I wish I hadn't skipped breakfast this morning," Sal remarked then frowned. "I wanted an appetite for clams on the beach at Monroe's house."

"I vote we don't talk about food," John muttered as he flopped onto the floor near Sal. He held his head in his hands and groaned.

"At least there's running water," Gil informed them as he finished his sweep of the large game room and approached the men on the floor. He drew a deep breath and held it. "You may not want what I have to offer." Gil reached into his pocket and removed four, small dog biscuits. He attempted a smile. "Beggars can't be choosers."

Sal and John stared at the dog biscuits in Gil's hand. Both men groaned and held out their hands. Gil gave each man a biscuit and returned the fourth to his pocket. He sat on the floor and joined them. All three savored their crunchy dog treat.

Sal eyed the biscuit while he chewed the dry treat. "You don't want to know what's in these things," he remarked.

"Whatever they scrape off the floor," John muttered while seemingly enjoying his biscuit.

"Back to our current situation," Gil announced not seeming at all bothered by the dog biscuit he ate. It was possible he'd eaten them before in his travels. "Whoever abducted us, all of us, went to a lot of trouble. There has to be a common foe in all this."

"Does it matter?" Sal asked while casting a look at Gil. "We're trapped in here with a bunch of cannibalistic nut cases and a predator waiting to shoot us in the head if we so much as take a step outside."

"Where the hell are we even?" John demanded and looked around. "I was unconscious for most of my trip, and I was blindfolded for the ground excursion."

"I'm guessing we're in Maine or Vermont," Gil replied while looking around. "I took a healthy peek out the window. We're definitely north of New York. It's cooler here. Higher elevation. I couldn't see where they flew my plane, but I know roughly how long we were in the air and approximately how fast we were flying."

"I'm afraid I'm not current on abandoned hospitals," Sal remarked.

"The back road they took us on wasn't paved. It was bumpy as hell," John informed them. "We must be pretty deep in the sticks."

"We have an idea where," Gil announced and finished his biscuit. "Now we need to know the who and why."

"You can imagine I have a lot of enemies," John muttered with defeat. "It could be anyone from my past."

"We're not exactly saints either," Sal informed John while sighing. "It stands to reason this person is someone we have in common."

"But was he after you or me?" Gil asked his friend. "We have two entirely different sets of enemies." He then eyed John. "With our similar military backgrounds, I'd be willing to guess I have more friends and foes in common with John than you do."

"If we're going to find that common denominator, we have a lot of ground to cover," John insisted as he shifted uncomfortably on the floor. "I've gotten around since my military days."

"Any mafia ties?" Sal asked John.

John smiled knowingly.

Sal groaned and rested his head against the wall behind him. "Okay, so let's review potentially common friends and foes starting in the mafia category."

Gil sighed and made himself comfortable. "It's going to be a long day."

"Possibly the most notable job I had involving the mob was when I worked for Giovanni," John remarked with a dramatic sigh.

Sal and Gil suddenly exchanged looks and immediately straightened.

"Maybe it won't be such a long day after all," Gil muttered.

"Giovanni?" Sal announced with surprise. "When and where?"

"His son's wedding," John replied then groaned. "What a bloody disaster that was. And I mean that literally."

Sal and Gil now stared at each other.

"What was it Giovanni said about his son?" Gil asked his friend.

"He's unstable," Sal replied then eyed John. "Did you interact with Marco, his son?"

"Of course," John replied. "That was sort of my reason for being there. Despite all of us working security for that wedding, it went south anyway."

"Yes, we know," Sal reported. "Gil and I were both there."

"Then all of this has to do with Giovanni?" John just about demanded.

"It seems that way," Sal muttered.

"What branch of the military did you serve?" Gil then asked.

"Special Forces," John announced and raised his brows. "Army Ranger."

"I'm a retired Navy SEAL," Gil reported.

John suddenly grinned. "You're with Whiskey Tango Foxtrot, aren't you? I remember your team being on Giovanni's island." he announced then laughed. "Our paths crossed on more than one occasion in and out of service."

Sal groaned with annoyance. "So we're back to square one then."

§

Sal, Gil, and John remained within the game room several hours longer. They were silently waiting, although none knew for what. It didn't seem as if there would be a rescue. No one even knew where they were, which included the three men themselves. John and Sal entertained themselves with an old deck of cards they found among the game room activities. The more entertaining games were either mostly rotted or would make too much noise. They had to keep quiet to avoid being found by the roving band of psychotic cannibals. It seemed impossible that those roaming the institution halls were once patients. None seemed old enough. Twenty years with a limited food source was also highly suspicious.

The more plausible explanation was equally chilling. The demented roving band of crazies were brought to the asylum by the same psychopath that brought the three of them there. Still, the level of crazy the others had achieved would take longer than a few months. How long could they possibly have been stranded at the institute? How much dedication would the sniper outside the gate need to have in order to patrol the outside area longer than a few days or a couple of weeks? None of it made any sense. While Sal and John played their card game, Gil once again searched the room. He routed through a box of useless items possibly used to entertain the mental patients decades ago.

The box mostly consisted of several pairs of glasses, funny hats, and assorted, creepy dolls. Gil examined several pairs of glasses. He removed a cheap pair of children's binoculars from the bottom of the box and stared at them a moment while deep in thought. He then turned toward Sal and John.

"When we were outside, I noticed the building was four stories high," Gil announced while eyeing his friend and his new partner. "Did either of you notice a staircase other than the one in the main lobby?"

"I thought I saw a sign for stairs near the infirmary," Sal informed him. "I wasn't actually paying attention since we were interested in getting out not going up."

"I would assume there are fire stairs on either side of the building," John informed him then appeared curious. "Why? What are you thinking?"

Gil flashed the binoculars. "They're not much to look at, but these binoculars will give us a better view of the tree line," he replied. "If we can get up to the fourth floor, we may be able to spot our sniper."

"It's going to be dark in another hour or two," John reminded him. "I'm venturing a guess that this place doesn't have any power. It'll be dark in the hallways in less than an hour."

"So we'll need to move fast," Gil reported. "We'll find a room on the fourth floor facing the gate and barricade ourselves in for the night. If we can see who's outside the gate and where they're hiding, we may be able to formulate a plan on getting past them."

"Personally, I vote we terminate them," John replied with little emotion.

"In order to do that, we have to make it to them without being seen," Gil added. "We're also going to need a better method of defending ourselves."

"So we're heading to higher ground?" Sal asked while standing with some stiffness.

"Yeah, you've got the keys?" Gil asked.

Sal removed the key ring from his pocket.

"We'll need to do this quietly," Gil reminded both men. "I don't know what condition the staircase is in, but we can use them to take us to the second floor. I doubt there's access to the fourth floor outside of the patient's areas, so we'll need to find our way back inside the main facility and find the closest fire stairs. We can then take them to the fourth floor."

"Well," John announced with a deep sigh. "What are we waiting for?"

Chapter 27

The three men peered out the game room door. When nothing moved, they crept out of their hiding place and entered the large gathering area of the once elegant lobby. John and Sal were only steps behind him. They approached one of the two large staircases. At second glance, the stairs seemed less sturdy then they had originally suspected. The large hole in the ceiling had allowed too much rain and dampness into the lobby, which had rotted the wood on the stairs.

"On second thought," Sal announced while staring at the deteriorating wooden steps, "maybe we should find one of the fire stairs."

"The railing is sturdy," John reported as he pulled on the thick railing. "Just keep to the outside. The steps are rotted from moisture, but the edge furthest from the hole in the ceiling should be solid."

John led the way up the staircase while keeping close to the railing. Gil indicated for Sal to go next. He then brought up the rear. Each step creaked beneath the men's feet, which indicated they needed to take it slow. A thump was heard from across the lobby. All three looked back as two men in tattered clothing entered from the lounge. Their hair was long and scraggly, and their bodies dirty and grimy. The two men immediately spotted the three on the stairs.

"Trespassers," the first man shouted in a raspy voice.

Both crazed men ran for the stairs. Gil motioned for John and Sal to go. The rotted wood splintered beneath Sal's foot, causing his foot to fall through, trapping him in the broken step. John returned to help him free his foot. Gil leaped over the sturdy railing and, without hesitation, engaged the aggressive men. He punched the first man in the mouth with his right fist, while still clutching his pocketknife, and then struck the second man across the face with the baton flashlight. The first man was only mildly dissuaded from the punch and again lunged for Gil. Gil kicked him in the side with his booted foot then cracked him over the head with the flashlight. He used a little too much force and snapped the metal casing at the joint, leaving the weapon useless.

At least it had effectively taken the man down. The second man came at Gil with a little less vigor now as blood streaked the side of his face. Gil punched him twice in the abdomen and then flipped him over his shoulder. The man hit the floor with a loud thump. John finally managed to help Sal free his foot. Both looked back at Gil, who had taken down the last of the two men. He motioned them to continue and ran for the stairs. Sal and John used the railing to support most of their weight as they headed up the rotted stairs. A little more than halfway up, they reached solid flooring and ran the rest of the way to the second floor.

Both men turned and looked back to check on Gil. Gil leaped onto the railing, stood upright on it, and teetered a moment. He caught his balance then ran up the banister past the rotted steps. He jumped off onto the solid steps and hurried to join the two men.

Sal turned to face John while breathing heavily and patted him on the shoulder. "Thanks for not leaving me back there to fend for myself."

"We don't leave our men behind," John informed him.

"You're okay," Gil announced then shifted his attention to the lobby.

More crazed men were now filtering into the lobby as the first two men recovered from their assault. Without hesitation, they attempted to follow the three men to the second floor. Several crazed men ran up the stairs without worry or care.

"We should probably get out of here," Sal remarked with noted concern.

Gil, Sal, and John were about to leave when they saw the first two crazed men crash through the rotted boards, taking out most of the steps as they fell to the floor beneath. With the steps out, the others had to stop their pursuit. The remaining crazies stopped at the large hole and stared at their battered and broken housemates on the floor beneath the stairs. The small group of men turned, ran back down the stairs, and hovered over their fallen men. Without hesitation, they lunged for the injured men and tore into their flesh with their teeth.

All three men on the stairs landing grimaced at what they had just witnessed.

"Okay," Sal announced. "I think we can go now."

Gil nodded and motioned them toward the patient's wing. The men's screams were the last Gil, Sal, and John heard as they ran through a set of doors.

§

Within one of the shared bedrooms on the fourth floor, John rigged the door in the event the crazies made it up the stairs and by some stroke of luck actually found them in the massive institute. The patient's room was mostly bland with white walls, although most of the paint was chipping to reveal the drywall beneath. In some areas, the drywall itself had holes, which looked suspiciously like fist dents or even dents from patient's possibly banging their foreheads into the walls. The room facing the front of the building had two, rusted metal framed beds with bare, stained mattresses. The room contained a toilet and sink within what looked more like a closet than a bathroom. The condition of both the toilet and the sink was gag-worthy but functional.

What was left of the curtains were mostly shredded over the cloudy, barred windows. Gil approached the window and observed as much as he could from their higher elevation. Despite the height, the view was pretty much the same. Wooded terrain as far as the eye could see. There wasn't much around them, leaving the building in total seclusion. It was nearly seven-thirty, which only gave them an hour or so to scan the area with the cheap binoculars. Gil placed the binoculars to his face and scanned the woods surrounding the gate and the chain link fence. Sal approached and stared out the window as well, although there wasn't much to see within the woods without the binoculars.

"Anything?" Sal asked.

"I see some movement," he announced while patiently scanning the area for their prison guards. "It's difficult to tell if it's animals or men."

"Assume the worst," John retorted.

Gil suddenly straightened and perked up. "What's this?" he announced with enthusiasm, alerting both men.

John hurried to join them at the window and strained to see what he saw. Both men scanned the woods but didn't see whatever it was Gil saw.

"What is it?" Sal asked while adjusting his glasses. "I don't see anything."

Gil handed the binoculars to Sal while grinning and indicated the sky. "Out there."

Sal looked through the binoculars and saw a private plane in the distance. It had to be a few miles away. "Is it Jackie?" Sal asked with hope.

"It's not her plane," he offered, "but she left that in Colorado. She had flown her helicopter to Virginia. If she somehow found our location, she'd need to rent a plane. It could be her."

Sal grinned and chuckled. John tapped Sal on the shoulder. Sal handed him the binoculars. He took the cheap binoculars and watched the plane a moment.

"What makes you think it's her?" John asked while watching the plane then lowered the binoculars. "It could be anyone for all you know."

"It's circling," Gil informed him and again secured the binoculars. Gil watched the plane in the sky and seemed hopeful. "Whoever is flying that plane is searching for something. It has to be Jackie and the guys."

"I hate to be a downer," John remarked while frowning. "How would your friends even know where to look?"

"They're good," Gil teased.

"That's probably me," Sal remarked and caught both their attention. He shrugged at the looks he'd received. "I let Othello install a GPS app of his own design on my cell phone, so I could be found in the event I ever, uh, went missing again."

"Again?" John asked.

Sal smirked. "It's happened on more than one occasion," he replied. "You start planning for it. I had him install it on my daughter's cell phone as well, but her husband went a little crazy and smashed her cell phone." Sal then considered the comment. "Well, more like he let Zack use it for target practice."

"Her cell phone wouldn't work at the lodge," Gil insisted while giving him a strange look. "Why would Beck be upset about it?"

"That's the beauty of Othello's GPS app," Sal informed his friend. "The phone doesn't need cell service. It doesn't even need to be turned on."

Gil grinned and resumed watching the plane in the near distance. "In that case, I don't blame Beck for 'bumping off' her phone," he remarked, "but at the same time, I'm encouraged that our rescue is closing in. If only we knew where they left your cell phone when they confiscated it." He lowered the binoculars and eyed Sal and John. "They won't be able to land too close. Our rescue is about four miles from here."

"Do you think they saw the building?" Sal asked with interest.

"There are a lot of thick woods around this area," Gil informed him. "I don't know what she saw from the sky."

"Your friends are going to be ambushed by those snipers near the gate," John remarked with concern. "Unless they brought an army, it could be a short-lived rescue."

"They don't need an army," Gil replied while smirking. "They just need a psychotic ninja leading the march, and we happen to have one of those."

"Two," Sal muttered then laughed at the comment that went over John's head.

"I doubt we'll see a rescue anytime tonight," Gil announced, "but we should take turns on guard duty, keeping an eye on the woods just in case. When they show up at that gate, we'll want to be ready."

Chapter 28

A little after seven-thirty that evening, the private plane Jackie rented in Kentucky flew over the vast woodlands just a few miles north of Bridgewater Corners, Vermont. The rental plane, a Grand Caravan EX, was a ten-passenger, single-engine prop plane with non-retractable wheels, wings attached on the top, and doors in the front and back. The body length was forty-one feet with a wingspan of fifty-two feet. According to the GPS coordinates they received from Sal's cell phone, they were close. Jackie circled the area while everyone kept watch for anything resembling a building, structure, or Gil's plane. Despite Bridgewater Corners being a small, remote town, they saw an even smaller town about ten miles beyond that. Another ten miles north of that town was a lone building, but it was too far from the GPS location to be what they were looking for. Jackie again circled the area as her frustration mounted. With all the woodland, it was like finding a needle in a haystack.

"It has to be around here somewhere," Jackie insisted. "Does anyone see anything?"

"There's a roadway," Rayner informed her.

"There's a clearing just beyond it," Bogart announced and glanced at Jackie behind the wheel. "It looks big enough for you to land."

Jackie flew toward the clearing further from where she had originally circled and strained to see the ground below. Her eyes suddenly lit up. "That's an abandoned airfield," she informed the others. "I see an old hangar."

Zack pointed past Jackie from the back seat. "Is that a plane?"

She grinned and laughed. "That's Gil's plane. I'm setting her down," Jackie announced with little hesitation then fiddled with several controls. "I'm going to circle around one more time," she informed them. "I want to take her down a little lower and slow her speed."

Zack leaped from his seat and grabbed his discarded duffel bag he'd left in the main cabin. Kane's team watched as Zack rummaged through the bag and removed automatic weapons. He passed them out to Kirk, Bogart, and Monroe in the front seat. Zack set one aside for himself and Jackie as well. He then removed several semiautomatic handguns and passed them out to each of his teammates. Zack hesitated then met Kane's gaze for the first time the entire day. He took a moment to consider his options then extended a semiautomatic to Kane. Kane tensed slightly and accepted the weapon. He then passed one to Stone and Maverick. When he handed one to Rayner, he eagerly accepted it. It was possibly the first time Rayner had been included as an option in a possibly dangerous situation. Typically, he was sidelined. Zack then extended a gun handle first to Scorpio. She eyed the gun and reluctantly accepted it.

Zack noted her reluctance. "You do know how to shoot, don't you?"

Scorpio avoided looking at him and nodded. "I'm not a very good shot."

Zack stared at her in possible disbelief. He shook off the comment then placed a semiautomatic in each of his shoulder holsters.

"Okay, everyone strap in," Jackie announced. "It's not much of a runway, so this could be a little bumpy."

Scorpio gasped at the frightening words and tightened her seatbelt then grabbed Rayner's hand for added measure. Monroe, who sat in the co-pilot seat, stared out the windshield and nervously watched the top of the trees.

"You're close to those trees," Monroe announced as his eyes widened dramatically.

"I see the trees, Monroe," Jackie snarled. She didn't appreciate him pointing out the obvious. "Hold on to something." She tightened her grip on the wheel.

Despite Jackie's assurance that the landing would be rough, Zack remained on one knee on the floor and placed a hand to the interior of the craft and the other to the nearby seat as the plane touched down. The plane landed roughly and jolted everyone. Zack somehow managed to remain in place with little effort. Once they hit the ground and the vibration decreased, Zack resumed stocking up on his firearms and other menacing-looking weapons. Kane and Scorpio watched him stuff things into his many jacket and pants pockets. Both seemed unusually tense now, and it had nothing to do with the terrifying landing in progress. The plane continued to vibrate as Jackie attempted to slow the plane on what barely constituted a landing strip. Scorpio, Maverick, and Rayner shut their eyes and held their breath as the plane seemed to skid haphazardly on the surface beneath the wheels.

"We're coming in hot," Jackie announced and clutched the vibrating wheel with a death grip.

Monroe saw Gil's plane and the hangar getting closer, causing him to shirk back in the co-pilot's seat while clutching the door and the vibrating panel before him.

"Fifty yards from Gil's plane," Jackie announced. "We're stopping in five."

The guys in the back cocked their assault rifles causing all five in Kane's team to twitch at the menacing sound. Kane and Scorpio appeared to be the most intimidated.

"Four," Jackie continued her countdown while fiddling with controls as the plane slowed enough to keep from crashing into Gil's plane. "Three."

Zack sprang to his feet, darted to the door, and looked back at Kane's team. "The five of you hold back and stick close to the steps," he ordered.

"Two," Jackie alerted them and threw another switch while slowing the plane.

Now that the plane had decreased speed and was rolling to a stop, Monroe leaped from his seat and joined his team in the back. He cradled his assault weapon in his arms and stood just behind Zack near the door. Kirk took his position on the opposite side of the door from Zack. Zack placed his hand on the door lever.

"One," Jackie announced as the plane rolled to a stop, again jolting everyone.

Zack swiftly opened the door, dropping the steps. Kirk charged down the steps, jumping over the side before he even reached the bottom. Zack charged out the door next with Monroe and Bogart bringing up the rear. Jackie cut off the engine and sprang from the pilot's seat while carelessly tossing her headset aside. She snatched her assault rifle and took a lookout position in the plane's doorway.

Jackie indicated Stone, Maverick, and Kane. "You three, follow me and keep low," she announced in a commanding tone. "Take a lookout position by the front wheel watching our right and left flank." Jackie then looked at Scorpio and Rayner. "You two keep low on the steps and watch for any activity from behind."

Jackie hurried down the steps. Kane, Stone, and Maverick ran after her. Scorpio exchanged looks with Rayner, held her breath, and then cautiously headed down the steps and remained at the base. Both kept their attention focused on the back of the plane. Kane, Stone, and Maverick crouched near the front wheel alongside Jackie. All three men stared in near disbelief as Kirk, Monroe, and Bogart scattered with their weapons while seemingly sneaking up on Gil's motionless plane. Zack was nowhere to be found.

"We are so far out of our league," Maverick muttered to Kane and Stone.

"I thought you guys were in the military," Kane remarked to his friends with some surprise. "Shouldn't this be familiar to you?"

"We were on a naval vessel," Stone informed him. "We didn't exactly leave the ship much."

"The only action we saw was from a bar stool," Maverick added.

Jackie cast a look of surprise at the three men crouched alongside her. "You two," she announced while indicating Maverick and Stone. "Stay here and guard the plane." She then met Kane's gaze. "Ninja boy, you're with me. Watch our asses."

Kane eagerly nodded. Jackie scrambled out from under the front of the plane. Kane was briefly startled by her sudden departure. He hurried after her with the semiautomatic in his hand and kept up with her while keeping his body turned to watch for anything behind them. Jackie stopped by the tail of Gil's plane. Unfortunately, Kane didn't stop and collided into her from behind. Jackie was thrown forward a step then spun and kicked him in the thigh with her knee.

"Pay attention," she snarled just loud enough for him to hear.

Kirk, Monroe, and Bogart were converging on the plane from both sides. Jackie crouched low and ran beneath the plane's underbelly with Kane directly behind her. She stopped near the plane's steps. This time Kane stopped short of running into her.

"Stay here," she instructed and pointed from her eyes to the nearby hangar.

Kane remained crouched near the backside of the steps and kept watch on the hangar. Jackie darted out from under the lowered steps in time to meet Zack, who had mysteriously appeared at the same time. Bogart crouched alongside Kane with his back to him. Zack silently crept up the plane's steps with Jackie only a step or two behind him. Kane shook his head while watching.

"Christ, she's hot," Kane muttered aloud.

Bogart cast a glare at the man behind him. "Watch it, kid," Bogart scoffed. "That's my sister."

"Oh," Kane whispered. "Sorry. No disrespect intended."

Kirk and Monroe appeared by the steps and kept their weapons aimed up at the open doorway and at the hangar. Zack peered in through the opening then bolted inside the plane. Jackie moved in after him. Kirk and Monroe didn't move from the steps. Gil's plane wasn't very big and didn't require more than two to check it out. Jackie followed Zack through the plane while keeping watch behind them. Zack approached the cockpit and peered inside. He turned toward Jackie and scanned the interior of the plane.

"Looks like we missed the party," Zack announced with annoyance.

Jackie frowned and picked up Sal and Gil's cell phones where they were left smashed on the first seat. "Whoever took them was hoping to keep their location a secret."

"Just be glad Othello is smarter than they are," Zack remarked then looked around. "We're in the middle of nowhere. Whoever took them couldn't possibly have taken them on foot."

"We should check the area for hostiles then search for tire tracks," Jackie announced.

Zack placed his transmitter into his ear and switched on his belt radio. "No one home," Zack announced to the guys through his transmitter. "Fan out and search the area."

"Kirk and I are heading to the hangar," Monroe remarked over his transmitter. "Bogart and the kid will keep a lookout position from beneath the plane."

"Roger that," Zack announced. "Jackie and I will check for a possible extraction scenario."

Chapter 29

While Kirk, Monroe, and Zack patrolled the area with their weapons, Jackie and Bogart checked over Gil's plane. Stone and Maverick were assigned to patrol the area around Jackie's rental plane. It was nearly eight o'clock that night, and the woods were starting to get dark. Jackie had the interior lights on within Gil's plane, which allowed Scorpio, Kane, and Rayner the opportunity to search for clues regarding who may have taken the two men and injured Mac. For the amount of blood Mac had lost, whoever stuffed her into the cargo compartment of the plane wasn't concerned that she would more than likely die before the craft reached its destination. Only Mac's quick thinking and self-preservation kept that from happening. If they didn't care about Mac's life, there was no doubt that Sal and Gil were in serious trouble.

Jackie collapsed into the pilot's seat of Gil's plane and attempted to start the engine. Nothing happened. Bogart stood in the cockpit doorway and stared at her.

"I'm guessing it's not just out of gas," Bogart muttered while frowning.

"No, it's been disabled," Jackie informed him even though she realized he already knew that. "Whoever is behind this must know Gil is resourceful. They have a backup plan in case he manages to escape from whatever prison they have him. Disable the plane, and he's not getting far."

"Are we assuming this was something personal against Gil?" Bogart asked.

"Unlikely," she replied. "Gil's not *that* guy. He doesn't have mortal enemies solely out to get him. It has to be someone with a grudge against the entire team. Gil's probably just the bait."

Bogart flopped into the co-pilot's seat, drew a deep breath, and eyed his sister. "There is one other scenario you seem to be forgetting."

She cast a look at Bogart. "Sal?" Jackie sighed and shook her head. "No, I haven't ruled out one of Sal's enemies crawling out from the woodwork, but this doesn't feel like revenge against Sal. Anyone after him would probably have killed him at the airport. This is thought-out, concise, planned. They knew what they were doing as well as when and where to hit."

"So it was someone with knowledge of their travel plans?" Bogart asked with some surprise. He cocked his head and revealed his disbelief in her theory. "That's a tall order on short notice. Those plans were only made a week or so ago. We didn't even know where we would be and when. I don't see how someone else could have known."

"Not to mention our little side trip to Virginia," Jackie remarked. "Those plans were less than a week in the making. Whoever jumped them had to have known they'd be at the airport in Virginia."

"A week ago, we didn't even know we'd be in Virginia," Bogart remarked.

"Exactly."

"Someone watching your house?"

"No," she replied with a deep sigh. "That wouldn't have given away any plans including their arrival at the airport in Virginia." She shook her head. "It keeps going back to Sal. He would have told his housekeeper about the trip. Who knows who she told?"

"What about Ellie?" Bogart suggested. "She had to ask for time off from work. Any number of people there could have known her plans."

"Well, we're never going to figure it out sitting around here," she announced with a defeated sigh before looking out the cockpit windshield. "It's going to be dark soon. I don't think we're leaving here tonight."

"Do you have enough runway to get us out of here?" Bogart asked while raising a brow.

"Yeah, it'll be fine," Jackie replied with little concern. "As long as everyone empties their bladders before we take off, it'll be fine."

Bogart suddenly groaned. "I hate your 'piss your pants' take-offs."

Jackie ignored the comment and sank into thought. "We'll need to consider hiking that road in the morning and see if it leads anywhere."

"If whoever took them had a car waiting, we're never going to find them on foot," Bogart remarked. "We won't even know if we're going in the right direction."

"Holden has our coordinates," Jackie informed him. "He's already contacting the state troopers working in this area on our behalf."

"On the surface, that sounds like a good idea," Bogart muttered, "but you know how those who play by the rules tend to slow things down."

"Which is why they won't show up until tomorrow afternoon," Jackie replied. "That'll give us a good six hours of daylight tomorrow to find them first."

"So what do we do tonight?" Bogart asked. "Build a campfire and roast marshmallows with Zack's kids?"

Jackie gave her brother a curious look. "Did you bring marshmallows?"

"No."

"Then I guess that's not an option, is it?" she huffed. "First thing tomorrow, I'll need to poke around inside the engine and see if I can figure out what's wrong with Gil's little princess."

"Which takes us back to tonight," Bogart announced with some concern. "What are we going to do about the uncomfortable situation with Zack's kids?"

"We're not going to do anything," Jackie informed him with little interest. "We're all adults here. Everyone is just going to have to get along."

"Solid plan," Bogart replied then casually leaned back in his seat. He raised his brow and cast a look at her. "Good luck telling Zack that."

Chapter 30

Despite that Gil's plane was more spacious and comfortable than the rental plane, the two teams intended to spend the night together in the rental plane. Perhaps it was just from years of paranoia, but there was a lingering concern that whoever abducted their men and sabotaged Gil's plane could potentially come back and do the same to them and the rental plane. They couldn't afford to have their only transport sabotaged. Two-man teams would have three-hour guard duty shifts at the base of the plane's steps. The team would make sure no one snuck up on them in the middle of the night. Zack was eager to take first watch between eight and eleven. It would give him an excuse to avoid Kane and Scorpio during the few hours everyone was awake.

Zack sat on the plane steps with his assault rifle cradled in his arms like an old friend. The emergency lights from the plane allowed light to spill out onto the steps, so those on guard duty didn't have to remain in darkness. Jackie joined him on the steps and squeezed alongside him. It was a tight fit, but neither minded.

"Did Monroe enjoy delegating guard duty teams?" Zack asked then offered a teasing grin. "I assumed I'd be alone, and he'd put you on guard duty with him."

Jackie drew a deep breath and placed her hand on Zack's leg. "He considered it," she replied. "Until I pointed out the more logical, two-hour per team idea."

Zack gave her a strange look.

She cast a look at him and smiled. "I mean; there are ten of us," Jackie informed him. "Why not include the others to make our lives that much easier?"

Zack's expression turned less jovial. "What did you do?" he snarled under his breath.

Jackie kissed Zack warmly on the cheek. "Play nice," she announced while grinning. "See you in the morning."

As she stood, Zack sprang to his feet and caught her wrist. His look was stern.

"You can't leave me alone with him," Zack insisted. "If he's anything like me at that age, we'll probably kill each other."

"Oh," Jackie announced as her eyes widened. "I had no intention of going there. I wanted you on your best behavior."

Zack gave her a strange look.

Jackie flashed a smile and headed up the plane steps. Scorpio appeared on the steps and walked down them with less enthusiasm. She cast a quick look at Zack then immediately looked away and sat on one of the upper steps.

"I was assigned guard duty with you," Scorpio informed him while insecurely shoving her hands into her jacket pockets.

Zack withheld his groan, cast a quick look at Scorpio, and then returned to the lower step. It would possibly be the longest two hours of both their lives.

§

Maverick leaned against the plane steps for his ten to midnight shift and surveyed the dark area surrounding the plane without use of the night vision binoculars. Kirk appeared from the edge of the woods while zipping his pants. He had his assault rifle slung over his shoulder and the night vision binoculars hanging around his neck.

"Nothing out there," Kirk insisted.

"You could have just said you needed to take a piss," Maverick announced with little emotion.

"I thought I was being polite," Kirk muttered.

"By pretending to hear something and storming into the woods with your rifle aimed?" Maverick asked while raising a cocky brow. "If I had to guess, I'd think you were trying to get a rise out of me."

Kirk leaned his back against the steps opposite of Maverick and stared into the woods. "Did it work?"

"No, Bogart warned me about you," Maverick replied.

Kirk frowned while shaking his head and cursed under his breath. "And he wonders why I can't stand him," he muttered.

"Yeah, well, he seemed grateful to be without your company on guard duty as well," Maverick announced.

"I'm sure your friend is no prize himself," Kirk remarked with little emotion.

"Are you kidding?" Maverick announced and cast a look back at Kirk. "Stone is hysterical and has a funny story for every occasion. Those two hours will go by fast."

"I tell funny stories," Kirk announced and seemed almost insulted. "I'm fun to be around."

"Oh?" Maverick remarked and cast a glance at Kirk with his back to his on the opposite side of the steps. "Share a funny story."

Kirk only gave it a moment's consideration. "We were on this one mission at a wedding reception in this mansion, and I needed to distract the mother-of-the-bride," he began while turning to face Maverick.

Maverick became interested and faced Kirk as well. Both leaned on the railing on their side of the steps.

"Just the tiniest bit of attention, and she's on me like Lassie in heat," Kirk continued. "I'm thinking to myself, 'fuck, this woman is old enough to be my mother'." He then became animated. "But the team needed her distracted, so I went upstairs to her bedroom with her." His eyes widened dramatically. "She comes out of the bedroom wearing this leather outfit with a whip in her hand. The whole time I'm thinking, 'fuck, I have to take one for the team'."

Maverick waved his hand in the air while giving him a strange look. "Where's the funny part to this story?"

"I'm getting to it," Kirk insisted. "I have the guys talking in my ear transmitter telling me it's time to pull out and this cougar is just about riding me to death." He threw his hands in the air. "It's not as if I could just toss her off and walk out the door."

Maverick stared in mild disbelief while rubbing his finger against his temple.

"So the team is waiting at the rendezvous while the mother-of-the-bride is using me as her personal trampoline," Kirk continued. "The entire time, my mic is on, and the guys can hear the whole thing going down. I mean; this woman is screaming profanities for all the guys to hear while her entire family is downstairs in the ballroom."

Maverick stared at Kirk, who now stopped talking, and then raised a curious brow. "Is that the end of the story?" he asked with some surprise.

"Well, you pretty much know how the story ends," Kirk insisted. "You've been with women. It almost always ends the same. Happy endings all the way around."

"Your story, although graphic, wasn't funny," Maverick informed him.

Kirk frowned and waved him off. "What the fuck do you know," he announced. "Fuck off."

§

Tuesday, July 15th. Monroe and Rayner had guard duty from midnight to two o'clock in the morning. Between keeping an eye on the area beyond the plane and occasionally scanning the surrounding woods with the pair of night vision binoculars, they played chess on Rayner's laptop. Rayner was able to charge his laptop from the plane's power source, which also kept the steps dimly lit as well.

"You and Scorpio seem pretty close," Monroe finally spoke out as he scanned the area with the night vision binoculars then resumed their chess game. He cast a quick look at Rayner before making his next move on the virtual chessboard. "Are you two a couple?"

Rayner studied the chessboard while only briefly glancing at Monroe. "Yes, we are," he replied. "And thanks for not adding the look of disbelief."

Monroe chuckled in his throat and again scanned the area with the binoculars while Rayner considered his next move. "Believe me; I get it," he announced. "It was pretty tough living in Kirk's extra buff shadow in our military days. Women are drawn to him like flies to shit. Never mind his deplorable attitude. It's easier catching a woman's eye by flexing muscles than luring them in with charm and intellect."

Rayner suddenly chuckled as if understanding completely. "Scorpio resisted, trust me," he remarked. "Her first boyfriend was very similar to your Kirk. I still sometimes wonder how I got her attention."

Monroe chuckled then made his next move and again scanned the area with the binoculars. "Don't question it; just enjoy it." He then fidgeted and eyed Rayner, who studied the virtual chessboard. "What's the story with Mac? How did she get involved with your team?"

Rayner laughed and finally met Monroe's gaze. "Trust me; it's not my team," he replied. "Kane sought out Mac because of her rumored connection with your team. I guess he liked her and wanted her to join him in his business venture."

"Private detectives?"

"I guess that's what he's attempting to pull off," Rayner replied. "He was obsessed with finding his father. Mac wasn't exactly forthcoming with him, which made him less than forthcoming with her. He claims they're so close yet he didn't trust her with his real reason for wanting to find your friend." He shook his head. "If they had some open dialog, it could have saved a very big misunderstanding."

"Are Kane and Mac--?"

Rayner cast a quick look at Monroe then smiled and laughed. "What? A couple?" He again laughed. "No, not even close. Kane loves her like a sister."

Monroe seemed to relax and smiled more naturally. "She's not exactly easy to win over, that's for sure."

"It's pretty one-sided," Rayner informed him. "Kane's extremely affectionate, and Mac's, well, not."

Monroe laughed at the comment. "We've had our clashes, believe me," he remarked then seemed to drift back to a different moment. "I think we've made some strides in the right direction." Monroe then frowned. "Although the other day probably set us back a thousand years."

"I've seen a significant improvement in her mood since she and Maverick got together," Rayner offered while studying the chessboard.

Monroe's expression dropped although Rayner didn't see it. "She's involved with Maverick?"

"Involved?" Rayner remarked then snorted a laugh. "Sex for the sake of sex is more like it. If they don't slow down, one of them is liable to get hurt."

Monroe frowned, lifted the binoculars, and again scanned the area. "I'm surprised to hear," he muttered with a tone of disapproval. "She prided herself on avoiding intimacy."

Rayner laughed, oblivious to the real conversation, and moved his bishop across the virtual board. "Maverick is something of a conman," he remarked. "She probably doesn't even realize she's in a relationship. Once he gets her back to Scorpio's hotel in Maine, it'll be a done deal." Rayner grinned smugly. "Checkmate."

Monroe snapped out of his thoughts and looked at the virtual chessboard. He frowned at the game he'd lost.

§

Stone and Bogart had the two until four in the morning shift. Both men hung out by the plane's steps and attempted to keep their voices down while laughing and having a good time. Bogart shook his head and wiped a stray tear from his eye after having laughed so long and hard.

"We have to hang out sometime," Bogart announced while chuckling. "Don't get me wrong; I love the guys, but they range from serious to deathly serious."

"When this is over, Maverick, Scorpio, Rayner, and I are returning to the hotel in Maine," Stone informed him then grinned. "You should come and visit." He then considered the comment and shrugged. "You'll probably be put to work, but we have a lot of fun."

"I might take you up on that," Bogart replied. "What about Kane and Mac?"

Stone shrugged then released a deep sigh. "Kane isn't on the same page as Scorpio," he remarked then shook his head. "I think he's trying to make his mark in the world. He's got the roaming itch. Mac will probably follow him as long as there's a paycheck involved."

"Being Zack is his father, you'll be lucky if roaming is the only itch he's got," Bogart announced then shook his head. "Zack is a whole other breed. I think he's finally warmed up to me, which basically means he doesn't plan on shooting me anytime in the near future."

"Kane is nothing like his father," Stone insisted. "I think he finally realizes that. Kane wears his heart on his sleeve. More of a lover than a fighter, although he can also fight like no man I've ever seen. He's got a good heart, which is probably his biggest downfall."

"Yeah, he's nothing like Zack," Bogart laughed. "Zack is pretty much emotionless. Well, except with Jackie. He'd kill and die for her."

"Are they a couple?" Stone asked.

Bogart laughed and shook his head. "Only in Zack's mind," he remarked. "Jackie's married to that fed, Holden."

"Oh, that one," Stone replied. "The one who questioned the shit out of us when we were in Colorado." Stone stared at Bogart as something suddenly seemed to click. "Wait a minute. I remember seeing your face on a target in that creeped out, abandoned slaughterhouse."

"Yeah, that's one of their playgrounds," Bogart reluctantly informed him. "It's where they, well, we train." He frowned. "My image as a hostage on that target is one of many tasteless jokes at my expense."

"You know, you could always come work for Scorpio at the hotel in Maine," Stone informed him. "She wouldn't treat you that way."

"I appreciate the offer," Bogart replied then managed a smile, "but I've been slowly gaining respect within the team. Being accepted by them is probably the greatest feeling in the world. Besides, I'd never leave Jackie. I never really had a family. Finding out Jackie was my half-sister was one of the happiest days of my life. Don't get me wrong, she and Holden took me into their home and their lives long before that, but it's nice knowing we have something that can't be broken."

"That's what Maverick and I have been searching for," Stone informed him. "That's why we intend to stick with Scorpio. She's our family now."

Chapter 31

Jackie and Kane had the four until six in the morning shift. After their shift, Jackie would check the engine on Gil's plane and see if she could figure out what needed to be fixed. Once Bogart woke her for her shift, she nudged Kane on her way to the plane doorway. Kane had occupied the plush seat next to his sister and managed to leave without waking her. Jackie was already at the bottom of the steps with her assault rifle and the night vision binoculars when Kane made his way down the steps. She couldn't deny being on guard duty with Kane was a little uncomfortable. She'd nearly killed his sister, which had to be in the back of his mind. She couldn't expect Zack to engage in something quite as uncomfortable as pairing up with the children he didn't even know he had if she wasn't willing to accept the same discomfort.

Jackie wasn't quite ready to face Scorpio after what happened in the cemetery. She could feel the tension with their team when they met up at the airport in Virginia. Everyone was uncomfortable after what had happened. In particular, Jackie felt she broke Scorpio's spirit. Scorpio had attacked Jackie like a demon possessed and now the young woman couldn't look any of them in the eyes. Pairing Zack with Scorpio on first watch was step one to breaking tension between him and his children. Although Scorpio was traumatized and quite possibly intimidated by Zack, Jackie knew he wouldn't go out of his way to make her more uncomfortable, and maybe she'd even relax after spending a couple of hours on guard duty with him. Jackie didn't expect much conversation between the two, but just hanging out in silence was a start.

On the other hand, Jackie didn't know what to expect on guard duty with Kane. Their interaction would be less explosive than pairing him with Zack. They'd blow up that bridge when they came to it. Jackie knew she needed to do some damage control with Zack's children, and she felt more comfortable starting with Kane than the woman she nearly piked. Jackie handed Kane the night vision binoculars then slung the assault rifle over her shoulder as she leaned against the railing of the steps. She wasn't sure what she wanted to say to rectify the uncomfortable situation with Kane, but she knew she had to say something. Jackie realized she had to find a way to ease into the conversation, although she was still debating how she'd do that.

"I'm sorry about all the trouble I've caused," Kane announced in a docile tone.

Jackie turned and looked at him where he stood on the opposite side of the steps from her. And maybe she didn't have to worry about opening up the dialog between them. Kane seemed perfectly willing to take the reins. He stared at her with sincerity but seemed to look away with shame when she met his gaze.

Kane raked his fingers through his hair then managed a tiny laugh. "To be perfectly honest; I've made better first impressions," he announced then lifted his eyes and met her gaze. "Can we move past all the unpleasantness from the other day?"

Jackie was slightly stunned that he easily took responsibility for everything and the humility he projected. "You're nothing like your father," she remarked, although she hadn't actually intended to say it aloud.

"I'm starting to realize that," Kane replied while looking away and seemed almost defeated.

Jackie approached the steps, removed the assault rifle from her shoulder, and sat on one of the lower steps. Kane stared at her and the massive weapon. She noted the expression on his face as he eyed the rifle.

"Not a fan of weapons?" Jackie asked while indicating the rifle.

"I've never actually seen one that big up close before," he admitted then hesitated. "I'm not sure which is more intimidating. That weapon or you."

Jackie eyed him with surprise by the comment. "You think I'm intimidating?" she remarked. "You have some pretty amazing fighting skills. I don't see how I'm intimidating to you."

"Are you serious?" he replied with surprise. "You're holding a weapon half my size like it's a handbag by Prada, you nearly killed my sister, and you could very likely kick my ass all the way back to Maine. You honestly don't think you're intimidating?" He hesitated only a moment and shook his head. "To put all that into perspective, you're the girlfriend of possibly the most frightening man I've ever met in my life, who also happens to be my father."

"I'm not Zack's girlfriend," Jackie corrected.

Kane eyed her. "Does *he* know that?"

"Of course he knows that," Jackie scoffed then made a face. "I met his girlfriend. Trust me; *she's* intimidating."

"I'm pretty sure I don't want to meet her," Kane announced.

"No, you really don't," Jackie countered then eyed him and smiled. She indicated the steps alongside her. "Come on over. I don't bite; honestly."

Kane seemed hesitant but was quick to join her on the steps. Jackie extended the assault rifle to him. Kane stared at it a moment then uncertainly accepted it. He immediately marveled at the weight. She then had him stand up and showed him the correct way to hold it, requiring her to place her hands on him. He seemed mildly distracted by her touch, possibly still a little nervous around her. Jackie pointed out the weapon's features and showed him how to use the sights, which the night vision scope was an impressive feature. Jackie then instructed him on how to fire the weapon, placing her hands on his hands, so he held it correctly. She didn't actually let him fire it since that would bring the rest of the team out with their weapons and itchy trigger fingers. She then showed him how to unload and reload it.

Kane then did what she had shown him without instruction. He aimed the weapon into the woods and looked through the night vision scope. A little red dot appeared in the center, although the laser pointer couldn't be seen anywhere but within the scope. He lowered the weapon and grinned.

Jackie offered a pleased smile. "So? Is it less intimidating now?"

He cast a look at her and nodded in response.

Jackie then indicated the clearing. "All right then," she announced. "Let's patrol the perimeter."

She showed him how to carry the excessively heavy weapon while patrolling, which would allow him ease of use at a moment's notice if necessary. Jackie used the night vision binoculars to scan the woods as they walked. Once they searched the area surrounding both planes, they returned to the steps. Kane returned the weapon to her, which she set aside, and both sat on the steps. He cast a quick glance at her and smiled.

"I appreciate the weapons lesson," he announced and seemed slightly uncomfortable. "Scorpio and I didn't spend a lot of time around guns. With the way our grandfather was, I suppose we're lucky he let us take karate lessons. I wouldn't have minded learning how to shoot."

Jackie couldn't even imagine a world where she didn't know how to fire, disassemble, and clean a weapon. "My father taught me how to shoot before I could walk," she informed him then laughed.

Kane realized it was a joke and laughed with her. "Your father was Zack's commanding officer?"

Jackie nodded and offered a warm smile. "They were best friends," she replied while sinking back into a different time. "I grew up with his team. My mother died when I was little, so I was raised as one of the boys."

"So Zack is like a father to you?"

Jackie cast a look at him and suddenly snorted a laugh. "I sometimes see him that way, but he doesn't share that sentiment," she replied. "We'll just go with my partner and best friend."

"I spent my entire life wondering what my father was like," Kane remarked then sank into his own thoughts. "Wishing I had him in my life growing up." He sighed with defeat. "I guess I was just setting myself up for disappointment. In a way, he's pretty much how I thought he'd be, yet somehow he's nothing like I imagined."

"That's pretty much the way everyone feels about Zack," Jackie admitted then grinned.

Kane caught her look then smiled in response. "I can see why he appreciates you the way he does," he remarked then fidgeted slightly and nervously scratched his beard. "After that morning in the cemetery, I likened you to a demon." He met her gaze with his blue eyes. "I feel a little bad about that."

"I've been called worse," she teased then chuckled as she looked away.

"That's beside the point," he announced, causing her to look back at him. Kane met her gaze and stared into her eyes. "I'm not like that. I hold myself to a higher standard, particularly when it comes to women. It's par for the course when you have a twin sister. At least for me it is."

"You and Scorpio are close, aren't you?"

"I'd like to think we can read each other's minds. It's a twin thing," he teased then reconsidered the comment. "Although maybe I'm closer to her than she is to me. She can be emotionally shut off at times. She thinks I'm too warm and personable."

Jackie snorted a laugh. "Well, I guess we know which of you takes after Zack," she teased.

"Funny," Kane muttered and managed a tiny laugh that almost sounded insecure. "I always assumed I took after my father."

"No, it's definitely your sister," Jackie informed him. "I see a lot of him in you, but she has his temperament." She then laughed. "Don't worry; you dodged a bullet on that one. You're much better off the way you are. The world can only handle one Zack in it."

Kane stared into her eyes a moment longer while enjoying the compliment. He suddenly tensed and looked away. Jackie stared at his profile a moment longer then looked back out to the dark woods. Her thoughts strayed to what could have been; what should have been. Zack intended to marry Maggie and move her to Virginia. Jackie would have been raised alongside

Kane and Scorpio. The young man sitting alongside her could very well have been one of her best friends growing up or even the little brother she never wanted. Zack wasn't the only one who missed out on seeing his children grow. It was a sobering thought and made her almost sad.

Chapter 32

It was a little before five in the morning and not long before sunrise. Kane prompted Jackie to talk about her childhood and life growing up on military bases. He was easy to talk with and seemed genuinely interested in her father and the team. Despite knowing Kane was Zack's son, Jackie didn't offer too much information about the team and gave no information about the lodge or any of their current homes and safe houses. Jackie hated being distrustful, but it was second nature. Even growing up, her father drilled it into her to keep anything about the team on a 'need to know basis'. It was only in later years that she understood why.

"Did Zack ever mention my mother?" Kane finally asked Jackie.

She glanced at him and felt slightly uncomfortable. He should be asking Zack questions about his mother; not her. Jackie stared into Kane's eyes and knew she needed to step in if Zack wouldn't.

"He confided in me, yes," she replied. "It's not something he found easy to discuss. He's a private person."

Kane obviously wanted to ask more, but, instead, he looked away and suddenly avoided the subject. Despite that he seemed mature and together, he appeared to be wrestling with demons of his own. Almost certainly, his demon went by the name Zack. Jackie took a moment to study his profile. Now she realized why she was troubled by him the first time they'd met back in Colorado. He looked a lot like his father, and she could see so much of Zack in him.

"I had a great childhood," Kane announced without looking at her. "Loving grandparents who gave me everything I ever wanted and the world's greatest sister slash built-in best friend." He hesitated a moment and drew a deep breath. "But there was always this empty void in my life. I somehow *knew* he was alive. At times, I even let it consume me. No one understood why I had to know; why I had to search." He finally glanced at her and met her gaze. "Do you have any idea what it's like feeling alone even when you're surrounded by people who love you?"

"No, I'm afraid I don't," she informed him then raised her brows. "But I've spent a large part of my life being there for someone else who felt that way."

"Zack?"

"Your father," she corrected. "You risked a lot finding him. Maybe you should try talking to him."

Kane frowned. "He doesn't want to talk to me," he announced and looked across the clearing. "I knew the sort of man he was, but I fooled myself into believing it'd be a happy reunion anyway."

"No, you don't know the man he is," Jackie insisted. "He rarely shows that side. It's not easy for him to show his feelings, but the man who sacrificed his happiness to protect the woman he loved is still in there." She hesitated then drew a deep breath. "Unfortunately, he's been guarding his game a long time. I'm convinced part of him died after Midnight Requisition."

The faint sound of movement was heard within the woods. Jackie and Kane heard the rustling sound at the same time. Jackie raised the rifle and looked through the night vision scope while Kane scanned the area with the binoculars.

"Anything?" Jackie asked.

"No," Kane replied. "Nothing. Maybe it's an animal."

Jackie sprang to her feet and kept the rifle cradled in her arms with her finger near the trigger. "I'm going to check it out."

Kane jumped to his feet and kept close to her as they approached the woods. "Not without me," he insisted.

Both scanned the woods with their respective night vision equipment. They heard a twig snap deeper within the woods. Jackie and Kane easily followed the sound for a visual on whatever they were hearing.

Kane stared through the binoculars. "I see a man at ten o'clock," he informed her.

Jackie spun with her rifle and stared through the night vision scope. She caught a glimpse of the man Kane saw as he darted through the woods. Kane lowered his binoculars and appeared surprised.

"Where'd he go?" he asked.

"Watch my back," she announced and headed into the woods.

Kane removed the semiautomatic from his pants, turned his back to Jackie's, and kept watch behind them.

"I see him. Seven o'clock," Kane announced then hesitated while gently clearing his throat. "You can relax. He isn't armed."

"Are you sure?" Jackie asked while spinning with the rifle aimed.

"Yeah, uh, pretty sure," Kane announced.

Jackie caught a glimpse of the man in her night scope. What little she saw was a naked, middle-aged man darting through the woods. Jackie lowered the rifle and groaned.

"You've got to be kidding," she scoffed.

"What do we do?" Kane asked.

Jackie flashed a mocking smile. "He's all yours," she announced. "See who he is and send him packing."

"Why me?"

"I'd answer that, but it would only sound sexist and possibly a little vulgar," she replied.

Kane frowned in response. "I'll give you that one," he replied then headed after the naked man. He paused a few feet away, looked around with bewilderment, and then looked at Jackie. "He's gone."

"I doubt he got far," Jackie insisted then looked around.

The naked man suddenly lunged for Jackie from out of nowhere. Jackie cried out with surprise by the animalistic sounds coming from the aggressive man as he attempted to take her down. Jackie punched him in the abdomen, although it didn't seem to deter him. He bolted around her as if he were a lion stalking its prey. Jackie slung her rifle, locked onto his position, and spun into a roundhouse kick. The naked man darted from her path mid kick. Her foot connected with Kane's shoulder as he darted closer to aid her and sent him backward into a tree. Jackie gasped with surprise, having struck Kane. When she turned to see where the man had gone, he leaped for her with a snarl and tackled her to the ground. Her assault rifle flew from her shoulder and across the forest floor. The naked man was now on top of her while pulling her hair and attempting to bite her neck.

Jackie was more shocked by the man's teeth coming at her neck than his animalistic snarls. She held his face back from her neck while considering her next move to get him off her. Kane suddenly kicked the man in the face and sent him backward across the forest floor. Kane ran to Jackie's side and crouched alongside her.

"Are you okay?"

"My weapon," she cried out while pointing at the naked man, who now grabbed her discarded assault rifle as he sprang to his feet.

Rather than attempt to shoot them, the man took off with the stolen rifle while cackling like a crazed maniac. Kane ran after the man and tackled him face first to the ground. Jackie sprang to her feet just in time to witness the hard tackle and cringed.

"Oh, that's gonna hurt," she muttered then joined Kane as he applied pressure to the naked man face down on the ground.

Jackie snatched her rifle that was now just out of the man's grasp and turned to look at Kane, who proudly sat atop the naked man.

"This is possibly the second grossest thing I've done in my life," he casually announced.

"What was the first?" Jackie asked while sneering at the struggling, naked man.

"Walking in on my grandparents getting it on," he announced then made a face. "Doggie style." Kane shut his eyes and shuttered. "That image will haunt me until I die." He drew a deep breath then eyed the man beneath him. "What do we do with our crazed streaker?"

Jackie removed a pair of zip ties from her jacket pocket and tossed them to him. "Knock yourself out." She watched as Kane swiftly zip-tied the man's wrists behind his back. "Sorry about knocking you on your ass."

"Wouldn't be the first time I *fell* for a woman," he announced while chuckling.

"Next time you'll want to stay out of the way," Jackie informed him.

"I'm usually pretty good at seeing a kick coming," he insisted. "You're a little faster than I'm used to."

"I've had a lot of practice," she informed him. "I've also been knocked on my ass a lot."

The naked man, who was obviously mentally unstable, rolled onto his back and laughed for some unknown reason. How he could laugh after having his naked body plowed across the ground was startling. The man then started singing commercial jingles and didn't even notice or care that he was captured. Jackie rolled her eyes and shook her head at the demented man. Kane touched his temple and eyed the blood on his fingers.

"You're bleeding," Jackie announced and hurried toward him.

"It's nothing," he replied. "I must have hit my head on the tree when you launched me into space."

Jackie reached for his temple and gently brushed his hair from the small cut. She frowned while studying his injury as he stared at her closeness to him in silence.

"There's a first aid kit in Gil's plane," Jackie announced then pulled back and met his blue eyes as he stared at her. "We'll need to clean that."

Without warning, Kane placed his hand to Jackie's face and kissed her quickly but passionately on the lips. Jackie was taken by surprise, although with the way he pulled back, he seemed almost equally surprised by his actions.

"I'm sorry," he quickly announced defensively. "I shouldn't have done that. I don't know why I did that."

Jackie stared at him, feeling somewhat tense and was uncertain how to respond. She shook her head and snorted a slight laugh.

"Yeah, you're Zack's son all right," she muttered.

Kane nervously raked his fingers through his hair while shifting uncomfortably. "Scorpio's never going to let me live this down."

"Relax," Jackie remarked and easily shook off what happened. "It's more important Zack doesn't hear about it. You should probably also know that the federal agent who questioned you at the slaughterhouse is my husband. He already has it out for you for lying about your name."

Kane stared at her and seemed stunned by the last comment. "You're married?" he suddenly gasped then groaned while holding his head. "When I screw up, it's go big or go home." He met her gaze with increased embarrassment. "I'm really sorry."

Jackie waved him off and offered a humored smile. "You've met my teammates," she informed him. "If I didn't have a sense of humor, I'd be as insane as this guy." She then indicated the happily clueless, singing man. "Let's get our naked friend back to the plane and wake the others."

Chapter 33

With their naked prisoner in tow, Jackie and Kane returned to the large clearing within the abandoned airfield, which was brightened by the rapidly rising sun. Someone darted out from beneath the plane and ran past the distant hangar.

"Who the hell was that?" Jackie suddenly demanded.

"I've got this," Kane announced and ran after the unidentified person.

Kane ran around the old hangar and saw the man attempting to make it for the darkened woods just on the other side. Headlights from an approaching vehicle caught his attention but didn't stop his pursuit of the man. The man appeared to be carrying something, although it was impossible to see what he was hiding in his arms. He just about made it to the woods and possible freedom when someone leaped from the moving vehicle and bolted after the man. The man was tackled to the ground with such force that both tumbled and rolled. The man scrambled to his feet as his attacker rebounded with catlike reflexes. Kane stopped his pursuit and assessed the situation rather than engage. The man left whatever he had stolen and ran into the darkened woods.

A dog jumped from the vehicle and raced into the woods after the man, disappearing into the darkness. As Kane approached, he saw it was a woman who had intervened, and she now clutched her shoulder while showing no attempt to pursue the man or the dog. Kane ran across the clearing, stopped a few feet short of the woman, and stared at her in disbelief. Mac met Kane's gaze with a difficult to read expression. She'd been betrayed by her friends, but in a way, she'd also betrayed them. Kane and Mac hadn't spoken since the cemetery double-cross, and it was difficult to tell what either was thinking.

"I'm so sorry, Mac," Kane whispered as tears glossed his eyes. "Please forgive me."

Mac released the anxious breath she'd been holding, and her shoulders sagged with relief. Kane took a quick step toward her and gathered her in his arms. He pulled her against him in a warm, snug embrace. Mac hesitated only a moment before returning the embrace possibly for the first time in all the times he'd shown affection toward her. Mac clung to Kane's neck despite the pain in her shoulder, buried her face against him, and sobbed softly. Her emotional response caused Kane to hold her even tighter while cradling the back of her head in his hand, keeping her face buried against his neck.

Jackie slowed her approach, eyed the tearful reunion, and then picked up what the man had dropped before taking off. She frowned when she realized it was a part from her plane. The familiar barking of a dog caught Jackie's attention. When she looked toward the woods, Darth ran for her at top speed with no intention of slowing. The dog excitedly plowed into her and knocked her to the ground. Darth whimpered and whined while licking her face like an excited puppy. Jackie sat up as best she could and attempted to keep up with Darth's enthusiasm to see her.

"Hey, boy," Jackie announced while affectionately petting the dog. "Where have you been?"

The dog continued to whine while rubbing against her and nearly bowling her over with his body. Jackie managed to pull herself to her feet and calm the dog. Darth suddenly barked excitedly and ran off across the abandoned airfield for an unmistakable shadow that could only be Zack. Despite his attempt to slow the dog, Darth knocked him to the ground as well. Kane finally loosened his grip on Mac, although he still held her, and met her gaze. He gently wiped the tears from her face with his thumbs then affectionately kissed her forehead. Mac clung to his wrists as he held her face.

"Are you okay?" Kane asked then took a step back, although still unwilling to release her, and checked her over for injuries.

"I've been better," Mac replied then managed a tiny laugh. "I've also been worse." She wiped additional tears from her face and stared at him. "What are you doing here?"

"Looking for you," he announced. "After we learned that you skipped out at the hospital, that Othello guy called and said you were tracking Sal Romano. We must have just missed you at the airport."

"You came looking for me?" she asked with surprise.

"Of course we did," Kane announced then offered a warm smile. "I had to make sure my little badger was okay."

Mac stared into his eyes and resisted crying further. "I'm sorry I wasn't completely honest about Zack," she announced while fidgeting. "I didn't know why you were looking for him. I was protecting you from him as much as I was protecting them from you."

"I know why you did it," Kane replied. "I understand."

"How can you understand when I don't even understand it myself?" Mac asked.

Kane shrugged and offered a tiny smile. "You're a complicated person," he replied. "And I understand that. I also know that you care more about others than you'd ever admit."

Mac tensed and glanced at Jackie, who remained nearby while observing their reunion. Mac moved away from Kane, took two steps toward Jackie, and projected a more serious attitude.

"Did you find Gil and Sal?" Mac asked then indicated Gil's plane, which was visible just beyond the old hangar. "The GPS on Sal's cell phone indicated he was here."

Jackie frowned and shook her head. "No, we didn't find either man. We found their phones on Gil's plane," she announced then sighed. "I'm assuming they didn't come here willingly."

"Three men jumped Sal and Gil on his plane in Virginia," Mac informed Jackie. "Last time I saw them, they were already being held captive. Whoever those men were, they were more interested in taking them prisoner than killing them." She then frowned. "Apparently, I was expendable. I'm convinced they're still alive."

Jackie stared back at Mac then offered a sincere smile. "I'm glad you're okay," she announced gently. "The man who found you in the cargo hold of his plane told us what happened."

Mac smiled more naturally and nodded. "I've survived worse," she replied then frowned. "Although I wouldn't turn down a handful of painkillers if you've got any."

"There should be some on Gil's plane," Jackie reported then nodded across the abandoned field.

Kane then noticed a young woman in her early twenties standing near the car that brought Mac to them. "Are you making new friends?" Kane asked and indicated the young woman.

Mac looked back at the car, appeared embarrassed that she had forgotten about her chauffeur, and motioned the woman to join them.

"This is Deidra," Mac announced then introduced the woman to Jackie and Kane.

Deidra was a beautiful country girl with a curvy yet toned body from years of farm work. Even without a pinch of makeup, she maintained a girl-next-door attractiveness. Despite her simple, country girl attire, her strawberry blonde hair was styled more city than country. Even pulled back into a simple ponytail, it was evident her haircut came from somewhere beyond the small town of Bridgewater Corners. It was possible she was attempting to break free from life on the farm while sneaking off to the city for fun. She was the right age for dance clubs.

"Izzy's friend dropped me off at the closest airport, so I had to thumb my way out here to 'no man's land'," Mac informed the others. "I met Deidra last night in Bridgewater Corners. She was nice enough to let me stay with her at her friend's house last night and offered to bring me out here first thing this morning."

"I was heading home early this morning anyway," Deidra informed them while seemingly sizing up Kane.

Kane's steampunk appeal seemed to attract young girls from tweeners to twenty-somethings. Although his magnetic blue eyes may have helped lure in women as well. Every young party girl on the planet seemed drawn to Kane.

"I live pretty far out in the country," Deidra announced while casting several looks at Kane and flashed smiles in an attempt to flirt with her eyes.

"Maybe you could help us with our other problem," Jackie remarked with little interest in Deidra's 'love at first sight' crush on Kane. "We ran into a crazy, naked man this morning. He tried to bite me."

Deidra slipped out of hormone overdrive and immediately groaned while rolling her eyes. "Not Sammy," she announced with a huff. "He's a sweet man, but when his sister leaves him alone, he tends to go off his meds, which is usually followed by his clothes. Did he eventually leave?"

"No," Jackie replied. "We felt it best to tie him up until he settled down. Can you give him a ride home?"

"Sure," she replied with a sigh. "I've hauled his naked ass around more than once."

"Deidra says there's a town up the line from here," Mac informed Jackie. "It might be a good place to look for Sal and Gil."

"I could take you there this morning," Deidra informed them and again batted her eyes at Kane. "We heard your plane flying overhead yesterday evening. Not too many planes flying this way."

"I assumed it was you," Mac informed Jackie while hiding her sly grin at her correct assumption. "I told Deidra you wouldn't have any ground transportation. Apparently, there's very little around this area."

"I have enough room for seven in my jeep," Deidra informed them. "How many of you are there? After Sammy and me, I can take five in my jeep. I'm sure someone will give you a ride back later." The young woman then looked at her watch and grimaced slightly. "We need to leave in an hour, though. I wasn't supposed to go out last night. If I'm not home by eight to do farm chores, my father won't let me use his jeep again."

"I'll talk to the guys," Jackie informed the young woman. "This town you mentioned seems like a good place to start our search."

"There's not a lot there," Deidra reported, "but someone there may know something about your friends. Strangers would be noticed this far out."

Jackie fiddled with the detached plane part in her hand.

Kane finally noticed what she held and became concerned. "Is that from your plane?"

She sighed deeply. "I'm afraid so," Jackie replied. "I'll need to see what other damage was done while we were off chasing the streaker."

Deidra shook her head. "I have a pretty good idea who you were chasing with that part from your plane," she announced. "There's a guy not far from here who rebuilds cars. Well, tinkers on them is probably more accurate. I wouldn't doubt he thought he could borrow some parts from your plane. You'll want to report that to the sheriff. Charlie is a menace. Steals anything he can get his hands on."

"Not to change the subject," Mac announced while shifting uncomfortably, "but I'd really like those painkillers now."

Chapter 34

Everyone was up and out of the rental plane by the time Jackie found some painkillers for Mac. Gil kept a medical bag stashed on his plane. Similarly, Jackie had one on her plane and her helicopter as well. There were times it was necessary to do quick patch jobs on their teammates. As Jackie, Mac, Kane, and Deidra headed across the field toward the rental plane, the others were already approaching to find out what Mac knew. No one was surprised at Zack's mysterious disappearance the moment Mac showed up. When it came to Mac, Zack was unwilling to forgive and forget. Although, it remained a mystery what had happened between them in the first place. Darth seemed to disappear with Zack. Gil's dog had become unusually attached to Zack recently, and it was quite possible the feeling was mutual. Both tended to spend a lot of time at Jackie and Holden's house.

The pair had quite possibly bonded during Zack's bouts of sleeplessness. Jackie would never share her thoughts, but she secretly believed Zack was recruiting Darth as one of his minions when he finally made his play for world domination. Scorpio, Rayner, Maverick, and Stone were happy to see Mac and greeted her with more affection than she had been anticipating or possibly wanted. Jackie watched the reunion and noted subtle looks of emotion on the hardened woman's face. It would seem she finally found the family she'd been searching for. Jackie also observed Monroe's general discomfort and inability to look at Mac.

There were any number of reasons for Monroe's anxiety. Possibly at the top of that list was the circumstances leading up to the incident in the cemetery. Mac was less likely to forgive and forget being bound and gagged, so the team could ambush her friends. Despite it not being Monroe's idea or something he wanted any part of, Mac would take it out on him more than the others because of his mild emotional attachment to her. Maverick played it cool with Mac, but it was more than obvious to their team that he wanted to smother her in his arms. In private, that would be acceptable, but he risked Mac's wrath attempting to do it in front of others, particularly in front of Whiskey Tango Foxtrot.

Once everyone was up to speed on what happened with Sal and Gil, they were introduced to Deidra, who was now eyeing her watch. They would need to leave soon if they wanted a ride.

"Only five of us can ride along with Deidra to the nearby town," Monroe informed those from both teams. "Jackie needs to stay behind and work on repairing the plane." He then looked around and sighed. "I'll go along to town to see if anyone knows anything about Gil and Sal. We have room for four more."

"I'm going," Mac immediately chimed in surprising her friends. She caught the strange look Kane gave her. "Sal and Gil aren't here, and I don't intend to sit around waiting for the state troopers to show up. I doubt they'll be much help anyway. Someone in town may know something."

"At the very least, we may be able to get a car and patrol the back roads," Maverick announced. "I'll tag along."

Rayner and Scorpio seemed to be having their own private debate.

"I should go," Rayner informed her. "If they have access to the internet, I can be of some use."

"Then I should go with you," Scorpio insisted. "I don't think you and I should split up."

"You should stay with Kane," Rayner remarked. "We need more eyes on the planes."

"He has this, Scorp," Kane assured her.

"I'm sure they'll be able to find someone to loan them a car," Deidra chimed in. "It's only a thirty-minute drive back here." She again eyed her watch. It was now seven o'clock in the morning. "It's going to take me an hour to get to my place, so we need to get going if I'm going to make it by eight."

"Let me grab my bag, and I'll join you by the car," Rayner informed them.

Monroe, Mac, Maverick, and Deidra headed for the car parked on the other side of the hangar. Rayner ran back to the rental plane for his laptop bag. Scorpio greeted him halfway and threw her arms around him.

Rayner returned the embrace and laughed warmly. "I won't be gone long," he insisted. "Nothing's going to happen in a small, one-horse town."

Scorpio pulled back just far enough to meet his gaze and stared into his eyes. "I just have a really bad feeling," she remarked with concern. "I wish you'd reconsider and let me go along."

"It'll be fine," Rayner again assured her then tensed. "I think you need to stay here and keep an eye on Kane. I'm more worried about another clash between him and, uh, your father."

"I suppose when you put it that way--" Scorpio muttered then managed a tiny smile. "Be careful."

Rayner nodded then kissed her quickly but passionately. He pulled away and offered a warm smile. "I'll see you in a few hours."

Rayner hurried to catch up with the others and the only transportation away from the abandoned airfield. Scorpio reluctantly joined the others, who were eager to hear what Jackie had to say upon inspection of the rental plane's engine compartment. Jackie stood on a folding stool Gil kept in the cargo compartment of his plane. She peered into the engine compartment and pounded the metal frame with disgust. Obviously, it wasn't a good prognosis.

"What is it?" Bogart asked as he eyed her frustration with his own concern.

She glanced at her brother while frowning. "They disabled our only communication." Jackie glanced around the woods that had lightened considerably. "Whoever did this wasn't some car enthusiast scrounging for parts; he wanted to make sure we lost communication."

"Yeah, that sounds about right," Kirk muttered and removed his rifle from his shoulder. He glared at Stone then indicated Jackie's discarded rifle propped against the plane. "You're patrolling with me. Lock and load."

Stone grabbed the discarded rifle, cast a quick look at Scorpio, and then hurried after Kirk.

"Can you fix the radio?" Bogart asked with concern.

"I think so, but it'll take some time," she replied then looked at the part on the ground. "Replacing that part should be fun too. I'm missing some inexpensive but important bolts." She looked around the ground. "That man possibly tossed them when he removed them, but they could be beneath the plane. Everyone start looking for nuts and bolts on the ground. I'm going to check Gil's plane and see if it's the same issue. If it is, that man who tried to steal the part probably has some connection to Gil and Sal's disappearance."

Zack and Darth returned in time to greet Jackie as she headed for Gil's plane with her folding step stool. "We're secure to the north and west," he informed her.

"Kirk and Stone are checking south and east," Jackie remarked then eyed Zack as she approached the engine on the front of Gil's plane. "We're missing some nuts and bolts in order to reconnect that part, and communication has been severed."

Zack groaned and shook his head. "Do you want the toolbox from Gil's plane?"

"If you don't mind," she replied then placed the step stool before the front left side of Gil's plane. She climbed on the step stool, opened the engine compartment, and stared at the engine. Jackie shook her head while vigorously running her fingers through her hair. "Son-of-a-bitch."

"What is it?" Zack asked.

"Gil's plane is missing the same part, and the radio has been disabled the same as the other plane," she informed him in a less than civilized tone. "That man who got away was key to whatever happened here."

"Want me to look for him?"

"No, it's too late for that," she replied with a defeated sigh. "He's probably long gone after Darth showed up."

"Darth had some blood on his muzzle," Zack announced. "I'm assuming he got a piece of your man."

Jackie nodded and indicated the bloodstains on her hands. "Yeah, Darth slobbered bloody saliva all over me."

Zack eyed her and gave a slight nod. "You got a little on your face too," he teased. "I'll get you that toolbox then take a look inside the old hangar. Maybe there's something useful left behind."

"Grab any size nuts and bolts you find," she announced. "Heavy wire will do in a pinch."

Zack suddenly grinned. "I've got plenty of duct tape," he proudly informed her.

"We'll call that plan 'b'," she muttered with less enthusiasm. "I may be able to steal some parts from Gil's plane to repair the rental."

Zack glanced across the old airfield to the rental plane where Scorpio, Kane, and Bogart searched for discarded nuts and bolts.

"Where's the rest of the gang?" he finally asked.

"They went with Mac's new friend to a nearby town," Jackie informed him. "They're hoping for internet and possibly a car to borrow. Someone in that town must know who lives around these parts. Abandoned buildings. Anywhere someone could have taken Gil and Sal."

"I'll leave you Darth while I'm in the hangar," Zack informed her. "He'll watch your ass for me."

Jackie cast a disapproving look at Zack after the comment. He barely flashed a smile before heading onto Gil's plane. Darth eyed her and tilted his head. Jackie looked back at the dog.

"You need a better class of friends," Jackie informed the dog.

Darth whined in response.

Jackie laughed. "Yeah, you're right," she announced. "So do I."

§

By the time Deidra's jeep reached the edge of town, it was close to eight o'clock. Despite Deidra's concerns about being late to reach her father's farm, she agreed to drop off their local streaker at his son's house, which wasn't far from her farm. To save time, she dropped Mac, Rayner, Maverick, and Monroe off at the end of the main street to town. Once they were out of the jeep, Deidra drove like a wild woman to make it home in time.

"That girl is at least as old as Kane and Scorpio," Maverick announced. "I'm surprised she adheres to a curfew."

"Just because she's working for her father, that doesn't mean he can't demand she show up for work on time," Monroe remarked.

"I don't think she's going to make it in time," Rayner muttered then looked at the town before them.

The town seemed oddly void of life even for eight in the morning.

As the four walked along the main street, which was the only street in town, they looked at the buildings with increasing concern.

"Something doesn't seem right," Monroe announced while studying each home.

Several homes had nearly a dozen, five-gallon water containers lining the porches. The four noticed the trend at nearly every home.

"What's with the water jugs?" Mac asked.

"Tainted water?" Maverick guessed although he appeared equally puzzled.

"If the water were contaminated, there would be notices," Rayner remarked and studied each home they passed. He then paused and eyed the trees, grass, and shrubs. "Looks as if they've suffered a severe drought."

Mac suddenly stopped within the road. "Anyone else noticing what I'm not noticing?"

The three men stopped and looked around.

"No cars," Monroe announced then appeared concerned. "They abandoned the town." He looked around and shook his head. "It's a ghost town."

"That's impossible," Mac remarked. "The homes are in good condition."

"Recently abandoned," Rayner informed her then shook his head. "Less than a year, I'd guess."

Mac suddenly spun to face Rayner and glared at him. "If the town has been abandoned six months or longer than that means--"

Rayner nodded while raising his brow. "Your new friend lied to us."

"Son-of-a-bitch!" Mac cried out.

"Then that means she's in on whatever happened to Gil and Sal," Monroe announced then turned angry. "She lured us out here to split up the team."

Monroe and Mac removed their semiautomatics from their shoulder holsters while Maverick removed his from the back of his pants. Rayner saw the others with their weapons drawn and removed his as well.

"Are we expecting an ambush?" Rayner asked while looking around.

"I'm not waiting to find out," Monroe muttered while scanning the area. "She purposely dropped us off a good thirty miles away from the others. We need to find a car or truck and return to the rest of the team. Either we're in trouble, or they are."

Rayner immediately tensed. "Scorpio," he gasped with concern.

"Zack and Kirk will keep their eyes open," Monroe insisted. "Especially after the plane was sabotaged. They'll be on their guard. Let's just concentrate on finding transportation."

Mac nodded down the road. "There's a garage," she announced. "We should try there."

All four cautiously made their way toward the garage while keeping watch on every window in every home. Once they reached the garage, Monroe tried the door, but it was locked.

"It's locked," Monroe announced. "That must mean they intended to come back but never did. They probably left a lot of things behind."

Maverick wiped dirt from the garage door window and peered inside. He looked back at the others. "I see a car in there," he announced. "Depending what's wrong with it, I may be able to fix it."

Mac tried the doorknob despite Monroe's insistence that it was locked. She then took a step back and kicked the door. The lock splintered the doorjamb as the door flew open with enough force to cause it to strike the opposing wall. Monroe aimed his weapon and cautiously entered first. Mac entered behind him with her weapon held in the same menacing manner. Maverick and Rayner exchanged looks then entered behind them in a less threatening fashion.

Chapter 35

Jackie worked on the plane a little after eight o'clock that morning with Darth sitting faithfully by her side. While she attempted to fix the plane, Kirk volunteered Bogart and Stone to join him on a five-mile hike along a back road he'd found. Since Deidra was already taking the others along what was considered the main road, Kirk thought they'd explore the even lesser traveled road in search of their friends. According to Kirk, they would be gone about three and a half to four hours, depending upon how often Bogart stopped to complain. Kirk's disrespect for Bogart would have bothered Jackie, but she knew his constant torment of her brother was actually Kirk's way of bonding with new guys.

Naturally, Zack patrolled the area near the plane to ensure Jackie could focus on repairs without fear of an ambush. She had two semiautomatics in her shoulder holsters as well as her wuss sticks and the assault rifle within grasp. Darth would also alert her to any potential danger. Kane removed his sword from the bag Rayner had brought with them and caressed it like an old girlfriend. He flipped it once in his hand and smiled at some old memories. Scorpio had seized his sword last year when he left on his little quest. He had a difficult time getting her to return it. He replaced his sword to its sheath and then handed Scorpio her sword. She eyed the sword then shoved her hands in her pockets.

"I think I'm done playing warrior," Scorpio informed her brother.

Kane stared at her with a strange look and some surprise. "Why? Because of what happened in the cemetery?"

She glared demandingly at him. "Yes, of course, it's because of that," Scorpio snapped back then indicated Jackie, who was far enough away not to hear their conversation. "That crazy woman just about impaled me in the face with my own sword. And for what?" Scorpio snorted an uneasy laugh. "So you could confront our father? We failed, Kane. We failed on every single level. You didn't want to talk to him; you wanted to humiliate him. You wanted to show him that you were tougher than he was, and you were wrong. He could have broken you in two anytime he wanted." The look in her eyes was cold and serious. "I'm going back to Maine, fix up my hotel, and never leave home. I don't want anything to do with that man or any of these people ever again. And if you don't come to your senses, that'll include you too."

Kane stared at her with surprise then immediately felt ashamed. "I'm sorry, Scorp," he gently announced. "You're more important to me than any of this. Once this is over, I'll go back to Maine with you and make your hotel dream a reality."

"Could someone help me over here?" Jackie announced from halfway inside the engine compartment toward the front of the plane. "I need an extra set of hands."

Kane stared at Jackie's exposed backside as she stood on the small step stool before the engine compartment. Kane drew a tense breath while staring at Jackie's backside, nervously rubbed the back of his neck, and had to look away.

"You'd better help her," Kane muttered.

"Me? Why me?" Scorpio suddenly demanded. "I don't want to be anywhere near that psychotic bitch. She wasn't hovering over you with a sword inches from your face. I can't be anywhere near her. She scares the shit out of me."

Kane glanced back at Jackie and again stared at her backside as she half leaned inside the compartment. Kane groaned and looked back at his sister.

"I already screwed up once with her," Kane announced then appeared flustered. "Her backside will practically be in my face. It would be inappropriate on so many levels."

Scorpio stared at her brother with surprise. "Oh, my God," she gasped in horror. "You want to bang your father's girlfriend."

Kane glared at Scorpio. "First off; that's rude," he insisted. "Secondly; she's not his girlfriend." Kane nervously fidgeted. "She's married to that federal agent we ran into at the slaughterhouse."

Scorpio raised her brows and folded her arms across her chest. "Rude or not, it's true."

Kane cast a glance back at Jackie's backside then turned to face Scorpio while rubbing his eyes. "Fine, I'm seriously attracted to her," he erupted then glared at his sister. "I already made a fool of myself once by kissing her. Can you show some mercy and let me have this?"

"You kissed her?" Scorpio suddenly gasped with surprise. "You? The king of restraint?"

"Yes, I thought we were having a moment, but I completely misread her intentions. Now let it go," Kane huffed while nervously raking his fingers repeatedly through his hair. "I'm wrestling with a lot here, and I don't know that I won't continue to make a fool of myself even knowing she's married. I just need some space between us for now. Can you understand that?"

"Yeah, I understand," Scorpio groaned then appeared almost humored. "Did she kick you in the gonads?"

Kane glared at her. "The fact that you ask that with such pleasure on your face both disturbs and offends me." He shook his head. "Sorry to disappoint you. She actually said it was no big deal and merely explained that she was married."

Scorpio appeared slightly surprised by the admission. "Huh? I thought she'd crush you for sure," she remarked. "I'd certainly cut Maverick or Stone a break if that happened, but I doubt I'd be *that* nice."

"Which is why I don't trust myself," Kane insisted then cast a quick look at Jackie's backside. "Maybe her husband is a jerk. Maybe their marriage is on the rocks." He looked back at Scorpio. "When she looks at me, I feel a definite vibe coming from her. It's as if she's staring into my soul." Kane groaned and again raked his fingers through his hair with vigor. "I'm out of my mind just thinking about her."

"Okay, enough," Scorpio groaned. "You're going to hurt yourself."

"Anyone out there," Jackie again called out. "I could really use someone's hands."

Kane groaned and placed his hand over his eyes. "That sounds so dirty."

"Fine," Scorpio huffed. "I'll help her. I'd rather not see you killed." Scorpio approached Jackie on the step stool and looked up at the engine compartment. "What can I do to help?"

"I'm sort of stuck," Jackie announced from partway within the compartment. "My shoulder holster is caught, and I can't move my arms."

"I've actually never heard that one before," Scorpio muttered. "What do you want me to do?"

"I need you to crawl inside and dislodge my shoulder holster from whatever it's hung up on," Jackie informed her.

Scorpio looked back at Kane, who watched in silence while chewing on his fingernail. Scorpio stepped onto the step stool with Jackie, squeezed in alongside her, and worked on freeing her caught shoulder holster. Darth tilted his head and watched the two women just about stuck inside the small opening in the engine of the plane. Kane stared at the sight; possibly imagining what would have happened if he had crawled into the compartment in that compromising position with Jackie. He immediately turned away and groaned.

"Yeah, that would have gone well," Kane muttered as he nearly collided with Zack, who stared past him at the scene in the engine compartment.

Kane was mildly startled by Zack's sudden appearance and possibly more so by the assault rifle casually resting against his shoulder. Zack stared at the sight of the two women dangling from the engine compartment then shook his head and walked away. Kane took only a moment to weigh his options then hurried after Zack.

"So, uh, Jackie and I were talking while on guard duty this morning," Kane began.

Zack paused by the plane steps and set his binoculars aside. He cast a look at Kane. "Yeah, I heard about it," Zack remarked then turned to face Kane with a disapproving frown. "If it happens again, there's going to be trouble."

Kane stared at him with surprise. "She told you?"

"We don't have any secrets," Zack announced while raising a brow.

"I can't believe she told you," Kane practically gasped. "After her insistence--" He then met Zack's gaze. "I don't know what possessed me to do it, and I apologized to her for it. Especially now that I know she's married--"

Zack's expression didn't change, but it was somehow more intimidating. "Did you make a pass at Jackie?" he suddenly demanded.

"You said you knew," Kane announced with surprise.

Zack pulled the assault rifle away from his shoulder, causing Kane to jump back and take a defensive position. Zack slung the rifle over his shoulder and shook his head.

"You're lucky she didn't tear you in half," Zack scoffed.

Kane seemed surprised by the reaction. "Actually, she was very understanding."

Zack's eyes narrowed with disapproval. "I blame the company she keeps," he snarled then raised an arrogant brow. "She's off limits."

Zack then turned and headed toward the woods. Kane hesitated only a moment then hurried after him.

"Duly noted," Kane replied as he kept pace with Zack. "You know, I get that you don't want anything to do with my sister and me. I honestly don't even care that you hate me. I do, however, believe you could give five minutes of your time to the children of the woman you supposedly loved."

Zack stopped and spun to face Kane. Kane stopped but didn't show any emotion despite the concerning look on Zack's face.

Kane then continued without prompting. "She suspected you were alive, and I have reason to believe she spent her last moments intending to find you," he announced. "That's why I came looking for you. I did it for her because even though I didn't know my mother, I loved her very much. Despite what my grandparents believed, I had hoped she actually meant something to you."

"I did what I did because I had to," Zack informed him. "I didn't do it because I wanted to. She believed I was dead. That botched Midnight Requisition mission was more than enough to convince her of that. She died knowing how I felt about her, and my feelings never changed. I can't change what happened to her, and I live with that guilt every day." Zack cocked his head. "What more do you want from me?"

"Nothing," Kane launched back and seemed instantly annoyed. "I don't want anything from you. I found out everything I needed to know about the man my mother thought she loved from our brief meeting and from Jackie. Scorpio and I have each other, and that's all we need." He glared at Zack. "My mother never knew how lucky she was that you abandoned her and us. I'm sure you would have been the world's worst father."

Kane saluted Zack with his middle finger then turned and headed back toward the plane.

Chapter 36

Bogart and Stone had been following Kirk for nearly an hour as the three men hiked the deserted back road. The sound of crickets chirping was nearly deafening. Kirk carried his weapon with purpose, prepared for action. Bogart and Stone looked less menacing with their weapons casually draped in their arms while they talked and joked.

"And she was your half-sister the entire time?" Stone asked then shook his head while laughing. "That's amazing. It was like fate or something."

"Yeah," Kirk muttered while in front of them. "It was or something all right."

Bogart waved off Kirk while grinning at Stone. "Ignore him," he announced. "Kirk is grouchy. Doesn't get laid enough."

"You're a prick," Kirk scoffed.

"I think he's hilarious," Stone reported regarding Bogart.

"Yeah, well," Kirk muttered with little emotion, "you're a prick too."

Stone chuckled at the insult then looked back at Bogart. "You spent a lot of time around Jackie before discovering she was your sister," Stone concluded then appeared curious. "Any awkward moments? I mean; she's a sexy woman." He immediately held his hand up. "No disrespect."

"None taken," Bogart replied then tilted his head. "That's the really weird part. I mean; I noticed she was attractive, but I was never actually attracted to her."

"Funny how that happens," Stone remarked.

"Tell him about the time you walked in on Jackie while she was in the shower," Kirk announced from ahead of them then snickered.

Stone looked from the back of Kirk's head to Bogart as his eyes widened. "You walked in on her in the shower?" he asked.

Bogart fidgeted slightly and was about to explain when Kirk held his fist in the air, indicating they should stop and keep quiet. Stone and Bogart immediately stopped, raised their weapons, and scanned the area for whatever caught Kirk's attention. Kirk signaled to an overgrown roadway in the woods that appeared to have been recently driven upon. The tall weeds were flattened, although still mostly green. Kirk motioned again. All three walked onto the old roadway and cautiously searched the surrounding area in silence. They traveled the recently driven roadway for nearly half a mile before seeing a tall, chain-link fence partially overgrown with vegetation. Kirk again stopped them and frantically motioned them into the woods.

All three bolted into the woods. Kirk removed his binoculars and scanned the area. When nothing moved, they continued quietly through the woods closer to the large fence and the closed gate. The old gate was held shut with a newer, heavy chain and large padlock. Now that they were closer, they could see newly laid barbed wire along the top of the fence. They proceeded with caution to have a better look. Stone nodded to the fence, silently indicating that some of the chain link was new as if being recently replaced. Kirk handed Bogart the binoculars, not wanting to be burdened with them so he could concentrate on the area surrounding them.

Bogart moved closer to the fence and scanned the cleared area beyond it with use of the binoculars. Beyond the large, overgrown field, Bogart saw an old, red brick building. The building itself was four stories and roughly the size of a fifty-bedroom hotel. It was obvious the old building wasn't a hotel. It looked more like an old-fashioned hospital. Despite the overgrown driveway, Bogart could see a carport of some sort in front, which allowed vehicles to park in order to drop off passengers or patients. None of the windows were boarded, which was unusual considering the age of the building and that it was almost certainly abandoned. Bogart then noticed the bars covering the windows. He tensed and zoomed in on the plaque on the front of the building. Bogart lowered the binoculars and cast a look at Kirk.

"It's an old mental institution," Bogart informed him and again peered through the binoculars at the distant building.

The familiar and frightening sound of parting air was suddenly heard, and the binoculars were jolted from Bogart's hand.

"Down!" Kirk yelled.

All three crouched to the ground and scanned the area with their weapons. Bogart glanced at the discarded binoculars and saw the indentation from where a bullet had struck them. It was unclear if it had been a precision shot for the inanimate object or if the shooter had been aiming for Bogart's head and missed.

"This is the place all right," Kirk informed Stone and Bogart while scanning the area through his riflescope.

"How many shooters?" Stone asked.

"Unknown," Kirk responded while keeping his attention on the area surrounding them.

§

Around nine o'clock that morning, Gil, Sal, and John remained within their fourth floor prison bedroom. Gil sat in an old chair by the window and appeared half-asleep while Sal and John had made themselves comfortable on the less than hypoallergenic beds. With his arms folded beneath his neck, Sal stared at the chipping plaster on the ceiling.

"I guess I've grown too accustomed to staying in four-star hotels," Sal announced to no one in particular. "I don't care for the service or the amenities in this one."

"Yeah, I'm hungry too," John announced from his bunk despite appearing as if he were asleep.

Sal cast a look at the man in the next bunk over. "Is that what you took from that comment?"

"I'll be honest," John remarked. "I didn't listen to a word you said. I was too busy daydreaming of an all-you-can-eat steak and seafood buffet."

Sal shook his head as if disappointed then drew a deep breath. "Lobster tail dripping in rich butter."

"Medium rare porterhouse steak," John added.

"With seasoned steak fries," Sal muttered.

Gil opened his eyes and glared at the two men with mild irritation. "Will the two of you knock it off," he snarled.

§

Kirk peered through the riflescope from behind the tree and attempted to get a fix on the shooter. Another nearly silent shot splintered the tree near him. Kirk disappeared behind the tree and eyed Stone and Bogart.

"We're out of radio range. We need to return to camp and regroup," Kirk announced then nodded toward one of the larger trees not far from them. "Bogart, hightail it for that tree. I'll cover you." He then eyed Stone. "You keep your eyes out for shooters. We need a fix on their location."

Bogart psyched himself for his sprint. Kirk secretly motioned for him to make his run. Bogart kept low and ran for the large tree. Several shots were fired. Stone and Kirk fired at two different locations where the nearly silent gunshots had originated. Gunfire from Stone and Kirk's weapons could be heard echoing throughout the entire area. Bogart made it behind the tree and waited for the signal.

§

227

Within the fourth floor bedroom of the asylum, Gil shot forward in his chair to the sound of echoing gunfire. John and Sal leaped out of their beds and hurried for the window to join Gil.

"Is it a rescue?" Sal cried out with renewed hope.

"Those are our guys," Gil informed the two men crowding him by the window as he scanned the area with the cheap binoculars. "That's not the sound of your average hunting rifle from some good ole' boys."

"Do you see them?" John asked while sharing Sal's enthusiasm.

"Not yet," Gil replied while carefully scanning the woods. "It's tough seeing anything." He then hesitated. "I see one of the shooters. He's wearing black and gray camouflage. Definitely professionals." Gil looked back at Sal and John. "Grab the sheet!"

Sal and John grabbed the white sheet from the floor, fumbled with it, and quickly tacked it to the inside of the window. From the outside view, the large words 'standing by' were written in red marker across the sheet. The message would be visible to anyone outside.

"We need to move," Gil informed the men. "We have to get to a lower floor and get ready for them."

The gunfire had ceased causing Sal to tense. "That's not good."

"The men in the woods have silencers on their rifles," Gil informed Sal. "Our guys are probably taking cover. A rescue is coming. We may need to exercise patience."

§

Within the woods, Kirk kept his back to the tree and looked at Stone alongside him.

"On my signal, you run for Bogart," Kirk announced. "Bogart and I will draw their fire. I'll be right behind you so don't stop, or I'll run over your ass."

Stone nodded with conviction. Kirk looked across the woods and signaled Bogart. Both men fired in the direction of the silent gunfire while Stone ran for the tree and Bogart. Kirk ran after Stone while firing at the second shooter. All three men made a run for a large group of trees. Another shooter appeared from behind the trees and shot at them. Bogart saw the man and returned fire. One of Bogart's rounds struck the man in the chest. Kirk switched direction and had the men cross the overgrown road and into the woods on the opposite side.

A man suddenly appeared from behind another tree and was only a few feet in front of the running men. Stone stopped when he saw the man aiming his weapon. Bogart didn't stop and charged for the man. He spun into a clumsy roundhouse kick and knocked the weapon from his hand. Bogart then rammed the butt of his rifle into the man's face, dropping him to the ground. Stone snatched the man's discarded rifle affixed with a silencer and took only a moment to marvel at it. He slung the weapon over his shoulder and followed Bogart while Kirk brought up the rear, firing at the men behind them.

As the three ran through the woods, the sound of nearly silent gunshots decreased. It didn't seem as if they were being followed. Bogart, who had been leading the pack, finally slowed and looked around. Stone kept his weapon aimed and scanned the area while Kirk brought up the rear, keeping watch. Kirk cast a look at Bogart, who appeared mildly puzzled.

"In case you were wondering. The road is that way," Kirk informed him while pointing in the direction of the road that would lead them back to the abandoned airfield.

"I smell something," Bogart informed Kirk.

"We don't have time for this," Kirk announced with some irritation.

Bogart ignored him and followed the foul smell.

Stone then smelled it as well and made a face. "He's right," Stone remarked. "That's pretty foul."

Stone and Kirk followed Bogart through the woods. A loud humming sound was now heard. It was familiar yet strange. The wafting odor became stronger, and the humming sound increased. All three saw a strange, dark cloud just up ahead. Bogart approached then hesitated. The strange dark cloud was the source of the humming, which was actually a buzzing sound. Stone swatted at dozens of flies then stared at the large, dark cloud.

"Those are flies," Stone remarked with some surprise while staring at the swarm with a bewildered look on his face.

"Must be thousands of them," Bogart remarked and continued closer to the buzzing swarm.

He gagged on the overwhelming smell and pulled his shirt over his nose and mouth. Stone used his sleeve to block the rancid smell and followed Bogart. Kirk didn't seem bothered by the smell, although he was easily annoyed by the swarm of flies. Bogart approached what appeared to be a large pit. Kirk then stopped and shook his head while showing little reaction.

"You probably don't want to do that," Kirk remarked as if privy to what his teammate would find.

Bogart peered into the pit while waving his arm at the buzzing swarm of flies. Stone paused alongside him and looked as well. Both men appeared horrified at the sight of nearly a dozen decaying men tossed into the pit. The level of decomposition ranged from severe to freshly killed. Each man was covered in blood and flies. There was no doubt their injuries were from gunshots. Some had been shot multiple times. Bogart saw the familiar profile of the man on top. He had a lean, athletic build with short dark hair, peppered with gray.

"Gil!" Bogart suddenly cried out, tossed his rifle aside, and slid partway into the pit for the man on top.

Bogart nearly lost his balance and just about tumbled onto the pile of dead men. Stone reached into the pit and caught Bogart's hand. Stone helped Bogart maintain his balance while he reached for the dead man and pulled him onto his back. Bogart stared at the freshly killed man and immediately realized it wasn't Gil.

"Christ," Bogart cried out then allowed Stone to assist him back up the steep bank to safety.

Kirk moved in closer while waving flies away from his face and finally peered into the pit. The flies were now buzzing around the three men as well. They hurried away from the pit to escape the buzzing pests. All three stared at the thick, buzzing cloud of flies then glanced back at the direction they had just come.

"Gil and Sal are in trouble," Bogart announced with concern then looked at Kirk for guidance. "What are we going to do?"

"There's nothing we can do at the moment," Kirk insisted while scanning the wooded area. "We need the rest of the team if we hope to get inside that building."

"He's right," Stone remarked and shook his head. "The three of us don't stand a chance against them. There's no telling how many are waiting inside the gates." He then looked around. "Or outside of them." A tree splintered near Stone's head causing him to shirk. "Fuck!"

"Move it out," Kirk announced and forced them onward. "Keep heading in the direction of the road."

All three darted through the woods to avoid the nearly silent gunfire.

"Keep in the woods," Kirk called to them. "We can't expose ourselves in the open. Move it; move it!"

Chapter 37

Gil and John unblocked the patient room door as quickly and quietly as possible. They gathered their mediocre weapons and prepared for their departure into the asylum. Gil took a moment to eye Sal and his injured ankle.

"Are you okay to move?" Gil asked.

Sal offered an unsettling smile. "If it means getting out of here," he announced, "I could carry your ass. Don't worry about me."

Gil managed a tiny, humored smile and nodded then turned to face John as well. "We'll need to avoid the main stairs and take the fire stairs," he informed the two men. "That'll take us through the patient's ward on first. We need to reach the lobby and wait for extraction."

"I don't mean to be a pessimist," John remarked, "but I haven't heard any gunfire in the last few minutes. What's our backup plan?"

"My friends are twice as deadly when you don't hear them," Gil insisted then added a throaty chuckle. "We wait in the lobby until we're unable to wait there. The game room can be our backup if we need to barricade ourselves somewhere until help arrives."

John nodded in agreement. Gil indicated for Sal to open the door. Sal grasped the door handle and pulled open the door while moving out of the way with it. Gil and John moved into the doorway with their weapons prepared for whatever they'd find on the other side. Both stared into the empty, fourth floor corridor. There wasn't any sign of the roving band of psychotic cannibals. Gil took the lead with Sal directly behind him. His ankle was bad enough that he walked with a limp, but he seemed to be managing the pain fairly well. John brought up the rear and kept watch behind them as they made their quick but cautious journey toward the fire stairs. When they reached the front fire stairs, they were unable to open the door. Sal attempted the key in the lock, but it became apparent that the door had rusted shut.

"This door is rusted just like the one on the second floor had been," Sal informed them then frowned because he knew what that meant.

"Then we'll need to head back for the fire stairs at the far end of the floor," John insisted. "That'll bring us to the rear of the building on the first floor near the infirmary."

Sal frowned at the thought of again crossing the entire fourth floor for the second set of fire stairs. It would also mean they'd have to cross the entire building on the first floor to get back to the lobby. His ankle was already giving him trouble. He didn't need the added hike.

"That's a long haul." Gil again glanced at Sal and appeared sympathetic. "You think you can make that journey?"

Sal snorted a laugh but maintained his sense of humor. "Do I have a choice?" he asked.

"Not really," Gil replied.

They headed across the entire ward toward the back of the building and finally reached the rear fire stairs. As the three headed down the stairs, Gil looked back and noticed Sal's difficulty with the steps. Although his ankle was just bruised and possibly only sprained, it was still enough to cause him tremendous pain and hinder his ability to move fast. It was a long journey down four flights of stairs. Sal saw the way Gil kept looking back at him on the stairs.

"I'm still behind you," Sal snapped with some irritation. "You just worry about what's in front of you. Let me worry about me."

Gil frowned and remained focused on the stairs, paying added attention to each landing of the next floor down. Considering John didn't know Sal, the self-proclaimed mercenary was surprisingly patient with Sal's struggle regarding the stairs. That wasn't to say John wouldn't sacrifice Sal at the first sniff of trouble, but for the moment, he was a team player. The three finally reached the first floor, which seemed to take forever. Gil opened the door partway and scanned the area. They were in the back of the building, which contained the staff areas, offices, and the infirmary. Gil shuttered at the thought of returning to where their journey into hell first began. On the plus side, they knew which direction would lead them to the lobby. Unfortunately, they had to cross the entire institution just because they wanted to avoid the fragile main stairs. There was no telling what would happen if they attempted to walk down them again.

"The corridor is clear," Gil informed his two teammates. "Every door between us and the lobby is wide open. We don't know what's in each of those rooms, so we need to proceed with caution."

"We should stop in the infirmary," John announced and immediately received looks from Sal and Gil.

"I'm not feeling nostalgic," Sal remarked.

John then nodded to Sal's injured ankle. "You're not getting far on that ankle," he insisted. "If it comes down to it, we may need to make a run for the woods. We need to get a wrap on that ankle to give it some support. I saw some medical supplies in the infirmary during our stint there. It'll take two minutes to wrap your ankle. It'll increase your odds of survival."

"We'll stop in the infirmary," Gil agreed.

Sal frowned but didn't comment. He obviously didn't want to burden the mission with his ill-timed injury, but his two travel companions weren't going to take no for an answer. All three crept two doors down the hall and entered the familiar room. The dead, slaughtered man remain strapped to his bed while his butcherer lay dead on the floor where Gil had taken him out. Despite everything Sal had seen and been through, he couldn't take his eyes off the sight. John sought the medical supplies he'd seen in an open drawer not far from where he had been tethered to his bed. He found an ACE wrap and tossed it to Gil. Gil caught the wrap and indicated for Sal to sit on the nearby rolling stool. Sal sat on the chair and removed his shoe with some discomfort. His ankle was possibly twice its normal size. Gil didn't bother removing Sal's sock to look at it. They'd already seen it last night, and it didn't seem any less swollen.

The entire team had extensive medical field training, and treating injuries while under extreme pressure came second nature. Gil wrapped Sal's ankle in under a minute and helped him slip back into his shoe, which needed the laces loosened to give him extra room for swelling and the wrap. Sal stood and was able to put additional weight on his bad ankle with less pain. They could hear the faint sound of something rolling along the corridor floor not far from the infirmary. John bolted away from the door and frantically motioned for them to hide. Gil and Sal dove beneath the closest bed while John darted into a nearby closet. The sound of something rolling along the floor got louder. Two psychotic looking men wearing dirty, frayed scrub uniforms entered the infirmary with a rolling, burlap laundry bin.

Gil and Sal strained to keep an eye on the two men. They appeared unarmed, as were most of the crazies running around the institution, but something seemed different about these two men. They picked up the dead man from the floor and tossed him into the bin. Gil glanced at the laundry bin and saw the entire bottom was covered in dried blood that had soaked through the burlap lining. The two unfamiliar men removed the second body from the bed and tossed it into the bin as well. Gil and Sal exchanged looks in silent question. The two men proceeded to remove the dead men from the first two beds then rolled the cart from the room. Once they left, all three slipped out of their hiding places and exchanged looks.

"What was that?" John demanded.

"I don't care how they were dressed," Gil announced while shaking his head. "Those men weren't part of the crazy brigade we've been avoiding."

"So you think they're behind whoever brought us here?" John asked, almost as if relaying what he had been thinking. "I assure you; they don't work here."

"We need to follow them," Gil insisted.

"What about the rescue?" Sal asked. "You said we needed to wait in the lobby."

"We don't know when that's coming," Gil informed him then indicated the door with conviction. "Those men will lead us somewhere."

"Maybe even to some weapons," John added then eyed Sal and offered no sympathy. "We'll secure you in one of the rooms until we get back."

"I'm fine," Sal insisted proudly and with a little too much conviction in his tone. "I'm going with you. I won't be a burden."

§

The two men dressed as deranged orderlies pushed the rolling laundry cart into the freight elevator. Once the door closed, Gil, Sal, and John watched the elevator light indicate it was going down.

"Apparently, some areas have power," John retorted and seemed surprised.

"That would have been nice to know on our way down from the fourth floor," Sal muttered.

"I assure you; there wasn't power in the front part of the building," John remarked. "There must be a backup generator in this section."

"We need to get down to the basement and see where they're going," Gil announced and hurried for the nearby fire stairs.

Sal limped after him while attempting to keep up. John brought up the rear and kept watch over Sal's back. Gil hurried down the stairs leaving John and Sal behind. He didn't want to lose sight of the two men once they left the elevator. John and Sal would catch up in their own time. Gil reached the bottom and quietly opened the stairwell door just enough to peer into the hallway. The two men and their bloodstained laundry bin headed down the basement hall, which was dimly lit with electric lights. They disappeared through one of the doorways. Gil motioned for Sal to wait in the safety of the stairwell before hurrying along the basement corridor. John was only a few steps behind him to provide backup.

They paused before the door that was labeled 'incinerator room'. Gil and John exchanged knowing looks. There was a loud humming noise coming from the room. The sound would be enough to cover the creaking of the door opening. Gil pushed the door open just far enough to peer inside. The no-frills room was entirely made of block stone and concrete. Apart from the incinerator itself, the only thing within the room was a large stack of dismantled cardboard boxes and a supply rack. The two men they had followed were across the room near the far wall where the large, iron incinerator was built into the wall. They talked above the loud humming sound of the flames while waiting for the fire to reach temperature. Gil and John slipped into the room and took cover behind the supply rack. They scanned the area then studied the two men, who laughed and joked around. The first man flipped a two-foot long, metal object in his hand. It resembled an unusually long flashlight. Gil's eyes lit up.

"What is that?" John asked.

Gil's smile increased. "It's a cattle prod," he announced. "They use it to keep the crazies off them."

John raised a clever brow and offered a sly, knowing grin. "You want that cattle prod, don't you?"

"I can do a lot more damage with that than a switchblade knife," Gil informed him.

"Army versus Navy," John teased while grinning. "You take the one on the right. I'll take the one on the left."

Gil smiled and nodded. Once the fire in the incinerator was up to temperature, the two men removed the first body and tossed it into the opening. The two men reached deep inside the bin for the second body. As they straightened, Gil and John launched their attack from both sides. John placed his hand over the man's mouth from behind and stabbed him in the neck with the scalpel. Gil appeared behind the second man, grabbed him by the head, and easily snapped his neck. The mutilated body fell back into the bin, and both men holding the body dropped to the floor. John eyed Gil, smirked, and nodded his approval.

"Not bad for a frogman," John teased.

Gil sneered at the comment then managed a tiny smile. He snatched the discarded cattle prod. Both men then searched the two dead men for anything useful. Other than a second cattle prod, they didn't find any other weapons on them. Gil then removed a hand radio, flaunted it to John, and grinned.

"I think I found today's entertainment," he teased.

John straightened and grinned while waving two protein bars. "I found breakfast."

Gil stared at the protein bars and subconsciously groaned. "I'm so hungry, I could eat an MRE."

Gil and John secured their new weapons and hurried from the incinerator room. As they quietly made their way along the basement corridor, they saw fresh blood pooling just outside the stairwell door.

Gil's expression dropped to concern. "No," he gasped. "Sal--"

They hurried to the stairwell door where the blood collected. Gil stepped over the blood and nervously opened the door. Two crazed men lay face down in large pools of blood surrounding their bodies. Sal sat on the second to last step, his shirt spattered with blood and the bloodied chest spreader on the step alongside him. Sal casually cleaned the speckles of blood from his glasses onto his shirt, placed them back on his face, and eyed both men.

"That didn't take long," Sal remarked with little emotion as if the two dead men weren't even there.

Gil and John eyed both dead men then the unaffected look on Sal's face.

"Should I ask?" John muttered to Gil.

"We find it best not to," Gil replied.

John tossed Sal one of the two protein bars, which he eagerly caught. "You've earned that."

Chapter 38

It was a little before noon by the time Jackie fixed the rental plane. The radios in both planes were a different story. She couldn't fix them. Jackie needed Monroe. He had the knack for fixing most communication issues. Zack could fix simple problems, but the damaged done to both radios was beyond his capability. Zack remained on patrol taking Darth with him while Kane checked the engine compartment and had a look at the radio in Gil's plane. Jackie knew it was worth a shot, but she was almost convinced it was beyond repair. Scorpio stood alongside Jackie while they watched Kane half dangling from the compartment with the toe of his boot touching the step stool. Jackie kept checking her watch then surveyed the area. Scorpio noticed Jackie's rising tension.

"Is something wrong?" Scorpio finally asked and looked around as well.

Zack was seen nearby with his rifle, so Jackie wasn't concerned about him.

"They should have been back by now," Jackie remarked although she didn't convey enough concern to worry Scorpio. "Monroe could be gone a little longer in that town they went to investigate, but Kirk and Bogart should have been back with your friend by now."

"Maybe they found something of interest," Scorpio suggested and remained uncomfortable around Jackie.

"That's possible," Jackie replied while scanning the area. "Wherever they are, they're out of radio range." She tapped her ear transmitter. "I'm not getting anything. Kirk wouldn't waste time on something minor, and he wouldn't launch a short-manned attack on something major."

"Meaning what?" Scorpio asked.

"Meaning he should have been back by now," Jackie muttered.

"I can't speak for your man," Scorpio remarked, "but Stone is the voice of reason. He wouldn't take on more than he can handle."

"Bogart too," Jackie insisted then brushed her concerns aside. "I'm sure they're on their way back. I'm just being paranoid."

Despite her attempt at sounding confident, Jackie again fidgeted.

"Is something else bothering you?" Scorpio asked then instinctively looked around as if sensing Jackie's concerns.

"Where's our backup?" Jackie remarked while sinking into thought. "My husband was calling the local authorities to come out here. I thought they'd be here by now."

"Small town," Scorpio replied. "Maybe they had another call. I wouldn't doubt there are only two or three local deputies in this area. We're not in any danger, so we're a low priority."

"True," Jackie replied although she wasn't convinced.

Scorpio seemed to tense at Jackie's inability to relax. "I'm curious. Why would Mac risk her life for this Sal guy?" she finally asked.

"It's complicated," Jackie announced. "Mac made some mistakes, and she's still begging for forgiveness."

Kane dropped onto the step stool then jumped to the ground. "Why won't anyone forgive her?" he asked. "What did she do?"

"As far as Sal is concerned, you should probably ask Mac that question," Jackie informed him. "Zack's problem with her remains a mystery. Something happened after she saved his life. Whatever it was; he's unable to forgive her. Considering Zack was able to get beyond a Russian spy attempting to lobe off his manhood, I'd say it has to be pretty significant."

"A Russian spy tried to cut off his pecker?" Kane asked before he could stop himself.

"His on-again-off-again Russian booty call," Jackie explained then gave a slight shrug. "His taste in women leans toward frightening and dangerous."

"He's dating a Russian spy?" Kane asked with surprise. It was tough to tell if Kane was disturbed or intrigued.

"No, they're not dating," Jackie corrected. "They just enjoy each other's company from time-to-time."

"Our mother would be so proud," Kane scoffed.

"Zack occasionally needs to blow off some steam," Jackie informed him. "He's less likely to blow up things." She then folded her arms across her chest. "And you need to cut him some slack. You have no idea what that man has been through and the sacrifices he's made. No matter your feelings for him, your father is a hero. He's put his life on the line for every man on this team, and he's personally saved my ass many times." Her eyes then turned demanding. "And if he had known about the two of you, he would have given up his entire career and the team to be the father you think he could never have been."

Kane tensed as if realizing she must have overheard parts of his earlier conversation.

Jackie glared at Kane with rising irritation. "He would have been a great father if he had been given the opportunity," she insisted. "I would know. He's been in my life since the beginning. Zack and the rest of my father's team helped raise me after my mother died. You can't blame him for falling in love with your mother. He did everything he could to protect her, including removing himself from the picture." She shifted her gaze between the two of them. "So while the two of you silently judge him, there are those of us who admire him and would lay down our lives to protect him."

Kane and Scorpio seemed uncomfortable at the lashing they'd received from Zack's biggest fan.

"Maybe you shouldn't be so quick to judge us either," Kane snapped back although lacking Jackie's irritation. He seemed almost emotional. "I spent years looking for my father, believing he was alive despite what I'd been told. You stand there and defend him to me, but you weren't the one he rejected. After all these years, I discovered my father was actually alive and risked my life to track him down only to be rejected."

Scorpio held her breath and gently placed her hand on her brother's shoulder. "Don't go there, Kane," his sister whispered.

"No, Scorp," Kane snapped back while quickly losing his patience. "It needs to be said." He then shifted his glare back at Jackie. "You *had* your father in your life. You grew up surrounded by an entire team of men stepping forward to be a father to you. You don't get to judge me for feeling rejected by the man you admire so much."

"Is that why you came looking for your father?" Jackie asked with less hostility and more compassion. "You want him to be proud of the man you've become?"

"Is that really asking so much?" Kane snapped back and attempted to hide his emotions but failed. "Scorpio and I were always different. We were outcasts among our own peers. Scorpio was never the little princess our grandparents wanted her to be. I didn't want to be the businessman in a suit." He let his emotions get the better of him. "I'd hear my grandfather tell my grandmother how disappointed he was in me. Over and over, I heard him complaining that I was too much like my father. I thought I was like him. I thought he'd understand me and what I'm going through, but he doesn't care. You couldn't understand. He never rejected you."

Jackie took a step closer to Kane while staring into his eyes. She placed her arms around his neck and pulled his head to her shoulder as she had with Zack so many times. Without a second thought, Kane wrapped his arms around Jackie's waist and clung to her. Unlike when he'd smother Mac, it was Kane's turn to be comforted. Jackie gently stroked his hair in an almost motherly manner.

"He is proud of you," Jackie announced softly while comforting him. "And even though he may never say it or show it, he loves you. Your mother was the love of his life, and the two of you are a product of that love. There's no doubt in my mind that he loves you."

Kane kept his face buried in her neck and tensed slightly by her words.

"It's time the two of you had some open dialog," Jackie announced.

"Yeah? Maybe you need to tell him that," Kane muttered while Jackie continued to comfort him.

"I *was* telling him that," Jackie replied.

Kane pulled away from Jackie, met her gaze, and then looked behind him. Zack stood only a few feet away while witnessing the entire scene. He'd obviously overheard everything. Scorpio saw Zack and immediately sidestepped, putting distance between them. At the moment, Zack was focused on Kane and Jackie. Jackie met Zack's gaze with a serious look.

"Talk to him, Zack," Jackie announced. "Tell him how you felt about Maggie. Tell him about Midnight Requisition. Tell him about the hurt and anger you felt when Abbott shot you in front of their mother." She drew a deep, tense breath. "Tell him the things you've told me. He needs to hear them from you, not me."

Zack unslung his rifle, fidgeted slightly, and then handed the weapon to Jackie. He looked back at Kane.

"I loved Maggie," Zack gently announced while struggling with his emotions. "We were going to get married and move into the house next to my commander, Jackie's father. I'd already put the down payment on the house. We were supposed to move to Virginia at the end of the month when someone from my past found me. He knew about Maggie. I received threatening notes. He threatened to kill your mother. Eliminating me from the picture was the only way to keep her safe. If a psycho from my past found me once, he'd find me again. I couldn't do that to your mother. I didn't think I could protect her. She was better off without me." Zack drew a deep, tense breath. "I didn't know she was pregnant. I doubt she even knew it yet. If I had known, I may have done things differently. If I knew the two of you were out there after her death, I would have come for you. *Nothing* would have stopped me from coming for you."

Kane threw his arms around Zack's midsection and hugged him like an insecure child. Zack was startled and immediately tensed, unprepared for the reaction. Jackie took Zack's hands and placed them against Kane's back. Zack uncertainly hugged

Kane. Kane pulled away, smiled as if a terrible burden had been lifted from his shoulders, and wiped the corners of his eyes.

"Thank you," Kane whispered then glanced back at Scorpio as if silently questioning whether she wanted to get in on the family reunion.

Scorpio frowned and walked away. Darth whimpered then ran after Scorpio. Kane held his breath then looked back at Zack, who stared after Scorpio with an unreadable expression.

"She'll come around," Kane insisted and managed a tiny laugh. "She's stubborn and bull-headed."

"I wonder where she gets that from," Jackie muttered.

"I have so many questions about you and my mother," Kane announced with enthusiasm. "My grandparents seemed to know very little about your relationship with my mother."

Zack remained slightly tense. Jackie flashed a smile and slung the rifle over her shoulder.

"I'll take guard duty," Jackie announced cheerfully. "And Scorpio just volunteered to take watch with me." She then gave a nod to Kane. "You two have a good talk."

"Not my strong suit," Zack remarked.

"I think Kane will gladly get the conversation started," Jackie announced.

Chapter 39

An hour later, Zack and Kane patrolled the area surrounding the planes and the hangar. Scorpio sat on a seat from an old aircraft they had recovered from the hangar and placed against the abandoned structure. Darth sat before her with his large head on her lap and whimpered softly. Scorpio subconsciously petted the dog's head while she watched Zack and her brother with their weapons as they walked along the edge of the woods. The two were talking and even occasionally smiling and laughing. Scorpio frowned at their interaction then leaned her head against the exterior hangar wall.

"Don't approve of your father and brother bonding?" Jackie asked from nearby.

Scorpio glanced alongside her and saw Jackie, who had approached from the opposite side of the hangar. Scorpio had exceptionally good hearing, which made Jackie's sudden appearance that much more surprising. Scorpio folded her arms across her chest, again rested her head against the side of the building, and eyed Jackie with indifference.

"It's not that I disapprove," Scorpio remarked. "I just don't understand it."

Jackie gave a tiny wave, indicating for the young woman to move down on the old bench seat. Scorpio remained tense around Jackie but did as she was instructed. Jackie sat on the edge of the bench and watched Zack and Kane bond over their patrol of the grounds. Scorpio cast a glance at Jackie's profile and attempted to relax around the woman that nearly ended her life. Jackie looked back at Scorpio, who pretended she hadn't been watching the woman.

"What's not to understand?" Jackie finally asked as Darth lay by her feet.

"My brother is a grown man seeking attention from a complete stranger that he blindly idolized since we were little," Scorpio replied and shifted uncomfortably. "That man may be our biological father, but he's a stranger to us." Scorpio frowned while considering the comment. "Kane's always been somewhat needy and co-dependent, but I don't understand why he's so eager to bond with some grown man he doesn't even know."

"I saw the way your brother interacted with Mac," Jackie remarked while eyeing the woman, who was only a few years younger than herself.

"What does Mac have to do with this?"

"Despite her 'lone wolf' attitude, your brother formed a bond with her in a short period of time," Jackie informed her. "He didn't know Mac either. It seems perfectly natural for him to want to know his father and even form a fast bond. I'm guessing that's Kane's nature."

"I suppose I don't understand because Kane and I aren't alike in that sense," Scorpio informed her. "If the roles had been reversed and we'd been searching for our mother, I still wouldn't greet her with open arms. In my mind, that person is still a stranger to me."

"I can relate to that," Jackie remarked. "I grew up with little female influence in my life. I don't interact as well with women as I do with men."

"I can't say I have that problem," Scorpio insisted. "I'm just, well, not a social butterfly like my brother. Growing up, most of my friends started out as his friends. I don't feel the need to have a large circle of friends."

"You get that from your father," Jackie informed her and appeared humored. "Once, while he was staying at my house, we spent the entire day together without him uttering a single word." Jackie then considered the comment. "Unlike my brother, who can't stand silence and chatters like a chipmunk on speed."

Scorpio smiled and laughed. "I like your brother," she remarked. "He's funny. I'll bet Stone's having a blast with him."

Scorpio subconsciously rubbed her cheek, brushing her fingers against the slightly bruised area around the scratch, and cringed with some discomfort. Jackie eyed the scratch on Scorpio's face and immediately frowned.

"Sorry about that," Jackie remarked and indicated the scratch.

"I suppose it was my own fault," Scorpio replied. "Kane went off the deep end, and I naturally felt the need to defend him. You didn't know we weren't sent to kill you, and we didn't know you had reason to believe we could possibly be hired killers."

"We get a little paranoid whenever anyone sniffs around looking for Zack," Jackie announced. "A lot of people want him dead."

"Why is that?"

"That's an extremely long-winded conversation," Jackie replied. "Zack was good at what he did. Because of it, a lot of people want him dead. Thankfully, most of them think he is dead." Jackie managed a tiny laugh. "I'm guessing he was pretty impressed with the way you handled those swords. He's been pressuring me to use swords more often. He doesn't approve of my 'wuss' sticks."

"I think you managed just fine with swords," Scorpio responded and again rubbed the scratch on her cheek. "I'm not used to coming in second. I thought Kane and I worked well as a team." She glanced at Jackie and revealed her insecurities. "I have to admit; I was pretty intimidated by you."

"You've obviously had a good teacher," Jackie informed her. "He just couldn't take you to the next level. I'm guessing you reached his level and stopped."

"Yeah, Kane and I just sort of challenged each other after that," she replied. "Who taught you?"

Jackie raised her brows and nodded toward Zack across the clearing. "My father was skilled enough to teach me in the beginning. When I reached a certain level, Zack took over.

While they were away on missions, I would train with some of their military friends."

"And your father and Zack were best friends?" Scorpio asked.

Jackie eyed the young woman. "Yes, my father and *your* father were best friends."

"I'll just stick with Zack for now," Scorpio remarked and cringed at the thought of calling Zack her father.

"Relax," Jackie scoffed. "No one expects you to start calling him 'dad'."

Kane approached them while grinning almost slyly. "Hey, Scorp," he announced excitedly. "Dad's going to teach us how to break a man's neck. Are you coming?"

Scorpio glared at Kane and raised her brow at the comment. "Dad?"

"No, he's not," Jackie launched hotly. "You tell him I said no."

Kane then focused his attention on Jackie. "He said you might protest, in which case, I'm supposed to tell you to try and stop him," he announced.

"Yeah, he'd love that," Jackie snarled.

Scorpio eyed Jackie. "Shouldn't your friends be back with Stone by now?"

§

It was nearly four o'clock that afternoon, and there was still no sign of the team storming the asylum. Gil, Sal, and John had once again barricaded themselves in the game room in order to keep an eye on the tall field between the building and the front gate.

"Please tell me your friends just enjoy a fashionably late, dramatic entrance," John remarked while he sat on the floor with his back against the wall.

"No, not really," Gil muttered then considered the comment and lowered the cheap binoculars. He turned away from the window and eyed John. "Well, maybe Monroe. He gets a lot of swagger out of his expensive clothes."

"I've been meaning to discuss 'less is more' regarding cologne with him too," Sal muttered from where he sat on a chair and had his injured leg propped up on the table to help reduce swelling.

"Well, in that case, at least you'll smell him coming," John retorted as he folded his arms across his chest and sighed in boredom.

The hand radio Gil had removed from his new, dead friend in the incinerator room crackled softly.

"Tyson, you copy?" the male voice announced over the radio startling all three men.

Gil snatched the radio and turned down the volume. John and Sal immediately came to life and listened.

"Leonard," the voice bellowed with conviction and some hostility. "Report."

"Do we tell them about their friends?" Sal teased while grinning in an unsettling manner.

"We're not ready for a firefight," Gil replied. "Let them send their men in one-by-one. If we're lucky; we'll liberate a firearm or two from them."

"I wonder how many of them are out there," Sal muttered more to himself.

"I'm guessing at least four men patrolling the fence and another four inside the perimeter," John replied with little emotion.

Sal raised a curious brow and eyed the casually reclined man. "Interesting guess."

"We've seen enough of the estate grounds," John remarked and straightened. "Two men wouldn't be able to successfully cover the entire area. You'd need one on each end watching all possible exits."

"I haven't ruled out tree stands," Gil added. "There's some organization to whatever they're doing here. They're in it for the long haul."

"Four extra men to keep an eye on things closer to the building or even inside would make sense," John informed Sal. "That's proven by the fact that they were burning bodies to keep them from rotting or being found."

"Perhaps they'll give up a little more information," Gil announced while eyeing the hand radio. "Maybe we'll learn something useful."

"Our time might be better spent surfing channels listening for the team," Sal remarked. "If they're nearby, we should be able to get ears on them."

"There weren't many shots fired," Gil informed Sal. "The team probably split up to conduct their search. Whatever radio chatter there was is done already. They're probably regrouping now. Our chances of catching the right frequency while they're mounting their rescue is pretty slim. We'll hear the gunfire before we hear them on the radio."

"Team one," the man on the radio announced. "Move in. Find our men."

"Roger that," another man responded over the radio.

Gil suddenly jumped to his feet. "Those were the magic words," he announced and glanced at John. "We need to get the jump on team one. That had a definite 'lock and load' overtone."

"I wouldn't mind a real weapon myself," John remarked while making a face as he eyed the cattle prod in his hand. "If I could get something with a scope on it, we wouldn't need to worry about those men patrolling the gate. I'd pick them off one at a time."

Gil smirked and extended his hand to the door. "It's a date," he announced. "Let's go."

Sal attempted to stand.

Gil pointed a warning finger at him. "You stay here," he ordered.

"What am I?" Sal demanded and appeared offended. "Some helpless old man?"

"No, you're an injured old man," Gil replied.

Sal sneered at his friend. "I'm only a few years older than you," he scoffed without humor.

"Yeah, and I'm old too," Gil informed him and again pointed his threatening finger while giving him a firm glare. "You stay here. Make yourself useful." He tossed Sal the binoculars. "Keep an eye out for the team."

"I want my dog back," Sal scoffed.

Gil ignored him and headed with John to the barricaded door.

§

Gil and John cautiously hurried along the first floor corridor with their cattle prods clutched firmly in their hands. The asylum was eerily silent despite a small horde of crazed cannibals roaming the building.

"We have no idea how they intend to get into the place," John announced in a loud whisper. "What makes you think we'll be able to find our captors?"

"We don't have to know their point of entry," Gil insisted while keeping his eyes on blind corners before him. "We already know where they're going."

"We do?" John asked and appeared puzzled. "Did I miss something?"

"We have to assume they only enter the building for two reasons," Gil announced and raised his brows. "To drop off new prisoners and--"

John groaned and nodded while offering a tiny grin. "To toss bodies into the incinerator."

"We just need to wait in the basement for them to check the incinerator room," Gil informed him. "That's where they're going to look for their missing men."

"That's where they're going to find their missing men," John muttered. "And they're not going to like what they find either."

"That's why we need the element of surprise before they can call in reinforcements," Gil remarked while scanning the empty corridor. "We need to pick them off before there are too many of them."

"That's a long haul to the basement stairs," John announced. "Once we're in the basement, we have to basically head back the way we came."

"We don't have a choice," Gil remarked. "I don't know where there's another set of stairs or a functioning elevator to the basement."

"I know a quicker way," John announced.

Gil stopped in the corridor, turned to face John, and gave him a surprised look. "You do?"

John grinned and nodded.

Chapter 40

Gil stood over the large hole in the middle of the lounge and stared at the debris-covered kitchen ten feet below. He looked over his shoulder at the grinning man alongside him and shook his head.

"I've heard of worse plans before," Gil remarked to John while eyeing the scene below. "Though a bit of a drop onto some unstable debris."

John moved closer to the edge of the rotted floor not far from the wall and sat on the edge that creaked beneath his weight. He then dropped down onto the top of the large, old refrigerator. John slipped on some of the debris covering it but easily caught his balance. He kicked away the debris, stood firmly on top of the refrigerator, and indicated the counter alongside it.

"Two steps and a jump," John teased.

Gil drew a deep breath then sighed and waved his hand. "After you."

John sat on the refrigerator then dropped onto the counter. He kicked away more debris to expose the countertop, making the jump easier for Gil. Gil lowered himself onto the refrigerator then sat on it while John jumped to the kitchen floor. John landed in some heavy debris and nearly lost his footing. He laughed at the prospect of almost falling then cleared more debris from the floor with his foot as Gil jumped onto the countertop. Once John moved from his cleared spot, Gil easily jumped to the floor.

"Add another point for Army," John teased. "That's two-one Army."

Gil sneered at the gloating man. "Don't get cocky just yet," he remarked. "The game is far from over."

John chuckled at Gil's irritation then led him across the disastrous kitchen. They carefully walked around the mound of ceiling debris on the kitchen floor and headed for the main entrance. John pulled on the steel door that creaked on rusted hinges.

"Check your corners," Gil remarked.

"Our insane friends haven't ventured down here," John informed him then pulled the door open.

A crazed woman screamed while lunging through the open doorway and tackled John to the dirty floor. Gil casually watched as the woman in tattered clothing straddled John and bitch slapped him like an angry wife. John attempted to stop the assault, but the woman delivered one strike after another. Gil smirked at the crazed woman's dedication to humiliating the former Army Ranger turned mercenary. Gil finally poked her in the shoulder with the cattle prod. She screamed like a banshee as she was thrown off John and onto the floor from the powerful charge that the cattle prod produced. She twitched a moment then panted from exertion. John sprang to his feet while staring at the exhausted woman then eyed Gil, who smirked.

"Your wife was really pissed," Gil teased and added a throaty chuckle. "That's two-two. Next time watch your corners."

John gingerly rubbed his reddened face. The red marks were clearly in the outline of a handprint. "For a small thing; she was aggressive," he announced with some surprise.

"*It's not the size of the dog in the fight, it's the size of the fight in the dog,*" Gil teased while quoting Mark Twain.

John glared at Gil and frowned. "After getting to know you," he announced. "I'm starting to wonder if your friends will actually bother saving your ass."

Gil chuckled then indicated the open, kitchen door. "Lead the way," he announced. "In case we run into any more of your ex-girlfriends."

Both men continued cautiously through the kitchen doorway with their cattle prods prepared for action. It didn't take long before they reached the incinerator room. Gil gently pushed open the door and peered inside. The incinerator continued to burn beyond the large, open door mounted on the wall. Beneath the incinerator, four crazed patients kneeled over the two dead men and devoured the flesh from the arms and legs. John and Gil grimaced at the sight. They then heard voices echoing through the basement corridor. Both men looked down the corridor and heard the men nearing the corner. Gil and John had no choice but to enter the incinerator room. They quietly hurried into the room, not wanting to attract attention to themselves, and slipped behind the supply rack. The psychotic cannibals never even heard them. The door opened to reveal two guards dressed in black and gray camouflage. They saw the four crazed cannibals devouring their men.

"Jesus," the first man snarled.

Both approached the four patients on the floor over the two dead men. The patients saw them, sprang to their feet, and lunged for them. The two men easily took all four down with their cattle prods. While the four cannibals twitched on the ground and recovered from the current surging through them, the two guards frowned at their two dead comrades. With little discussion, they picked up each man and tossed him into the incinerator. Once the four crazed cannibals gathered their strength, they darted from the incinerator room. The two guards threw the last remaining bodies from the laundry bin into the fire as well and shut the heavy, iron door.

"I hate this job," the second guard huffed in disgust. "The boss is as demented as the crazies kept locked away in this Godforsaken place."

"What was in the water in that little town anyway?" the second man demanded and appeared curious. "Why did they all go insane?"

"I don't know, and I don't care," the first man responded. "Wouldn't doubt that psychopath had something to do with the tainted water. At least the pay is good."

Both men turned and came face to face with John and Gil. They flaunted unsettling smirks as they simultaneously zapped the two guards with the cattle prods. The men twitched and dropped to the floor. With little time to celebrate their victory, Gil and John eagerly searched both men for weapons and other useful items.

Gil removed a semiautomatic from the guard's hidden shoulder holster and grinned. "Now that's more like it," he announced then worked on removing the man's shoulder holster, which contained extra magazines.

The second guard had a shoulder holster as well, which John removed. They found zip ties, which they used to tie the men's wrists behind their backs, a few more energy bars, and a hand radio each. Now Gil, John, and Sal would all have hand radios.

"What do you want to do with them?" John asked as the two men started coming to their senses.

"I don't know about you," Gil announced with little emotion, "but I want answers. How are you with interrogations?"

John grimaced at the question. "Moderately squeamish," he replied honestly. "It takes a special breed of psychopath to effectively interrogate prisoners."

"We just call ours Zack," Gil remarked then drew a deep breath and met John's gaze. "We don't have all day. One of us has to do it."

"You're more intimidating than I am," John insisted while taking a step back.

Gil stared at John with some surprise. "You're closer to a psychopath," he launched back defensively. "What sort of mercenary are you? This sort of depraved behavior should be right up your alley."

"I shoot people," John insisted while seemingly taking offense to the comment. "We need someone who instills fear in men."

Gil then tensed and eyed John. A strange grin crossed his face. "Actually, I think we have one of those. We'll take one of them back to home base with us."

"What about the other?" John asked.

Gil shrugged. "He'll have to sort that out on his own," he replied. "I'm not babysitting two of them."

§

Sal crouched before the man tied to the old chair in the game room and met his gaze. The tied guard easily looked away and gave the impression he wasn't going to say a word. Sal drew a deep breath, shook his head, and then adjusted his small, round glasses.

"I'm a desperate man, son," Sal announced to the guard, who showed no emotion to the man hovering over him. "If your boss thought he could fuck with my friends and me, he's sadly mistaken."

The man didn't respond and finally looked away as if ending the discussion that never began.

Sal straightened and sighed. "I'm sorry it has to be this way," he announced and held his hand out to Gil.

Gil appeared unaffected but was slightly rigid as he placed the pliers in Sal's hand.

John grimaced as Sal fiddled with the pliers without showing any emotion. "Not the fingernails," John muttered. "I don't think I can stomach that."

"I'm more comfortable with ripping out his molars," Gil added then cast a look at Sal. "Let's go for the molars instead."

Sal groaned and looked at the man standing on either side of him. "You boys lack nerve," he muttered. "I'm very disappointed." Sal eyed the pliers while snapping them together and showed no emotion. "Remove his pants."

Gil and John stared at Sal with horror on their faces. Their mouths simultaneously dropped open.

Sal glared at both and raised his brows at their reactions. "What? I'm not nearly as patient as I used to be," he informed them. "Wisdom isn't the only thing that comes with age. I've grown increasingly impatient. I want to know what this thug knows, and I don't feel like asking twice. Pop one of his testicles like an engorged tick, and he's going to tell us everything he knows." Sal considered the comment and shrugged. "After he regains consciousness, that is." Sal offered little emotion as he turned toward the now frightened, bound man. "Remove his pants and let's get this over with." Sal again snapped the pliers together.

The man jumped at the sound. Gil and John exchanged looks, inhaled deeply, and then approached the bound man. As they reached for his pants, he thrashed and cried out.

"She has us call her Madam Director," the man shouted. "She says she runs this place."

"Madam Director?" Gil just about gasped and eyed Sal and John. "We were targeted by a woman?"

Sal cast his gaze upon the bound man. "Why did she want us?"

"She didn't," the man insisted while nervously twitching. "She gives us a list of names with descriptions and target locations. We find the men she wants, and we bring them here."

"For what reason?" John demanded.

"The obvious one," the man insisted. "They're left here to rot or die. I don't know why she chose any of them. She just gives a list of names."

"How long has she been doing this?" Gil demanded.

"Around six months," he insisted. "I've only been here a month or two, but one of the perimeter guards has been close to six months."

"How many guards?" John asked.

"Six per shift," the man informed him.

"So that means there are at least eighteen guards," John filled in the blanks.

"She has a small army working inside the building as well," the man offered.

"How many on the inside?" Gil demanded.

"There are fifteen of us working the inside patrol," the man readily informed him while remaining tense.

"What else do you know about Madam Director?" Sal asked while showing little emotion.

"She's smart," he replied nervously while shifting looks from the men to the pliers Sal held. "Attractive too."

"How old is she?" Gil then asked.

"Early twenties," the man responded.

"No real name?" John pressed.

"She didn't offer; none asked," he countered without taking his eyes off the pliers in Sal's hand.

The three men exchanged looks.

"That's an interesting twist," Sal muttered to his friends. "We could be looking at any number of scenarios involving this woman."

"A psychotic, attractive, twenty-something-year-old woman?" John remarked and raised his brows. "Sounds like every woman I've ever dated."

Chapter 41

It was nearing eight o'clock that night, and sunset would soon fall on the lifeless town. The old jeep left behind within the abandoned garage was still in disrepair, although Maverick seemed confident he'd be able to fix it. Unfortunately, there wasn't enough light to safely continue working on the jeep's engine. Mac and Monroe had searched the house alongside the garage, but there was little in the way of emergency lighting. They found a kerosene lamp and several candles but nothing that would enable Maverick to see within the already dark engine compartment of the vehicle. Rayner had found a mostly full container of water within the garage that would get them through the night. Despite that the garage had running water; they assumed it was contaminated after seeing all the water containers around town. Monroe lit the kerosene lamp, which brightened the garage office considerably. Mac sat in the leather chair behind the desk and spun herself back and forth with boredom.

"If we're going to be stranded here the night," Mac announced. "We should probably forage for food."

"Do you think there would be anything left that's edible?" Maverick asked while wiping his hands after finishing what he could with the broken down jeep.

"The town hasn't been abandoned that long," Rayner insisted. "There are several houses along the street. We should check them for useful items. Someone must have left some canned goods behind."

"We should go before the entire town is dark," Monroe insisted then looked at the others. "We'll split into two teams and search the houses on both sides of the street." He eyed Maverick then indicated Rayner. "You and Rayner can search the houses on this side of the street. Mac and I will take the far side of the street." He then looked at his watch before glancing at the others. "We'll gather anything of use and meet back here in an hour."

"Excellent plan," Maverick announced while revealing little emotion as he leaned in the doorway to the office. "Except I'm going with Mac."

Mac and Rayner both groaned in unison. Monroe glared at Maverick and raised his brows while folding his arms across his chest.

"Any particular reason?" Monroe asked.

It was a bit of a loaded question, and Monroe knew it. If Maverick responded incorrectly, Mac would undoubtedly bite off his head. She made it perfectly clear she wasn't in a relationship so anything Maverick said could be used against him. Maverick carefully considered his response while Mac tilted her head and waited to hear what he had to say.

"I'm not the one who abducted her, tied her up, and used her as leverage to get to Kane," Maverick announced boldly.

Mac smirked at Monroe and withheld her laugh. "He's got you there," she replied then sprang up from her seat. "And now that he's reminded me of that, I think he's right. I should go with Maverick." Mac playfully linked onto Maverick's arm and smiled mockingly at Monroe. "Don't worry. Rayner is extremely useful, and I'm 95% confident he won't kick you in the nuts."

Rayner nodded while eyeing Monroe. "She's right on both accounts," he replied. "I am useful, and there's only a five percent chance I'll kick you."

Monroe frowned at the playful look on Mac's face before she turned and guided Maverick toward the garage door.

"One hour," Monroe called after them. Once they disappeared, he shook his head. "She's messing with me on purpose."

Rayner shrugged and offered a tiny smile. "I'm sure she is," he replied with some humor. "Trust me; with the mood she's in, you should be glad she's avoiding you. That wasn't just playful banter. I'm convinced she has every intention of kicking you in the nuts."

"What else is new?" Monroe muttered then motioned Rayner to the garage door. "We already searched the house to the right of the garage. Let's check out the house to the left and work our way down the street."

§

Mac easily picked the lock on the front door of the house directly across the street from the garage. There was just enough light coming through the many windows to brighten the lower rooms. Maverick closed the door behind them and turned the bolt, catching Mac's attention. She gave him a look and raised her brow in question. He caught her glare and gave her an innocent look.

"I don't want anyone sneaking up on us while we search for necessities," Maverick insisted.

She nodded and smirked. "And that should be all that's going through your head," Mac announced then checked out the living room while deep in thought.

The living room was completely furnished, and framed family photos still hung on the walls. Despite a layer of dust, the place was in excellent condition.

"It's going to be uncomfortable sleeping in that garage," Mac announced. "Maybe we could find a couple of sleeping bags and some pillows."

Maverick indicated the sofa and loveseat within the room. "Plenty of throw pillows," he remarked.

"Let's check the kitchen first," Mac insisted. "We can raid the closets after we find food for tonight. I don't know about you, but I'm starving."

Maverick followed her into the tidy, modern kitchen where each proceeded to search the cupboards for anything left behind. To their surprise, the pantry was just about stocked.

"That's strange," Maverick remarked and shook his head. "I'm starting to think the people in this town left in a hurry. Don't you find it odd that they left all their furniture and family photos behind?"

"This entire town gives me the creeps," Mac informed him as she pulled canned goods from the pantry. "Check the drawers for a manual can opener."

Maverick routed through the drawers and finally found what he was looking for. He removed the manual can opener and a few spoons and forks as well.

"We need a shopping bag or something," he insisted while placing the items on the counter.

"Maybe there are some garbage bags in the lower cupboards," she announced then nodded to the stairs not far from the kitchen. "I'm going to check upstairs and see if they left some pillows behind."

Mac left the kitchen leaving Maverick to fill a garbage bag with canned goods and some utensils. The staircase was dark, but Mac could see light coming from the upstairs hall window. She then removed her semiautomatic and cautiously made her way down the second floor hallway. There was enough light still invading the master bedroom that she could see the furniture and neatly made bed. She made sure the room was secure by checking the bathroom, under the bed, and in the closet before returning her weapon to her shoulder holster. Mac saw a rolling suitcase inside the closet buried beneath some boxes.

A few things about the room bothered her. The bed being neatly made and including decorative throw pillows was just the beginning. Why had the homeowners left their suitcase behind? There were personal items on top of the dresser, including a woman's jewelry box. She opened one of the drawers and found it filled with clothing. Mac proceeded to open a few more drawers and found they were all filled. She considered their situation again then brushed her thoughts aside. For now, they needed to concentrate on the current situation. They had to get through tonight and make it back to the abandoned airfield. Mac again looked at the suitcase in the closet.

"That'll come in handy," she announced and pulled the suitcase out from under some boxes.

Several boxes clattered to the floor before she freed the rolling bag. Mac grimaced at the sound. A floorboard creaked behind her. She spun around while reaching for her weapon and nearly collided with Maverick.

"Trying to wake up the entire neighborhood?" Maverick teased.

Mac gingerly rubbed her sore shoulder. "I thought we could use the suitcase to carry the supplies back to the garage. It has wheels. We can just roll it on over," she informed him. She again rubbed her sore shoulder and grimaced. "I wish I had a few more of Jackie's pain pills."

"I'll check the medicine cabinet," Maverick announced then entered the bathroom.

Mac approached the bed, which contained two pillows. "I doubt you'll find anything in the medicine cabinet--"

"Found some," Maverick announced as he appeared from the bathroom and flashed the bottle. "That's odd. They are prescription painkillers." His look was concerning. "There's an entire medicine cabinet of goodies in there including someone's blood pressure medication. It doesn't seem as if they took anything with them when they left."

"Not even their clothes," Mac insisted and indicated the dresser drawers. "I wonder why?"

She took the bottle of pills from him, removed one, and took it without use of water since she didn't trust the tap water. Mac then placed the pill bottle in her jacket pocket.

"Let's get these pillows and that comforter," she announced. "We'll need two more pillows from the other bedrooms. I think we'll have everything we need to get us through the night in some comfort."

Maverick glanced at his watch. "Well, we've made good time," he announced. "You wait here. I'll find some more pillows. Rest your shoulder."

"Thanks," Mac replied and watched Maverick leave the rapidly darkening room.

With the light fading fast, Mac spotted a candle left behind on the dresser. She found a cigarette lighter and lit the candle to brighten the room, giving it a romantic glow. Mac gingerly rubbed her shoulder as she looked around the bedroom while deep in thought.

§

Maverick entered the smaller bedroom across the hall from where he'd left Mac in the master bedroom. He approached the double bed within what was almost certainly a teenager's bedroom. He removed the pillows, tossed them into the center of the bed, and then folded the comforter over them to form a bundle that he could easily carry. The nearby closet door creaked, alerting Maverick. He swiftly removed the semiautomatic from the back of his pants and aimed it at the closet door. Nothing moved. Maverick cautiously approached the partially open door with the gun aimed, reached for the knob, and threw it open. A shelf broke, and several items crashed to the floor. Maverick jumped back with a groan then relaxed.

"Everything okay?" Mac called out with concern from across the hall.

"Yeah," Maverick called back and eyed the mess, which consisted of an entire box full of girly magazines. "Apparently, I found their teenage son's room." He eyed the scattered magazines depicting half-naked women. "A very horny teenager."

Maverick replaced his gun to the back of his pants, grabbed the comforter bundle from the bed, and left the room. He entered the room across the hall where he'd left Mac. Mac's clothes were discarded on the floor, and she lay on her side facing him, naked beneath the covers, while propped on her good arm. Maverick dropped the bundle when he saw her on the bed within the romantic glow of the candlelight. A sly grin crossed Maverick's face.

"I thought you said 'no' to any other thoughts going through my head," he teased as he practically ripped off his shirt and dropped it to the floor near her clothes.

Mac grinned slyly. "You did point out we have a lot of extra time on our hands," she teased.

Maverick removed his semiautomatic and set it on the nightstand before pulling off his boots containing his matching knives. The moment his shoes hit the floor, his jeans were only a second behind them. He dived beneath the covers and moved against her. Maverick then hesitated when he saw the gauze dressing over her shoulder injury and met her eager gaze.

"I don't want to hurt you," he insisted while indicating her shoulder.

"I think you can manage around it," she insisted then flung her leg over his hip and pulled him on top of her as she rolled onto her back without using her injured arm.

Maverick chuckled while caressing her body beneath his. "Okay then--"

He eagerly kissed her without further prompting. Mac responded with rising aggression and set the tone. While they kissed and groped each other beneath the covers, neither noticed the outline of a man in the bedroom doorway. Mac writhed beneath Maverick's body as he aggressively kissed her neck and good shoulder. Her eyes opened and strayed to the open doorway. She stared at the empty doorway, almost as if something caught her attention. Maverick eagerly pressed against her with a pleasurable grunt. Mac let out a sharp groan and clung to him.

Chapter 42

The woods were already mostly dark despite that it wasn't officially sunset. Bogart and Stone slouched on the ground behind a large rock while attempting to remain still and silent. They had managed to lose Kirk nearly thirty minutes earlier and, since they were still taking enemy fire, going back to look for him wasn't an option. They couldn't see much as it was, they didn't know where to look, and whoever had been shooting at them was too close for comfort.

"What do you think happened to Kirk?" Stone whispered to Bogart with concern in his tone.

"I'd like to believe he has some epic master plan he's working on," Bogart muttered while peering across the dark woods, "but that might be wishful thinking."

"How many do you suppose are out there?" Stone asked in hushed tone.

"At least two," Bogart replied while clinging to his assault rifle. He then fiddled with the scope. "You should be able to switch the scope to night vision."

Stone strained to see the dial on the scope and turned it. A red light shot up into the trees. Bogart gasped and placed his hand over Stone's scope.

"Are you trying to get us killed?" Bogart cried out in a harsh whisper.

Bogart frantically fiddled with Stone's weapon in order to turn off the laser pointer when they heard the sound of someone rapidly moving through the woods.

"Shit," Bogart softly cried out and fixed the scope. "They're coming."

Bogart returned the rifle to Stone then rolled onto his stomach and peered out from behind the large rock with his weapon just about on the ground in front of him and his finger on the trigger. He peered through the scope with use of its night vision. While Bogart's back was turned, a man dressed completely in black suddenly appeared behind them with his rifle aimed. Stone saw the intruder first, since he had been facing that direction, and gasped. Stone didn't even have time to aim his weapon as the man's finger tightened on the trigger. Kirk suddenly appeared alongside the armed intruder and placed his large hand over the man's mouth while jerking his body upward. The nearly silent shot from the man's rifle fired into the air.

Kirk plunged his Bowie knife into the man's neck before he even had a chance to defend himself. The intruder muffled a gasp in pain and surprise. As the man's eyes rolled back into his head, Kirk gently assisted him to the ground to keep his falling body from making too much noise. Kirk pulled his knife free, released the man, and wiped the blood from his blade on the dead man's shirt. Kirk looked at the horrified expression on Stone's face.

"Good to see you," Stone gasped while attempting to sound confident.

Kirk snatched the dead man's weapon containing the silencer. Bogart turned from where he lay on the ground and stared at the dead man not far from them. Kirk approached the rock and aimed the guard's weapon in the area where they suspected the remaining men were lurking. Kirk fired two nearly silent shots that struck some trees in the distance. They heard a loud rustling within the woods. Kirk fired another two shots. The rustling sound decreased by one. Kirk lowered the rifle, straightened, and cursed under his breath. He then faced Stone and Bogart.

"The last one got away," Kirk informed them. "We should probably get back to the airfield and secure the planes. There's no telling if they've made it that far."

Stone nodded although he was clearly stunned after seeing the way Kirk took down the man, who was now swiftly bleeding out not far from him. Stone then noticed something. He suddenly lunged forward and grabbed the hand radio from the man's belt.

"Think we could use this to hear what's happening out there?" Stone asked.

Kirk took the radio from Stone and fiddled with the knob. He finally found a static-filled response from the man fleeing the area.

"Two men are down," the man on the other end announced over the hand radio while sounding out of breath, indicating he was running. "I think we scared them off for the moment."

Kirk turned the radio volume down then looked across the woods. "You two stay here and cover me," he announced and indicated the area where he shot the other guard. "I'm going to retrieve the dead man's radio and weapon. We could use a second radio and another rifle with silencer."

Stone and Bogart aimed their weapons across the dark woods while staring through their night vision scopes. They scanned the area but didn't see any sign of armed men. Once Kirk was in position, Bogart nodded for Stone to keep an eye on the area surrounding their teammate, who ventured out from behind the rock. While Stone covered Kirk, Bogart searched the dead man's pockets for anything useful. He removed a set of old keys and eyed them with bewilderment. Stone cast a look at the keys before returning his focus on Kirk.

"What did you find?" Stone asked.

Bogart appeared surprised then grinned. "I'm guessing these are the keys to the building," he announced. "This one looks like a padlock key. It'll probably open the front gate. The others are extremely old keys. I'm guessing at least one opens the front door." He placed the set of keys in his jacket pocket then searched the man. He removed a semiautomatic and laid it on the ground near the body. Kirk returned with extra weapons, a second radio, and some additional magazines for their new weapons.

"Let's go," Kirk announced then pointed. "The road should be that way."

Stone joined Bogart and nodded at Kirk in the lead. "Is he just guessing or is his sense of direction that good?" Stone asked with a curious look.

"He'll tell you he's that good," Bogart muttered, "but his watch has a built-in compass. Tells latitude and longitude. Even gives pulse rate."

"Then we'd better follow him," Stone remarked. "Because I have no clue where we are."

"You and me both," Bogart muttered.

Chapter 43

Scorpio whimpered and thrashed in her sleep then felt a hand touch her. She cried out with surprise and flew up within the plush plane seat. Scorpio panted breathlessly and stared at Zack, who stood over her. Despite her sudden movement, Zack wasn't startled.

"You were having a bad dream," he announced gently then returned to his seat on the opposite side of the plane.

Scorpio remained tense a moment then slowly straightened while attempting to control her breathing. She held her head with a trembling hand then glanced at Zack, who still kept his eyes on her.

"Where's Kane?" she asked while looking around the fuselage. She remembered her brother had been in the plane when she closed her eyes.

"Outside trying to impress Jackie with his charm," Zack replied. "Very poorly, I might add."

Scorpio didn't seem the least bit surprised and avoided looking at Zack while she attempted to shake the nightmare from her mind.

"Are you okay?" Zack asked while keeping close watch over her.

"I have a sleep disorder," she remarked. Scorpio attempted to keep her hands from shaking while avoiding looking at the man across from her. "I barely sleep, and when I do, I have intense nightmares."

Zack frowned at the comment. "Sorry," he replied gently. "You get that from me."

"I get that from my life," she scoffed and finally looked at the man in the seat across the aisle from her. "I have a lot of pesky demons festering inside my head."

Zack continued to stare at her and raised his brows as if making some silent comment.

Scorpio caught his look and straightened. "Yeah, I suppose you would have that too."

"I've seen a lot," he reassured her. "When I close my eyes, everything I've seen and done returns to haunt me." Zack then shrugged. "I've learned to embrace the horror. There are a few people I don't mind repeatedly killing night after night. I'm guessing I have just a little more experience with that sort of thing than you."

"Yeah, I'm sure you do," she replied and shifted uncomfortably. "I watched the man I love die in my arms. It was difficult enough the first time around. Then there's the whole thing with my grandfather, but I'm sure Kane told you all about that."

"No, I don't think he did," Zack replied.

"He has a strange way of putting unpleasant things out of his mind, especially when he has goals to accomplish," she announced. "On those rare occasions when he actually has a girlfriend, life is nothing but puppies and kittens for him. I don't know how he does it."

"We all have our security blankets," Zack remarked and actually smirked, relaying some hidden meaning behind the comment.

"Yeah? Well, I'm a little worried about my security blanket," Scorpio remarked. "He should have been back by now."

Zack appeared interested while studying her. "That big guy, Stone?" he asked with a curious look. "Are the two of you a couple?"

She stared at Zack with some surprise then snorted a soft laugh and shook her head. "No, I'm not dating Stone," she replied.

Zack's expression then dropped into something resembling a sneer. "Not the pretty boy," he muttered then made a face. "We already have our Bogart. We don't need another in the family."

Scorpio stiffened while glaring at Zack. "No, I'm not dating Maverick either," she insisted then ran her fingers through her hair while shaking her head. She groaned softly. "You wouldn't understand."

"The computer geek?" he asked while raising a curious brow.

She rolled her eyes and avoided looking at him. "Just drop it, okay? I certainly don't need your approval."

"I didn't say you did," Zack replied then shrugged. "You could do worse. I can name six or eight men right off the top of my head."

"Your friends?" she teased while eyeing him.

"I suppose some of them are my friends," he remarked while considering the comment.

"And which of your 'friends' would you least like to see me with?" she teased.

"Is this one of those things where you go out and do exactly what I tell you not to do?" he asked while tilting his head. "Because I'm still mad at Jackie for her brief romance with Monroe when she was younger."

"No," she replied. "Sorry to disappoint you. I'm happy with Rayner."

"In that case," Zack announced and turned serious. "Kirk would probably be number one on that list inching out Bogart by a hair. When it comes to women, Kirk is basically a mutt in heat. At least Bogart has that clueless country boy charm to fall back on."

"You don't like Kirk, huh?"

"Actually, Kirk and I get along just fine," Zack replied. "We share the same disdain for scum of the earth."

Scorpio managed a tiny laugh. "Why am I not surprised?" she muttered.

Zack shrugged with little care regarding the insult. "I won't deny what I am. Most of what you've heard about me is pretty much true," he informed her without emotion. "I'm an intolerable prick."

"Are you?" she asked with a curious look.

Zack met her gaze and nodded without hesitation. "Yeah, pretty much," he offered. "I have Jackie fooled into believing I'm not so bad."

She stared at him a moment in awkward silence. "Did you have my mother fooled too?" Scorpio asked while offering a curious look.

Zack tensed and drew a deep, uncomfortable breath. "No, but I wasn't as big of a prick back then. She brought out the best in me." Zack drifted out then frowned. "Then I got her killed." He remained lost a moment. "I live with that guilt every day of my life."

Scorpio shifted uncomfortably. "Yeah, well, you may want to check your guilt at the door."

Zack met her gaze and gave her a puzzled look.

"You had nothing to do with my mother's death," Scorpio informed him while shifting in her seat.

"The men who killed her were after me," he insisted with little emotion. "They threatened to kill her in order to hurt me. It took years to find and neutralize that threat, but I accomplished that mission."

"I don't doubt you have people who want to kill you," she informed him, "but you weren't responsible for my mother's death. Not even a little."

He stared at her with a strange look. "How do you figure?"

Scorpio hesitated then drew a deep, tense breath. "Because I killed the man responsible," she informed him then sank into her own thoughts. "He never even felt my blade cut through his neck." She then sneered with disgust. "He was still smiling at me thinking he'd beaten me."

Zack stared at the distant look in her eyes. "I feel oddly close to you right now," he announced almost proudly. "Who was he?"

She frowned and met his gaze. "It was my grandfather," Scorpio informed him.

Zack's expression suddenly turned cold. "Newman?" he just about gasped. "Maggie's own father killed her?"

"Not with his own hands," Scorpio replied, "but he hired the man who did. He also tried to have Kane bumped off as well."

Scorpio could tell Zack was having a difficult time processing what she'd just told him. He undoubtedly found and killed the man who had threatened to take Maggie from him, but he was nowhere near the man who had actually completed the task. Zack slipped out of his own thoughts and studied Scorpio a moment.

"I'm sorry you had to be the one to do that," Zack gently informed her then cocked his head. "I would have gladly done it for you."

Scorpio wiped a stray tear from her cheek. "I wish it had been anyone but me too," she whispered then attempted to put the nightmare behind her and finally managed an uneasy smile. "Please tell me Kane isn't really out there attempting to charm your friend."

Zack offered a tiny grin and indicated the open plane door. "See for yourself."

She shook her head and held back her laugh. "He's pathetic," Scorpio remarked. "He can have almost any woman he wants, and he goes after the only one he can't have. She's married to that fed too, isn't she?"

Zack nodded.

Scorpio groaned. "Honestly, I need to kick his ass around a little," she remarked then met Zack's gaze. "That usually straightens him out."

Zack chuckled in his throat. "That's what Jackie does with me," he teased.

She met his humored gaze then laughed. "I'll bet she does."

Chapter 44

Within the deserted town, Monroe and Maverick had secured the garage bay doors and the main door to prevent any unwanted visitors. Placing the garage on lockdown would also keep them from having to take turns on guard duty throughout the night. After a healthy dinner of cold baked beans and fruit cocktail, the four played an hour or more of poker before settling in for the night. A second kerosene lamp brightened the first, empty bay of the garage where the four had made makeshift beds out of comforters and some sleeping bags Monroe and Rayner had found. A tarp over the garage windows kept any light from escaping and alerting potentially unwanted visitors from learning their location.

Mac was the first one knocked out of the poker game. She made herself comfortable on one of the comforters and looked through an old magazine she'd found within the garage. Monroe made a wild bet, and he was knocked out of the game only twenty minutes after Mac. Maverick and Rayner were now going head-to-head for the win. Monroe joined Mac in their temporary sleeping quarters and sat on the empty sleeping bag next to hers. He lay on his side, propped on his elbow, and glanced at Mac while she flipped through the magazine.

"So," Monroe announced while raising his brows. "You and Maverick, huh?"

She cast a look at him then returned to her magazine. "It's not a big deal," Mac casually informed him.

"Oh, really? What happened to your 'once and done' rule?" Monroe asked with a curious look. "Or did that only apply to me?"

Mac cast her magazine aside and glared at Monroe. "Not that it's any of your business," she announced, "but I was bored, and Maverick was handy."

"So you're not dating?"

"Again, not that it's any of your business," she announced, "but, no, we're not dating. We're just scratching each other's itch."

"You know; I'm not opposed to being handy when you're bored," Monroe announced in all honesty. "I have no problem being someone's wild fling."

"We both know that's not true," she informed him as she reclaimed her magazine. "You're the kind of guy who wants exclusive dating rights."

"Says who?" Monroe demanded.

Mac raised her brow while staring at him. He shifted uncomfortably.

"That's not to say I couldn't do the whole casual sex thing," Monroe insisted then seemed offended. "You wouldn't even consider the possibility."

"I know better," Mac remarked. "What happened between us was a mistake. One time and you want to turn it into dating. Next, it'd be dating exclusively. I know how you think."

"Oh, so you were talking to Jackie," he scoffed with irritation.

"I don't need Jackie to tell me how to read men," Mac insisted. "Even now, you can't let it go. You can't even get past your fling with Jackie. This is exactly what I wanted to avoid."

"Hey," Maverick casually announced, catching their attention.

Mac and Monroe looked up and saw Maverick now standing over them. His tense body language conveyed his irritation with Monroe.

"Everything okay?" Maverick asked while shifting disapproving looks at Monroe.

"We're just talking," Monroe informed him and offered a slightly humored smile. "Mac and I go way back."

Maverick cocked his head and daringly raised his brows at the comment. "Sounds like she's not in a nostalgic mood," he remarked, revealing his irritation.

"You can put the overly protective boyfriend routine away," Monroe announced with an unusual calmness about him. "She'll let me know when the conversation is over."

Mac eyed both men with some irritation. "I'm not sure I want to talk to either of you right now," she remarked.

"Okay," Maverick announced to Monroe. "You heard her. The conversation is over."

Monroe stood without taking his eyes off Maverick and faced him. Mac placed her hands over her eyes and groaned. Rayner stopped cleaning up the cards and chips and now watched as well.

"What is your problem?" Monroe scoffed while locking eyes with Maverick.

"My problem is you and your friends," Maverick informed him without hesitation. "I don't particularly care for the way you treated Mac prior to and including the incident at the cemetery."

"That was a misunderstanding," Monroe snapped back. "I've apologized, and we've moved on. You seem to be the only one with a problem."

"A misunderstanding?" Maverick scoffed then smirked while shaking his head. "You and your friends threw her under the bus and then used her when it suited your needs, but since you've *apologized*, that makes everything all better."

"I think Mac can defend herself just fine," Monroe informed him while folding his arms across his chest. "She doesn't need some jealous boyfriend sticking his nose in where it wasn't invited."

"It doesn't matter if she can defend herself," Maverick boldly announced. "Friends stick up for friends, so they don't have to fight their battles alone. Probably something you should have done a long time ago. Instead, you and *your* friends cast her aside. She deserved better than that."

Monroe stared at Maverick and possibly took his words to heart, but his irritation seemed to get in the way.

"I get it," Monroe remarked in a calm tone. "You're afraid we'll work things out, she'll be embraced by my team, and then she'll switch sides."

"Doubtful," Maverick scoffed. "Kane treats her better than your team ever had. We're her family now. You had your chance, and you blew it."

"And you're mistaking a good time for a relationship," Monroe announced. "She'd leave you and your team in a heartbeat to join us. Why do you think she's so hell-bent on finding Sal? She wants her old job back."

Maverick punched Monroe in the mouth without warning, leaving Monroe no time to see it or attempt to block it. Before Maverick had even straightened from the swing, Monroe went for the return hit. He punched Maverick in the abdomen and then across the face, sending him back a step. Rayner sprang up from his seat and stared at the fight in progress with surprise. Mac remained comfortably seated on the floor with her hand over her eyes and shook her head. Monroe straightened and pointed a warning finger at Maverick, who dabbed the blood from the corner of his mouth.

"Don't ever--"

Before Monroe could finish his sentence, Maverick tackled him to the sleeping bag on the floor, allowing a semi-soft landing on the otherwise hard concrete. Mac watched the two men wrestle on the floor while attempting to punch each other not far from her. Rayner approached and looked from the fighting men to Mac.

"Shouldn't you say something and break that up?" Rayner demanded.

Mac threw her hands in the air and seemed almost disinterested. "Who am I to stand between two idiots who want to pummel each other?"

Rayner glared his disapproval at Mac then looked around the garage. He snatched an air horn from the nearby counter and approached the men rolling around the sleeping bag, attempting to punch each other. Mac cringed and covered her ears. Rayner placed the air horn closer to the men and pressed the button. The loud, shrill wail echoed throughout the garage.

Maverick and Monroe leaped apart and held their ears while crying out. Both looked at Rayner with surprise.

"Are you finished acting like a couple of hormonal teenagers?" Rayner demanded.

"I think I'm deaf," Monroe gasped.

"What?" Maverick cried out while holding his ears as he looked at Rayner.

Rayner set the can down on the counter and cast a look at Mac. "That wasn't so difficult, now was it?"

Mac eyed him then managed a smile and chuckled. "Nicely handled."

Chapter 45

The old, abandoned airfield was dark and quiet a little after ten o'clock that night. A faint glow from the rental plane's interior lights could be seen, although the area surrounding the plane was dark. Zack sat on the plane steps with Scorpio. Both had their night vision binoculars and kept watch on the woods. Within the plane, Jackie slept on one of the plush, reclining seats. She was curled up with a blanket over her, which had fallen partway off her shoulder. Kane slept in the seat across the aisle from her and woke, seemingly for no reason. He looked around with some disorientation then glanced at Jackie and the peaceful state in which she slept. He couldn't help but stare at the attractive woman a little longer than acceptable.

Kane stood, took two quiet steps closer to where Jackie slept, and gently pulled the blanket back up over her shoulder. He took one more moment to admire her peaceful look then returned to his seat. He attempted to get comfortable, but he seemed unusually troubled. When Jackie woke, Kane turned his head and stared out the nearby window. Jackie allowed the blanket to fall from her arm and looked at her watch. She groaned then glanced at Kane in the seat across the aisle.

"Can't sleep?" Jackie asked.

Kane looked at her and acted as if he didn't realize she was awake. "I'm worried about the guys," he replied. "They've been gone all day. It's possible Mac and the others found a place to crash for the night in that town, but what about Stone and your two friends?" He shook his head. "They should have been back by now. You don't think they're lost out there, do you?"

"If it were just my brother out there, yeah, I'd believe that," Jackie replied, "but Kirk doesn't get lost. That fancy watch of his tells him his longitude and latitude."

"So we should be worried about them?" Kane asked with concern while straightening in his seat.

"We can't exactly go out there looking for them in the dark," Jackie replied.

"Those sounds you heard earlier," Kane announced with a curious look. "They were gunshots, weren't they?"

Jackie nodded. "A couple of miles away," she replied. "There were only a few. That doesn't mean they came from our guys."

"I doubt anyone was hunting this time of year and so close to dark," Kane informed her.

"I know that too," she replied.

"Why didn't the police arrive?" Kane asked and now turned on his seat. "If your husband called them, they should have been here by now."

"There's nothing we can do at the moment," Jackie insisted. "We can't call anyone, and we can't run around in the dark looking for our friends either. Our only option is to remain here and wait for them to return. Once the sun is up, we can look for them."

§

Scorpio set her night vision binoculars on the step alongside her then glanced at Zack on the step near the bottom. She stared at his profile a long moment then tensed and looked away. Her attention suddenly shifted to something deep within the woods. They'd heard animals roaming about within the woods, but this sounded bigger. Scorpio snatched her binoculars at the same moment Zack lifted his rifle while straightening. He peered through the night vision scope and scanned the same area as Scorpio. He'd heard it too.

"Stay here," Zack ordered gruffly just loud enough for her to hear.

He darted toward the woods with his rifle in position and prepared to fire. Scorpio continued to scan the woods in the direction Zack headed. She suddenly tensed to another sound. This one came from beneath the plane. She silently set down the binoculars, making as little noise as possible, and then leaped over the railing, facing the underbelly of the plane. A man dressed in black jumped with surprise to her stealthy appearance. He had a wrench in his hand while heading toward the front of the plane and the engine compartment. The man raised the wrench and lunged for Scorpio. Due to the limited space beneath the plane, Scorpio snap kicked him, hitting him beneath his chin. His head snapped upward and struck the underbelly of the plane with a loud clunk. Jackie and Kane were suddenly heard moving around within the fuselage almost certainly having heard the clunk.

The slightly dazed man straightened and reached inside his jacket for what Scorpio was certain would be a weapon in a shoulder holster. Scorpio kicked his arm, preventing him from reaching whatever he intended to remove. She then punched him twice in the face before going low and sweeping his legs out from beneath him. The man crashed to the ground just as Darth leaped off the plane steps while loudly snarling. He was already too late and had missed the excitement. Jackie and Kane were only steps behind the dog and leaped over the plane steps on opposite sides like a synchronized militia. They hurried for Scorpio.

"He had tools. He was going to sabotage the plane," Scorpio announced then pointed to the woods behind her. "Zack went that way into the woods. I'm certain there are more of them out there."

Before the words even left Scorpio's mouth, Darth took off for the woods, possibly having heard something or maybe understanding the word 'Zack' and reacting to the direction she pointed. Jackie removed her semiautomatic and was about to speak when Kane bolted for the woods in the direction the dog had gone. Jackie stared after him and shook her head. She then looked at Scorpio and indicated the opposite side of the plane.

"Take a lookout position, in case there are more of them near the hangar," Jackie instructed.

Scorpio uncertainly removed the semiautomatic from the back of her pants and approached the opposite side of the plane while Jackie swiftly zip tied the man's wrists to the plane's front wheel. Scorpio's attention shifted to the hangar.

"There's someone inside the hangar," she announced while glancing back at Jackie.

Jackie hurried to join Scorpio while replacing her semiautomatic to her hidden holster and removed the assault rifle slung over her shoulder. She raised the weapon and peered through the night vision scope.

"Stay here," Jackie ordered then cautiously approached the hangar.

Despite Jackie's orders, Scorpio silently moved alongside Jackie with the semiautomatic in one hand and the night vision binoculars in the other. Jackie glanced over her shoulder to the woman following her.

"I told you to stay with the plane," Jackie insisted. "These people are playing for keeps."

"I've played that game more than once," Scorpio informed her, "and I'm still alive."

Jackie groaned and reluctantly gave in. She paused by the open hangar door, placed her back against the wall, and looked at Scorpio. She motioned Scorpio lower, indicated the binoculars, and then the hanger. Scorpio moved closer to the opening, pressed her back against the wall, and crouched down. She peered into the hangar with the binoculars and scanned the cluttered area.

"Nothing," Scorpio whispered. "Someone could be hiding among the clutter."

"Keep low, stick close, and cover me," Jackie ordered in a stern whisper.

Scorpio nodded and watched as Jackie stepped into the open doorway with her large weapon aimed while peering through the night vision scope. As Jackie entered the hangar, Scorpio followed while keeping watch on their backs as well as to their sides. While looking to her right through the night vision binoculars, Scorpio heard a sound from her left. The moment she caught a glimpse of someone lunging for her, she spun into a roundhouse kick. She struck the man in the chest and sent him backward into a pile of clutter with a loud crash. Jackie spun with her weapon and aimed it at the man now on the floor. The unarmed man leaped to his feet. Rather than shoot him, since he was unarmed, Jackie kicked him in the groin then in the face, dropping him back into the clutter on the floor. Scorpio heard a faint clunk to her right. She spun while peering through the binoculars and saw a man with a large wrench in his hand now lunging for Jackie's turned back.

Scorpio gasped with surprise, raised her semiautomatic, and fired three times at the man, missing with each shot. Jackie spun with her assault rifle, saw the man through the scope and took him out with one shot. The man was thrown to the hangar floor. Jackie stared with disbelief at Scorpio through the darkness.

"That has to be some of the worst shooting I've ever seen," Jackie gasped.

Scorpio fidgeted. "Kane and I haven't handled firearms much," she admitted.

Jackie shook her head then handed Scorpio a pair of zip ties. "Tie that up," she announced while indicating the man on the floor.

§

Kane followed Zack through the woods while Darth now took the lead and sniffed the entire area in search of something to chase. Zack had his assault rifle aimed while staring through the night scope. Kane kept watch behind them while holding his semiautomatic. Whatever they had seen or heard seemed to have vanished. They heard several shots fired from the old hangar, alerting both men.

"Scorpio," Kane gasped with alarm.

"Darth," Zack announced then pointed back to the abandoned landing field and commanded the dog in German. "Suchen Jackie."

Darth snarled and raced back toward the abandoned airfield with a mission in mind. Zack motioned Kane back to the clearing containing the planes. As they hurried back for the airfield, nearly silent shots were fired at them from beneath the plane, sending them back into the woods and behind some trees for shelter. The man carrying an assault rifle with a silencer darted out from under the plane and hurried toward the woods not far from them while following his freed teammate. Kane aimed his semiautomatic and fired several shots missing both men. Zack watched the second man through the scope of his assault rifle, caught him in the crosshairs, and squeezed the trigger just before he was about to disappear into the woods. The man's head nearly exploded from the shot, dropping him to the forest floor. The man in front got away. Zack lowered his assault rifle and glared at Kane, who stared with shock and horror at the shot Zack made.

"Please tell me your sister is a better shot than you," Zack remarked.

"Actually, she's worse," Kane shyly admitted while fidgeting.

"Your mother was a better shot than that," Zack huffed and snatched the gun from Kane. "You'll get this back when you learn to shoot worth a shit."

Kane frowned and seemed somewhat ashamed. Zack headed into the clearing with his assault rifle leading the way and scanned the area. They hurried past the planes and for the hangar. Jackie and Scorpio appeared from the hangar with the bound man and Darth keeping a watchful eye on him for added measure.

"How many friends do you suppose he has out there?" Jackie asked while looking toward the dark woods.

"One less than before," Zack remarked. "No thanks to the boy who can't shoot to save his life." Zack then indicated the bound man. "Are you going to let me ask the prisoner how many friends he has out there?"

Jackie tensed, eyed the prisoner, and then looked back at Zack. "Normally, I'd say not a chance," she announced, "but we need to know what happened to the rest of our team, and I'm tired of asking nicely."

Zack suddenly grinned while staring at Jackie. "You finally grew a pair," he announced then grabbed the man by his shirt collar and pulled him away from Scorpio.

Scorpio suddenly tensed and eyed the situation. "What's he going to do?" she asked.

Jackie shook her head and groaned. "Don't ask," she remarked. "You don't want to know."

As Zack pushed the man toward the planes, they heard the sound of four-wheelers approaching. All four became alert and aimed their weapons, except Kane, who had lost his weapons privileges. As they watched the clearing with anticipation, Kirk, Stone, and Bogart rode the four-wheelers into the area near the planes. All four relaxed when they saw it was just their teammates. Kane and Scorpio ran to greet Stone, relieved he was okay.

Scorpio hugged Stone. "I was worried about you," she announced then pulled back to meet his gaze. "What happened? Why were you gone so long?"

"We ran into some trouble that kept following us," Stone informed her then indicated the four-wheelers. "We were hiking back when we found these bad boys parked half a mile from here."

"We heard gunshots," Kirk announced and eyed the man in Zack's custody. "There has to be others. There were four more quads where we found these."

"We only ran into four of them," Jackie remarked.

"One got away," Zack muttered with disapproval, although he refrained from glaring at Kane.

Kane shifted uncomfortably at the comment.

Bogart looked around with concern. "Monroe hasn't returned yet with the others?"

"No," Jackie informed her brother. "The local law never made an appearance either."

"I was just going to question the prisoner about Gil and Sal," Zack informed them.

"I think we know where to find them," Kirk announced, "but we're going to need a plan. That place is heavily guarded."

"That's okay," Zack announced while grinning and indicated the bound man. "I think we'll have all the information we need in the next hour."

"Really?" Kane asked with surprise. "You think you can get him to talk?"

Zack sized up the man, who appeared emotionless and unwilling to give up any information. "I give him two pinkies before he tells us everything we want to know."

The man's expression dropped as he eyed Zack. Zack grinned with a little too much enthusiasm. Jackie grimaced at the thought. Scorpio, Kane, and Stone stared at Zack with horror and hoped he was only joking.

Chapter 46

Wednesday, July 16th. The small repair garage in town was dimly lit by the kerosene lamp that had been turned down to half its brightness. It was a little after one o'clock in the morning. Mac remained restless while in something resembling a light sleep. Despite the garage being locked up tight, she remained anxious about their situation. Maverick occupied the comforter on the floor not far from hers. Mac woke from her light sleep when she heard movement not far from her. The sound she heard was just Maverick moving around. Not surprising, Maverick moved alongside her and spooned against her from behind. For appearance sake, he had waited until the others were asleep.

Mac tensed slightly as if anticipating Maverick's visit. "Not a good idea," she scoffed just loud enough for him to hear.

"It's okay," Maverick announced close to her ear while clinging to her. "Rayner and Monroe are asleep. I'll move back before they wake."

"That's not what I meant," Mac snarled while remaining tense.

There was a moment of silence. Maverick moved to his elbow without releasing her and attempted to look at her profile where she lay.

"You aren't still mad about that incident with Monroe, are you?" he asked. "He deserved to be hit."

Mac pulled away from him and sat up. She glared at Maverick, who sat up as well while staring at her with a puzzled look.

"You behaved like a jealous boyfriend tonight," she scoffed just loud enough for him to hear while glaring demandingly at him. "I made my position regarding our extracurricular activity clear."

"I wasn't acting like a jealous boyfriend," he insisted. "Kane would have defended you the same. What we do in private has nothing to do with what happened with Monroe. It had nothing to do with jealousy."

Mac stared at him a moment then raised her brows. "I'm sure you realize I'd had sex with Monroe," she announced.

Maverick stared at her but didn't react to the comment. He seemed to cast it aside and managed a tiny shrug. "It's none of my business," he replied. "I was just defending my teammate. That's all."

"You didn't like that he was talking to me," Mac informed him. "You didn't want him partnering with me on our little field trip, and you attacked him when he insinuated I'd dump Kane to join their team. That sounds like a jealous boyfriend to me."

"He was the one acting like a jealous boyfriend," Maverick remarked while studying her in the dim lighting. "He was purposely pushing my buttons."

"And you let him," Mac quietly launched back. "You're becoming too attached, and I need you to back off. We agreed to fulfill each other's sexual needs and nothing more. If I want to have sex with Monroe or every man I meet, it's none of your concern."

Maverick tensed a moment while staring at her. He nodded in agreement then suddenly turned angry and shook his head. "No, I'm not playing that game," he finally blurted out a little louder than anticipated. "You're right. I've become too attached. I've enjoyed our time together and sex for the sake of sex, but it's no longer enough."

Mac raked her fingers through her hair, frowned, and looked away.

Maverick sprang to his feet and no longer cared about waking the others. "If we're not in a relationship, the exclusive kind, I'm through hooking up with you."

Mac turned her head and stared at him with some surprise, although she probably shouldn't have been.

"So go ahead, fuck Monroe," Maverick lashed out in anger while pulling on his boots. "Fuck your way through his entire team for all I care. When you finally come to your senses and realize it was a relationship you actually wanted--" Maverick held his breath and straightened proudly. "I'll be there to take you back."

Maverick headed across the dimly lit garage for the door. He unlocked it, opened the door, and left, shutting the door behind him. Mac held her head a moment then glanced at Monroe and Rayner, who were now sitting up as well. Both men appeared slightly uncomfortable then acted as if nothing happened and lay back down.

§

Maverick sat on the curb not far from the garage, held his head, and seemed to collect his thoughts as well as his emotions. He rubbed the back of his neck, groaned softly, and then cursed under his breath. He lifted his head, and his eyes instinctively strayed to the house across the street where he and Mac had found supplies and shared an intimate moment. He squinted at what appeared to be a light coming from one of the upstairs rooms. Had they not properly extinguished one of the candles? He stood and headed across the street for the house. Maverick entered the house and removed his borrowed semiautomatic from the back of his pants just in case. He paused within the foyer and listened a moment.

When he didn't hear anything move or any creaks coming from the house, he approached the stairs and headed up them. Despite that he was almost certain he was alone, he still walked cautiously and quietly up the stairs. Maverick paused just outside the master bedroom and saw the glow of a candle coming from the room. Maverick stepped into the doorway with his gun aimed, saw the burning candle, and then swept his eyes across the room. The room was empty. Despite being positive they blew out the candles, it would appear as if one hadn't been properly extinguished. Maverick replaced the weapon to the back of his pants as he approached the dresser and blew out the candle. The room darkened considerably. As he was about to turn, he saw someone else's reflection in the dresser mirror. Maverick spun around while reaching for his weapon.

§

Mac curled on her side on her makeshift bed and stared across the dimly lit garage. She frowned with frustration, rolled onto her back, and eyed the vacant pillow alongside hers. She groaned, scratched her mussed hair, and sat up. Rayner and Monroe appeared to be asleep, although it was difficult to tell in the dim lighting. Maverick had only been gone twenty minutes. How it was possible for guys to fall back asleep so fast was a mystery. Mac sighed with defeat then slipped into her shoes and sprang to her feet. Monroe opened his eyes and looked at her, indicating he hadn't been asleep after all.

"You may want to let him cool off a while longer," Monroe informed her.

"I'm not going after him," she insisted defensively. "For safety reasons, we need to keep that door locked. If he wants to brood, he can do it in the garage."

"Yeah, that won't start another argument," Monroe muttered and shut his eyes.

Rayner groaned and sat up. He pulled on his shoes, catching Mac's attention.

"Where do you think you're going?" she demanded.

Rayner glared at her as he stood. "I'm going to talk to Maverick," he insisted. "If you talk to him, we're going to be subjected to another round of who's fucking whom."

Mac folded her arms across her chest while glaring her irritation with Rayner.

"It's really none of your concern," she informed him. "This is between Maverick and me."

"No," Rayner announced with a sigh. "You made it perfectly clear that there's nothing between you and Maverick. Truth be told; you barely even know him. I've known him longer, and we have something in common. Scorpio tore my heart out and trampled upon it once too. Trust me; it's better if I talk to him than you."

Mac frowned as Rayner left the garage.

Monroe sat up on his sleeping bag and groaned then eyed Mac. "Even the computer geek is mad at you," he remarked. "You certainly know how to alienate yourself."

She glared at him with annoyance. "Fuck off, Monroe."

"Three out of three," he muttered. "That's the Mac we all know."

§

Rayner stood outside the garage and looked around the dimly lit town. There was no sign of Maverick, and every building was dark. A faint, dull clunk came from the house across the street. Rayner eyed the house a moment, assumed it had to be Maverick, and ventured across the street. The front door was partially open to the dark interior. Rayner pushed the door open further, removed his cell phone from his pocket, and used the light to see inside the foyer. Rayner entered the foyer and shined the light from his cell phone around the dark hallway and into the nearby rooms. A floorboard creaked behind him. Rayner spun around with his cell phone lighting the way. A large man dressed in black was startled by the reversal of his sneak attack but wasted little time throwing his large fist for Rayner's face.

Rayner gasped with surprise and threw himself to the foyer floor. There was a clunk on the stairs followed by the parting of air. When Rayner looked at the large man hovering over him, he saw the man clutching his bleeding leg where a knife was embedded in his upper thigh. Rayner caught a glimpse of Maverick on the stairs as he leaped over the railing and landed on the hallway floor. Unfortunately, he wasn't alone. Another man thundered down the stairs behind him. As the large man in the foyer cried out in agony while clutching his bleeding thigh, Rayner sprinted into action. He leaped to his feet, ripped the knife from the injured man's thigh, and rammed his knee into his groin. The large man fell to his knees in agony.

When Rayner turned, Maverick was fighting the man who had been chasing him. Maverick grabbed the man's wrist, keeping his gun pointed away from him, and punched him across the face. Rayner saw the weapon and lunged for the armed man while Maverick punched him again. Rayner stabbed the man in the hand, forcing him to drop the weapon. As it fell to the floor with a clatter, Rayner dove for the gun. Maverick simultaneously yanked the knife from the man's hand and plunged it into his neck. The man gasped and dropped to his knees. Rayner spun with the semiautomatic toward the big man, who had been temporarily rendered immobile, and aimed the weapon.

The large man had already recovered from the groin shot, and, despite his bleeding thigh, he found the strength to punch Rayner in the face. Rayner was thrown back several steps and struck the hall table with a crash. Maverick was about to throw his knife at the big man, when his attacker turned and punched Maverick as well. Maverick flew against the banister with enough force to crack the rung. The big man knocked the knife from his hand and punched him in the stomach, doubling him over.

Chapter 47

Mac hurried to the garage door, moved the tarp, and looked out the window. She scanned the dark town attempting to figure out where the sound had come from.

"I thought I heard something," she announced.

"Yeah, me too," Monroe announced while slipping hastily into his shoes.

Mac continued to scan the area when the house across the street caught her attention. The front door stood open. She looked back at Monroe.

"The front door to the house across the street is open," Mac informed him and threw open the door.

Monroe grabbed his shoulder holster and slipped into it while running toward Mac and the door. Mac ran out of the garage with Monroe only a few steps behind her. She drew her weapon on her sprint across the street. As she leaped onto the porch, Monroe was directly on her tail. Mac positioned herself alongside the open doorway to the dark house while Monroe took a flanking position behind her. She bolted into the foyer and looked around with her gun aimed. Monroe shined his flashlight around the small foyer and allowed it to fall upon the dead man not far from the stairs. Except for the dead man in the foyer, the house seemed unusually quiet. Monroe shined his light in several directions.

"There," Mac cried out and pointed to the floor.

Monroe shined his light at the decorative knife on the floor. Mac grabbed Maverick's knife, which was covered in blood. She then saw a discarded cell phone not far from it. Mac grabbed the cell phone, hit a button, and stared at the familiar picture of Scorpio and Rayner.

"This is Rayner's cell phone and Maverick's knife," she informed Monroe then used the light from the cell phone to scan the foyer. "Something's happened to them."

Monroe followed droplets of blood along the hallway toward the kitchen. "I have a lot of blood here," he announced. "Someone's been injured badly."

As he followed the trail of blood, Mac kept watch on their backside and hurried after him. They entered the kitchen where the blood continued out the back door. Both heard the familiar sound of a car's engine in the distance. A vehicle could be seen near the edge of the woods despite the absence of headlights. Monroe and Mac ran for the woods as a jeep took off for the dirt road. They were nearly to the road when headlights from another jeep came on and temporarily blinded them. The open top jeep raced for them in an attempt to run them down. Mac and Monroe jumped in opposite directions from the jeep's path. Both rolled across the ground and sat up with their weapons aimed, firing simultaneously upon the men in the jeep.

The man in the back of the jeep attempted to fire at them, but he was struck in the chest by Mac's gunfire. Monroe sprang to his feet, aimed carefully, and fired, striking the driver. The driver took the bullet to the back of his head and slumped against the wheel. The jeep swerved and struck the corner of the house, successfully stopping it. Mac and Monroe ran for the banged-up jeep and checked on the men. Both were dead. Mac grabbed the driver and pulled him from the seat while Monroe flung the dead man from the back.

"They have Rayner and Maverick," Mac announced while leaping into the driver's seat. "We have to go after them."

Monroe jumped into the back of the jeep as Mac threw the vehicle into reverse. He attempted to keep his balance as the jeep backed up several feet. As she turned the vehicle, Monroe jumped into the passenger seat.

"They took the road Deidra used to bring us here," Monroe announced and pointed toward the woods. "They could be heading to the abandoned airfield."

Mac threw the jeep into drive, slightly grinding the gears, and headed for the dirt road away from town. Mac was obviously in pain while attempting to steer with her bad arms, but she didn't let it stop her. Despite the speed Mac drove on the bumpy back road, there was no sign of the other jeep. She finally slowed down, keeping the high beams on, and both scanned the area.

"Do you think they turned off?" Monroe announced while looking around.

"Turned off where?" Mac demanded while keeping her eyes peeled for any hidden paths. "There was no place to turn off or even pull over."

"You'd better take it easy," Monroe informed her. "This road is in bad shape and so is the jeep."

"They have to be ahead of us," she insisted. "If I slow down, we'll lose them for sure."

There was a loud pop, and the jeep suddenly jerked to the left. Mac struggled to maintain control of the jeep, which sent shockwaves of pain through her bad shoulder. The vibration and sound told both they had blown the front tire. Mac stopped the jeep, threw it into park, and leaped out on her side. She checked the flat front tire. The damage done by the crash into the corner of the building had caused enough damage that the tire was shredded by the bent metal. Monroe rounded the vehicle and eyed the damage.

"We need to pull that metal away from the tire," Monroe informed her. "I'll do that while you get the jack and remove the spare tire off the back."

Mac cursed and kicked the front fender before hurrying for the tire attached to the back of the jeep. Monroe just about had the metal pulled away from the shredded tire by the time Mac rolled the spare tire toward the front of the jeep. Despite being in pain, she didn't let her injured shoulder slow her down. Monroe leaned against the jeep while panting from the effort it took to pull the metal away from the tire. As Mac feverishly loosened the lug nuts on the flat tire, Monroe watched her. She was clearly irritated and took it out on the lug nuts.

Monroe shifted uncomfortably and frowned. "I'm sorry about what happened with you and Maverick," he announced almost timidly.

She didn't bother looking at him and concentrated on her work. "What do you have to be sorry about?" she snapped. "It wasn't your fault he turned all jealous."

"It may have been," Monroe remarked while frowning. "It's possible I egged him on a bit." He groaned and shook his head. "Sometimes, I do dicky things."

Mac cast a look at Monroe and raised her brows as if silently agreeing with him.

"I guess I was still a little bothered by the way we left things that day at the airport in Colorado Springs," he announced. "You were adamant about once and done yet there you were carrying on with Maverick. I suppose I was the jealous one."

Mac resumed changing the tire. Once she had the lug nuts removed, she used the jack to raise the front of the jeep. Monroe stepped in and removed the tire for her. She'd put enough strain on her injured shoulder, and although she didn't complain about it, Monroe knew she had to be in pain. Mac didn't protest. Monroe placed the new one on, and hand tightened the lug nuts.

"That's nice of you to defend Maverick," Mac announced then lowered the jack.

Monroe took over and tightened the lug nuts the rest of the way to give Mac's shoulder a break. Mac straightened and watched him work on the tire.

"Even if you were jealous and had egged him on," Mac continued, "that doesn't change the fact that Maverick got too attached."

"What is it with you?" Monroe asked while shaking his head. He finished with the tire iron then stood and faced her. "What is so wrong with being in a committed relationship? No one says you have to get married and pop out a dozen kids. Is there something wrong with attachments?"

"Yes," Mac replied, which surprised Monroe. "Eventually, everyone leaves. They die; they skip out. Does it matter? I don't want to be burdened with feelings toward others, and I certainly don't want my life complicated with them having feelings for me."

When Monroe didn't respond, Mac seemed compelled to look at him. He stared at her with a strange look.

"Then you're already screwed," Monroe informed her. "Kane loves you. Maybe not in a sexual sense, but he does. Deny it all you want, but I know you feel the same way about him. You're so consumed with not getting attached to a lover; you completely missed that brotherly love coming from your new friend."

Mac tensed slightly then wiped her hands on a rag. "I don't love Kane."

"I was there, Mac," Monroe informed her while raising a clever brow. "When Zack was beating his ass, you were frightened for him."

"That doesn't mean I love him," she scoffed. "He's a foolish boy."

"A foolish boy whom you love," Monroe replied. "Stop denying your feelings toward others. If you never let anyone in, you're going to die alone and lonely."

Mac raised her brows along with a tiny smirk. "And yet I'm okay with that."

Monroe groaned and shook his head. "I tried, Mac," he announced with defeat. "I honestly tried. We need to get to the airfield, collect the others, and search for the guys."

Chapter 48

It was nearly three o'clock in the morning. Maverick opened his eyes to dark nothingness surrounding him where he lay against a cold, hard metal surface. The stench of decay was overpowering, and it caused him to gag. Maverick reached above him and immediately met the same smooth metal just a few inches above his body. His hands then moved to the side where he was met by more metal just beyond his shoulders.

"Oh," Maverick groaned with concern while feeling the walls while choking on the foul stench. "This is not good."

He pressed his hands beyond his head and felt the metal just inches behind him. Maverick pressed his hands against the metal alongside him and pushed his body. Instead of his body sliding on the metal beneath him, the entire tray slid and struck the enclosure beyond his booted feet.

"Please don't tell me I'm in a fucking morgue," Maverick muttered loud enough to hear his voice echo within the metal container surrounding him.

"You're in a fucking morgue," Rayner's voice announced dryly from somewhere nearby.

"Rayner?" Maverick cried out and turned his head toward the familiar voice despite not being able to see anything. "Where the hell are you?"

"Judging by the sound of your movement," Rayner announced with little emotion, "I'm guessing I'm in the drawer beneath you."

"What sort of crazy shit is this?" Maverick demanded and pounded on the metal wall. It echoed loudly. "And how the hell did you get into this nightmare?"

"I'm not sure," Rayner replied. "I vaguely remember hitting a wall."

Maverick then groaned and placed his hand over his eyes. "That's right," he muttered. "We had our asses handed to us in that house."

"I'm going to assume we're no longer in that house," Rayner remarked with little emotion.

"Maybe a funeral home or a doctor's office," Maverick insisted. "Although I don't remember seeing either when we walked through town." He again gagged on the stench within the confined space. "What the hell is that smell?"

"I could venture a guess, but I don't think you really want to know," Rayner informed him in a dry, flat tone. "Any idea how to escape our little tubes of death? I'm not exactly claustrophobic, but this is mildly terrifying."

"You don't sound terrified," Maverick commented while looking around despite not being able to see anything.

"Probably because I'm trying to keep from pissing my pants," Rayner replied. "Tell me you have a plan."

Maverick felt the area beyond his head. "The wall is solid behind my head, so the door must be at my feet."

"There's no interior handle, if that's what you're hoping for," Rayner informed him.

"Not exactly," Maverick replied. "I'm going for brute force."

Maverick slid further down on the metal tray, pulled his knees up as high as the ceiling would allow, and kicked the door with both feet. The tray shot backward and hit the wall beyond his head. The force was enough to rattle the tray as well as jolt Maverick.

"The trays slide, you know," Rayner announced matter-of-factly.

"Yeah, I realize that now," Maverick huffed. "Can you offer any *useful* information?"

"Apply *bruit* force to the right side of the door," Rayner replied. "That's where the latch is located. It's the most vulnerable part of the door."

"How would you know what side the latch is on?" Maverick asked while running his foot against the metal door. "I don't feel anything different from the right and left."

"The ping test."

"The ping test?"

"Yes," Rayner replied.

Rayner pounded on the metal to his left. There was a low thump. Rayner then pounded on the metal to his right. It sounded hollow.

"That hollow sound means there are freezers to our right but not our left," Rayner insisted. "Morgue doors latch to the inside."

"How would you know that?" Maverick asked with some surprise.

"I installed security cameras in several hospitals before moving to your town," he announced. "Every morgue door I've seen latched inward not outward."

"You're like an encyclopedia of useless knowledge," Maverick remarked.

"And yet here I am giving you useful advice," Rayner replied. "Brace your arms against the sides of the drawer. I'll push up on your tray with my feet. Together we'll hold your tray in place while you kick the door."

"Okay," Maverick announced.

Rayner thrust his legs against the tray above him while Maverick braced his hands against the walls on either side. He coiled his legs back as far as possible and thrust both feet into the door to the right. The door flew open with almost no resistance, struck something, and a sharp yowl followed. Maverick heard the male cry and thrust the tray from the drawer with added vigor. The tray fully extended with a bang, but Maverick was already toppling off before it stopped. He sprang to his feet and prepared for a fight. John writhed around on the cold floor while Gil stood nearby and aimed the cattle prod at Maverick. Maverick saw Gil and breathed a sigh of relief.

"I never thought I'd be happy to see you again," Maverick announced.

"Who's out there?" Rayner called from the lower drawer. "What's happening?"

"It's the guys we were looking for," Maverick called back then eyed Gil and the cattle prod that he had yet to lower. "You know we came here to rescue you, right?"

"I'm not getting a strong 'rescue' vibe right now," Gil remarked.

Maverick was quick to help John to his feet. "Sorry about, you know, hitting you with the morgue door," he announced. "You must be Mac's former boss, Sal."

John clutched his shoulder and gave Maverick a puzzled look. "Mac?"

"No, that's John," Gil informed Maverick. "Sal is holding down the fort in the front of the building."

"Maverick," Rayner scolded from his lower drawer.

Maverick managed a tiny smile, held his finger up in the air, and then opened Rayner's drawer. He pulled the tray out, allowing Rayner to spring to his feet.

Gil finally lowered the cattle prod. "Is Mac okay?"

"Yeah, she's fine," Maverick insisted. "I mean, she was pretty banged up after the attack, but she's fine now." He then considered the comment. "At least, she was until we were captured."

"My God, stop your babbling," Rayner scoffed then looked at Gil. "We arrived with your friends."

"So they're planning a rescue?" Gil asked.

"We had split up while searching for you," Rayner admitted. "Things sort of went sideways, and we were separated from Mac and Monroe. The others were back at the plane waiting for some federal agent to send some local deputies."

"As encouraging as that sounds, it's not safe here," Gil informed them while casting looks around the morgue.

"Where exactly is here?" Rayner asked. "We were unconscious when they brought us here."

"Some old mental asylum deep in the woods," John informed them.

"We need to get the two of you back to the security of the game room," Gil insisted.

"How did you know you'd find us here?" Maverick asked as they headed toward the morgue door.

"We saw a vehicle approach and head around back," John informed them while gingerly rubbing his shoulder. "We had hoped to reach the men dropping you off, but we arrived too late to catch them."

"We assumed they were up to something, so we checked here and the infirmary," Gil concluded.

"Okay, that's not at all dark and mysterious," Maverick muttered.

"We'll explain everything once we're back in the game room," Gil informed them.

Chapter 49

Four o'clock in the morning. Jackie sat in the cockpit of the rental plane and stared out the windshield into the darkness. She was supposed to be sleeping, but she couldn't close her eyes for more than a few minutes at a time. After hearing Kirk and Bogart's accounts of what happened near the abandoned building they'd found, she was even more concerned for Monroe, Mac, and Kane's other friends. They still had no idea what happened to Gil or Sal, and Holden's backup never made an appearance. She hated to admit that they were flying alone and blind. Zack collapsed into the co-pilot's seat and just about startled her. Jackie had been halfway between dozing off and stranded in her own thoughts. She eyed Zack as he propped his feet on the console. He folded his arms across his abdomen and shut his eyes as if about to nap.

"Did you get anything from our prisoner?" Jackie pressed for an answer.

"What do you think?" Zack teased and didn't bother opening his eyes.

Jackie held her breath at the next question. "And?"

"And what?" he asked while casting a look at her. "Are you actually asking about my methods?"

Jackie shifted uncomfortably in the pilot's seat. "You didn't actually cut off his pinkies, did you?"

"No, of course not," Zack announced with little emotion then flicked two molars across the console. "Too much blood and screaming."

Jackie eyed the molars on the flight console and made a face. "What did he tell you?"

"Three dozen armed men guarding the institution Kirk found," Zack informed her. "A few rifles with scopes but no automatic weapons."

"So we're only outmanned not outgunned, huh?" she teased although she still couldn't seem to relax.

Zack opened an eye and cast a look at Jackie. "I like our odds."

"You always like our odds," Jackie remarked then shifted uncomfortably. "The four of us can't take on that many armed men."

"Seven," Zack informed her. "You forgot Stone and the kids."

She suddenly raised her brows. "They may be your kids," Jackie announced, "but they're not you. They can't shoot worth a shit. You're not dragging them into a war without proper weapons training."

"And what's your big plan?" Zack just about demanded now returning to life and straightening in his seat.

"We need to fly this piece of shit to the nearest airport and call for backup," she insisted with some irritation. "The backup that never came."

"Probably because the law is helping whoever is behind this," Zack informed her. "We've wasted enough time. Gil and Sal could be in serious trouble. There's no telling what's happened to them within the walls of that building. With or without you, I'm going in."

"Without your kids," Jackie firmly insisted.

"If the boy wants to go, he's in," Zack countered.

Jackie glared at him in disapproval.

"The girl isn't ready," he agreed. "You can take her with you to the nearest airport for backup."

Jackie was about to protest Zack's decision to take Kane with him when they were interrupted.

"You want me to go with you on your mission?" Kane asked from the cockpit doorway.

Jackie didn't even look back when she heard Kane's excited voice. She glared at Zack revealing her annoyance. Zack stared back at her and tensed.

"Now I know how annoying it is when I do that," Zack remarked. He drew a deep breath and climbed out of his seat to face Kane. "If you think you're ready--"

Kane hugged Zack. "I'm touched--deeply."

Zack remained rigid and somewhat stunned by Kane's affectionate reaction. "Must that really involve touching me?" he remarked.

Kane jumped back and laughed while grinning. "Sorry," he announced and held his hands up. "I'm guilty of being overly affectionate. Just ask Mac."

Zack frowned at the comment. "Thanks, I'd rather not," he muttered.

"Sorry," Kane remarked while tensing. "I forgot the two of you had a falling out. Personally, I love her to death. The feeling isn't exactly mutual."

"Enough with Mac," Zack snarled then returned to his seat and rubbed his temple.

"Yeah, sure," Kane announced and backed out of the cockpit. "I'm going to catch a few winks before we relieve Stone and Bogart."

Kane left the cockpit, once again leaving Jackie and Zack alone. Zack groaned and rubbed his eyes. Jackie just glared at him. He avoided looking at her.

"I don't want to argue with you over this," Zack remarked under his breath.

"I'm not ready?" Scorpio suddenly demanded loudly from the cockpit doorway.

Zack lowered his hand from his eyes, looked at the pilot's seat, and met Jackie's gaze.

Jackie raised her brows and offered a cocky smirk. "I'm guessing it's not me you're about to argue with," Jackie informed him then leaned back in her seat and closed her eyes.

§

Kane sat in the front seat closest to the cockpit with one foot on the seat and his knee against his chest while watching his sister and Zack engage in a shouting match.

"How can you say I'm not stable enough to handle your little coup d'état?" Scorpio lashed out in anger from where she stood facing Zack in the cockpit doorway.

"Your immature outbursts speak for themselves," Zack replied with little reaction to the irate young woman.

Scorpio squinted at Zack. "Apparently, I get that from my father," she snapped back.

"Right from the terrible two's to a rebellious teenager, huh?" Zack muttered.

"Typical man," Scorpio scoffed as her eyes narrowed. "Propping up the son while discarding the daughter as unworthy and fragile."

Zack stared at Scorpio with surprise. "I assure you; that is not the case," he snapped back. "Jackie's my partner, and I'm pretty sure she's a woman. I helped train her myself. She's the best there is."

"Thank you," Jackie called out from the cockpit.

"Shut up," Zack snarled back at Jackie. "You're not helping!"

"Will all of you shut up," Kirk shouted from the back of the plane. "Some of us are trying to sleep on this flight from hell!"

Kirk was easily ignored by Scorpio and Zack.

"Out of the two of us," Scorpio announced while indicating Kane, "I'm the better fighter."

"I wouldn't go that far," Kane muttered from his front row seat.

Scorpio sneered at her brother. "Shut up," she snarled then looked back at Zack and folded her arms across her chest. "If he's going; I'm going."

"It could be dangerous," Kane informed his sister with some concern. "If Jackie's not going--"

Scorpio shot a look at Kane. "Oh, now you think I'm fragile and helpless too?" she launched hotly. "You *know* what I'm capable of doing."

Kane eyed Zack and shrugged. "She does have a pretty impressive 'psycho' mode."

"That's it," Zack snarled and waved his hands firmly. "Neither of you are going."

"What the hell--?" Kane lashed out in a mild temper tantrum as his feet hit the floor. He glared at Scorpio. "Look what you've done now!"

"Jesus, Kane," Scorpio shouted back in annoyance. "It's not as if he can send you to your room. Stop trying to impress him. He may be our biological father, but he's nothing to either of us."

Kane's expression dropped. "Scorpio," he scolded. "The man has feelings."

"Not really," Mac muttered from the plane doorway.

Everyone looked at the plane steps and saw Mac standing in the doorway to the fuselage.

"What the hell is going on here?" Mac demanded. "We could hear you arguing a mile away."

Kane leaped from his seat and rushed for Mac. She attempted to take a step back to avoid him but bumped into Monroe, who blocked her only escape. Kane threw his arms around Mac and hugged her as if he'd never let go.

"I was worried when we didn't hear from you," Kane announced without releasing her.

Mac remained stiff then gently patted Kane's back. "I'm fine," she replied. "But we have problems."

Kane released her, took a step back, and stared into her eyes with concern. "What happened?"

Jackie appeared in the cockpit doorway and stared at Monroe, who frowned while attempting to hide his look of shame. Scorpio's expression dropped as she stared behind Monroe then looked at Mac.

"Where's Rayner?" Scorpio suddenly asked.

"That's part of the problem," Mac delicately replied.

§

Scorpio rushed down the plane steps with Kane on her heels. Her mood was mounting rage, leaving Kane mildly apprehensive about chasing after her. Scorpio approached Stone, who was on guard duty with Bogart.

"I know you're upset, Scorp," Kane announced while attempting to keep up with her, "but you have to get your head on straight. We're talking about three dozen, highly trained, heavily armed men."

Scorpio snatched the assault rifle from Stone, startling him. She tossed the weapon over her shoulder and headed for the nearby four-wheeler.

"What's going on?" Stone asked and hurried after them.

"They took Rayner and Maverick," Kane informed his friend.

"What?" Stone gasped while keeping pace with them.

Scorpio mounted the four-wheeler and glared at her brother. "I'm going after him, Kane," she lashed out then pointed an angry finger at the plane. "And *your* father isn't going to stop me."

"Stop this," Kane scolded. "You're not going in there by yourself. That's insane."

"I'm not being sidelined," she snapped back. "Rayner and Maverick are out there, and I'm getting them back. I don't need anyone's permission."

"You may not need anyone's permission, but that doesn't mean we won't stop you," Jackie announced now standing only a few feet away.

"You can try," Scorpio snapped and reached for the key to start the four-wheeler.

To her surprise, the key was gone. She looked back at Jackie, who dangled the key.

"I'm pretty sure I'll succeed," Jackie replied.

The banged-up jeep pulled alongside the four-wheeler, startling everyone. Mac sat behind the wheel, eyed Scorpio, and raised an arrogant brow.

"Get in," Mac snarled at Scorpio.

Scorpio leaped off the four-wheeler and ran for the jeep. Kane and Jackie lunged for Scorpio but missed her as she leaped into the back of the jeep.

"Meet you there," Mac announced then stomped on the gas pedal.

The jeep burned out on the deteriorating macadam. Kane, Scorpio, and Stone watched as the jeep careened for the dirt road and vanished into the darkness.

"That is not going to go over well," Jackie muttered and ran her fingers through her hair. "Anyone but Mac." She shook her head. "Zack is going to kill her."

"We need to go after them," Kane insisted with rising concern.

"We will," Jackie announced then turned to face Kane. "Mac may be a bit of a hot head, but she's not going in there alone. She has more sense than that."

"I'd better go after them," Stone insisted while extending his hand to Jackie for the keys. "They can't just drive up to the front gate. We need the element of surprise."

Jackie held her breath a moment then gave Stone the keys to the four-wheeler. Stone jumped on the quad and raced after the jeep. Jackie looked back at Kane.

"We have to rally the troops," Jackie informed him. "Come on."

Chapter 50

Gil and John escorted Rayner and Maverick through the hospital by the glow of the flashlight built into their cattle prods. All four headed in the direction of the game room. The two newcomers reacted with the same expressions as Gil and Sal had when they first ventured through the house of horrors. John and Gil were already indifferent to the experience.

"This is like the fun house from hell," Maverick muttered while casting looks at old and new bloodstains on the floors and walls.

They entered the lounge with its massive hole in the floor, which caught both men's attention.

Maverick eyed the hole and nodded with little emotion. "And just when I thought this place couldn't get any worse--" he remarked.

"You haven't seen the worst of it yet," John informed him while bringing up the rear.

Rayner strayed closer to the opening as they crossed the room and peered down into the messy kitchen below. "What's worse?" he mumbled.

"Roving bands of crazed cannibals," John replied matter-of-factly.

Maverick and Rayner exchanged looks then hurried after Gil to keep from being left behind.

"That was a joke, right?" Maverick asked while managing a tiny chuckle.

"Yeah, I wish," Gil muttered while lacking emotion. "Stay close and keep quiet."

All four left the patient's lounge and entered the massive, filthy lobby. Rayner and Maverick followed Gil into the game room while John brought up the rear. He then barricaded the door behind them.

Sal eyed the two new recruits and appeared curious. "Where'd you find these guys?" he asked.

"Oh, just lying around in the morgue," Gil replied with a straight expression. He then indicated Sal to Rayner and Maverick. "This is Sal." Gil then pointed to the two men. "Rayner and Maverick are Mac's new cohorts in crime. They came with Jackie and our rescue party."

Sal looked at both men and seemed surprised. "Oh, so they're the ones--?"

"Yeah," Gil replied and nodded. "They introduced themselves at the cemetery."

Sal then nodded with understanding. Rayner and Maverick eyed the man tied to the nearby chair, who seemed relaxed while watching them.

Maverick indicated the bound man. "Who's that?"

"That's Boris," Gil casually replied.

"Boris?" Rayner asked with some surprise and again eyed the bound man.

"He wouldn't give us his name, so we made one up for him," Sal informed him then eyed both men. "Is Mac okay? She'd been injured at the airport."

"A little more pissed than usual," Maverick replied then nodded. "But, yeah, she's fine."

"Thank God," Sal whispered then shifted uncomfortably. "Mac and I had a slight falling out. It's a long story."

"You're her former employer," Maverick remarked then raised his brow. "She mentioned you."

"For the record," Sal announced. "I'd forgiven her for attempting to steal my fifty million."

Maverick tensed and seemed unable to move while staring at Sal. "Fifty million?"

Rayner covered his eyes and groaned.

"She didn't mention that?" Sal asked him with some surprise.

"How exactly did she steal fifty million dollars?" Rayner asked with interest.

"Digital money," Sal explained. "There was this flash drive from my accountant." He then waved off Rayner. "She seduced Zack and tried to steal it. She never even made it out of the motel room with the thing. Water under the bridge. I understand temptation. She's been trying to make amends since, but no one wants to piss off Zack, so she's been on the outside looking in for quite some time."

Maverick stared at Sal with a somewhat befuddled look on his face. He seemed unable to grasp what he was hearing. "Mac *seduced* Zack?"

"I think the fifty million is the bigger picture here," John muttered.

"Mac trying to kill Zack for the money should be the bigger picture," Gil countered.

Maverick shot a look at Gil. "She seduced him then tried to kill him?"

"Most women Zack sleeps with try to kill him," Gil casually replied. "He's used to it."

Maverick shook his head with disbelief. "Mac slept with Scorpio's father?"

"Why are you so hung up on that?" Sal asked with a curious look.

"Because he's dating Mac," Rayner casually replied.

"No, I'm not," Maverick insisted.

"Sorry," Rayner replied then eyed Sal. "She dumped him earlier tonight."

"Can we get back to what's important here?" John demanded while glaring at the others. "What about this rescue?"

"Since we didn't find Mac and Monroe anywhere inside the asylum, we should assume they weren't captured," Rayner remarked.

"Then they'll attempt to regroup with the rest of the team," Gil insisted.

"Jackie's FBI husband contacted the local law to meet them there," Maverick added.

"I'd think they'd be able to follow the jeep tracks and find us here," Rayner announced.

"They already know we're here," Gil informed them. "The snipers in the woods were shooting at someone who was shooting back. I assumed the team had split up to find us. Once they regroup, they should be back. John and I have the guard's guns, so when they arrive, we'll be able to assist them from this end."

"Apart from the more than two dozen armed men guarding this facility," Sal began, "how many crazies do we think are trapped inside with us?"

"Hard to say," Gil responded. "They seem to travel in small packs."

"I've yet to see the same faces twice," John offered. "I think there's more than a dozen."

"We can't do much about the men outside the facility," Sal announced while conspiring, "but we can round up those inside and perhaps lock them somewhere. We don't need to be ambushed during our ambush. We have two cattle prods and keys to the kingdom."

"I noticed locks outside the door in the patient's lounge," Rayner informed him. "Back when this was a mental hospital, they must have locked the patients in that room during the day. I saw a nurse's station encased in shatterproof glass."

"If we could lure them into the lounge, we can lock them inside. Great idea," John announced then appeared curious. "So how do we lure them into the lounge?"

There was a long moment of silence. Gil and John cast looks at Rayner.

Rayner immediately turned defensive. "I'm not doing the whole live bait thing anymore," he launched defensively.

All eyes were suddenly on Maverick.

Maverick rolled his eyes and groaned. "Of course, why not?" he huffed. "I'm expendable."

John grinned and patted Maverick on the back. "That's the spirit."

§

Maverick poked his head inside the dimly lit lounge and scanned the large area. When he didn't see anyone, he hurried across the room while carrying three plastic buckets stacked inside one another. He approached the hole in the floor and peered into the mostly dark kitchen below. Apart from two dead patients sprawled on the floor, the debris-covered kitchen was void of life. Maverick lined the buckets on the floor, sat on one of the buckets, and removed two large screwdrivers from his pocket. Using the plastic ends of the screwdrivers as drumsticks, he pounded on the two plastic buckets before him. The loud, rhythmic drumming echoed throughout the room, sounding like a small rock concert. As he played his makeshift drums, the sound of running feet could be heard coming from several directions. Maverick tensed but continued to play.

Four crazed cannibals ran into the lounge from the lobby while six more entered through the back corridor. The doorways on each end of the lounge slammed shut. Maverick leaped up from his bucket and ran for the nearby hole in the floor. He jumped down to the top of the refrigerator and then onto the counter. Two men attempted to follow him. One fell to the floor with a loud thud. The other was only a few steps behind Maverick. Maverick jumped to the floor and ran across the kitchen. He bolted through the kitchen door and slammed it shut behind him. He flipped the lock into place then took a moment to lean his back against the door while panting.

"That was too close for comfort," he muttered.

Maverick opened his eyes and saw two psycho patients standing just a few feet in front of him.

"Crap," he groaned.

Both men lunged for him. Maverick ducked beneath them, spun around, and skillfully flipped the screwdrivers in his hands, so he was now holding them by the handles. The first man leaped for him. Maverick rammed the screwdriver into the man's neck then kicked the second man before he could reach him. Maverick turned and ran down the basement corridor. The second man chased after him and was keeping pace. Maverick saw another crazed patient step out of the incinerator room just up ahead. He cursed and skidded to a stop while dodging out of the path of the man chasing him. He straightened, flipped the screwdriver in his right hand, caught it by the tip, and threw it at the patient running toward him. The screwdriver struck the man through his eye.

The man that had run past him spun around and lunged for him from only two feet away. Maverick plunged his last screwdriver into the man's abdomen while simultaneously flipping him over his shoulder. The man was thrown over Maverick and struck the floor face first, driving the screwdriver further into his midsection. Maverick grimaced then ran down the hall toward the patient on the floor with the screwdriver protruding from his eye socket and blood collecting around his head. Without even slowing, Maverick snatched the screwdriver from the man's face and continued along the hall for the stairs at the opposite end of the basement.

Maverick barely slowed as he threw open the stairwell doorway. He nearly collided with Deidra. Maverick skidded to a halt and clutched the blood-covered screwdriver in a threatening manner. He hesitated and lowered the screwdriver when he saw it was Deidra.

"Deidra, what are you doing--?"

Deidra rammed the cattle prod into Maverick's side, instantly dropping him. He thrashed on the floor a moment then became motionless.

Chapter 51

Gil stood outside the lounge door within the corridor that eventually led to the infirmary. He stared down the crumbling hallway, frowned, and then raised the hand radio to his mouth.

"I'm going to meet Maverick halfway and make sure he's safe," Gil announced into the radio. "I'll meet you back at our home base, John."

"Roger that," John responded over the radio.

As Gil hurried down the long corridor, he returned the radio to his mouth and spoke into it. "Keep watch for the outside patrol. Maverick's drum solo may have attracted some attention."

"Way ahead of you, buddy," John replied.

Gil continued in the direction of the stairs at the far end of the corridor. Out of the corner of his eye, he saw something move in the connecting corridor. Gil spun and looked down the hallway. A woman dressed in black pants, jacket, and boots entered one of the back rooms. Gil appeared puzzled a moment then hopeful.

"Mac?" he gasped.

Gil hurried down the connecting corridor in the direction the woman headed. He paused outside the open doorway and glanced at the sign. Administration. He passed through the doorway and headed down the long corridor with offices on both sides. A clunk was heard from the room halfway down the hall to the right. Gil slowed his approach and paused outside the office doorway. He held the gun in one hand and the cattle prod in the other. Gil stepped into the doorway and quickly scanned the room. When he didn't see anyone, he kicked the door with his right foot with enough force to send it against the wall. A woman cried out.

Gil leaped into the room with his gun aimed and pulled the door away from the wall. The woman dressed in black met Gil's gaze. He stared at the unfamiliar woman with some surprise. The somewhat tall woman was in her early twenties with an athletic build beneath her black combat fatigues. Her light brown hair was pulled back into a neat ponytail. She suddenly lunged for him with her own cattle prod. Gil leaped from the path of the high voltage weapon and immediately swung backward with his own cattle prod, striking the woman alongside the head. She took the hit and dropped to the floor. Gil frowned and was obviously not pleased by what he had done to the woman. Just because she wasn't dressed like the other guards, that didn't mean she wasn't one of them, and he couldn't take any chances. Unfortunately, she could also be a recent arrival brought to the asylum against her will.

He immediately crouched before the unconscious woman and searched her pockets. When he found several zip ties in her pocket, he knew he'd made the right call. He was certain she was one of them.

§

The woman slowly came to and looked around the office. She immediately fought the plastic strips binding her wrists to the office chair then looked up and saw Gil sitting on the desk in front of her.

"Who are you?" Gil demanded without showing any emotion.

"Fuck you," she launched back while sneering at him.

Gil placed his foot against the seat of the chair and thrust it backward. The chair struck the wall with enough force to jolt her. Gil casually straightened.

"Sorry," he snarled as he took a step toward her and stared down at the bound woman. "I can't afford to be a gentleman under the circumstances. Answer my questions." His look was commanding. "Don't make me ask twice. I'm not in the mood."

She suddenly smirked. "Gil, right?"

Gil nodded in response. "And you are--?"

"None of your fucking business," she snapped back while grinning.

Gil held up her hand radio in front of her face and pressed the talk button. She gave him a strange look as if wondering what he was attempting to convey with his unusual actions. He poked her leg with the cattle prod. She cried out as the current jolted through her just enough to cause her to thrash and scream. She panted and glared at him as he released the talk button on the hand radio.

"Regina," a man announced with concern over the radio. "Report."

Gil eyed her and raised his brow. "Well, now we're getting somewhere, *Regina*."

Neither spoke for the next few seconds as the woman stared at Gil in silent rage.

"They're going to kill you, motherfucker," she informed him.

"Yeah, what else is new," Gil scoffed. "Tell me something I don't know. Who are 'they'?"

She maintained her stare but refused to speak. Gil turned toward the desk, opened the drawer, and removed a pair of scissors. He gently caressed the seemingly sharp blade without looking at her.

"You can either tell me," he announced then met her gaze with a mildly psychotic one. "Or I give you a Navy haircut to go with that sailor's mouth of yours." He glared at her and snapped the scissors together three times. "Snip snip."

"My father and sister," she snarled.

"Care to elaborate?"

The hand radio crackled. "I have your man," the male voice announced.

Gil didn't take his eyes off the woman. "Did you want to answer that or should I?"

§

John hurried across the dimly lit lobby and headed toward the game room. The crazed patients could be heard pounding on the door between the lounge and the lobby. The game room door opened, and Rayner poked his head out. John was about to speak when the front door was thrown open. Two men stood in the doorway, saw John, and aimed their weapons at him. John gasped with surprise and bolted across the lobby as bullets struck the wall beyond him. He ran for the lounge door, unlocked it, and yanked the door open while using it as a shield. Nearly a dozen crazed cannibals spilled out of the lounge and ran for the men in the doorway. As the guards fired their weapons at the rampaging men, John slipped into the lounge and shut the door behind him.

The crazed men storming across the lobby were mowed down by the semiautomatic rifle fire, but the guards couldn't fire fast enough to take them all down. Two tackled the first man to the floor and sank their teeth into him while he screamed and thrashed. The second man continued to fire at them while running for the rotting stairs. He attempted to run up the stairs while firing back at the last three men chasing him. Sal and Rayner peered out the partially open game room door and watched the three men chase after the guard firing at them. The guard hit a bad floorboard, and his leg went straight through the steps, pinning him. He fired several shots, but the three men were soon on top of him. Two of the crazed patients went through the stairs with the guard. The third man thought better of it and ran back for the fallen guard in the doorway.

Sal motioned Rayner for the nearby corridor. They hurried into the first floor patient's wing and shut the door behind them. Sal attempted to jog alongside Rayner despite his pronounced limp. They could hear someone attempting to break down the ward doorway from the lobby.

"Guards or patients?" Sal asked with concern.

"Does it really matter?" Rayner asked as panic seemed to fill him. "Either way we're screwed. We need a new hiding place."

"I have to be honest," Sal announced while casting a serious look at Rayner as they hurried along the corridor. "I'd much rather be shot then eaten alive."

"Thanks for sharing that with me," Rayner muttered while grimacing at the confession.

Rayner directed him into the first floor nursing station. They hurried into the security of the enclosed nurse's station, locking the door behind them, and then headed into the back break room. Rayner shut the second door behind them as well and flipped the lock. He exhaled then saw Sal speed limping across the breakroom with purpose.

"What is it?" Rayner asked with concern.

Sal removed a wooden baseball bat from the corner of the room hidden behind one of the tables. He grinned and studied the bat.

"Now we're back in business," Sal announced without taking his eyes off the bat.

Rayner gave him a strange look. "Why am I suddenly concerned?"

§

John hurried across the lounge and approached the door leading to the infirmary, which was the direction Gil had reportedly been heading to find Maverick. He paused before the door, used his key to unlock it, and aimed his weapon into the corridor. Even though nothing moved, he didn't let down his guard. John removed his hand radio and placed it closer to his mouth.

"Gil, you copy?"

"Yeah, John," Gil announced from the other end. "I copy. Any good news?"

"You wish," John scoffed. "Our friends from the outside made a guest appearance and spoiled the entire party. I hate party crashers."

"I hear you," Gil replied over the radio. "I'm making new friends myself. Maverick's been captured. You know that place where we first met?"

John considered the comment and appeared curious. "Uh, yeah," he replied. "Feeling nostalgic?"

"A little," Gil remarked from the other end. "Meet me there. I don't want to give away my location. I don't know how secure this channel is."

"Copy that," John replied. "On my way there now. I expect flowers and champagne."

"I'll do my best."

Chapter 52

The jeep with Mac at the wheel and Scorpio riding shotgun stopped nearly half a mile from the entrance to the asylum. Stone pulled up behind them on his four-wheeler and jumped off. It was around four-thirty in the morning and still an hour until sunrise. Mac and Scorpio climbed out of the jeep and eyed the dark, overgrown lane that used to be a paved driveway. Scorpio removed the assault rifle from the back of the jeep and immediately received a sharp glare from Mac. Scorpio frowned and handed the weapon to Mac, who was undeniably the better shot. All three still had semiautomatics on them as well.

"We need to wait for the others," Stone insisted while watching the two women preparing as if about to head into battle.

"We will," Mac reluctantly agreed then raised a cocky brow. "If they don't take all day about it." She then cast a sharp look at Stone. "Those are our friends in there. I'm not waiting around very long."

"I understand," Stone replied. "Maverick and I have been friends since we were kids, but getting ourselves killed storming the fort isn't going to help them any either. The three of us can't take on three dozen armed men."

"Maybe *you* can't--" Mac muttered without looking at him.

Stone groaned and shook his head. "You haven't even fully recovered from your last outing," he insisted and indicated her shoulder. "Can you fight like that?"

"We're going to find out now, aren't we?" Mac announced with little emotion.

"Everyone needs to just take a couple of deep breaths," Stone insisted while eyeing the irate women. "Our backup is the same group who ambushed us at the cemetery. Those are the guys we want leading the charge."

"Unfortunately, he does have a point," Scorpio muttered while folding her arms across her chest.

§

Only a few minutes had passed when the first three quads arrived. Zack leaped off his quad in an aggressive and threatening manner. Jackie sprang from her four-wheeler and attempted to cut Zack off before he reached Mac. Mac didn't flinch, and her expression didn't change as Zack nearly plowed down Jackie to reach her.

"Hasn't your hot temper and lack of judgment gotten enough people killed?" Zack snarled in anger then pointed demandingly at Scorpio. "You want to risk her life now as well."

"We're not getting into this now," Mac launched back but managed to keep her temper in check.

Kane jumped off his quad, grabbed a duffle bag from the back, and approached the others gathered by the jeep.

"Oh, we're doing this," Zack shot out in anger. "I won't allow my team, my family, be more collateral damage fueled by your reckless pursuit to achieve your selfish desires."

"Selfish desires?" Mac suddenly snarled in anger. "My selfish desires kept your ass alive!"

"At the expense of other innocent lives?" Zack shot back in a rage not often seen.

"I did what I had to do!"

Zack suddenly lunged for Mac, who immediately took a defensive stance, prepared for his attack. Kane jumped between the two while facing Zack.

"Everyone needs to calm down," Kane announced while holding his hands in the air with his back to Mac and kept his focus on Zack.

Zack's eyes were locked on Mac just behind him. Without warning, Zack shoved Kane from his path and snap kicked at Mac. She easily dodged his booted foot and took a more aggressive stance, prepared to strike back. Kane spun into a backward roundhouse kick and nailed Zack in the chest. Zack was thrown back a step from the hard-hit, but he easily caught his balance. He glared at Kane, who again stepped between him and Mac. Kane suddenly took an aggressive attack stance and stared down his father.

"Don't *ever* touch her," Kane threatened in a stern, serious tone.

Zack's eyes burned into Kane's with a frightening rage. "You don't know what she did," he snarled. "You don't know what lengths she'll go to in order to achieve what she wants. Collateral damage means nothing to her."

Kane didn't flinch or look away. "I don't care," he announced boldly while locking eyes with Zack. "Don't *touch* my badger."

Jackie and Scorpio watched the scene with tense anticipation as neither man flinched. When the remaining three quads were heard nearby, Zack relaxed his aggressive stance. As the four-wheelers approached, Zack turned and walked away. Jackie hurried after him. Kane relaxed then turned to face Mac. She met his gaze and frowned in disappointment.

"You should have let him attack," Mac remarked with little emotion while folding her arms across her chest. "Delaying the inevitable is just going to make it worse."

"Whatever happened between the two of you can wait," Kane informed her. "We have other things to worry about right now. Maverick and Rayner need us to keep our heads and work together." Kane then shot a glare at Scorpio. "*All* of us working together."

"Yeah?" Scorpio snapped while glaring at her brother. "Tell that to your father."

Kane rolled his eyes and groaned. Monroe approached them with Kirk and Bogart only a few steps behind.

Monroe glared at Mac. "Oh, good," he snarled sarcastically. "You actually waited."

"We should be in Maine right now," Mac scoffed under her breath.

Kane tossed his duffel bag onto the hood of the jeep and unzipped it. He collected a handful of throwing stars and placed them in his pocket then removed the samurai swords in the leather, dual holster and handed it to Scorpio.

"You're going to need these," he announced.

Scorpio stared at the swords a moment and seemed to relive her failure in the cemetery. Kane gently touched the healed cut on her cheek and met her gaze.

"Getting knocked down doesn't make us a failure," Kane informed her. "Not getting back up does."

Scorpio stared into her brother's eyes a moment then timidly accepted the swords.

"Okay, we need a plan," Monroe announced and motioned everyone toward the jeep.

Chapter 53

It was a little after five o'clock in the morning and getting close to sunrise. The area surrounding the asylum was already becoming lighter and allowed better visibility, although the woods remained mostly dark and would stay that way for quite some time. Nothing seemed to move, and it appeared as if the asylum had truly been abandoned. The sound of a jeep broke through the early morning silence. Bright headlights shined upon the closed asylum gates as the jeep rocketed closer. Silent gunfire, seemingly out of nowhere, fired upon the speeding jeep. Despite the barrage of bullets, the jeep didn't slow and plowed down the front gate. Armed men appeared from the woods and ran after the jeep while still firing their weapons, attempting to stop it. The jeep didn't stop until it crashed into a tree not far from the building itself.

The two, armed men hurried to reach the crashed jeep and aimed their weapons only to discover the jeep was empty. Two more men hurried from the side of the building and ran to join the first two by the crashed vehicle with its engine still running on full throttle. The first man approached the jeep and saw the gas pedal had been jammed down with a metal rod. He turned it off to cut the sound from the engine. Despite turning off the engine, they still heard the sound of something running. By the time the four men turned toward the gate, Kirk and Stone raced through the opening on their four-wheelers and fired at the four men. The guards immediately took cover and attempted to fire back.

Kirk and Stone stopped their four-wheelers near a small cluster of trees, leaped off the all-terrain vehicles, and took cover while returning fire. While the four guards were busy shooting at Kirk and Stone, the three remaining teams closed in on the asylum from the south, east, and west. Zack and Kane headed toward the side door, which would take them to the administration wing. Jackie, Mac, and Scorpio headed across the back for the basement entrance. That left Monroe and Bogart approaching from the west with the more difficult task of making it to the main entrance without being seen by the men taking cover near the crashed jeep.

"I see them," Stone announced to Kirk and indicated Monroe and Bogart, who reached the first pillar just under the overhang.

"Twenty bucks says you can't hit the gas tank on the jeep," Kirk announced while smirking.

Stone gave Kirk a surprised look then grinned. "You're on."

Stone stared through the riflescope, carefully aimed the weapon, and fired. The bullet pierced the gas tank causing the entire vehicle to explode and erupt into a ball of flames. All four men near the jeep dove for cover from the explosion. Monroe and Bogart used the diversion to their advantage and ran for the front door. Monroe removed the set of keys Bogart had found on the dead guard and attempted to find the one for the front door. Bogart kept watch as Monroe fumbled with the keys, unable to find the right one. Bogart cocked his head then reached for the knob and turned it. The door opened surprising both. Monroe sprang to his feet as Bogart aimed his weapon inside. Both men slipped into the lobby and shut the door behind them.

§

At the same time Monroe and Bogart reached the front door, Zack and Kane approached the west side of the asylum.

Bars covered the windows on the patient's wing on each level. Zack and Kane flattened themselves against the side of the building to keep from being seen by the guards that Kirk and Stone were keeping distracted.

Kane pulled on the bars covering the window nearest him then looked at Zack. "What's the plan?" he asked. "Those bars are encased in brick."

Zack pointed up the side of the building to a window that was missing its bars. "I can get in through that window," he insisted. "There should be a firehose I can tie off and toss down to you."

Kane looked up the side of the building to the window without bars on the second floor. "That window?" he asked and gave him a curious look. "Do you really think you can scale the side of the building?"

"I've been scaling buildings for decades," Zack informed him. "Watch and learn."

Zack backed away from the building, keeping close to the side, took a running start, and used various protrusions in the side of the building to aid him in scaling it. Kane watched Zack make it to the barred window alongside the one missing its bars. He clung to the bars and kicked with both feet, breaking the window next to it. Zack then tossed himself feet first through the open window. He rolled across the floor littered with broken glass, sprang to his feet, and brushed the shards of glass from his clothes. As he hurried for the patient's room door, he heard the crunching of glass behind him. Zack spun around, prepared to attack. Kane stood just inside the window and grinned at Zack.

"I've been scaling walls since grade school," Kane teased in response.

Zack stared at Kane a moment then grinned and laughed. "Can your sister do that?"

Kane made a face and waved his hand in a gesture of so-so. "She didn't break curfew as often as I did."

§

Jackie, Scorpio, and Mac reached the back entrance with little resistance. The back door contained a padlock and seemed impenetrable, but there was a service entrance leading to the basement. While Jackie checked out the back door, Mac sought out the service entrance.

"This way," Mac announced. "This must be the way they sneak in and out."

Jackie and Scorpio joined Mac down the short ramp by the partially open, service entrance door. All three slipped in beneath the garage door in order to maintain an element of surprise. There was just enough light peeking in from the partially open garage door to make out a newer jeep. There was also a large panel truck. The rear building entrance was just beyond the storage area. The three women hurried for the closed door across the room. Mac tried the door and discovered it was unlocked. Scorpio removed one of the swords from her back holster and took a defensive stance as Mac opened the door. Jackie and Mac aimed their weapons into the dimly lit corridor. To their surprise, the hallway had power. Several bulbs were either burned out or fluttered on and off, but they had enough light to watch for an attack in the basement corridor.

§

Stone caught a glimpse of the rest of the team entering the building from the front and the side. They didn't need to worry about the women heading in through the back since all the activity was happening out front.

"They're in," Stone announced while grinning then eyed Kirk. "What now?"

"We bag our limit of bad guys," Kirk replied and fired several shots at the guards now running for cover behind the tree.

Stone heard a strange cracking sound from the tree branches above him and looked up. He saw the bottom of a man's boots dangling above them just before the body crashed to the ground, nearly striking them. Stone and Kirk jerked with surprise at the bloated, rotting corpse missing its head.

"Oh, shit!" Stone cried out in horror. "Where's that dude's head?"

The head dropped from the tree and nearly fell into Stone's arms. He cried out again and fell onto his backside. When Stone looked up, he saw several men hanging by their necks within the trees.

"This place is fucked up!"

Kirk looked up as well and stared with surprise at the sight. "Hell, no," he scoffed.

Stone scrambled to his knees while retrieving his weapon then saw more men approaching behind them. "Oh, crap," he cried out. "We have company up our ass."

Kirk saw the men approaching from the rear and fired at them. "Mount up," he cried out.

Stone and Kirk jumped onto their four-wheelers and sped away from the approaching men coming through the open gate.

Chapter 54

Darth positioned himself at the top of the steps just within the rental plane doorway. His front paws dangled over the first step while his head rested on his legs. It may have appeared as if Darth was slacking in his duties, but he was ever watchful on the mostly dark woods beyond the clearing of the abandoned airfield. Faint movement was barely heard within the woods. Darth's eyes shifted. Although he didn't stir, a low growl escaped his throat. Without lifting his head, he listened to the increasing movement within the woods. As the sounds grew closer, Darth lifted his head, again growled in his throat, and then crept down the plane steps. Two men with assault rifles affixed with silencers paused within the woods and assessed the area surrounding the two planes.

"Remember," the first man announced quietly to the second man. "As soon as you've replaced the missing part, start her up and head for the rendezvous. We need to get these planes out of here. We can't keep the state troopers at bay forever. We don't want them finding these planes and searching the area for the pilots. It'll ruin everything."

"Are you sure you can handle those left on the other plane?" his partner asked.

"There are only four of them onboard," the first man insisted. "The rest are scattered around the area. I think I can handle four sleeping men. I'll have them out of the way before you finish reinstalling that part." He then indicated the rental plane. "We'll use that plane as our getaway and meet you in a day or two at the rendezvous."

They watched the area a few minutes longer. When they were convinced no one had heard their arrival, they parted ways. The first man headed for the rental plane while the second headed for Gil's plane. Darth hid behind the front wheel of the rental plane, remaining within the shadows, and watched the first man silently creep up the steps to the open doorway. Darth slinked across the area beneath the plane and hid just behind the steps as the first man paused before the open doorway. The man bolted inside the plane. Darth crept up the steps with some speed, looking more like a stalking tiger than a German shepherd. The dog peered inside the dark plane. The intruder had his weapon aimed and scanned the empty fuselage. He seemed bewildered when he didn't find the four passengers who had almost certainly been left behind.

Darth remained low to the floor and pattered across the aisle. He hid behind one of the passenger seats and poked his head back out to watch the armed man. The intruder again scanned the plane then headed toward the back for the bathroom. He paused outside the bathroom and slowly pushed open the door with the muzzle of his rifle. The bathroom was empty as well. Darth crept across the aisle and hid behind another seat. The intruder turned around, again scanned the fuselage, and noticed the cockpit door was partially closed. He raised his weapon and quietly approached the front of the plane, his sights set on the cockpit.

The armed intruder pushed open the door with the muzzle of his rifle and aimed the weapon into the cramped cockpit. It was empty! He slowly lowered his weapon and appeared baffled.

"What the hell?" he muttered aloud. "Where did they go?"

He approached the steps and headed down them. Darth darted for the doorway. The intruder reached the bottom of the steps, aimed his weapon, and scanned the area through the night scope. Darth stood at the top of the plane steps. As the intruder was about to search the area, Darth leaped off the top step while snarling. The intruder spun around but not fast enough. Darth tackled him to the ground, landing on him with enough force from his jump to knock the wind from the man. Darth snarled while standing on top of the man and tore into his right arm with his teeth, keeping him from securing his weapon. The man cried out while attempting to throw the dog off of him, but Darth kept him pinned to the ground. Using his left hand, the intruder removed a semiautomatic containing a silencer from his shoulder holster and attempted to aim it at the dog. As his finger squeezed the trigger, Darth changed position and landed on his left arm.

A nearly silent shot was fired. Darth yelped and released the man's right arm. The dog sprang off the man, who gasped and looked down at his bleeding abdomen. The man appeared almost stunned while gasping to catch his breath then looked at the dog standing over him.

"Fucking dog--"

Darth exposed his bloodstained teeth and snarled in response. The man's eyes rolled back in his head, and his body became limp. There was a faint metallic clunk from Gil's plane. Darth looked up then bolted back into the shadows beneath the rental plane. He again hid behind the front wheel and watched the man in the distance as he climbed up the step stool before the engine compartment to Gil's plane. As the second man opened the compartment and worked on the engine, Darth tilted his head while listening to the faint sounds of a wrench turning. When the man's back was turned, and he was focused on his work on the engine, Darth bolted across the open area between the two planes. The dog took cover behind one of the back wheels. The man turned and scanned the area. When he didn't see anything, he resumed working.

Once the part was installed, the man climbed off the step stool and replaced his tools to the tool belt on the ground. He collected the tool belt, the step stool, and his assault rifle then headed away from the plane. Darth silently watched the man. The man set the items on the ground just below the closed fuselage door and reached up to open it so he could lower the steps. As he reached for the strap before him to pull down the steps, he heard a dog's low woof. The man hesitated then looked a foot away from him where Darth sat happily panting and wagging his tail. The man stared at the dog with some surprise.

"Are you lost?" the man asked the dog then laughed as he crouched down to Darth's level. "Come here, boy. I won't hurt you." He held his left hand out to Darth while removing his Bowie knife from his boot with his right hand.

Darth again woofed and stood. Without warning, Darth lunged for the man. The man just about had the knife from his boot when Darth leaped onto his shoulder and jumped up for the dangling strap above him. Darth grabbed the strap in his teeth and allowed his body to pull down the steps. The man looked up just as the steps crashed on top of his head. He fell the rest of the way to the ground with the base of the steps crushing his skull. Darth landed on the ground, backed away from the dead man, and barked several times. He then ran for the steps, raced up them, and entered Gil's plane. Darth trotted through the plane, stopped by Gil's discarded leather jacket, and pawed at the pocket until he freed a bag of beef jerky.

Darth grabbed the bag of jerky, jumped onto one of the plush passenger seats, and worked on opening the bag. Once the bag was open, he made himself comfortable and happily chewed on the succulent treats.

Chapter 55

Bogart and Monroe stood inside the lobby behind the closed door while listening to their men returning fire. Both men scanned the lobby with their weapons aimed while stepping around the dead man on the floor just inside the doorway. Bogart crouched down and briefly examined the dead man while Monroe continued to scan the room. Monroe casts several glances at Bogart where he crouched over the blood-soaked body.

"Well?" Monroe asked while attempting to focus on the dimly lit lobby. "Anyone we know?"

"It's hard to tell," Bogart just about gasped then briefly met Monroe's gaze while grimacing. "Something tore off his face."

Monroe turned his head and looked from Bogart to the dead man. "What?"

Bogart quickly straightened and looked around while raising his weapon. "Maybe I've seen one too many horror movies, but I'd swear this is the work of zombies."

"Okay, now you're just being ridiculous," Monroe scoffed then shined the light from his rifle on the dead man partially sticking out of the broken stairs.

Monroe stared at the dead man a moment then uncertainly approached while keeping his weapon trained on the area surrounding the body. Bogart remained behind Monroe with his back to his and watched behind them. Monroe cautiously walked up the first two steps and eyed the dead man. His throat had been torn out, and chunks of flesh were missing.

"Christ," Monroe bellowed. "What did that?"

"I'm telling you," Bogart gasped while nervously looking around then whispered, "zombies."

"There aren't any zombies," Monroe snarled back although it did seem as if Bogart's crazy talk was starting to unnerve his partner.

As Monroe moved away from the stairs, a man snarled and lunged for him. The man had blood running down his chin, bloodstained teeth, and a chunk of flesh in his hand. Monroe saw the frightening man and the teeth coming for him. He cried out at what almost certainly appeared to be a zombie and fired two shots into the man. The man instantly dropped to the floor.

"You have to shoot them in the head," Bogart cried out. "It's the only way to kill a zombie."

Monroe hesitated and looked at the dead man on the floor. He tapped his booted foot to the man's dirty, bare foot.

"He wasn't a zombie," Monroe scoffed then studied him more closely. "Just a deranged lunatic."

The man suddenly cried out and just about shot up from the floor. Monroe screamed and shot the man in the head. The man again went down and no longer moved.

"Told you so," Bogart huffed.

They approached the closed lounge door and attempted to open it. It was locked. Monroe took a step back, removed his semiautomatic, and shot out the lock. He easily kicked the door open. Monroe and Bogart then took cover and aimed their weapons into the dimly lit lounge. When nothing moved or jumped out at them, they entered the massive room. The lounge was empty, but the door on the far side of the room was partially open.

"Through there," Monroe announced while motioning with his weapon.

"Keep an eye out for more zombies," Bogart whispered nervously.

Monroe groaned at the comment. Bogart kept an eye on their backside while Monroe led them across the lounge to the open door, which would take them into the broad corridor.

Monroe and Bogart entered the corridor and cautiously followed it. As they neared the back of the corridor, a man with a semiautomatic suddenly stepped into the hallway, saw them, and aimed his gun at them. Monroe fired at the man. John leaped back into the infirmary.

"Toss your weapon down and come out with your hands up," Monroe called out. "Tell us where our friend is, and we won't kill you."

"Monroe?" Gil suddenly called out.

Monroe took his eye away from the riflescope and suddenly perked up. "Gil?"

Gil stepped out of the infirmary with his hands raised and the semiautomatic still in his hand.

"Did I just try to shoot you?" Monroe asked with some surprise.

"Uh, no, that was our new friend, John," Gil remarked then looked back into the room. He glanced back at Monroe and managed a smile. "He forgives you. He's even giving you a one-finger salute."

Monroe and Bogart lowered their weapons and hurried down the corridor to join their missing teammate. All three exchanged manly hugs.

"Glad you're alive," Monroe announced while grinning at his friend.

"Where's Sal?" Bogart asked with concern. "Is he okay?"

"Yeah, Sal's fine," Gil informed him. "A little moody these days. Nothing a steak dinner won't cure."

"He wasn't bitten, was he?" Bogart asked as his eyes widened.

"Bitten?" Gil asked with some surprise. "No. Why?"

"On account of the zombies," Bogart remarked.

Gil raised a brow then glanced at Monroe. Monroe waved off the comment.

§

K ane followed Zack and his assault rifle to the fire stairs on the second floor. Zack attempted to open the door but discovered it was rusted shut. He slung his rifle over his shoulder then pushed on the door several times, attempting to find its weaknesses. Zack located the rusted area that prevented the door from opening. He took a step back and kicked the door twice before it creaked then flew open. While Zack peered into the stairwell, Kane eyed the building's structure. Dirt and debris floated to the floor.

"The building is literally rotting out from under us," Kane remarked.

"Decades of water damage," Zack responded. "Keep your grenades in your pockets. One explosion could bring the entire building down on us."

Zack removed his rifle that had been slung over his shoulder then entered the stairwell. Kane stared after him with a befuddled look.

"Uh, I didn't pack any grenades," he remarked then hurried into the stairwell after Zack and appeared curious. "Did you?"

Zack didn't comment. They hurried down the fire stairs to the patient's wing on the first floor. Zack easily tackled the steps while keeping his weapon aimed and ready for a firefight. Although Kane had been given his own rifle, he lacked his father's confidence while handling it. He attempted to mimic Zack's posture with the weapon and seemed to marvel at the man's nerves of steel. The moment they entered the first floor patient's wing, they could hear loud thumping sounds. Zack slowed his approach and signaled for Kane to follow suit. As they closed in on the sound, they saw six men in tattered clothing pounding on the shatterproof glass while attempting to gain access to what appeared to be an empty nursing station.

Zack lowered his weapon and stared at the unarmed men with bewilderment. "What do you make of that?"

Kane slung the rifle over his neck and shoulder. "They're not armed," he announced. "They look like homeless people. Aggressive homeless men."

Zack slung his rifle over his shoulder as well. "Whoever they are, they want access to that room."

"Drugs?" Kane asked.

"Maybe our friends," Zack replied while remaining curious about the men. "Non-lethal engagement."

"Yeah, way ahead of you on that one," Kane muttered.

Kane and Zack quietly approached the six men, who were preoccupied with gaining access to the nurse's station. Once they were within striking distance, Zack kicked the first man in the knee, driving him to the floor while Kane swept his adversary's legs out from under him. The first two men no sooner went down when the remaining four were aware of the men behind them. As all four men spun around, Kane and Zack were already striking with high kicks and fast punches. Zack knocked his second opponent into the man attempting to get up off the floor, sending both men down. When the two men hit the floor, they became angry at each other and started fighting between themselves.

Kane delivered two hard punches to one of the men before him then focused his attention on another, not giving him an opportunity to get the upper hand. Zack resisted his signature move, which was breaking his rival's neck, and instead delivered a throat punch. The third man was now grasping his throat and wheezing. Without even waiting to recover, the man stumbled away and hurried from the wing. Kane attempted to punch his last adversary, but he chased after the man leaving the wing rather than stay and fight. Kane kicked the remaining man in the abdomen as he attempted to stand, just about driving him back to his knees.

Zack didn't wait for the two men fighting on the floor to return their attention to him. Instead, he engaged the men by kicking both while they were still on the floor fighting. Both men stopped their fight, scrambled to their feet, and ran away as well. The last two followed without further bodily harm to themselves. Once they were certain the six crazed men were gone, Zack and Kane peered into the empty nurse's station then noticed the door in the back. Whatever the men had been seeking had to be beyond the second door.

Zack eyed Kane and raised a curious brow. "Want to take this one?"

Kane grinned in response then took a step back then kicked the door inward. It flew open with tremendous force. Zack removed his semiautomatic from his shoulder holster and approached the closed breakroom door. Kane followed suit and did the same. Zack paused alongside the door and motioned Kane to the opposite side. Once both were in position, Zack lightly knocked on the door.

"Anyone home?" Zack announced through the door.

The door was immediately unlocked and thrown open. Zack and Kane aimed their handguns at Sal, who now stood in the doorway while holding his baseball bat in a non-threatening manner. Sal's grin increased when he saw Zack.

"I knew you'd find us," Sal announced and gave Zack a manly hug.

Zack tensed and eyed the happy man. "Why is everyone hugging me?" he demanded.

Rayner moved into the doorway, saw Kane, and appeared relieved. "Thank God," he gasped. "We need to get out of this place."

Kane appeared offended while staring at Rayner. "What? No hug from you?"

"Who's this guy?" Sal asked Zack while indicating Kane.

Zack cast a look at Kane, drew a deep breath, and then looked back at Sal. "This is my son, Kane."

Kane cast a quick look at Zack and had to hide his emotions at the introduction.

Sal immediately grinned and laughed while extending his hand to Kane. Kane accepted his hand and was caught off guard when Sal pulled him in for a manly hug.

"Pleasure to meet you, son."

Kane returned the manly hug then pulled back and eyed Sal. "You must be Sal," he announced. "Mac's former boss. She went to great lengths to find you."

"I know," Sal replied while nodding. "I owe her a few dozen apologies."

Zack rolled his eyes at the comment. "Before we meet up with the others," he announced. "What's the situation here? Who were those whack jobs we chased off?"

"That's a long story," Sal announced.

"I don't do long stories," Zack remarked. "I'll give you ten words or less."

"Psycho cannibals from hell," Rayner remarked with little emotion. "Can we go before they come back for an early morning snack?"

Chapter 56

Jackie, Mac, and Scorpio quietly crept along the dimly lit basement corridor. Mac led the way while Jackie brought up the rear, leaving Scorpio and her sword in the middle of the women with the intimidating weapons. The dim lights continued to flicker, giving the already creepy basement corridor an even creepier appeal. They passed the fire stairs and headed toward the laundry room. Mac paused by a junction in the corridor, flattened her back to the wall, and peered around the corner. Two armed men forced a bound Maverick toward the elevator. Deidra was directly behind them. Mac again flattened her back to the wall and looked at Jackie.

"Two men and Deidra have Maverick," Mac announced in a soft, concerned tone.

Jackie wasn't surprised to hear that Deidra was in on it. It had been too convenient that the woman showed up to assist Mac and even offer a ride to the remote location. They heard more voices. Mac again looked around the corner and saw Deidra, Maverick, and two guards enter the elevator. More men appeared from the laundry room.

"Four more men," Mac remarked and then eyed the fire stairs. "They're getting into the elevator. I'm going to cut them off upstairs. I need a diversion. Break up that party for me."

Jackie nodded. As Mac ran back for the fire stairs, Jackie remained partially hidden behind the corner and fired at the four men within the corridor. Bullets ricocheted off the concrete walls. The four guards fired back while the two with Deidra and Maverick took the elevator to safety. Jackie hit one of the men, although it wasn't one of her better shots. The four men, including the injured man, darted back inside the nearby laundry room and returned fire despite not seeing their intended target. Scorpio looked around the corridor as if disinterested in the gunfight.

"Do you know what I love about these old buildings?" Scorpio announced.

Jackie cast a strange look at Scorpio and appeared bewildered. "No, enlighten me."

Scorpio grinned and pointed up at the ceiling to the large vent. "Extraordinarily large vents."

Jackie's expression suddenly dropped. "You want to crawl through that old air vent?" she asked with a look between surprise and repulsion.

"Yeah, I want to crawl through the air vent," Scorpio replied while returning her sword to her back holster. "Kane and I would play war with the neighborhood kids in abandoned buildings. I've been in plenty of dirty air vents."

"Don't expect me to follow," Jackie informed her. "Probably filled with spiders and rats."

"I'll get behind them," Scorpio announced then indicated the vent opening in the ceiling. "Give me a stirrup."

Jackie fired several rounds down the corridor then slung her rifle over her shoulder and spun to face Scorpio with her fingers from both hands laced together. Scorpio leaped into Jackie's hands with one foot and allowed Jackie to boost her upward. Scorpio sprang the vent door and grabbed the edge. Jackie then gave her an added upward thrust, helping project her into the vent. Jackie immediately removed her rifle from her shoulder and fired another few shots down the corridor to keep the men hole up in the laundry room.

§

Mac darted up the stairs and through the fire doorway. She spun the corner and ran for the elevator as it dinged, alerting her to their arrival. Mac didn't even slow down. As the doors opened and the first man stepped out, Mac tackled him to the floor. She violently elbowed him in the face and was on her feet by the time the second man realized what had happened. Mac kicked the gun from the man's hands. Deidra raised her own weapon. Maverick plowed into Deidra despite his bound hands and took her to the corridor floor just outside the elevator. Deidra punched Maverick in the mouth and easily scrambled out from beneath him. Mac took on both men at once with kicks and punches.

While still on the floor, Maverick kicked Deidra's feet out from beneath her before she could reach her discarded weapon. She again crashed to the floor. Mac removed Maverick's dagger from her boot and threw it across the hall. The knife struck the wall near Maverick and became embedded in the drywall. Maverick saw the dagger and leaped to his feet. He turned his back to the weapon lodged in the wall and worked on cutting through the zip ties binding his wrists behind his back. The moment Maverick's wrists were free, Deidra changed course and fled down the hall, leaving her discarded weapon and the two guards to fend for themselves.

Maverick snatched the knife from the wall and lunged for the guard now retrieving his weapon. He stabbed the guard in the throat and successfully stopped him. Mac took the second man down, snapping his neck on the way to the floor. She straightened and looked around.

"Where did Deidra go?"

Maverick pointed down the hall. Mac cursed under her breath then looked back at Maverick. She picked up one of the guard's discarded weapons and tossed it to Maverick.

"We have to go back to the basement and make sure Jackie and Scorpio are okay," Mac announced.

Maverick nodded and jumped into the elevator with her. They rode the elevator to the basement in silence. When the doors opened, both were prepared with their weapons aimed. The men inside the laundry room had just poked their heads out to fire another round at Jackie when they saw Mac and Maverick with weapons on the other side of the hall. The men darted back into the laundry room and shut the door. Mac and Maverick ran for the door and attempted to open it, but it was locked. Jackie saw them and hurried down the hall to join them.

"We need to get in there," Jackie announced with some concern.

"There's no other way out," Maverick informed her. "They're trapped."

"No," Jackie responded and nodded to the door. "In two minutes, we're about to have a situation. Scorpio needs backup."

"She's in there?" Mac gasped with horror.

"She will be soon," Jackie replied then pointed at the air vent.

"Son-of-a-bitch," Mac cried out and violently kicked the door. She darted out of the way just before the men fired at the door.

§

The four, armed guards faced the laundry room door with their weapons aimed. They no longer heard movement on the other side of the door, leading them to believe they had shot the person attempting to get inside. The vent panel in the ceiling silently opened behind them. Without a sound, Scorpio dropped down behind them into a crouching position. As she straightened, she removed both swords from her back holster. One of the men heard the sound made by the sword and spun around. Scorpio was already in attack mode and lunged for the man. She struck the man's rifle, knocking it from his hands. The metallic clang was enough to alert the remaining three men of her presence.

Scorpio kicked the unarmed man in the chest, knocking him out of the way as she engaged the remaining three men. She slashed the first guard across the throat with her left sword while slashing the second man's arm with her right sword, forcing him to drop his weapon. The third man fired his weapon. Scorpio was already rolling across the floor to avoid the gunfire. She sprang up not far from the man and snap kicked him in the crotch. He released his weapon while clutching himself. Before he sank to his knees, she stabbed him in the chest with her left sword. The first man lunged for her from behind. She easily flipped her sword in her hand and rammed it back behind her, piercing the man through the midsection, successfully stopping his surprise assault. The last man attempted to reclaim his weapon despite his bleeding forearm. Scorpio slashed simultaneously with both swords in a crisscross, slicing the man's throat and chest at the same time.

Chapter 57

Outside the laundry room, Jackie moved Mac aside and aimed her semiautomatic at the door lock. She easily shot it out with two rounds. Mac kicked open the door, bolted inside, and stopped when she saw Scorpio straightening as she lowered her blood covered swords.

"What took you so long?" Scorpio asked then saw Maverick.

Relief swept over her as she hurried to him with open arms despite her bloodied sword in each hand. Maverick was a little leery of her swords dripping with blood but allowed her to hug him anyway. She pulled back and met his gaze with a concerned look.

"Where's Rayner?" Scorpio asked. "Is he okay?"

"He was with Sal in the game room," Maverick informed her.

"And Gil?" Jackie asked.

"We were locking the crazies in the patient's lounge," Maverick announced. "Gil and I were supposed to meet up. That's when I ran into Deidra. Gil has one of theirs. The plan was a hostage exchange."

"Let's find the others," Scorpio announced and walked past them.

Mac, Maverick, and Jackie just stared after the young woman. Jackie looked back at the dead men on the floor and raised her brows.

"Not bad."

Jackie entered the corridor behind the three and looked both directions.

"This place is massive," Jackie announced then looked at Mac. "Why don't you and Maverick take the elevator, and Scorpio and I will take the stairs. We can cover more ground that way and then meet in the middle."

"Solid plan," Mac replied then nodded Maverick back to the elevator.

§

Within the infirmary, Monroe and Bogart cast several glances at the woman sitting in an old, rusted wheelchair with her hands and wrists bound to the chair. Monroe glanced at Gil and appeared curious.

"Who is she exactly?" Monroe asked.

"Her name is Regina," Gil informed them. "But I assume she prefers to be called Madam Director."

Regina sneered at Gil obviously realizing he'd gotten to one of her men.

"I believe she's here with her father and sister," Gil remarked. "Other than that, she's not saying much."

"I certainly don't know her," John announced with little interest.

"We're going to trade her for Maverick," Gil informed Monroe. "We're just waiting for them to come up with a way to double-cross us first."

"Sounds counterproductive," Bogart muttered.

"We need to flush out the head honcho," Gil replied and sat on the nearby bed.

"I thought you just said she was the head honcho," Bogart remarked.

"I think she gave orders to the men, but I'm pretty sure it's her father who's in charge," Gil announced. "If we intend to stop whoever is in charge, we need to let them come to us. If it's her father, he'll do anything in his power to rescue his daughter."

"You'll never escape," Regina hissed in anger. "You and your friends are all going to die slow and painful--"

John ripped a piece of duct tape from the roll and just about slapped it across the bound woman's mouth. "You talk too much," John scoffed.

Monroe removed his hand radio and pressed a button. "Kirk, you copy?"

There was a moment of silence. The radio crackled, and gunfire could be heard.

"We're a bit busy at the moment," Kirk shouted back through the radio.

"Do you need backup?" Monroe asked.

"That might be nice," Kirk snarled over the radio. He was clearly irritated.

"Okay, keep your shirt on," Monroe muttered in response. "We'll be out in five." He then looked at Gil. "Do you have everything under control in here?"

"The rest of the team is around?" Gil asked.

"Yeah, they're cleaning house," Monroe replied. "Bogart and I should go out and help Kirk and Stone."

"I'll go with you," John announced while springing forward. "I was an Army Ranger."

Monroe eyed John and raised his brow as if he was impressed. "Army Ranger, huh?" he remarked then shrugged. "Well, beggars can't be choosers. At any rate, you're probably a better shot than Bogart."

"Funny," John and Bogart scoffed in unison.

"Take John," Gil announced. "He'll be more useful out there. Bogart and I can handle the hostage swap."

Monroe eyed John and cocked his head. "You're up, brother."

Bogart handed John his assault rifle.

John accepted the weapon, lovingly caressed it, and then grinned. "Lead the way," he announced.

Monroe headed for the partially open infirmary door and nearly collided with Mac. Both raised their weapons, saw the other, and relaxed. Gil was surprised to see Maverick. He cast a look at the bound woman and grinned.

"Well, looks like your father and sister have one less bargaining chip," Gil teased.

Although it was difficult to tell beyond the duct tape covering her mouth, the woman sneered at him.

"Deidra is her sister, huh?" Mac remarked.

"Who's Deidra?" Gil asked.

"We ran into her when we first got here," Mac replied. "She dumped us in an old, abandoned town. I'm guessing in an effort to divide and conquer."

"Almost worked," Maverick remarked and eyed the woman with some hostility.

"You still have this?" Monroe asked.

Gil nodded. "Yeah, go," he replied, seeming unaffected. "We're good."

Monroe then nodded to John, and both hurried from the room.

Gil then eyed Mac and Maverick. "Bogart and Maverick will stay here and guard the prisoner," Gil announced then eyed Mac and grinned. "Ready to kick some?"

"Absolutely," Mac replied.

"Then let's do this," Gil insisted.

Mac grinned, raised her weapon, and nodded. "After you," she announced and indicated the door.

Maverick and Bogart watched both leave while appearing offended. "Were we just given babysitting duty?" Maverick asked.

"Yeah, that's about right," Bogart muttered. "I'm always picked last."

"Join the club," Maverick scoffed.

Chapter 58

Jackie and Scorpio cautiously headed along the first floor corridor while watching the open doorways on either side. Despite the number of people within the asylum, the building seemed almost too quiet. Scorpio paused and nudged Jackie, stopping her. Scorpio gave a slight nod to one of the nearby rooms. Jackie slung her rifle and removed her semiautomatic from her shoulder holster. She positioned herself along the wall just outside the open doorway. Scorpio clutched her sword and watched the remaining corridor and rooms to prevent a surprise attack. Jackie swiftly spun into the doorway with her weapon aimed. A naked, unwashed man cried out while leaping on top of her.

Jackie didn't even have time to fire her weapon as the man tackled her to the floor with his hands on her throat. The gun flew from her hand. Jackie easily broke his grip from her throat while the naked man straddled her. He swung at her with both fists. She blocked the first two punches. Scorpio kicked the man in the shoulder, sending him across the corridor floor. Jackie sprang to her feet at the same time as the crazed, naked man.

"What the hell--?" Jackie cried out with confusion just before the unarmed man again bolted for her.

Scorpio turned her head just in time to see a second man dart from the same room. Before she could react, he knocked her into Jackie, sending both women crashing into the opposing wall. The man bolting for Jackie tackled them against the wall along with the second man and attempted to bite them. Jackie and Scorpio punched both men to put some distance between them and keep the men from biting them. Scorpio kicked the naked man in the thigh, sending him further back. Jackie punched the man about to bite her, striking him twice in the face, and then kicked him in the abdomen.

"Does this happen to you often?" Scorpio cried out with surprise.

"Not exactly," Jackie replied.

The naked man lunged for Scorpio, who immediately grimaced before kicking him in the leg and sending him to the floor.

"Why do I get the naked one?" Scorpio cried out. "I don't want to see that!"

Jackie spun into a high, roundhouse kick and struck her man in the face, sending him into the naked man. Both men were thrown to the floor. Scorpio reclaimed her swords while Jackie threw herself to the floor and snatched her discarded semiautomatic. The naked man grabbed her assault rifle that had fallen to the floor when she earlier hit the wall. He aimed the weapon at her. Jackie rolled with the handgun, sat up, and fired two shots into the man's chest. The second man saw the bullets rip into the naked man's flesh, thought better of the attack, and ran down the hall. Jackie drew a deep breath then snatched the assault rifle from the floor.

"Okay, that wasn't just me, right?" Scorpio demanded. "That was weird."

Jackie eyed the naked, dead man on the hall floor then looked around. "Yeah, that was weird," she replied. "I'm guessing these people have been stuck here for quite some time. Although they can't possibly be from when this place an actual mental facility."

"No, this place has been abandoned at least ten years," Scorpio agreed.

"Maybe twenty years," Jackie added. "It just doesn't make sense. Why bring Gil and Sal here? Obviously, one of them was the intended target. There's no way it was just a random abduction."

"No, not when the abduction happened in Virginia," Scorpio added. "That would have to take planning."

"And I doubt they forced Gil to fly here," Jackie added. "A skilled pilot such as Gil would have seized the opportunity even if it meant crashing the plane."

"So whoever brought them here also has piloting skills," Scorpio announced.

Jackie nodded while deep in thought. "That tells me Gil was the intended target," she announced. "Sal has plenty of enemies, but what are the odds any of them are pilots. Gil knew dozens even hundreds of pilots over the years."

"It has to be bigger than your friend," Scorpio informed her. "This is one elaborate setup. The guards both outside and in. Time. Manpower."

"I have to agree with you," Jackie announced while looking around. "Whoever did this has been guarding his game for months or years. It has to be someone the team had crossed at one time, but not just my team. This man is seeking revenge on all his enemies."

"Do you know anyone fitting that description?" Scorpio asked.

Jackie groaned and shook her head. "I know plenty of people fitting that description," she replied. "Even more that were before my time."

"Maybe we should find the others," Scorpio announced while looking around with concern. "Maverick said Rayner was last seen in the game room with Sal. We need to find the game room."

"That should be on this level somewhere," Jackie remarked. "Let's follow this corridor and see where it leads. Keep an eye out for more crazies."

§

Bogart stood near the partially open infirmary door while Maverick paced the length of the room. Maverick nervously eyed the bloody mess left behind by the recent attack then seemed to realize that the bound and gagged woman was watching him. He eyed Regina several times then glanced back at Bogart.

"Any idea who this woman is?" Maverick asked.

Bogart glanced back only briefly and shook his head. "Gil said her name is Regina, but other than that, she's not talking," he announced. "We'll find out exactly who she is when we turn her over to the authorities."

"Give Mac five minutes alone with her, and we'd know now," Maverick remarked while eyeing the woman.

"I'm not really onboard with that," Bogart informed Maverick.

"Well, you're not the one she locked in a morgue drawer," Maverick announced while glaring at the woman.

Despite the duct tape covering her mouth, it was apparent Regina was smirking at him.

"I suppose I'm not really cut out for this type of thing," Maverick informed Bogart while glaring at the bound woman. "I'm resisting the urge to push her into the corridor to meet her little crazy, cannibal friends."

"If it comes down to them eating her or me, she's going first," Bogart announced without looking back. "That's a given."

Maverick nodded and smirked back at the woman bound within the wheelchair. "Sounds like a plan to me," he announced.

She stared back at him and no longer smirked.

§

Jackie and Scorpio continued along the corridor then entered the lounge. Both looked around. Scorpio's attention suddenly shifted to the doorway across the room.

"Kane," Scorpio gasped and hurried for the connecting doorway.

Jackie ran after her not even certain what the young woman had actually heard. Both entered the lobby where they discovered Kane, Zack, Rayner, and Sal as they entered the lobby from the patient's wing. Scorpio saw Rayner, appeared relieved, and ran for him. She jumped into his arms and clung to him. Rayner returned the embrace then pulled back just far enough to meet her gaze and scanned her for injuries.

"Are you okay?" he asked.

"Me?" she gasped then laughed nervously. "You were the one who was missing." Scorpio gently touched his face then quickly kissed him on the lips.

Sal limped toward Jackie, grinned happily, and gave her a warm embrace. She returned the hug.

"I'm glad we found you," Jackie announced.

Sal pulled back, met her gaze, and chuckled warmly. "Thanks for looking."

"Time to bring this party to an end," Zack announced then indicated the front door. "Sounds like the guys are still taking care of the guards outside." He then eyed Kane, Scorpio, Sal, and Rayner. "The four of you need to find a break in the action and make it to the woods. Hike back to the airfield and wait for us there."

"Shouldn't we stick together?" Kane asked and seemed unwilling to leave.

"Once we find our men, we're out of here," Zack informed him. "Jackie and I will be right behind you."

"Uh, speaking of right behind us," Kane suddenly announced and indicated the patient's wing doorway.

Three crazed patients charged through the doorway and ran for them. They heard movement coming from the lounge and saw four more patients heading their way.

"Everyone out," Zack announced and indicated the front door.

They ran for the main entrance. Kane yanked open the door to see four guards in the doorway. He attempted to slam the door on them but met resistance.

§

Gil and Mac crept along the corridor and glanced inside each room as they passed. The back wing seemed eerily silent despite the commotion outside. Even though they had been keeping alert for any patients or guards, Gil felt obligated to make small talk with Mac.

"Did you see Darth at all?" Gil asked Mac as they checked rooms.

"We were locked in the cargo hold of a private plane together," Mac informed him. "He saved my life. Got to ride in an ambulance and have some adventures in the hospital in Kentucky."

"I'm glad he's okay," Gil remarked and shook his head. "Not sure what I'd do without him."

"The guys left him at the abandoned airfield a few miles from here," Mac announced then shrugged. "I guess he's guarding the planes."

"He can be a little territorial about my plane," Gil countered then cast a glance at Mac. "Any idea who this Deidra actually is?"

"No, but she's young," Mac informed him. "Not even the legal drinking age yet." She cast a look at Gil. "I don't think she's anyone from Sal's past. I met a lot of people he'd interacted with, and she didn't seem the least bit familiar to me."

"Do you remember Giovanni?"

"Of course," Mac muttered while frowning. "That island wedding from hell isn't exactly something a person could forget."

"His son went off the deep end after the wedding massacre," Gil informed her. "Giovanni stopped by Sal's place the night before we left and told us about Marco's fragile state of mind. Does she seem like Marco's type? Someone he possibly knows?"

"If Marco is still crazy from what happened at his wedding, he didn't seek alternate company, I promise you that," Mac informed Gil. "Besides, Deidra is too backwoods for someone like Marco."

"Backwoods?"

"Yeah," Mac announced with little reaction. "You know. A hick. Redneck."

"I hadn't considered that," Gil responded. "The woman I found is less city and more rural too. I'm not sure how much that really helps though."

A crazed patient silently slipped from one of the offices behind them and crept up on Mac, who was bringing up the rear. He continued his quiet approach until he was just within striking distance. Mac kicked out behind her without seemingly looking and struck him in the chest. He was thrown to the floor. Mac didn't even bother looking back. The crazed man scrambled to his feet and took off in the opposite direction.

"Rules out Marco," Mac informed Gil while seeming unfazed by what had just happened. "He's a bit of a spoiled rich boy. You'd never find him in the woods of Vermont, particularly a place like this. He's too stuck-up to play this game."

"This is actually my first trip to Vermont," Gil informed Mac while keeping watch ahead of them. "I can't say I'm enjoying the visit."

"The skiing is great," Mac informed him. "Plenty of historical sites and amazing hiking trails. I don't think abandoned mental institutions are really what Vermont is famous for."

Two crazed patients ran down the hall for them. Gil lowered himself and rammed the first one in the abdomen with his shoulder, sending him airborne before crashing to the floor. Mac spun into a roundhouse kick and just about launched the second man into the opposing wall. Both men picked themselves up with some unsteadiness and ran away from the pair. Gil and Mac continued along the hallway.

"That happens a lot," Gil informed Mac while resuming their conversation as if nothing had happened. "I mean; I go to beautiful tropical islands and never really enjoy the beaches or the scenery. Maybe if people would stop shooting at me, I could enjoy myself a little."

"To be honest," Mac remarked while considering the comment. "That happens to me a lot too. Giovanni's island was quite nice until the bunch of you showed up. Went to hell after that."

Gil paused and cast a glare at Mac. "That shit show didn't follow us there, you know."

"I know," Mac replied then raised her brows suggestively. "But you have to admit; whenever you guys show up, things tend to go sideways pretty fast."

Gil stared at her a moment, considered the comment, and nodded. "You do have a point."

Chapter 59

The front door jolted against Kane's body and tossed him across the lobby. The four, armed guards forced the door open and fired randomly. Everyone, including the crazed patients, scattered from the gunfire. Rayner and Sal bolted into the nearby game room along with one of the cannibals, who had been directly behind them. They no sooner closed the door when the deranged man lunged for them. Sal coiled back with the baseball bat as Rayner ducked the attacking patient. Sal clocked the man alongside the head and sent him back several feet. Rayner took a step back for the closed door to avoid getting in the way of Sal and his baseball bat.

Sal suddenly appeared alarmed and tackled Rayner to the floor just as bullets riddled the door from the other side. The barrage of bullets easily penetrated the wood and entered the game room. As the crazed patient attempted to stand, he was struck multiple times, as was the prisoner they had left tied in his chair on the opposite end of the room.

§

Jackie and Kane ran from the lobby and into the lounge where they took cover just inside the doorway from the explosion of bullets. One of the patients had chased after them into the lounge and took the brunt of the gunfire meant for Jackie. The bullet-riddled man collapsed to the floor in a bloody heap just several yards inside the room. Jackie cast her back alongside the open door and fired back at the men in the lobby. Kane remained on the other side of Jackie while clutching his gun and seemed uncertain of his next move. Jackie didn't have time to check on Kane's condition, but she knew he was quite possibly shell-shocked.

"Is Scorpio still out there?" Kane asked with concern, although unable to move.

Jackie fired another couple of rounds and again sought shelter alongside the door. "I don't see her or Zack," she informed him. "Rayner and Sal made it into the game room, but they took some unwanted company with them."

"I'm not cut out for this," Kane suddenly announced.

Jackie cast a look at the once confident man alongside her. He met her gaze and seemed to be entering panic mode.

"I can't shoot worth a damn," he blurted out while trembling. "My sister and friends are out there, and I can't do a damned thing to help them."

Jackie didn't have time to keep Kane from falling apart, but she also couldn't afford to have him question his confidence in a life-or-death situation. Jackie partially turned to face him and stared into his eyes.

"Don't lose your shit on me, Kane," she announced firmly. "I need you to keep it together."

Kane stared back at her and nodded. "I'm good," he replied, although he didn't sound it.

She continued to stare into his eyes, knowing she needed to keep him focused even if it was on her.

"It's easier to gamble with your own life than with the lives of those you love," she informed him. "In cases like this, when I don't have a plan; do what I do."

"What's that?" Kane asked as his brain seemed to snap back into focus.

"Wait for it," she replied.

Kane stared at her with a strange look. "Wait for what?" he asked.

"One of Zack's infamous diversions," Jackie replied then offered a tiny smile.

§

As one of the guards ran across the lobby toward the lounge, Zack leaped from the railing of the stairs, rolled across the rotted floor, and sat up while firing his assault rifle. The man took multiple hits before falling to the floor. Scorpio somersaulted off the stairs on the opposite side and landed behind the man shooting the game room door. The man must have felt the gust of air and spun around with his weapon aimed. Scorpio swung with both swords in an outward crisscross and just about cut the man in two. Another guard appeared and fired multiple rounds at her. She leaped across the floor into a forward roll and vanished behind the steps. Two deranged patients ran for the guard and attempted to overpower him. The guard shot both patients with several rounds.

When the guard rounded the stairs to find Scorpio, Jackie fired at him from the lounge doorway. He ducked alongside the stairs, fired back at her, and ran for the second set of stairs, taking cover behind the banister. He aimed his weapon at the lounge and waited for Jackie to poke her head out once more. Scorpio leaped out from behind the first set of stairs and swung with her sword. A crazed patient tackled her to the rotted floor between the two sets of stairs before she could decapitate the guard. The guard spun around as Scorpio attempted to fight off the crazed man on top of her. He aimed his weapon with his finger on the trigger.

Zack appeared at the top of the landing and fired multiple rounds into the guard. His body jerked and jolted from several shots before he collapsed in a bloody heap to the floor. Scorpio kicked the crazed man off her and sprang to her feet. As she reached for her discarded sword, two more crazed men lunged for her and attempted to take her down. She spun into a roundhouse kick and kept the first one back, but she was grabbed by the second one. Zack leaped from the second floor landing and knocked the man off her. The floorboards groaned under the weight and collapsed, taking both crazed men, Zack, and Scorpio through the floor and into the basement below.

Within the basement dining hall, Zack lay motionless on the pile of debris. He slowly opened his eyes then saw a moderately banged up patient make it to his feet and lunge for him. A booted foot struck the man in the chest and sent him backward onto the debris. Scorpio ran for Zack and helped pull him to his feet. He clutched his bleeding head with some disorientation. Scorpio grabbed one of her discarded swords then looked up to the hole in the ceiling. It was a long way up, and the floorboards were severely rotted. The ceiling groaned above them.

"We need to move," Scorpio informed Zack.

The ceiling moaned again. Zack saw Scorpio's second discarded sword, grabbed it, and hurried off the mound of ceiling debris. The rest of the ceiling gave away and crashed into the dining room with a cloud of dust.

§

Jackie and Kane took two steps into the lobby and watched as the entire floor and both sets of staircases collapsed into the basement. A large, thick cloud of dust filled the entire room. The second floor groaned above them. Kane and Jackie stared at the ceiling.

"Oh, that's not good," Kane announced.

"This whole section is coming down," Jackie informed him then looked across the lobby.

The entire lobby was just about gone. They were stranded on their side with no way across the massive pit. Rayner and Sal hurried from the game room and stood not far from the front door. Both stared at Jackie and Kane from across the chilling scene in the lobby.

"Where's Scorpio?" Rayner cried out.

Jackie glanced at the large pit. Rayner's eyes shifted as well, and horror crossed his face.

"No," Rayner gasped.

"This entire section is about to come down," Jackie called out to them across the massive pit. "You need to get out. Find the guys outside. We'll evacuate out the back way."

Rayner protested while staring at the hole before him. "But Scorpio--"

"I can't leave without my sister," Kane insisted while staring at Jackie.

"We're not leaving without them," Jackie informed him. "We'll head to the basement and find them." She again looked across the lobby at Sal and turned commanding. "Get him out of here!"

Sal nodded and ushered a belligerent Rayner toward the main entrance.

"We'll find her, Rayner," Kane called out in an attempt to reassure him.

Jackie ran with Kane across the lounge while clutching his shirtsleeve, forcing him to pick up speed as they raced for the corridor on the opposite side. They had just about reached the corridor when there was a tremendous cracking sound, and the floor vibrated beneath their feet. Kane suddenly tackled Jackie through the doorway, landing on top of her. He shielded her with his body as a massive cyclone of dust and debris flew over them.

Chapter 60

Monroe and John joined Kirk and Stone who had now taken refuge alongside the patient's wing of the asylum. A loud rumbling sound caught their attention. They'd heard the familiar sound too many times before. The building began to vibrate. Kirk and Monroe exchanged horrified looks although Stone and John seemed mildly puzzled by what was happening. They hadn't been around for one of Zack's farewell parties during covert missions.

"Move, move!" Monroe shouted while wildly flinging his free arm toward the woods.

All four ran for the nearby woods as the ground literally rumbled under their feet. They darted into the woods and ran for several yards when they heard the nearly deafening sound. Monroe and Kirk tossed themselves to the ground. John and Stone saw the two men dive to the ground and immediately did the same, although they didn't seem to know why. There was a tremendous surge of wind followed by a large cloud of debris that reached the edge of the woods. It took a second for the dust to clear. The four men slowly moved onto their sides and looked back at the building. All four stories in the front section of the building were now reduced to a large pile of rubble. Monroe's expression dropped as he stared at the partially destroyed building.

"Oh, shit!"

Kirk just about sprang to his feet. "Our men are still in there," he cried out. "We need to get inside!"

As they looked across the overgrown grounds, they saw Sal and Rayner picking themselves up just beyond the destroyed jeep.

"It's Sal and Rayner," Monroe yelled while pointing. He snatched his discarded rifle and sprang to his feet. "We need to give them cover."

Kirk grabbed his rifle and ran after Monroe. Stone and John recovered a little less quickly but grabbed their rifles and hurried after them. Not surprisingly, they didn't come across any guards on the outside. They too were probably just as stunned with the collapse. Monroe and Kirk helped Sal to the woods as Rayner brought up the rear while keeping an eye behind them. He seemed preoccupied with the downed front half of the building.

"Scorpio is in there," Rayner gasped and seemed unable to focus on anything else.

They reached the safety of the woods.

"I'm sure she's fine," Stone announced while attempting to remain positive despite his outward appearance.

"No, she was in the lobby when it collapsed," Rayner just about cried out. "She and Zack fell into the basement. We need to get emergency crews out here. They could be alive under the rubble."

The remaining five men exchanged concerned looks then eyed the destroyed front half of the building. None was willing to admit what they all were thinking. If they were under the lobby when the rest of the building collapsed, there was little chance they survived.

§

Maverick and Bogart felt the entire building rumble beneath their feet. They grabbed onto the nearby walls to support themselves as the entire building vibrated. A loud thunderous crash was heard, and it felt as if they had experienced an earthquake. The violent tremor even caught their prisoner's attention. The building finally stopped shaking. Maverick and Bogart exchanged surprised looks.

"What the hell was that?" Bogart cried out.

"It felt like an earthquake," Maverick announced while looking around.

Regina was attempting to cry out while thrashing in the wheelchair where she had been restrained. Bogart approached the woman and removed the duct tape from her mouth.

"You idiots," she cried out. "That was the building coming down!"

Maverick and Bogart again exchanged looks, uncertain if they should believe her or not.

"We need to get out of here before the entire structure comes down," she screamed at them.

§

Once the building stopped vibrating, Mac opened her eyes from where she had been pinned against the doorframe. Gil had his body pressed against hers while holding her against the solid frame. Both looked around without moving.

"What the fuck was that?" Mac gasped in horror. "Did Zack blow the building?"

"Felt that way," Gil muttered and finally released Mac from the doorway.

Mac turned her back to the doorframe and held her head a moment. "Jesus," she gasped and looked around. She then eyed Gil, who was just as curious about the vibrating building. "Thanks."

Gil glanced at her and gave a slight nod. "Think nothing of it."

Mac again looked around and insecurely rubbed her arms. "Which part of the building was that?" she asked.

"I'm guessing the front," Gil informed her and removed his hand radio. "Anyone copy?"

"Gil?" Bogart announced through the radio. "I copy. Maverick and I are still here. You okay?"

"Yeah, Mac and I are fine," Gil announced. "Do you have a location of impact?"

"Came from the front of the building," Bogart announced through the radio.

"Gil," Monroe announced through the radio. "We have visual. The entire front of the building has collapsed." There was a moment's pause. "Zack and Scorpio were last seen at ground zero."

Gil shut his eyes a moment and held his breath. Mac's expression turned to horror. She snatched the hand radio from Gil.

"Any word on Kane's location?" she shouted into the hand radio. "Anyone seen Kane?"

"Mac, it's Rayner," Rayner announced over the hand radio. "Jackie and Kane were heading deeper into the building looking for a way into the basement. There's a good chance they made it out of the way in time."

Mac held her breath then shut her eyes and returned the hand radio to Gil.

"Jackie," Gil announced into the radio. "You copy?"

There was no response.

"Zack, you copy?"

Gil cursed under his breath and met Mac's gaze. Her concerned look turned angry.

"We need to head for the basement," Mac insisted. "If we're lucky, we'll run into Jackie and Kane on their way to find Zack and Scorpio."

Gil nodded then returned the hand radio to his mouth. "Monroe, sweep the estate grounds," he announced. "Mac and I are going to find Jackie and Kane."

"Copy that," Monroe responded over the radio.

"Bogart, you copy?"

"Yeah, Gil," Bogart replied over the radio. "We're still here."

"Head for the basement," Gil informed him. "We'll meet you down there."

"What about the prisoner?" Bogart asked from the other end.

"I don't give a fuck what you do with her," Gil replied then returned his hand radio to his belt. He looked at Mac and removed his slung rifle from his shoulder. "Let's go find our friends."

§

Moments later, Bogart and Maverick stood within the doorway and listened to the loud thumping sound. They exchanged looks as if attempting to read the other's expression.

"You feel guilty about this?" Bogart asked while cocking his head slightly and offering a tiny grimace.

"Not in the least," Maverick replied.

Bogart sighed with relief and managed a tiny laugh. "Good," he remarked. "I was afraid it was just me."

"Come on," Maverick announced and nodded toward the corridor. "Let's join the others."

Bogart and Maverick walked out of the morgue while Regina screamed profanities and pounded from where she was locked away inside the freezer drawer.

Chapter 61

A small pile of rubble moved, knocking dirt and debris off Kane. Kane coughed several times then rolled off Jackie with a loud groan.

"Fuck that hurt," he cried out.

Jackie slowly moved onto her hands and knees then collapsed into a sitting position while rubbing her hip. "Can't say I enjoyed it much either," she moaned then removed the broken hand radio.

Jackie frowned and cast the broken device aside. Kane pulled the lounge door partway open with his foot and peered into what was left of the large common area. He shook his head at the mound of debris covering half of the lounge. The morning sky could be seen beyond that. Kane then looked around the corridor.

"I think the rest of the building is structurally sound," he informed her as he slid closer to where she sat and panted after her ordeal. Kane gently brushed the hair back from her temple that bled freely. He eyed the laceration then met her gaze. "Are you okay?"

Jackie nodded and reached for her discarded handgun. She placed it in her shoulder holster then slowly moved to her feet. Kane stood and helped steady her.

"We need to get to the basement," she announced without looking at him then indicated the hallway. "The stairs are at the end of this corridor."

Jackie stumbled along the hall then realized Kane wasn't behind her. She turned and looked back to see what happened to him. Kane remained standing in the same spot while staring at the collapsed building behind them. Jackie drew a deep breath and approached him. She placed her hand on his shoulder, catching his attention. He glanced at her with a moderately traumatized look in his eyes.

"If she's dead, it's my fault," Kane announced in a slightly shaken voice. "I dragged her out here. She should have been in Maine."

Jackie placed her hand on his face and forced him to meet her gaze. "She's okay, Kane," Jackie insisted.

"How do you know?"

"Because she's with Zack," Jackie replied. "When it comes to knocking buildings down, Zack's practically an expert. If he's not dead; she's not dead."

Kane stared into her eyes a moment longer then nodded in response. "I believe you."

§

Jackie and Kane hurried down the fire stairs. They had both lost their assault rifles and now only had their semiautomatics with limited rounds. As they raced to the bottom of the concrete steps, Kane paused to look at the slightly crumbling concrete. Jackie realized Kane wasn't behind her and ran back up the few steps to join him. She then saw what had him concerned.

"How much time?" she asked while tensing.

"I'm not an expert," Kane informed her. "Ten minutes to two weeks."

Jackie rolled her eyes and nudged him with her elbow. "Let's go. We need to find Scorpio and Zack before the entire building falls down on our heads."

Kane hurried after her. She paused before the basement stairwell door with her weapon in her hand. Kane held his gun with less conviction. She eyed him as if secretly signaling her intention. His brows knitted with uncertainty to what she was conveying.

Jackie groaned with annoyance. "Cover me," she informed him.

Kane nodded with some embarrassment and aimed his weapon with a little more confidence. Jackie opened the door and aimed her gun into the corridor. The basement hallway seemed sturdy enough, but that wasn't to say the upper levels wouldn't collapse above them causing a domino effect. Kane followed Jackie along the quiet basement corridor while watching their backside. Jackie heard faint voices coming from the laundry room. She paused outside the door and listened a moment. She looked back at Kane, raised her brows, and then showed him four fingers while flexing her thumb. She was conveying at least four men and possibly a fifth man. Kane nodded with understanding. The voices trailed off, indicating the men were heading deeper into the laundry room.

Jackie silently signaled to Kane by raising her brows. He gripped his gun and nodded. Jackie slowly pushed open the door and peered inside the massive room. There were racks of old, dusty deteriorating linen, industrial sized washing machines and dryers, and many bins. There wasn't any sign of the men she had just heard moments earlier. The bodies of the men Scorpio had earlier taken down were gone. All that remained were large pools of fresh blood. Jackie darted into the laundry room and ducked behind a rack of linen. Kane was directly on her heels and joined her. They listened for any sounds of the men. Their voices were heard from deeper in the laundry room and getting louder.

"Ready?" Jackie whispered while staring into Kane's blue eyes.

Kane drew a deep breath, exhaled, and nodded with a little more confidence. Jackie and Kane peered above the old, dusty linen folded and piled on the rack and waited for the men to come into view. Two of the men appeared in the area near the washing machines while pushing linen carts. Kane moved away from Jackie, she assumed to get a better view. Jackie strained to see what was in the linen cart. She then saw the cache of weapons. She was about to motion to Kane when she felt something strike her hip. Jackie spun around and saw the naked man from the abandoned airfield. Kane rode on the man's back with his arm around his neck, choking him into silence. Jackie kicked the naked man in the testicles, dropping him to his knees. Kane rode the man down to the floor. Unfortunately, the man struck the linen rack and jolted it enough for it to rattle.

Kane rolled off the naked man. Jackie then heard a gun cocking behind her. She immediately tensed at the sound and realized Kane was already out of sight. Jackie slowly turned to face the guard aiming his weapon at her.

"Well, well," the guard announced. "What do we have here? Drop the weapon."

Jackie frowned and allowed her gun to fall from her fingers to the floor with a loud clatter. She just hoped Kane wouldn't do anything stupid while she did something stupid. Zack knew her moves and her capabilities, and Jackie was good at predicting where and when Zack would make an appearance. It's how they kept from accidentally killing each other during missions. Unfortunately, Kane wanted to be a knight in shining armor. As proven in the woods, he didn't know how to read her body language, and she feared another accidental collision with him while both attempted to reach the same goal. The guard's expression hardened as he motioned her out from behind the rack with his weapon.

"Move it," he snarled.

Jackie took her time walking out from behind the linen rack while secretly casting glances around the room in search of Kane. Just a few feet away from the linen rack, she shifted her eyes to where she would normally look for Zack high on a perch. To her surprise, she spotted Kane crouched low on top of the linen rack. She had to give him credit for his stealthy climb in the few seconds that had passed. As the second man got close enough, Jackie heard a tiny, metallic creak from the linen rack near them. Kane was about to make his move, and she needed to make hers. Jackie spun around while grabbing the man's rifle muzzle to keep it away from her and kicked the weapon from the second man's hand.

Kane leaped from the linen rack while spinning his body through the air and kicked the guard in the head. The man and his rifle were thrown clear across the room. He struck the cart filled with weapons and knocked the entire bin to the ground. They heard the clatter of hundreds of rifles. The man had successfully made enough noise to bring the others back in a hurry. Kane went with the roll then sprang back to his feet and faced Jackie.

"You could have just shot him," Jackie cried out and went for the return kick on the second man, who fell into the pile of weapons.

"I'm sure I would have missed and hit you," Kane yelled back as he ran for the nearby linen rack just as the two remaining men appeared with their weapons.

Kane kicked the first man and successfully knocked him into the second man, forcing both to drop their weapons. With all the stolen weapons strewn across the floor, it was impossible to tell which ones were loaded. Jackie didn't bother attempting to figure it out and ran for the first man who stood. She flipped herself over the man's body, caught him around the neck with her legs, and threw him to the floor while keeping her legs locked around him. As much as she hated doing it, Jackie gave an added twist and snapped the man's neck. The sound of his neck breaking was almost enough to nauseate her.

"Oh," Kane suddenly cried out in horror while staring at the dead man with his head turned in an unnatural position. "Oh, how could you do that?"

Jackie kicked the next man as he stood then glared at Kane and the horrified look on his face. "You said Zack was going to teach you," she launched.

"Yeah, but that's him," Kane cried out. "That's not something hot women should *ever* do!"

Jackie stared at him with surprise then shook her head, expressing her disapproval. "Have you met Mac?" she demanded. "She'd tear off your testicles without thinking twice."

"Well, we don't really have that sort of relationship," Kane announced.

Jackie gave a slight nod with little reaction. "Behind you," she casually announced.

Kane spun around into a kick and struck the man in the chest.

"Can we discuss your sexist attitude later?" Jackie demanded then turned to the man alongside her as he attempted to return to his feet.

Jackie kicked the man in the face with her foot and sent him crashing onto his backside. Kane was now confronted by both men behind him. He punched the first man and kicked the second.

"I'm *not* sexist," he insisted and punched the man in the stomach. "I'm warm--" He then punched the man in the eye. "Cuddly--" Kane kicked the guard in the groin and turned to face Jackie as the man fell to his knees while clutching himself. "And adorable."

The second man tackled Kane to the floor with a hard hit. Jackie caught a glimpse of the two men hitting the floor and grimaced.

"Clearly you lack focus," Jackie remarked and swiftly kicked an approaching guard. She rammed her elbow into the man's abdomen and then threw him over her shoulder. He crashed to the floor not far from where Kane wrestled to free himself from his attacker. "Focus is better than cuddly."

Jackie was suddenly tackled to the floor by the man she thought she had incapacitated. Jackie and Kane managed to throw their attackers off them at the same time. Both sprang to their feet.

"How about we continue this debate later?" Kane remarked while breathing heavily.

"Good idea," Jackie replied.

Jackie resumed her assault on the man who had just moments earlier taken her down. As the other guard lunged for him, Kane spun into a kick. Before he was able to connect with his target, Kane was struck on the back of the head. Kane dropped to the floor and appeared unconscious. Jackie spun around and saw a gun aimed at her just out of striking distance. The first thing she saw was the man's missing pinky and ring finger on the hand that held the gun. Her eyes strayed to the man's face. Horror swept over Jackie as she stared at the familiar man from her past.

"Abbott," Jackie gasped as all of the color drained from her face.

Abbott managed a mocking smile and cleverly raised his brows. "Thought I was dead, didn't you?" he announced while grinning almost deviously. "Not for lack of trying by you or Zack."

As Jackie stared at the man who had killed her father, the rage increased inside her.

Chapter 62

Approximately four years earlier. Vernon Heights, Virginia. It was nearly midnight in the small development, and most of the houses were dark. Jackson's funeral had been earlier that day, and the last of the guests had left the wake, which was held at the commander's house. The front door opened and Monroe stepped onto the porch. He turned to face Jackie in the doorway and offered her a sympathetic smile.

"Are you sure you don't want me to stay?" he asked while holding her hand affectionately in his. "I hate leaving you alone like this."

"I'll be fine, Monroe," Jackie gently replied and offered a warm smile while squeezing his hand. "I appreciate everything you've done for me and for my father's funeral, but I just want to be alone right now."

It was only a partial truth. Jackie knew she was vulnerable and letting Monroe stay was just asking for trouble. She'd possibly do something she'd later regret and couldn't risk breaking his heart again with another misunderstanding.

"I understand," Monroe responded then pulled her in for a quick kiss on the lips.

Jackie met his gaze and almost reconsidered the offer. She wanted someone to hold her, but that wouldn't end well. Jackie resisted asking him to stay.

"You know where to find me if you need me," Monroe assured her.

She smiled warmly and nodded in response. "Goodnight, Monroe."

Monroe turned, headed off the porch, and approached his rental car. Jackie watched Monroe back out of the driveway. He honked the horn as he drove away. Jackie smiled and was about to return inside when she looked across the yard. She thought she heard something, but she didn't see anything. She stared a moment longer then went back inside and closed the door behind her. The front light went out. Within a few minutes, the downstairs lights went out as well. The upstairs light came on, and Jackie's silhouette could be seen in the second floor window. Someone moved within the bushes and watched the house. The bedroom light finally went out. Abbott stepped out of the bushes and stared at the house with a merciless look on his face. He looked across the back yard and signaled toward the rear bushes.

A large man, who stood over six-foot-six with a muscular body to match, stepped out of the bushes and darted toward the house. Abbott took a moment to survey the neighborhood then hurried to the side of the house and joined the large man.

The large man smiled in a mildly sinister manner. "She's cute," he announced. "Do I have to kill her right away?"

"Torture her slowly for all I care," Abbott announced and sneered at the man. "Make it as messy and painful as you want. I don't care. I just want her to suffer."

The man chuckled. "Not a problem." He turned toward the house when Abbott stopped him.

"Just make sure you have her subdued properly," Abbott informed him. "She's not as sweet as she looks. She's a feisty thing."

"That's okay," the man announced and grinned. "I like them feisty."

"Text me when you have her prepped," Abbott announced. "I want to see the look on her face for myself."

The man grinned and laughed. "It's your money, you pervert," he remarked then headed for the side door.

Abbott approached the front bushes, slipped behind them, and made himself comfortable with his back against the house.

He closed his eyes for a few minutes and just about dozed off when his phone vibrated. The text message read, "All clear." Abbott looked at his watch and appeared impressed.

"That wasn't so difficult," he muttered then slipped out from behind the bushes and headed for the side of the house to use the same entrance as his hired goon.

Abbott paused before the side door and attempted to open it, but it remained locked. He appeared slightly surprised. Abbott then saw a man's reflection behind him through the glass door. He spun around in time to be struck in the face by a booted foot.

§

Abbott slowly woke and looked around what appeared to be a junkyard. As his vision cleared, what looked like wrecked cars turned out to be junked airplanes. He slowly sat up and almost immediately clutched his head. A clunk was heard from nearby. Abbott lowered his hand from his head and looked up. The haunting wreckage of Old Marge was just a few yards from him. The plane had taken one hell of a beating during her emergency landing, and a bold, bloodied handprint was visible inside the windshield. Abbott immediately tensed and scanned the area. There was a clunk from within the old wreckage. Abbott again looked at the plane. Zack stepped out of the side opening that was missing its door. Abbott scrambled backward on his backside while staring at the man only a few yards from him.

"Zack?" he gasped. "You're supposed to be dead."

"A dozen times over," Zack announced then shrugged with little emotion. "Give or take a time or two. You, of all people, should know that. You helped me die once."

"They found your toe," Abbott gasped.

"Plenty of toes in the world, Abbott," Zack informed him. "They're easy to find if you know where to look."

Zack removed the Bowie knife from his boot and studied it a moment.

Abbott tensed and slowly moved to his feet while holding his hands defensively in front of him. "Take it easy, Zack," he announced while scanning the area around him for any sort of weapon. "Let's talk about this."

Zack eyed him past the shimmering blade of his knife. "Have you ever known me to be the talkative type?"

"What happened with Jackson was an accident," Abbott informed him but didn't lower his hands. His eyes shifted to a metal pipe on the ground not far from the wreckage. Unfortunately, he'd have to go through Zack to reach it. "I was showing him a gun I'd acquired when Jackie suddenly decided to show off with some fancy flying moves. The gun accidentally went off. I swear."

"And then she kicked you out of the plane, huh?"

"She went insane," Abbott insisted. "It wasn't my fault, but she told everyone I'd killed her father. In reality, she'd killed him by showing off in the air."

Zack again studied the Bowie knife blade. "In reality," he announced without looking at Abbott, "you murdered our former commander, who also happened to be my best friend, and attempted to kill his daughter." Zack shot a look at Abbott and showed no emotion. "Any one of these acts by themselves would be enough to spark my wrath. But hearing the words 'torture her slowly'--?" Zack shook his head. "I'm not one to let my emotions own me, but every psychotic thought I've ever had has plagued my mind after hearing those words." He raised his brows and cocked his head slightly. "After I broke your goon's neck, I thought some of that rage would diminish, but instead, it's been festering inside of me. Then, I had an epiphany also inspired by your words tonight." His eyes narrowed and burned through Abbott. "Make it *messy* and *painful*."

Abbott was about to speak when Zack threw the knife with speed and force at him. The knife pierced Abbott's booted foot causing him to scream in agony. Abbott endured the pain and pulled the knife from his foot. He straightened while clutching the knife in his hand and stared at Zack.

"Underestimating me was your first mistake," Abbott informed him while panting from the pain in his foot. "Arming me was your second and last mistake."

Abbott took an aggressive fighting stance and lunged for Zack with skills that came from years of military training. Zack easily deflected Abbott's first couple of shots. When he swung the knife for Zack's face, Zack caught his arm, twisted it, and forced Abbott to stab himself in the side. Zack followed through with a foot to his abdomen and sent him backward against the side of Old Marge. There was a loud, empty metallic clang. Abbott touched his bleeding side, eyed the blood, and then glared at Zack. He was purposely playing with him, keeping his promise to make it messy and painful.

Abbott panted a moment while considering his next move against the highly skilled fighter. Abbott suddenly threw himself to the ground and rolled for the discarded metal pipe. Zack saw him going for the pipe and attempted to cut him off before he reached it. Instead of grabbing the metal pipe, Abbott threw a handful of loose dirt into Zack's eyes. Zack was temporarily blinded and halted his approach. Abbott sprang to his feet and lunged for Zack with the knife clutched in his hand. Zack managed to catch his wrist but couldn't stop his forward momentum. Abbott slammed Zack into the wrecked plane across from Old Marge while Zack held back the hand with the knife.

Zack saw the ring made from the Purple Heart Abbott received and sneered. "You're a disgrace," he snarled in anger. "You only received that Purple Heart because of your cowardliness. If Jackson hadn't saved your worthless ass, you'd be dead right now."

"If the commander hadn't put our lives in jeopardy, I wouldn't have been shot in the first place," Abbott snarled in response.

"Putting our lives in jeopardy *was* our job!"

Zack cracked Abbott in the head with his own forehead and mildly disorientated him. Zack snatched the Bowie knife from his hand, spun him around, and slammed him against the plane. Before Abbott could even gain his bearings, Zack violently slashed with the knife severing Abbott's right ring finger and pinky from his hand. Abbott bellowed out in agony while clutching his bleeding hand. Zack picked up the severed ring finger still containing the ring made from the Purple Heart. He then straightened and stared at the screaming man and showed no emotion.

"See you in hell, old friend," Zack announced then turned and walked away.

Abbott clutched his bleeding hand and stared at Zack's turned back, possibly surprised that he let him live. There was a distinctive, familiar metallic scraping sound. Zack tossed the grenade over his shoulder. It landed just before Abbott's feet.

"Jesus--" Abbott cried out.

As Zack walked away, the grenade exploded, taking most of the plane with it. As a lone car drove away from the plane boneyard several minutes later, smoke wafted from the barely burning, wrecked plane. On the opposite end of the smoldering plane, a panel of metal fell to the ground. Abbott, gasping and coughing, crawled out from under the wreckage.

Chapter 63

Present day. Abbott kept his gun aimed at Jackie while maintaining his smirk despite the venomous look in her eyes. Abbott chuckled in his throat, mocking her anger.

"You know," he announced in an almost jovial tone. "That's the same look Zack gave me right before he tried to kill me. Didn't work out for him either. You see; Zack's not the only one with nine lives. To be honest though; I thought he was really dead the last time. Where was that? Giovanni's island?"

Jackie stared at Abbott, silently killing him with her eyes. Although she didn't show it, she shouldn't have been surprised that he somehow knew about their little mission on Giovanni's island, but she was. What happened at Marco's wedding had made its way through every crime family on every continent making Whiskey Tango Foxtrot a known name in *certain* circles. Despite the team gaining notoriety, their actual names never surfaced, making it strange that the rumor of Zack's death seemed to spread. Mostly everyone believed he had been dead years before that.

"Do you want to know what happened after that?" Abbott asked while grinning.

"Not really," Jackie muttered while hiding her emotions. The sound of his voice made her want to kill him even more, if that were possible.

"Not too long ago, someone starts shopping around Midnight Requisition," Abbott announced then shook his head. "You can't imagine my surprise to hear that name after all these years."

Kane suddenly became alert and pulled himself up to his hands and knees. He sank back on his feet and stared at Abbott. The look on Kane's face was somewhere between horrified and guilt-ridden.

"Obviously someone was attempting to flush out Zack," Abbott continued. "Which meant someone knew something I didn't. That's when I realized the bastard was still alive." He grinned and chuckled. "What better way to flush him out than snatching one of his own." He stared at Jackie and raised his brows. "Going after you would be the direct approach but akin to suicide. I tried that once and failed. You've gained quite the reputation since then, and I thought it best to avoid the wife of a federal agent. Beck and Ross keep themselves off the grid and hidden away from the world. Even if I knew where to find them, they'd see me coming a mile away. The paranoid little shits."

"Not quite so paranoid when people *are* actually out to get you," Jackie remarked without taking her eyes off the man.

"Which brings us to Mr. Paranoia himself. Your former flame, Monroe. Well, Monroe is a bit like a ghost. He flies so low under the radar; it'd be more work to find him than it's worth." He then hesitated and chuckled. "But Gil--?" Abbott appeared pleased with himself. "Gil's been off and on with that ex-wife of his since I've known him. Like an old dog in heat, he travels the same route from Colorado to Virginia. All I had to know was when he left the Colorado Springs airport. That gave me his entire flight to set up a plan I already had in place." He then hesitated and eyed Kane. "I'll admit; I wasn't expecting quite so many guests to be joining us. Who's your new friend?"

"He's not a friend," Jackie informed him. "More like a stowaway."

Kane darted a look at Jackie. It was obvious she didn't want Abbott thinking Kane meant anything to anyone on the team. He was already an expendable prop for Abbott to use against Jackie. Abbott couldn't be allowed to know Kane had any association with Zack.

"We'll find out soon enough," Abbott remarked while casting a look at Kane then smirked. "The kid's looking a little guilt-ridden about something."

Kane held his bleeding head a moment then frowned while glaring at Abbott. "Why does everyone think I'm a kid?" he scoffed with irritation.

"Shut up and stay down," Jackie growled in response.

"Believe it or not, kid, she's just trying to keep you from getting shot," Abbott teased. "She must think you're helpless and need protecting."

"He's baiting you," Jackie snarled at Kane. "Don't do anything stupid."

"I'm not helpless," Kane snapped back and pulled himself to his feet. He swayed slightly and clutched his head. "I'll agree that I'm a little stupid sometimes."

One of Abbott's goons aimed his weapon at Kane. Jackie stepped in front of Kane, shielding him with her body, and faced Abbott's goon.

"So stop being stupid," Jackie snarled back at Kane. "Let the grown-ups talk."

A strange grin suddenly crossed Abbott's face. "Oh, I see," he announced, almost pleased with himself as he chuckled. "I'd heard you'd recently discovered a long lost brother. This must be him. The commander's bastard son."

Jackie glared at Abbott but didn't comment. Better for him to think Kane was her brother than Zack's son. She then felt something press against her hip and tensed when she realized it was Kane's gun. He nudged his semiautomatic against her, so she'd know he had it. She feared his lack of confidence with a handgun and hoped he wasn't thinking about taking matters into his own hands.

"If he were my brother," Jackie scoffed, "he wouldn't be such a lousy shot."

Kane understood the secret message loud and clear. It was obvious she didn't want him attempting to shoot anyone since he wasn't that good with firearms. Kane gently stuck the gun down the back of Jackie's pants and took a step to her left with his hands in the air.

"Let's find out how important this young man is to you," Abbott announced and aimed the gun at Kane's leg.

Jackie gasped with horror as Abbott pulled the trigger. The gun clicked empty. Abbott sneered, tossed his gun aside, and snatched the gun from one of his two goons. That split second was all Jackie needed. Jackie pulled the gun from the back of her pants while simultaneously diving to the floor to avoid the second, armed goon before he could aim his weapon at her. Kane leaped for the armed, hired goon while all attention was now on Jackie. Jackie sat up and fired at Abbott, grazing his hand, and forcing him to drop his weapon in response. Jackie squeezed the trigger again for the kill shot, but her gun clicked empty.

Abbott offered a sinister smile and went for his discarded weapon. Jackie threw the empty gun at him and struck him in the back of the head. He stumbled several steps and clutched his head. Jackie leaped to her feet and lunged for Abbott, throwing herself into the air, and kicking him in the face. Abbott struck the linen rack behind him with enough force to shift the entire rack, causing it to sway. He recovered faster than anticipated, but he was met with Jackie's right and left fist to his face. Abbott stumbled back and again hit the linen rack jolting it.

"You bastard," Jackie screamed and punched him again. "You killed my father!"

Jackie's mounting anger startled Kane. Abbott's goon sucker punched Kane in the gut and then hoisted him up into the air above his head. As Kane fought the man's hold on him, Abbott's goon tossed him into the empty laundry bin. Jackie punched Abbott two more times before his second goon lunged for her in order to stop the assault. Jackie spun into a kick and nailed him in the chest, sending him back several feet. Kane jumped out of the linen cart and tackled the goon, knocking him away from Jackie. Jackie returned her attention to Abbott, who finally retrieved his loaded handgun. Jackie leaped up Abbott's body, wrapped her legs around his neck, and flipped him onto the floor with her entire body. She landed a little rougher than intended, but it didn't stop her from gripping his neck between her legs in an attempt to strangle him or break his neck, whichever came first.

His gun had slid across the floor, and it was just inches from Jackie's grasp. Kane spun into a high roundhouse kick and knocked Abbott's man to the floor with enough force that he rolled twice, nearly striking Abbott's thrashing legs as he fought Jackie's killer grip around his neck. Kane was tackled face first against the far wall by the second goon and immediately reversed their positions despite that his arms were pinned to his side. Kane cast his body backward and rammed his captor twice against the concrete wall in an attempt to loosen his grip. The man still on the floor scrambled for his discarded weapon. Jackie kept her legs locked around the slowly strangling Abbott while she attempted to reach his discarded gun not far from her fingertips. She then saw the man on the floor grab his own weapon and aim it at Kane.

Kane saw the same thing Jackie did and attempted to free himself from the man holding him immobile. Jackie cried out in anger, released Abbott, and rolled across the floor closer to the man with the gun. While still on the floor, she kicked him in the side of the knee and dropped him. As he fell from her kick, the gun fired, and the bullet tore into her side. Jackie cried out and clutched her bleeding side as the man with the gun crashed to the floor not far from her. He no sooner hit the floor when he attempted to regain control of the gun. Kane saw Jackie clutching her bleeding side and became enraged. He rammed the back of his head into the nose of the man holding him, which caused the man's head to strike the concrete.

Kane broke free from his grip and bolted across the room. He kicked the second goon in the face before he could reach the discarded gun. The man clutched his bleeding, broken nose and writhed in agony. Kane leaped to Jackie's side to check on her injuries. Abbott kicked Kane in the temple, sending him backward onto the floor not far from Jackie. He writhed in agony a moment then saw Abbott aiming the gun at him. Kane barely acknowledged the gun as he slid closer to Jackie, who was now on her knees holding her bleeding side. Kane placed one arm around her and held her against him while cradling her face to his chest.

"Jackie, please don't die," he whispered. "I'll get you out of this. Just hang on, okay?"

Jackie clutched Kane's shirt with her free hand while enduring the pain. "If you have any tricks up your sleeve," she announced softly and met his gaze while panting, "now would be a good time."

Kane placed his forehead against hers while holding her head. "I'm sorry I'm not my father," he whispered. "This is all my fault. None of this would have happened if it hadn't been for me."

"It's not your fault," she whispered back while Kane seemingly lost control of his emotions.

"It is," he insisted. "I started something I was incapable of finishing. I've waged countless wars on men more skilled than I am. What did I bring?" Kane removed her hand from his shirt and held it in his. "I brought a *knife* to a gunfight and expected to win."

Jackie's heart pounded as she looked at her hand and saw the tips of the throwing star he'd held against her palm. Jackie lifted her head and met his gaze. Kane's expression turned stern.

"I'm sorry I stole your revenge against the man who killed your father," he announced gently and raised his brow in silent gesture. "An eye for an eye, Jackie."

She stared back into his eyes and nodded. "An eye for an eye," Jackie whispered.

Kane smiled and warmly kissed her forehead. He'd barely pulled his lips from Jackie's forehead when he thrust his hand away from his body and released several throwing stars at one time. Three of the four throwing stars hit their intended targets. The first guard took one throwing star to his chest while the other grasped one lodged in his throat as blood poured between his fingers. The third throwing star struck Abbott in the hand, forcing him to drop his weapon. Abbott clutched his bleeding hand then saw the rage in Jackie's eyes as she spun toward him while on her knees. Abbott didn't even have time to look for his discarded gun as Jackie threw the throwing star at him. The pointy, metal object struck him in the eye. Abbott cried out and clutched the spiked weapon lodged in his eye.

Jackie moved to her feet with a little less exuberance while clutching her side and took two steps toward Abbott. He managed to jump back a step and put distance between them. Despite her pain, Jackie spun into a high roundhouse kick and struck the throwing star protruding from his eye. The pointy object was shoved through his eye socket and into his head. Abbott barely had time to gasp as he hit the wall then sank to the floor. Jackie cringed and again clutched her bleeding side. Kane sprang to his feet and immediately held his hand over hers on her injured side.

"We need to get pressure on that," he announced with concern.

She pushed his hand away and groaned. "I'll live," Jackie scoffed. "It's just a graze, but it stings like a bastard."

"I'm sorry," Kane announced and shook his head. "That was my fault. I need more practice shooting."

Jackie found an old washrag that was somewhat clean then lifted her shirt and placed the rag to the bleeding laceration. She applied pressure to the rag and cringed.

"Oh," Kane announced and felt his pockets. "Zack gave me the first aid kit." He removed a roll of duct tape and proudly held it up.

Jackie eyed the gray roll of tape then met Kane's serious look. She suddenly smiled and laughed.

"Rip off a four-inch piece," she instructed then painfully removed her jacket and shoulder holster.

Kane ripped off a piece of tape as instructed and held it between his fingers. Jackie removed her black tank top with some discomfort. Kane stared at her in her black bra and immediately tensed.

"Uh," he announced and attempted to look away. "Oh--"

She cast a glare at him. "Don't be shy on me now," Jackie huffed and removed the washrag from her bleeding laceration. She ripped a long piece of rag with her teeth, handed him the shredded cloth, and took both the tape and roll from him.

"Pinch the wound closed and place the cloth over it," Jackie ordered.

Kane looked back at her and stared at the six-inch graze bleeding freely on her side. He nervously held the laceration together and placed the strip of washrag over it. Jackie handed him the ripped piece of duct tape.

"Now tape it shut," she announced.

Kane placed the tape over the rag covering the laceration so it would hold it together. Jackie ripped more tape with her hand and teeth and handed it to him one strip at a time. Once he had the entire laceration held in place with the smaller strips of tape, she handed him two larger strips.

"Now two strips the other direction for added protection," she informed him.

Kane did as she asked. Jackie tossed him the roll of tape and grimaced as she picked up her discarded tank top.

"Congratulations," she announced. "You're officially a field medic."

Kane allowed his eyes to stray across her bra-clad body, which allowed him a view of her scars. "You, uh, have a lot of scars," he announced timidly.

"I've seen a lot of action," she replied and gingerly slipped into her tank top.

Kane handed her the shoulder holster and then her jacket. "Mac has a lot too."

"She's seen a lot of action too," Jackie informed him then met his gaze and offered a warm smile. "Thank you, Kane."

"For what?"

"Saving my life."

"Yeah, after nearly getting you killed," he remarked then snorted a laugh.

Jackie drew a deep breath then gently touched his face while staring into his eyes. "No one expects you to be perfect," she informed him. "Your heart is in the right place, and that's all that matters."

"I'd rather be like my father," Kane informed her while touching her hand.

Jackie smiled warmly. "You are."

Chapter 64

Zack slowly opened his eyes to a thick haze around him. Maggie lightly brushed his cheek while staring down at him with a concerned look on her face.

"Zack," she whispered. "Zack, wake up."

"Maggie," he moaned and reached up to touch her face. "I had the worst dream."

"It's far from a dream," Scorpio scoffed and looked around. "More like a nightmare."

Zack's vision cleared and Maggie morphed into Scorpio. He shut his eyes and smiled.

"You're beautiful, just like your mother."

Scorpio stared at him a moment then gently touched the hand still on her face. She drew a deep breath and removed his hand.

"I need you to wake up," she insisted and lightly tapped his face.

"I'm awake; I'm awake," he moaned and attempted to open his eyes once again although barely succeeding. "I feel like a fucking house fell on me."

"Well, you're not entirely wrong," Scorpio admitted.

Zack's eyes popped open, and he looked around. He immediately groaned from the action. "Where are we?" he asked.

"I remembered seeing a very old stove as we ran for our lives," she informed him. "I'm guessing we're just on the other side of what was once the kitchen."

Zack attempted to get up and groaned without moving. "Am I standing?"

Scorpio glanced at him where he lay on the floor surrounded by rubble. "Not exactly," she replied. "Can you move?"

He attempted to sit up then groaned. "I think I'll just stay here until the world stops spinning so fast."

Scorpio moved to her feet while attempting to gain her footing and took both his hands in hers. "Come on," she announced. "Upsy daisy."

Zack groaned and allowed her to help him into a sitting position. "God, don't use baby talk on me," he muttered. "That's all we heard from Jackson the entire first year after Jackie was born."

"I don't get your relationship with Jackie," Scorpio remarked while attempting to keep him in an upright position. She sank to her knees facing him and sat on her heels. "Is she like a daughter to you or what? You two seem awfully chummy."

"Really?" Zack groaned while casting a look at her. "This is the conversation you want to have right now?"

"I don't see us getting more than five feet in the next ten minutes, and you seem just loopy enough to spill your guts," Scorpio insisted. "Besides; Kane's testosterone levels increased by two hundred percent the first time he looked at Jackie's ass. The thought of my father and brother both lusting after the same woman is kind of gross."

He gave her a strange look as if not understanding a word she'd just said then groaned. "Jackie was like a daughter to me until the day she first kicked my ass," Zack announced candidly. "I was gone for quite some time after one of the many times I'd faked my death. Jackie's father, my best friend and former commanding officer, was killed in my absence. When I reconnected with Jackie after her father's death, something was different. There was nothing left of the little girl I remembered. We bonded in a way I never thought possible. Sometimes I forget she's a woman. Other times--" Zack shrugged. "I'll admit; something's fucked up in my head. I've been a little too close to a few explosions back in the day. I'm sure there's some brain damage going on up there." A humored smile crossed his face. "Jackie doesn't seem to mind, and it hasn't harmed her relationship with Holden. If they can put up with me, I'm certainly not complaining." He hesitated and seemed to consider his next words carefully. "I need a reason to live."

Scorpio stared at Zack a moment and seemed to latch onto the last sentence. She shifted uncomfortably. "The universe provides, huh?" Scorpio insecurely rubbed her arms. "After my boyfriend was killed, I didn't think I could survive. Kane was off to God knows where. That's when Stone and Maverick showed up out of the blue. Then, after we thought Kane had died, I hit rock bottom. That's when Rayner entered my life. I guess, in a way, we all need someone to keep us from falling apart."

Zack studied the lost expression on Scorpio's face as she stared at the rubble beneath her. He gently touched her face causing her to meet his gaze.

"I'm sorry I wasn't there for you and Kane," he announced gently. "I thought Maggie was better off without me. If I had known, I would have done things differently. Not even your grandparents could have kept me away."

Scorpio stared into his eyes then placed her hand on his and sniffed. She offered a tiny smile. "I forgive you," she whispered then leaned closer and touched her forehead to his. "Dad."

Zack pulled her into his arms and held her against him. Scorpio clung to his neck and fought her tears. They held each other a long moment before Scorpio pulled away and wiped the tears from her eyes.

"I wish I knew my mother," she announced gently and again sniffed.

Zack wiped a stray tear from her cheek and smiled warmly. "You do know her," he announced.

She gave him a strange look. Scorpio realized it was possible he'd suffered a nasty concussion when the building came down on them.

"Kane is exactly like her," he announced, "but with my deplorable attitude."

Scorpio stared at Zack a moment then burst out laughing. "Oh, God," she gasped. "Please don't tell Kane that. It'll destroy his fragile ego."

"Let me guess," Zack announced and raised a brow. "He's the organizer, and you're the destructor."

Scorpio grinned with humor and nodded. "Yeah, that's about right."

"Sorry," he announced while chuckling. "I'm afraid you're me; he's Maggie."

Chapter 65

Zack leaned heavily on Scorpio as they walked through the debris-covered corridor past the storage room. He held his head in one hand while keeping his arm securely over Scorpio's shoulder. Scorpio clung to his waist in order to keep him on his feet. His unsteadiness didn't seem to get much better once they hit level footing. They had been lucky enough to find both swords, which weren't far from them in the rubble. Scorpio had returned them to her back holster in order to assist Zack. Unfortunately, they had successfully lost the last of their semiautomatics, so they couldn't afford to lose the swords. The building creaked and groaned, causing both to look up to the basement ceiling.

"Oh, that's not good," Zack muttered. "We should probably pick up the pace."

"Do you think the rest of the building is coming down?" Scorpio asked with concern.

"I have some demolition experience. Trust me; she's coming down with a vengeful wrath," he announced then met her gaze. "I don't suppose you know where we are."

"Yeah, the maintenance shop is just down the hall and around that corner," she announced.

Zack glanced at her with some surprise. "When did you have time for sightseeing?"

"I didn't," she replied then nodded to the plaque on the wall.

The blue plaque had the word 'maintenance shop' embossed on it with an arrow pointing down the hall.

Zack groaned and rubbed his temple. "Great," he huffed. "Jackie's going to make me see a doctor when we get back."

"I hate doctors," Scorpio muttered while making a face. "They always want to stick me with needles."

"Mine gives me psychotropic drugs to induce hallucinations in order to shoot me and throw me over cruise ship railings," Zack announced.

Scorpio gave him a surprised and bewildered look. "Does that happen often?"

"Eh, I exaggerate," he remarked. "Just the one time, but it was enough to swear me off doctors."

"Yeah, I'd guess so."

As they continued down the hall a moment in silence, both listened to the building groaning above them. Scorpio's attention suddenly shifted down the hall. She released Zack and removed both swords from her back holster. He eyed her in silent question. She nodded up the hall.

"I hear someone up ahead," she whispered.

He extended his hand to her and indicated one of the swords.

Scorpio gave him a strange look as he seemed to sway slightly. "You can barely stand on your own two feet," she whispered. "I'm not giving you any sharp, pointy objects. Stay here."

She hurried down the hall with her swords in attack position. Zack stumbled along the hall behind her and bumped into the wall. He turned to face the wall while taking an aggressive karate stance. When he realized it was just a wall, he appeared puzzled as if wondering what happened to his imaginary opponent. Scorpio paused outside the maintenance shop as the voices got louder and peered inside. She moved back against the wall and nearly bumped into Zack, who now stood alongside her. Scorpio jumped with surprise then shook her head. Even with his brains mildly scrambled, he was still quite the predator.

"It's Deidra, another woman, and a man," Scorpio whispered. "I couldn't tell if they were armed, so we'll have to assume they are."

"I'll slip in and get behind them for a rear assault," Zack announced. "When you hear the signal, you attack from the front."

"I don't think you're in any condition to slip anywhere," she insisted.

"I've got this," he announced while grinning. "I do it all the time." Zack raised an arrogant brow. "Watch and learn."

Before Scorpio could stop him, Zack entered the room and casually strolled across the maintenance shop to the other side. Scorpio watched in disbelief. She didn't doubt he actually thought he was sneaking across the room. Deidra, her sister, and the guard raised their weapons at Zack as he passed through then appeared bewildered.

Deidra frowned and lowered her weapon. "Just another crazy person," she muttered. She hadn't actually seen Zack at the abandoned airfield, so she didn't recognize him, especially covered in building debris.

Zack no sooner disappeared on the other side of the maintenance shop when they heard a loud crash.

"I've got this," the guard informed the two women and then hurried after Zack.

Deidra shook her head in annoyance. "I can't wait to get out of this place," she scoffed.

"I don't think you have to worry," Regina retorted and cast a look around. "This place is about to fall down on our heads."

"I hope the guys got the last of the weapons into the truck," Deidra remarked. "The sooner we get out of here; the better."

"If we're lucky, that Zack guy showed up and Dad can have his revenge," Regina announced while frowning. "Our entire life he's been harping about that guy. Once he's dead, maybe we can return to a normal life."

"I don't remember a normal life," Deidra remarked while sneering.

"Fathers, huh?" Scorpio scoffed from nearby.

Both women turned to see Scorpio standing only a couple of feet away from them. They attempted to aim their weapons at her, but she slashed with both swords, knocking the semiautomatics from each of their hands. Regina grabbed a pipe from the nearby bench and swung at Scorpio. She easily deflected the pipe with her sword. Deidra suddenly kicked her in the abdomen and sent her back a step, forcing her to drop the sword from her left hand. Deidra rolled across the floor, snatched the sword, and lunged for Scorpio. Scorpio deflected the sword blade with her own.

"Didn't think I could defend myself, huh?" Deidra demanded then grinned. "You'll find I'm pretty tough to kill. My father taught me well."

Scorpio was taken back to that moment at the cemetery when Jackie had disarmed her. She couldn't allow that trauma to shake her confidence. Regina and Deidra came at her at the same time. Scorpio deflected the sword with her own and kicked Regina in the arm, knocking the pipe from her hand. Scorpio spun just in time to keep Deidra from slicing her with her own sword. A strange, overwhelming sense of confidence swept over her.

Scorpio sneered back at Deidra. "Yeah?" she launched. "Well, I'm pretty sure my father is a sociopath."

Deidra twirled the sword and attempted to strike Scorpio twice without success. "Your point?" she snarled.

As their swords again clashed, Scorpio sneered at Deidra. "I take after my father," she snarled.

Regina swung the pipe at Scorpio while Deidra clashed swords with her. Scorpio kept pressure on Deidra's sword while ducking the pipe. She then plowed her shoulder into Deidra's abdomen, launching her over her shoulder and into Regina. Regina screamed as Deidra's sword impaled her in the chest when she landed on her. Scorpio spun around and resumed her attack stance. Deidra rolled off her sister and stared at the sword sticking through her chest. Deidra cried out in anger, yanked the sword from her dead sister, and sprang to her feet. She spun to face Scorpio with the sword clutched in her hands and savagely attacked her. Scorpio deflected each strike.

As an enraged Deidra coiled back with her sword, Scorpio slashed with her own sword then jumped back a step. Deidra tensed a moment while holding the sword in her hands and stared at Scorpio almost as if unable to move. Deidra's eyes suddenly widened in horror as blood poured from her neck. She dropped the sword and collapsed to the floor. Scorpio twirled her sword into a less threatening position as she stared at the dead woman in the nearly silent room. The building suddenly rumbled loudly. Scorpio gasped and looked around with concern.

"Shit," she cursed and grabbed the sword Deidra had dropped. Scorpio replaced it to her back holster then looked around. "Zack?" There was no response. "Dad?"

Scorpio ran across the maintenance shop in the direction Zack had last headed with the guard following him. She paused near a blind corner behind a rack of machinery parts and gripped her sword. The guard lay on the floor with his head twisted indicating his neck had been broken. Scorpio cringed. There was a gust of air behind her. Scorpio spun with her sword clutched in an aggressive stance. Zack landed gracefully, having jumped from his perch on top of the tall rack, and then fell onto his backside. He moaned and held his head.

"Why did you hit me?" he demanded.

Scorpio relaxed her fighting stance, replaced her sword, and helped him to his feet. "We need to get out of here," she insisted. "The building is coming down."

"Then we should probably leave," Zack informed her.

"That's a wonderful idea," she remarked and indicated the door while attempting to keep him on his feet.

Scorpio managed to get Zack into the corridor, but he was starting to weigh heavily upon her.

"You have to help me," she insisted. "I can't carry you."

Despite the rumbling of the building, the sounds of someone within the corridor ahead of them could be heard. Scorpio cursed under her breath while attempting to keep Zack steady in one arm while removing her sword with her free right hand. Gil and Mac appeared in the corridor, saw them, and were relieved. Scorpio breathed a sigh of relief as Gil took Zack from her.

"He received a concussion from the collapse--or the fall--or both," Scorpio insisted. "The building is coming down. We need to get out."

"We know," Mac assured her and nodded down the hall. "Everyone else is out."

"Is everyone okay?" Scorpio asked as they hurried along the hall.

Gil had Zack in a fireman's carry and was straining while attempting to pick up the pace. Mac moved to Zack's free side and took some of the weight. Thankfully, Zack didn't even seem to notice her.

"They're fine," Mac informed her. "It's us I'm worried about."

"Maverick and Bogart got Jackie and Kane out a few minutes ago," Gil assured Scorpio. "We're it."

Chapter 66

Several yards from the back of the building, Bogart fussed over Jackie while Kane and Rayner nervously paced the area not far from the woods as they waited for word on Scorpio and Zack. John, Sal, Maverick, and Stone watched the unstable building with nervous anticipation. There was no doubt it was coming down any minute. Kirk and Monroe raced around the building on the four-wheelers and approached the anxiously awaiting team.

"All the guards have been taken down," Monroe announced as he climbed off the ATV and eyed the others. "Any word on them?"

Everyone shook their heads in response while revealing their concern for their friends. The hand radio on Monroe's belt suddenly crackled.

"We have Scorpio and Zack," Gil announced over the hand radio, allowing everyone to breathe with relief. "We're at the basement entrance now. Mac found--"

The building groaned loudly and started to shake, keeping them from hearing the rest of Gil's response. Monroe placed the hand radio to his mouth.

"Gil, get the hell out of there," Monroe announced into the radio. "It's coming down. I repeat; the building is coming down now!"

There was a cloud of cement dirt wafting from the remaining structure.

"They need extraction!" Monroe cried out.

Kirk, who remained on his four-wheeler, didn't need further prompting and raced on the quad to the building. Kane jumped on Monroe's quad and rode after him. Both four-wheelers approached the building and reached the ramp to the basement loading dock. There was a thunderous rumble, and the building suddenly collapsed on itself. Rayner gasped and ran toward the building with Stone and Maverick on his heels. Bogart shielded Jackie from the large, thick cloud of dirt and debris that rushed outward in every direction. Sal leaped to Jackie's side and helped Bogart shield her.

Monroe ran for the building after the others despite the thick cloud that made it nearly impossible to see. A panel truck plowed through the dust and debris with the two quads racing after it. Monroe and Bogart grabbed their rifles and aimed them at the approaching truck. The truck slowed then stopped along with the two men riding on the four-wheelers. The truck door opened to reveal Scorpio. Scorpio jumped out the passenger side then helped Gil assist Zack from the truck. Mac climbed out of the driver's side, seeming pleased with her driving skills.

Jackie saw Zack and attempted to stand from where she sat on the ground. Sal managed to stand despite his sprained ankle and helped Jackie to her feet while she held her injured side. She sighed with relief upon seeing Zack and rushed to him. Zack released Scorpio, threw his arms around Jackie, and held her in a warm embrace.

"You promised you wouldn't knock down any more buildings," Jackie lightly teased while keeping her head on his shoulder.

Zack chuckled near her ear. "If it had been me who brought that building down, you would have known it."

Jackie clung to him and shut her eyes while hiding her concerns. She managed an uneasy laugh. Not far from them, Kane pulled Scorpio into his arms, held her a moment, and then released her into Rayner's awaiting arms. Rayner held Scorpio and stroked her hair while whispering his concerns for her. Once Scorpio was safe and secure with Rayner, Kane turned toward Mac and opened his arms to her. Mac seemed reluctant at first then offered a tiny smile and sank against him. As Kane held her, Mac returned the embrace and clung to him as if her life depended upon it.

"Admit it," Kane teased while clinging to her. "You love me."

Mac groaned and attempted to push him away, but he refused to release her. She eventually gave up and allowed him to hold her. While Kane continued to smother Mac, she saw Sal standing near them, silently watching her. Mac released Kane and stared back at Sal in what could only be described as a tense moment. Sal suddenly smiled and opened his arms to her. Mac released her breath and threw her arms around him.

"I'm sorry, Mac," Sal whispered in her ear. "Can you forgive me?"

"I forgive you," she whispered back.

"Any time you want to come back," he announced while holding her in a tight embrace, "there's a position available for you."

Mac slowly pulled away from Sal and met his gaze with some surprise. "Really?" she just about gasped. "You'll take me back?"

Kane suddenly tensed while witnessing the exchange but didn't interrupt.

Sal smiled at Mack and nodded. "You let me worry about Zack," he announced then managed a tiny laugh. "I can handle him."

Mac smiled and chuckled warmly. "Thank you, Sal," she announced. "That means a lot to me."

When Mac looked alongside her, Monroe offered a warm smile and opened his arms to her as well. She returned the smile and hugged him affectionately.

"The same goes for us," Monroe informed her then pulled back to meet her gaze. "I think I have enough votes to override the voices of opposition."

Mac stared at Monroe with some surprise. It was possibly what she'd been waiting to hear for a long time. Jackie left Zack with Kirk and approached Monroe and Mac. She patted Mac reassuringly on the shoulder.

"You have my vote," Jackie announced.

Zack overheard the comment from where he now sat on the four-wheeler and frowned although he didn't comment.

"Mine too," Bogart added.

Gil smiled and raised his finger in the air, signaling his intention while nodding his approval.

Kirk groaned and rolled his eyes. "Yeah, whatever," he muttered and waved them off. "She can stay."

Zack rolled his eyes.

Monroe looked back at Mac and shrugged. "That's five to three," he insisted then grinned. "You're in if you want in."

Kane's expression just about shattered as he watched the scene unfold. Maverick seemed equally tense and was unable to look away. Mac smiled just about overjoyed and kissed Monroe quickly on the lips. She pulled back and warmly caressed his face.

"Thank you," Mac replied while just about choking on her emotions. "I appreciate that." She hesitated then offered a tiny smile. "But my new family needs me more."

Mac cast a sly look at Kane, who released the breath he'd been holding. He was quick to pull her into his arms and affectionately kissed her forehead. When the moment became awkward, she had to push him away.

Mac then cast a look at Maverick, who seemed relieved but tense. She smiled slyly at him. "What do you say to a romantic bubble bath for two and some room service?" she asked.

Maverick appeared surprised, glanced at the group that had obviously overheard her question, and then looked back at her. "You realize everyone heard that?"

"So?" Mac remarked with little care and offered a sly smile. "They should assume I'm going to have romantic plans with my boyfriend."

Maverick stared at her a moment, appeared relieved, and pulled her into his arms. "Of course they should," he whispered while holding back his emotions.

Mac pulled back just far enough to meet Maverick's gaze and kissed him warmly but passionately. Maverick eagerly returned the kiss as their first public display of affections. Monroe frowned as he watched the happy couple. Jackie placed her hand on Monroe's shoulder and gave it an affectionate squeeze.

"You okay?" Jackie asked.

Monroe placed his hand on Jackie's hand on his shoulder and patted it. "I'd be lying if I said I wasn't a little jealous," he remarked then drew a deep breath and sighed. "But he'll be good for her."

"I have no doubt," Jackie replied then eyed Monroe, who couldn't seem to take his eyes off the happy couple. "There's someone out there for you, Monroe. I have no doubt."

Monroe finally looked away from Mac and Maverick and met Jackie's gaze. He smiled and placed his arms around her. Jackie returned the warm embrace.

"Thanks, Jackie," he whispered close to her ear. "You're a good friend."

Chapter 67

As the truck and four-wheelers pulled up to the abandoned airfield, they saw an FBI helicopter, several federal SUVs, and a few state police cars surrounding the once desolate area. As the team stopped and dismounted their four-wheelers and climbed out of the truck, Darth barked excitedly and ran for them. He just about knocked Gil to the ground while excitedly jumping on him. Gil laughed and affectionately played with the dog.

"I missed you too," Gil announced while coddling the excited dog.

Darth then made his way around the team, affectionately greeting everyone. When John saw the feds and state troopers crawling all over the abandoned airfield, he grabbed one of the guard's baseball caps from the truck and pulled it over his head in an attempt to cover his face. Sal saw the action and laughed. He wouldn't be the first man looking to avoid that many law enforcement officers in one place. Jackie held her injured side and headed past the men looking over Gil's now fixed plane. Holden saw Jackie and returned the state trooper's tablet to him. Holden appeared relieved and ran to greet his wife. He was about to pull her into his arms when he hesitated and saw the way she was holding her side.

Holden immediately fussed over her. "Are you okay?" he asked with concern.

She smiled and waved him off. "It's just a graze," Jackie announced and eagerly placed her arms around Holden's waist while resting her head against his chest.

Holden pulled her into his arms and held her against him, although he was careful not to squeeze her too tightly. The rest of the team looked at the two sheet-covered bodies on the ground.

"What happened?" Monroe asked one of the federal agents who happened to be standing nearby.

The agent snorted a laugh and indicated the playful dog. "Apparently, the dog stopped some would-be thieves. Nasty ones too," the federal agent announced. "I recognized the one man as an underworld mercenary."

"Not to make your paperwork load any larger," Monroe announced then indicated the panel truck, "but our rescue vehicle is loaded with weapons. It would seem the dead guy's buddies were into a lot of dirty dealings."

One of the state troopers was talking on his radio as he approached the federal agent who was speaking with Monroe. "We just received word that the old asylum a few miles from here collapsed on itself," the trooper announced. "We need to send a few men to investigate."

"You'll find the rest of your mercenaries there," Monroe informed him. "Buried under a pile of rubble."

"How do you know?" the state trooper asked.

"We just came from there," Monroe informed him. "Their cohorts abducted some of our friends. When we came to rescue them, they tried to kill us." Monroe then hesitated and appeared tense. "There were some people living in that old mental institute. They were out-of-their-minds crazy. Looked like they'd been there a while."

The state trooper gave Monroe a strange look. "That place had been closed down for almost twenty years," he remarked.

"And yet there were still a couple of dozen crazies roaming the halls," Monroe insisted. "I'm not sure who they were or how they got there--"

The state trooper tensed a moment as realization must have struck him. "Over six months ago, the town about thirty miles from here had an incident," he announced. "The water had been contaminated. CDC hadn't ruled out deliberate sabotage. Half the town had been taken away. They were supposedly shipped to some mental institution for evaluation. The rest of the town cleared out overnight. We never heard what became of any of them. Nothing was ever reported after that."

"Were there two sisters living in that town?" Monroe asked. "A Deidra and a Regina?"

The state trooper's eyes suddenly widened. "Regina?" he gasped. "Regina was psychotic long before the water was contaminated. We thought she was hauled away with the others to that mental home."

"I'm guessing she was hauled away, but not to the home you thought," Monroe remarked.

"I'll be damned," the trooper muttered.

The federal agent heard all he needed to hear then nudged the state trooper. "These men are with a special task force working with the Colorado Bureau," the agent announced. "We'll handle questioning them. You'd better gather some men and a salvage team to check out that collapsed building. There could be survivors."

The state trooper seemed slightly skeptical then reluctantly nodded and walked away.

Monroe smiled at the agent. "Thanks."

He nodded, returned the knowing smile, and then returned to his work. Not far from Gil's plane, Holden released Jackie and fussed over her injured side.

"We need to get you to the nearest hospital," Holden insisted.

"I'm fine," she informed him. "I'll seek treatment in Virginia after I drop off the rental plane at the airport. Gil can't fly two planes, and I'm the only other pilot." Jackie offered a warm, cunning smile. "Meet me at my father's house afterward?"

Holden smiled and cocked his head. "Are all these people going to be there?"

Jackie smiled and laughed. "Well, you never know," she announced.

Holden drew a deep breath then laughed. "Sounds like one hell of a poker game," he teased. "By the time I'm finished here, I'll probably make it back to Vernon Heights around the time you're finished at the emergency room. I'll meet you at the house." He then looked across the abandoned airfield where Kane and Scorpio fussed over Zack. "That looks encouraging. Family reunion?"

Jackie eyed Zack and his kids together then smiled and nodded. "Yes, it's very encouraging," she announced. "All three of them grew up a little today."

"Does that mean you can cut back your therapy sessions with Zack?" Holden asked.

Jackie considered the question then smiled. "I think it's safe to say we found a new form of treatment to cure what's been ailing him."

"Will we be getting our spare bedroom back anytime soon?" Holden teased.

Jackie laughed and affectionately patted Holden's chest. "Don't hold your breath," she replied.

"I know better," Holden announced then kissed her warmly on the lips. He pulled away and met her gaze. "I guess our quiet getaway alone is getting pushed back again."

"Seven to ten days," she teased. "As soon as the stitches come out, I'm all yours."

"I can handle seven to ten days," Holden replied while grinning. "I'd better get to work so we can clear you for takeoff."

"We need to fix Gil's plane first," Jackie informed him. "Those bastards snatched a part."

"The guys were looking over it," Holden informed her. "Your bad guys must have been interested in taking Gil's plane. It's working now."

Jackie gave him a surprised look. "Well, wasn't that nice of them."

"Darth didn't share your sentiment," Holden replied then indicated the two covered bodies.

"Yeah, well," Jackie announced under her breath, "that dog has issues."

Holden then glanced across the abandoned airfield. "I can't help but notice the condition of the landing strip and the short distance to the trees," he remarked then raised a curious brow. "Do you have enough runway to clear those trees?"

Jackie grinned slyly. "With maybe an inch to spare," she teased then laughed. "It'll be fun. Gil's taking bets on who'll piss their pants first. Care to get in on it?"

Holden frowned and shook his head. "That's terrible," he remarked then hesitated, looked around, and handed her twenty dollars. "Twenty on Bogart."

Jackie chuckled and took the money from him. "Wise investment."

Chapter 68

Despite having rented the plane in Kentucky, Jackie was able to return it to the airport in Colorado Springs due to connections she had with other pilots. Gil refueled his plane since his plans still included taking Sal, Othello, and Ellie to Monroe's island for a little fun in the sun. Their trip was much deserved. Othello and Ellie were already on their way to the airport once they received word that the team was safe and the trip was still scheduled. Monroe approached Gil as he finished refueling, paused beside him, and then nodded across the tarmac toward the private airport's small terminal. Some of the team joked around with their new friend, John.

"Something you forgot to mention?" Monroe asked with a curious look.

Gil eyed those outside the terminal then looked back at Monroe and shrugged. "Not that I'm aware."

"You invited John to my beach house," Monroe announced. "We don't even know this guy."

"He stuck his neck out for the team and us," Gil insisted. "I thought inviting him along was the least we could do. The poor guy needs a little R&R."

"You still should have talked to me first," Monroe protested.

Gil drew a deep breath, eyed Monroe, and raised his brows. "Monroe, can John come along to your beach house?"

Monroe groaned, rolled his eyes, and then walked away. Gil smiled and chuckled.

§

A little while later, Mac hugged Sal before he boarded Gil's plane for his trip to Monroe's private beach. Darth ran down the plane steps, barked happily, and excitedly jumped up at Mac. She crouched down and playfully scratched Darth's scruff.

"You keep an eye on them for me," she announced to the dog then held Darth's face and met his gaze. "If you feel the urge to bite Monroe in the ass, go with your instincts."

Darth happily licked her face. Mac affectionately hugged the German shepherd.

"Thanks for saving my life," she whispered then kissed the dog on the head.

Darth again licked her face. Gil whistled from the plane. Mac straightened and watched the dog run back for the plane and race up the steps. Gil gave a wave to Mac then pulled up the steps and secured the door. Mac insecurely folded her arms across her chest and took a few steps back from the plane. The plane's engine started, and it was soon rolling away from the private terminal. Mac remained on the tarmac and watched the plane leisurely rolling toward the nearby runway. She hesitated a moment then looked behind her. Zack leaned against the terminal building and appeared to be silently watching her. She drew a deep breath but refrained from speaking or attempting to make contact with him. Zack turned and headed inside without a word. Apparently, all was not forgiven.

§

Jackie stood near one of the hangars and watched as her helicopter landed not far from her. As the helicopter shut down, she approached and was relieved to see it again. Jackie lovingly ran her hand along the nose then approached the pilot's seat. Mac's friend, Izzy, got out of Jackie's helicopter and grinned at her. Oddly enough, Izzy looked a lot like his name sounded. His spiked hair was bleached white, and his skin was somewhat bronzed from too many tropical destinations for wealthy clients. For a man in his late twenties, Izzy seemed more like a scrawny, hormonal teenage boy. Izzy removed his steampunk sunglasses when he saw her and took in a sweeping eyeful of her.

"Jackie!" he announced a little too cheerfully and opened his arms to her.

She returned the smile while raising her brows and held her hand up to him. "Not happening, Izzy."

Izzy also had roaming hands, and Jackie didn't particularly feel like having his hands on her ass today. She was too sore to kick him in the gonads. Kane worked his way closer to the helicopter and watched the exchange between Jackie and the strange man. Izzy laughed at her reaction and patted the helicopter.

"Got her here in one piece for you," he announced excitedly. "That sexy girl is a dream to pilot."

"What do I owe you?" Jackie asked while praying he had kept both hands on the stick and off his own stick during the flight.

"I'll work something out with Mac," Izzy replied then laughed. "She said there's a plane that needs to go back to Kentucky."

Jackie pointed across the tarmac where Mac and Maverick shared a moment outside the rental plane. "She's waiting by the plane for you," Jackie announced, a little too eager to send the wayward pilot packing. "Thanks for bringing my helicopter to me. My husband wasn't too happy when I told him I had to go to Kentucky first before my emergency room visit."

Izzy suddenly grinned and held back his laugh. "Had another *accident*, did we?"

"You could say that," Jackie replied.

"Shot or stabbed?" he teased.

"I don't know what you're talking about, Izzy," she replied while grinning slyly.

"One day, you'll tell me all the juicy details," Izzy teased. "Catch you later." He then headed across the tarmac for Mac and the rental plane. Izzy was then heard shrieking from across the tarmac. "Mac, baby doll!"

Kane approached Jackie as she looked over her helicopter and checked it for any imperfections caused by Mac's questionable pilot friend. Jackie held her breath as she opened the pilot's side door and inspected the seat and controls for any foreign DNA. She was grateful when she didn't see anything, although she hadn't ruled out grabbing her black light and double-checking.

Kane paused a few feet behind Jackie and tensed slightly. "I, uh, didn't want to miss you before you headed off to the hospital," he announced.

Jackie glanced back at Kane and offered a slightly humored smile. "Who said I was going to the hospital?"

"You told your husband--"

Jackie laughed and waved off Kane. "I said I'd get it treated," she informed him.

Without prompting or embarrassment, Jackie lifted the side of her tank top and showed Kane the freshly stitched bullet graze. Kane tensed slightly at her lack of modesty and eyed the neatly stitched injury. She lowered her shirt, and he met her gaze.

"Looks great," Kane announced although slightly puzzled. "When did you get that stitched?"

"Monroe has a field kit on Gil's plane," she informed him. "He stitched me up the moment we landed here at the airport." She then rolled her eyes. "Zack insisted on offering his moral support." She shook her head and considered her next project. "We're going to have one hell of a time getting him to the hospital for a CAT scan. I'm afraid he really needs one this time. He called me Jackson three times, and he wasn't trying to be funny."

"Did you want some help with that?" Kane offered with a little too much enthusiasm. "We're in no rush to get to

Maine." He immediately back peddled and contained his eagerness. "I mean, Scorpio's been ready to go home for a few weeks now, but I don't mind helping."

"No, it'll be fine," Jackie replied and offered a warm smile. "He'll go quietly. I still have some happy drugs that I used on your sister." She then laughed. "If you thought your sister was amusing, you should see him on that stuff."

Kane studied Jackie a moment then fidgeted. "Well, then, I guess this is goodbye, uh, for now," he announced. "I, uh, hope we'll see you again sometime." He then offered a slightly humored look and nervously chuckled. "Just not in anymore condemned buildings." Kane again fidgeted. "I'm usually much better at saying goodbye and don't normally feel this awkward." He offered a timid smile and opened his arms as if asking for a goodbye hug then reconsidered and extended his hand.

Jackie eyed him, laughed, and moved into his arms for a warm embrace. Kane appeared relieved and affectionately hugged her, clinging to her with added warmth. The loving way his hands lightly caressed her back was enough to convey this embrace was different from his usual displays of affection. Jackie attempted to pull away, but he was reluctant to release her.

"Okay, getting a little weird," she informed him.

Kane released her and just about jumped away from her while fumbling over himself. "Sorry," he replied while hiding his embarrassed smile. "It's just--" He hesitated and attempted a smile that seemed strangely nervous. "I guess I finally see what my father sees in you."

"Okay, that makes me nervous," Jackie reported then leaned against the helicopter. She studied Kane a moment, hid her humor, and smiled almost mockingly. "I guess Zack forgot to mention that we're flying you back to Maine."

Kane stared at her with some surprise. "Oh," he responded and again fumbled over himself. "Uh, no, he didn't mention that." He nervously raked his fingers through his hair then managed a tiny smile. "Well, now I feel a little silly."

"Embarrassing the guys is one of my specialties," she teased while grinning.

"I think I can manage that fine on my own," Kane remarked with a tiny laugh. "Your assistance is not required."

Jackie smiled and laughed. "You're okay, Kane."

Kane drew a deep, tense breath while staring at her. "I know this may be inappropriate," he began and instantly caught Jackie's attention. A sly grin crossed his face. "Can I fly the helicopter?"

Jackie rolled her eyes and groaned. "I can't handle two of you."

§

Jackie's helicopter flew along the coast of Maine, allowing for a magnificent view of beaches, cliffs, and the ocean. A twenty-bed hotel sat atop the hill nestled against the bluff. Although the large, old building was in desperate need of repairs, the view of the ocean was spectacular, particularly during sunrise. The helicopter gently set down in a large clearing. Once it shut down, the passengers got out. Bogart and Kirk decided to wait at Jackie's house in Virginia before she took them back to Colorado in the morning. Maverick was eager to show Mac around the hotel and the grounds, despite that both needed a lot of work. Rayner and Stone offered to show Jackie around as well, giving Zack a few moments in private to say goodbye to Scorpio and Kane.

Zack seemed oddly preoccupied as he walked closer to the cliff. He stood on the edge and looked at the horizon beyond the ocean. Kane and Scorpio joined him. Kane seemed almost as mesmerized as Zack.

"I'd forgotten how much I loved this place," Kane announced almost too soft for Scorpio to hear.

"I bet Maggie loved this spot," Zack whispered while staring off.

"Our grandmother said she had spent a lot of time up here," Scorpio gently replied. "She and my uncle practically grew up here."

"Same as Scorp and I," Kane replied then cast a slightly tense look at Zack. "Will we see you again?"

Zack snorted a laugh then glanced back at Kane. "If you only realized how difficult it is to get rid of me," he teased.

He again looked out at the ocean. "I haven't felt Maggie in a long time, but she seems so close right now."

"Promise you'll come back," Kane insisted.

Zack turned to face Kane and offered a gentle smile. "I promise I'll be back."

Kane appeared relieved and threw his arms around Zack, clinging to him. Zack groaned then reluctantly placed his arms around his son.

Zack hesitated then held him a little closer and whispered in his ear, "I'm proud of you."

Kane pulled away, fought his emotions, and then backed away while attempting to keep from crying. "I, uh, better keep Mac out of my room," he announced. "She's liable to go through my things."

"I guarantee she will," Zack announced with a sigh.

Kane hurried away and secretly wiped the tears from his eyes. Scorpio stared at the ocean a moment longer. When she realized Zack was staring at her, she cast a look at him. She finally turned to face him and folded her arms across her chest. Scorpio didn't know why she wasn't as openly affectionate as her brother was, and it sometimes bothered her.

"Don't expect an emotional outpouring from me," she informed him. She hesitated and attempted to reveal her true feelings, but she couldn't manage it. "I'm not like my brother. I'll see you when and if you decide to come back."

Zack smiled and nodded. "Yeah, you're me all right," he teased.

Scorpio held her breath while staring at him. For a moment, she felt almost helpless and desperately wanted his approval the same as her brother had. She couldn't do it. Scorpio shook her head and managed a tiny smile.

"At least I finally know why I am the way I am," she announced.

Zack grinned almost humored by the remark. "And there's nothing wrong with that at all," he replied then turned to leave. He hesitated alongside her but didn't look at her. "You don't need validation from me or anyone else. You know who you are."

Zack's fingers grazed her hand as he passed. Scorpio hesitated from the slight touch and looked back. She watched Zack head for the hotel as a tear rolled down her cheek.

After he was out of sight, she whispered, "Thanks--Dad."

Chapter 69

Two weeks later. Mac stood on the back patio of the rustic hotel in Maine. The patio was just one of many areas within the hotel that needed refurbishing. Some of the stones were chipped, and the furniture was mismatched. Still, it was a beautiful view. Mac stared at the distant horizon over the ocean and seemed to be off in her own world. Within the hotel, Kane paced the front sitting room, which had originally been the hotel lobby, and would be again once it was functional. The lobby had an antique, wooden carved check-in desk with a polished marble top. The check-in desk took up nearly the entire back wall. The furniture was also antique, being the original furniture from the hotel's heydays. The antique furniture was part of the reason Scorpio didn't use the lobby to entertain much.

Kane continued to pace with the cordless phone to his ear while Scorpio sat slouched in a nearby chair and watched her brother wear out the already worn carpet.

"When I spoke to you last week, you told me you couldn't even ship the tile I ordered until the end of this week," Kane shouted at the man on the other end. "Now you're telling me you can't even find my order?"

"Kane," Scorpio moaned from where she sat in her chair with her temple resting against her fist. "Let it go. The contractor can't get to us until next month."

Kane ignored his sister and continued to pace with the phone to his ear. "If you can't find my order, I want my money back."

Scorpio groaned and covered her eyes at the commanding way her brother was dealing with her suppliers. He wasn't used to playing bad cop, and, unfortunately, he wasn't very good at it either.

"One hour," Kane snapped into the phone. "If you don't call me back in one hour, I'm sending my second in command out there to help you find my order."

Kane disconnected the call and caught Scorpio's stare. "You're not sending Mac to the Florida Panhandle to argue with our marble and tile dealer."

"What the hell is going on around here?" Kane demanded. "Why can't we get anyone to even deliver supplies, let alone do the work we're paying them to do?"

"Welcome to my world, Kane," Scorpio muttered with little reaction. "I've been living this nightmare since I acquired this place."

"I don't remember all these problems when I was here," Kane insisted.

"That's because you always let Cal and I deal with the bullshit," she announced. "Why do you think it's taking so long to fix this place?"

"I thought it was because you were cheap," Kane remarked with added irritation. "I just assumed you didn't want to pay anyone to do the work."

"I'm not you, Kane," she informed him. "It's hard to pay people to work when you can't even get them out to do the work."

Kane frowned and flopped into the chair with her. He showed little regard for her personal space and just about crushed her.

"I change my mind," he groaned. "I hate this place."

Scorpio hesitated and looked around the room with a bewildered look on her face. She heard something unusual in the distance. "Do you hear that?"

"Hear what?" Kane asked then glared at her. "Why do you have such freakishly good hearing? It's creepy."

Scorpio struggled to get out of the chair with Kane practically sitting on top of her. She headed for the side door and hurried outside. Scorpio stepped onto the patio and joined Mac, who now stared at the horizon. There was a faint rumbling in the sky.

"What is that?" Scorpio asked.

Mac had a strange look on her face. "I'm not entirely sure," she replied and hurried from the patio toward the front of the hotel.

Scorpio chased after her. Kane soon appeared on the patio and followed them. The rumbling sound became louder and now sounded more like a rhythmic thumping. Mac approached the front of the hotel and stared at the sky. Stone, Rayner, and Maverick hurried out the front door and looked around with the same puzzled looks. Mac suddenly snorted a laugh, although the others weren't certain why.

"What is it?" Kane asked.

"I could be wrong," Mac announced while grinning, "but it sounds like an invasion to me."

Scorpio and Kane exchanged looks not understanding the comment. Two helicopters suddenly appeared over the treetops and flew over the hotel. They landed in unison a safe distance from each other and the hotel itself.

Kane suddenly grinned. "It's Jackie," he announced with a little too much enthusiasm.

Mac cast a look at Kane and raised a skeptical brow. "You may want to tone down your enthusiasm," she informed her friend.

All five approached the clearing where the helicopters now shut down. Once the rotors had just about stopped, the side doors on both crafts opened, and the men spilled out onto the lawn. The entire team of Whiskey Tango Foxtrot and their wives joined Holden, Sal, and Othello as they crossed the lawn to greet those at the hotel. Zack approached Kane and Scorpio gave them a serious look.

"We heard you needed a construction crew," Zack announced then indicated the men and women with him. "We thought we'd lend you a hand, Navy SEAL style."

Kane grinned when he saw Zack and hugged him with enthusiasm.

Zack groaned, although he resisted pulling away. "Are you going to do this every time I stop by?"

Without releasing him or looking up, Kane laughed. "Yep."

Jackie casually walked past them and placed Zack's hand on Kane's shoulder for him. "Hug your son, you big baby," she muttered.

Scorpio met Jackie halfway and offered a thankful smile. "I really appreciate the offer and the dramatic entrance, but our material won't be here for a few weeks," she insisted then frowned. "Apparently, there are some stubborn bastards in the Florida Panhandle."

Sal grinned from nearby and adjusted his glasses. "Your materials should be here within the hour," he announced and grinned in a slightly chilling manner. "I had a word with your suppliers three days ago. You know; one stubborn bastard to another." He then raised his brows. "I thought they were *surprisingly* accommodating."

"How did you know--?" Kane began then cast a look at Mac.

Mac grinned and cleverly raised her brows. "Your second in command is connected," she teased.

Kirk and Gil unloaded the tools and some supplies from the back of his helicopter while Jackie unloaded duffel bags from her aircraft.

Zack offered a sly grin at Kane and Scorpio then indicated the team. "There's your crew," he announced. "Put them to work."

Monroe and Beck were already arguing over the layout of the patio. Kane and Scorpio eyed the men then looked back at Zack as Jackie paused alongside him.

"I don't know what to say," Scorpio announced while just about down to tears.

"You don't need to say anything," Zack replied then cocked his head. "Just show me the basement."

"The basement?" Scorpio asked with some surprise to the comment. "We didn't have any plans for the basement. Mac knew that."

"Which is why it'll make the perfect gym slash indoor shooting range," Zack informed her. "The two of you can use all the target practice you can get."

As Jackie and Zack headed for the front patio door while discussing plans for the indoor shooting range, Scorpio and Kane exchanged surprised looks.

Kane suddenly grinned and became overly enthusiastic. "We're getting an indoor shooting range," he announced then hurried after Zack and Jackie.

Scorpio groaned and covered her eyes while shaking her head. "I know I'm going to regret this," she muttered then hurried after them.

The End

Other books by Holly Copella!
Reviews left on Amazon are appreciated!

"The Battle for Andrea Maria"

A cruise ship attack turns six survivors into overnight celebrities after they take credit for the heroic act of a stowaway who died saving them.

The cruise is just what Jess needed--a bit of harmless fun far from her daily grind. But what begins as a relaxing vacation turns into a desperate fight for her life when terrorists take over the ship and start piling up bodies. Teaming up with a mysterious stowaway, Jess attempts to send out a distress call but knows they cannot wait for help to come. If she or the few remaining passengers have any hope for survival, Jess must act now. The papers dub it "The Battle for *Andrea Maria*," but to Jess it is the moment she fought side-by-side with her enigmatic Romeo, saving the ship--and losing him. She thinks the story ends there, but really, the nightmare is just beginning...

"Insanely Deadly"

When the dead return to life, it's up to an admiral's daughter and a mildly insane, former war hero to save their small town.

Jetta Cross, a Navy Admiral's daughter, is tasked with keeping her father's comrade, a former war hero turned town crazy, grounded in the real world. Capt. John Hunter is still fighting the war in his head, where imaginary dead people are part of his world. When a viral outbreak brings about a zombie uprising, Hunter is left to his own devices. He must resume his role as a one-man commando unit in order to destroy the ravenous undead. With Hunter still fighting his own inner demons as well as the undead, the townspeople fear their zombie neighbors may not be the only threat. Stranded at the island's luxurious resort with a handful of workers, Jetta is forced to live up to her father's reputation and take charge of the deteriorating situation at the hotel. She must wage her own war against the infected before the government declares her hometown a total loss.

"Deadly Institution"

A town recluse suspected of killing his wife teams up with a young woman in order to stop a killer.

After being accused of murdering his wife, Konrad Churchill turns his back on the town that once adored him. Ten years later, he still holds his grudge and the title of the most feared man in town. With the reopening of the burned mental institution, where his wife had died, former employees are now murdered one-by-one, throwing suspicion back on Churchill. A young local reporter, Jacey, is forced to reveal her long-time friendship with the infamous recluse in order to clear his name not only in the recent murders but to exonerate him in the death of his wife as well. Will Jacey's relationship with Churchill invite the killer closer to her? Or is the killer already in her life?

"Death Displacement"

A grief-stricken man travels back in time to seek revenge on the woman who murdered his girlfriend but inadvertently falls in love with her.

Kane is about to marry the woman he loves. His life is perfect. A few weeks before the wedding, a vindictive woman from his girlfriend's past mysteriously arrives and kills her. He learns of a traumatic accident that happened five years earlier, which triggers Riley's hatred for his girlfriend. Distraught over his girlfriend's death, Kane uses an antique time machine to travel into the past in order to find and destroy the woman responsible. When he runs into Riley's younger self, he realizes she's not the monster she later becomes, and he can't bring himself to destroy her. With a little help from his oddball friend from the past, they formulate a plan to prevent the accident that sends Riley down her destructive path. Kane's plan backfires when he falls for the younger Riley. His new tortured existence is further complicated when future Riley, his girlfriend's killer, shows up with her own devious agenda that doesn't include him. Will he be able to stop the time ripple, which ultimately ends with his girlfriend's death? Or will future Riley take him out of the timeline forever--

"Dead Village"

After strange happenings isolate a small resort town from the rest of the world, nearly one hundred residents seek refuge at the closed hotel. Only eight survive the night. And that's just the beginning...

One day after the entire population of Fox Ridge Village disappears, a car wreck forces several unsuspecting crash victims to seek help at the closed summer hotel. Within the hotel, they discover the grisly aftermath of a brutal slaughter. Crash victims Vander and Devon, a reluctant clairvoyant, team up to solve the riddle of the "haunted hotel" and the mass hysteria plaguing the remaining survivors. By the time they discover the hotel's secret, they're already drawn into the hysteria. As the body count continues to climb, it's a race to isolate the source and bring everyone back to reality before they kill one another. Will Devon be able to communicate with the traumatized spirits before their fate becomes her own?

"Town Darling"

After surviving a brutal attack that claims the lives of those she loves, a young woman seeks revenge on a corrupt town.

Going back home is never easy, but for Casey, it means returning to her corrupt hometown where she barely survived a brutal attack. Accompanied by two family friends, she seeks justice for the night that destroyed her life. Her physical scars are nothing compared to her emotional ones, forcing the local sheriff to believe that the town darling is back for revenge. As the conspiracy for her revenge appears to be leading up to the coveted town fair, the sheriff is determined to stop her from fulfilling her vengeful scheme...but guilt over his role on that fateful night continues to haunt him. Will his desperate need for Casey's forgiveness be his undoing? Or will Casey's desire for revenge destroy them both?

"Basement Dwellers"

A viral outbreak at a hospital leaves a mortician, sheriff, and coroner fighting for their lives against a horde of undead and the CDC.

After a massive car wreck leaves several survivors in critical condition at the local hospital, a surgeon uses experimental drugs on his critical patients and accidentally causes a zombie outbreak. When local mortician, Lexx, receives an infected corpse as her client, she becomes stranded in the hospital basement during CDC quarantine along with the local sheriff and the coroner. The infamous surgeon struggles to find a cure for his infectious blunder by using the other survivors as test subjects. Meanwhile, Lexx and the sheriff attempt to locate his missing sister, who's stranded somewhere in the battle zone that once was the emergency room. It's a race against time and the ravenous undead. Can they survive the undead before CDC sanitizes the hospital of all infection?

"Misfits, Inc."

A seemingly ordinary, young woman meets four misfits who claim she has given them supernatural powers.

While on a business trip to a remote island paradise, a bored secretary, Hailey, has her world turned upside down when her path collides with a psychic freak, Skyler. He attempts to convince her that they had met in his dreams, and she had chosen him as one of her four mystic warriors. After Skyler foresees a woman's death, they discover an unidentified creature has killed one of the guests. They are joined by a lounge pianist and a rich playboy, who also claim they had met her in their dreams. If Skyler's prophecies are genuine, the evil entity controlling the ravenous creatures needs to destroy Hailey to ensure its survival. Reluctantly accepting her fate, Hailey has to locate the last and most powerful of her chosen warriors, The Guardian. Their fate is in doubt when The Guardian turns out to be a self-absorbed, former cat burglar with a bad attitude. Can Hailey turn her company of misfits into an elite team of mystic warriors? Or will The Guardian's secret agenda destroy them all?

"Deadly Institution 2"

When blackmail turns into murder, a young woman finds herself caught in the killer's crosshairs.

The small town of Stony Ridge is no stranger to scandal and persecution of the innocent. When a brutal killing shakes the town's prestigious country club, Jacey McMurray seeks help from a self-proclaimed vigilante, Konrad Churchill. As her professional and personal worlds collide, Jacey fears the stress of the country club killings have finally taken their toll on Churchill. Can a stressed out vigilante stop the killer before he strikes again?

"Witness Protection"
Also available in audiobook!

After witnessing an execution, a resourceful young woman attempts to disappear while being pursued by a hitman and a handsome federal agent.

A helicopter pilot, Jackie Remus, reluctantly agrees to go on a date with one of her clients, but her date is unexpectedly cut short when she witnesses a man being murdered. After narrowly escaping with her life, she is placed into protective custody. When the safe house is breached, Jackie makes a daring escape from both the hired killers and the handsome FBI agent, who wants to return her to protective custody. With a little help from her sly and crafty friend, Monroe, Jackie is convinced she can disappear until the trial. While on her journey to meet with her friend, she solicits help from a few shady but lovable characters along the way. Although she manages to stay one-step ahead of the hired killers, the federal agent remains in hot pursuit. Will Jackie reach Monroe before she's captured by the FBI and returned to protective custody? Or will the hired killers silence her first?

"Unconditional"

A young woman puts her life on hold to care for an unstable, highly skilled combat soldier, who believes someone is trying to kill him.

A botched military coup leaves a team of elite fighters injured with one clinging to life in a coma. When Harlan wakes from his coma, he's left with no memory of his past life. His commander's daughter, Indy, takes it upon herself to care for the fallen war hero. She's challenged with more than just his physical care as she combats with not only his memory loss but also his newly found desire for her. His infatuation with her becomes the least of her worries when he sinks back into his role of a combat soldier. Believing his life is in danger, his fighting skills surface, turning him into an unpredictable and dangerous man. Will his memory return to him before Indy is forced to commit him? Or will he finally find his nemesis, "the coyote", and possibly claim the life of an innocent person?

"The Pen Pal"

In order to save her friend, she must enter the mind of a serial killer.

When her best friend is abducted, no one believes Jolynn saw it in a psychic vision. With nowhere to turn, Jolynn reluctantly joins Agent Harris Slade and his team on their hunt for a sadistic serial killer known only as "The Pen Pal". Finally confronted with the killer, Jolynn realizes she must enter the mind of the psychopath in order to stop the brutal killings. But when her vision reveals a particularly disturbing death, can Jolynn sacrifice her lover for her friend?

"Witness Protection 2"
The Return of Whiskey Tango Foxtrot

Believing she holds the clue to millions in missing laundered money, a young woman is placed into the protective care of a former Navy SEAL team.

Feeling sorry for her recently separated co-worker, Leeann invites Wiley to join her and her friends on their night out. Little does she know that finding her co-worker murdered is just the beginning of her nightmare. Leeann unknowingly holds the key to fifty million dollars in potentially laundered mob money. With hired killers pursuing her, the FBI places her into a different kind of protective custody. Former Navy SEAL team Whiskey Tango Foxtrot reunites to keep Leeann alive at their secret hideaway. What should be an easy assignment takes an unscheduled turn when secrets, lies, and betrayal threaten to derail their mission. Is the team prepared for a war on their own doorstep? Will Leeann's misguided trust endanger the lives of those sent to protect her?

"Witness Protection 3"
Alpha Mike Foxtrot

A helicopter pilot risks her life to help a team of retired Navy SEALs rescue two girls from a killer.

When former Navy SEAL team Whiskey Tango Foxtrot asks for a simple favor, Jackie reluctantly offers her air-taxi services. What could go wrong? What begins as a search and rescue for two girls turns into a fight for survival against a heavily armed drug cartel. Wanted by the law with the cartel in hot pursuit and their home base breached, the team is forced to call in a favor from a questionable ally. Unfortunately, their new safe house isn't what it seems. Without knowing who the real enemy is, can Jackie and the team save their young witnesses from the hands of a killer?

"Already Dead"
Supernatural Collection

From the already dead to the undead. Three supernatural tales of "things that go bump in the night".

"Bloodletting" - A vampire themed resort allows guests to *participate* in their Bloodletting Ritual to celebrate the island's legendary vampires.

"Reaper of Souls" - A young woman must outwit an evil sorcerer in order to save her brother or become one of his minions forever.

"Already Dead" - When Flight 220 crashes, ten passengers make it to an isolated island, but only one man lives to tell the lie.

"Witness Protection 4"
O-Dark-Hundred

A simple assignment turns deadly when a retired Navy SEAL team uncovers a plot to kill a notorious mob boss.

When Whiskey Tango Foxtrot embarks on a simple stalking case, they're not prepared for a trip to a private island paradise owned by an infamous mobster. With one of their own suffering from traumatic head injuries, the team is left scrambling to decide what is real or imagined. The situation escalates even further when they uncover an assassination plot where everyone is a suspect. Now targets themselves, can the team survive their trip to paradise?

"Witness Protection 5"
Outside the Wire

After suffering several casualties on their last assignment, a retired Navy SEAL team discovers their misery is just beginning.

When Whiskey Tango Foxtrot returns home after suffering a devastating loss, they're hit with even more bad news regarding the rest of their team. Their grief is cut short when they discover their names are all on the same hit list. Hunted by relentless assassins, the scattered team must decide whether to remain safely hidden or find the man who put the price on their heads. Against the wishes of her teammates, Jackie strikes out on her own in order to save a friend who wants her dead. In a kill or be killed situation, will Jackie's emotions finally betray her?

"The Murder of Emily Fisher"

After finding their favorite teacher murdered, the lives of two teenage girls are forever changed.

Everyone loved Emily Fisher. While walking home one afternoon, two teenage girls, Sidney and Trisha, stumble upon a gruesome murder scene. The brutal murder of Emily Fisher, a young, attractive schoolteacher, shocks the small town of **Marilina**. After graduation, Sidney moves far away from the memories of the small town while Trisha retreats deeper into denial. Eight years after the murder, Sidney receives a desperate call from her childhood friend, forcing her to return home. Trisha believes Emily's killer was falsely accused and she manages to turn the entire town against her while attempting to prove it. When Trisha receives a death threat, Sidney realizes there may be some credibility to her friend's wild accusations. Is Trisha's mental breakdown a result of childhood trauma? Or is the real killer actually attempting to silence her? In order to save her friend, Sidney must answer the eight-year-old question. Who murdered Emily Fisher?

"Once Upon a Disaster"

A young homicide detective finds herself at the mercy of a hitman in the aftermath of an earthquake

While investigating the murder of a hitman, Detective Jade Wesson pursues a lead connecting the dead man to a break-in at a computer programming company. She's drawn into the world of nightclub owner and front man for the mob, Cody Riley. Her investigation keeps pointing to Cody's right-hand man and possible hitman, Vahn Lott. Despite her efforts to keep her investigation on track, Vahn has plans of his own for the attractive detective. When an unprecedented earthquake rocks their east coast town, Jade must put her life in Vahn's hands if she wants to survive. Can she trust a man who might be the killer she's hunting?

"Awaken the Dead"

A grieving innkeeper struggles to keep her haunted hotel out of foreclosure.

After losing her parents in a suspicious boating accident, Harley Brandon is determined to keep the family hotel out of foreclosure. Unfortunately, the hotel ghosts have other plans. Built with tainted money, the century old Horizon Hotel thrives on a tradition of murder, scandal, and suicide. As the paranormal activity increases to alarming levels, Harley discovers the truth about the hotel and its residents. Can Harley save her friends from the hotel's frightening hidden secrets?

"Castle Bloodshed"
Murder Collection

From a deadly island paradise to haunted castles. Three novella length tales of murder, mystery, and malicious intent.

"Castle Bloodshed" – A tour of Wesley Castle turns into a fight for survival as six stranded tourists discover the haunting secrets within the castle walls. A mystery writer teams up with an uptight butler in order stop a killer who may already be dead. Novella length paranormal murder mystery.

"Fleshies" – Is Uncle Rutger crazy? Five years ago, four business partners died within their newly purchased, fixer-upper castle. Their bodies were never found. The surviving partner, Rutger, claims a demon keeps him as its slave. Rutger's nephew schemes to save his uncle by sacrificing the lives of a group of stranded motorists and a high-profile novelist. Novella length supernatural murder mystery.

"Demon Island" – A group of strangers are invited to a remote island for the reading of a will. The guests soon discover they were brought to the island to be executed one-by-one. It's up to a private detective and a tenacious young woman to solve the murders and find a way to escape paradise. Novella length murder mystery.

"Brighton Island"

When a psychic visits a haunted island mansion, he inadvertently awakens the ghosts' tortured souls.

Something's not right with Simon. When Jacklyn brings her eccentric friend to her uncle's island mansion, she didn't expect him to slip into psychic overload. As Simon attempts to solve a decade-old, double homicide, Jacklyn is confronted with the possibility that she could be next to join the mansion ghosts. When they find themselves stranded on the secluded island, her Uncle Hyland wages his own war to save them from a flesh and blood killer. Will her uncle's "shock and awe" military tactics save them or get them killed? Can Simon bring peace to the tortured souls or unexpectedly join them?

"A.L.F. Resort"

A fantasy vacation turns into a nightmare when the resort's artificial life forms are compromised.

Welcome to A.L.F. Resort where you can live out your fantasies with safe, state-of-the-art artificial life form robots! When a young journalist and a photographer are sent to A.L.F. Resort to do a story for their magazine, Shay and Becka believe they've hit the jackpot of all work-cations. The engineers pull out all the stops to make their fantasies memorable. Unfortunately, the newly designed A.L.F., the Gen X, is smarter than his programming and creates havoc within Shay's fantasy. A computer malfunction removes their safety inhibitors and the A.L.F.s play out their own hostile fantasies. Zombies, bikers, and mobsters run amuck, turning fantasies into nightmares. Shay gets more of a story than she anticipates, but will she survive long enough to write it?

"Jungle Princess"

While stranded on a prison island, a young woman discovers a creature of "unknown" origin.

After their cruise ship sinks, Alex and two of her shipmates are stranded on a deserted, tropical island. Unfortunately, the castaways soon realize they're not alone. They discover an abandoned prison with over two dozen inmates living on the island's south side. While avoiding the prison on the far side of the island, Alex discovers a strange but loveable creature of unknown origin. When one of her fellow castaways is in trouble, Alex reluctantly seeks help from the prisoners. After the brutal murder of several inmates, their questions surrounding the abandoned prison are about to be answered. What really killed over one hundred prisoners? And is it still out there?

"Murder in Wax"

A series of brutal murders plague a quiet farming community when beautiful women audition for the same acting job.

While all the young women in town are fighting over a once-in-a-lifetime acting opportunity, Devon Vincent is excited about her new job at the local wax museum. Although supportive of her friend's acting aspirations, Devon has a hard time understanding the rivalry among the women in town. When the aspiring actresses are brutally murdered one-by-one, Devon fears her friend may be the next victim. Devon finds herself in the middle of a murderous revenge plot that leads back to the wax museum's doorstep and possibly implicates her boss as the killer. Will Devon's newly found feelings for her boss bring a killer closer to her? Or is the killer already in her circle?

"Witness Protection 6"
Alpha Dogs

An easy rescue turns into a wild ride for retired Navy SEAL team Whiskey Tango Foxtrot when everyone wants to kill their client.

It was a simple task. Rescue a young woman from her mob boss father-in-law. Little did Jackie and company realize that rescuing the young woman was the easy part. Keeping her alive would be a massive undertaking, especially when everyone wants a piece of the mafia heiress. The team fights for survival against their toughest adversaries yet. How many innocent people must die in order to save one woman? Can the team survive the ultimate battle between mercenaries and assassins?

"Midnight Requisition"

A series of brutal murders leaves a traumatized young woman on a hunt to find a killer.

When they were just babies, Scorpio and her twin brother, Kane, tragically lost their parents under mysterious circumstances. Refusing to accept his father was dead, Kane set off on a mission to find a man he'd never met. A home invasion gone wrong leaves Scorpio grieving the loss of those she loves. Out of the tragedy of her loss, two fallen heroes are thrust upon her. Scorpio soon realizes someone wants her dead and the killer may already be in her circle. As her entire life unravels in a web of betrayal and lies, can Scorpio trust her new, slightly questionable friends?

"Until Death"

Liars, cheaters, blackmail and murder. It would be a wedding no one would forget.

Despite knowing he's making the biggest mistake of his life, Raina Steele reluctantly attends her father's third wedding. What should have been a boring reception turns into a web of lies, betrayal, and murder. With no one above suspicion, Raina must put aside her feud with the arrogant yet insanely handsome butler in order to catch the killer before he finds his next victim. With a murderer waiting to strike and lives hanging in the balance, the real question remains...the bride is wearing white? Seriously?

"Tainted"

What happens at the Dark Forest Hotel, stays at the Dark Forest Hotel...for all eternity.

What secrets surround Dark Forest Hotel? After her parents die under mysterious circumstances, sixteen-year-old Jeri escapes foster care and seeks refuge at a "closed for the season" hotel. Over the next six years, Jeri graduates from teenage runaway to the hotel's assistant general manager. When she learns a convention is secretly held every year in her absence, she demands answers from her boss, friends, and co-workers. After getting conflicting stories, Jeri sets out to discover the truth. She's suddenly thrown into a horrifying new world where vampires and vicious creatures are craving her virgin blood. After six years of everyone lying to her, is there anyone she can trust?

Coming Soon!
"Jumpers"

ABOUT THE AUTHOR

Holly Copella has been writing since the age of twelve when her frustration at a book's poor plot drove her to author her own story. Over the last decade, she's written a number of screenplays, some of which she's now adapting into novels. Her fascination with zombies and other darker material lends an edge to her writing, which tends to lean toward horror. As a fan of Agatha Christie, she appreciates the craft of a good plot and the importance of creating significant characters.

Hailing from Pennsylvania, Copella lives in the Endless Mountains on a farm with her rescue horses and other animals. In addition to writing and reading fiction, she enjoys riding horses and traveling to Las Vegas and Disney World.

www.ingramcontent.com/pod-product-compliance
Lightning Source LLC
Chambersburg PA
CBHW071637260626
47170CB00001B/136